루시 몽고메리의
빨강 머리 앤 스크랩북

루시 몽고메리의
빨강 머리 앤 스크랩북

엘리자베스 롤린스 에펄리 지음 | 박혜원 옮김

더모던
Themodern

공중누각

노력과 갈등에 지치면
걱정거리를 좇다가 지치면
나는 현실의 삶을 벗어나
공중에 누각을 짓는다.

경이로운 저택을 높고도 아름답게 지으면
그곳에서는 시들지 않는 장미가 꽃을 피우고
볕이 드는 마당과 우아한 거실은
아라비아의 향수로 흠뻑 젖는다.

가장 감미로운 음악이 울려 퍼지고
끝 모르는 여름이 서성이는 곳,
이곳에서 나는 여왕이자 성주이다.
이곳, 나의 공중누각에서.

웃음과 젊음으로 매력을 엮고
사랑은 언제나 환영받는 손님이다.
두려움이 속이지 않고 희망이 현혹하지 않는
그곳에서는 꿈꾸고 쉴 시간이 있다.

일이 잘못되고 하늘이 흐려지면
나는 마법에 이끌려 그곳을 헤매다가
평범한 세상을 벗어던진다.
나의 아름다운 공중누각에서.

—조이스 캐번디시Joyce Cavendish라는 필명으로 《스토리 페이퍼》에 발표한 시, 1904년 9월 24일

L. M. Montgomery.

루시 모드 몽고메리의 중요 연보

1874   11월 30일에 클라라 울너 맥닐과 휴 존 몽고메리 슬하에서 태어났다. 어린 몽고메리의 어머니가 결핵에 걸려 1876년에 사망하자 아기는 외조부모와 함께 캐번디시에 남겨진다.

1890 – 1891   친할아버지와 함께 서스캐처원 프린스앨버트로 아버지와 의붓어머니를 찾아갔다. 첫 시를 샬럿타운에서 발행되는 《패트리어트Patriot》지에 발표했다.

1893 – 1894   샬럿타운에 있는 프린스오브웨일스 대학에서 공부하여 1급 교사 자격증을 취득했다. 《레이디 월드》지에 시를 발표했다.

1894 – 1895   프린스에드워드섬에 있는 비더포드 학교에서 학생들을 가르쳤다.

1895 – 1896   노바스코샤 핼리팩스에 위치한 달하우지 대학에서 일 년 과정으로 영문학을 공부하며 그동안 핼리팩스 여학교(현재 암브레 아카데미)에서 생활했다.

1896 – 1897   프린스에드워드섬 벨몬트 학교에서 학생들을 가르쳤다.

1897 – 1898   프린스에드워드섬 로어 비데크 학교에서 학생들을 가르쳤다. 1898년 3월에 외할아버지가 사망했다. 몽고메리는 캐번디시로 돌아간다.

1901 – 1902   1901년 9월부터 이듬해 6월까지 핼리팩스 신문사 《데일리 에코》에서 일했다.

1905   6월에 《빨강 머리 앤Anne of Green Gables》을 쓰기 시작했다(여러 차례 퇴짜를 맞은 끝에 1907년 보스턴의 L. C. 페이지 출판사에서 출간하기로 한다).

1906   이완 맥도널드 목사와 비밀리에 약혼했다.

1908   《빨강 머리 앤》이 출간되고 곧바로 호평이 쏟아졌다.

1909 – 1911   《에이번리의 앤Anne of Avonlea》(1909), 《과수원의 킬메니Kilmeny of the Orchard》(1910), 《스토리 걸The Story Girl》(1911)을 출간했다. 외할머니가 사망했다. 1911년 7월 5일, 파크 코너에서 이완 맥도널드 목사와 결혼했다. 맥도널드 부부는 온타리오 리스크데일로 이사했다.

1912 – 1921   몽고메리와 이완의 아들 체스터 캐머런이 1912년 7월 7일에 태어났다. 둘째 아들 휴 알렉산더는 1914년 8월 13일에 사산했다. 셋째 아들 이완 스튜어트는 1915년 10월 7일에 태어났다. 《에이번리 연대기Chronicles of Avonlea》(1912), 《황금의 길The Golden Road》(1913), 《레드먼드의 앤Anne of the Island》(1915), 《파수꾼과 그 외의 시The Watchman and Other Poems》(1916), 《앤, 꿈의 집Anne's House of Dreams》(1917), 《무지개 골짜기Rainbow Valley》(1919), 《두 번째 에이번리 연대기Further Chronicles of Avonlea》(1920), 《잉글사이드의 릴라Rilla of Ingleside》(1921)를 발표했다.

1923   몽고메리는 영국왕립예술협회 회원으로 선정됐는데 캐나다 여성으로는 최초로 얻는 영광이었다. 《초승달이 뜰 무렵의 에밀리Emily of New Moon》를 발표했다.

1925   《에밀리가 오르다Emily Climbs》를 발표했다.

1926 – 1933   맥도널드 부부가 토론토와 가까운 온타리오의 노발 지역으로 거처를 옮겼다. 《블루 캐슬Blue Castle》(1926), 《에밀리가 추구하는 것Emily's Quest》(1927), 《매리골드를 위한 마법Magic for Marigold》(1929), 《뒤엉킨 거미줄A Tangled Web》(1931), 《은빛 숲의 팻Pat of Silver Bush》(1933)을 발표했다.

1935   대영제국장교훈장Officer of the Order of the British Empire을 받았다. 《여주인 팻Mistress Pat》을 발표했다. 맥도널드 부부가 온타리오의 토론토로 은퇴했다.

1936 – 1939   《바람 부는 버드나무 집의 앤Anne of Windy Poplars》(1936), 《랜턴힐의 제인Jane of Lantern Hill》(1937), 《잉글사이드의 앤Anne of Ingleside》(1939)을 발표했다.

1942   4월 24일에 세상을 떠나 캐번디시의 초록 지붕 집에 안치됐고, 그 후 캐번디시 공동묘지에 묻혔다.

프롤로그

내가 여덟 살쯤 되었을 때 우리는 오타와의 어느 아파트에 살다가 다른 아파트로 이사했다. 새로 이웃이 된 집에는 젊은 가족이 살았고, 그 집에는 정말 예쁜 사내 아기가 있었는데 나는 매일 그 아기를 보러 갔다. 아기 이름은 제이미였다. 세상에서 가장 빛나는 금발과 가장 파란 눈을 가진 아기였다. 다행히 내가 아기를 돌볼 일은 없었다. 당시에 어머니는 내가 밖에 나가서 하는 일들을 별로 믿음직하게 여기지 않으셨기 때문에 아기 돌보는 일도 허락하지 않으셨을 것이다. 내가 다섯 살 때부터 꾸준히 읽었던 책이라는 렌즈로 세상을 바라본다고 어머니는 생각하셨다. 그리고 아기라는 탈을 쓰고 다가온 현실을 접하면서 내가 보일 모습도 과히 좋은 모습만은 아닐 것이라고 확신하셨다.

하지만 제이미와 가까운 이웃이 된 덕분에 더없이 소중한 선물도 받게 됐다. 제이미의 엄마가 나의 아홉 번째 생일에 루시 모드 몽고메리의 《빨강 머리 앤》을 선물한 것이다. 나는 그 책에 푹 빠져들었고, 그 뒤로 앤이 나오는 책을 전부 읽었다. 내 앞에 열린 세상은 캐나다라는 제2의 조국이었다. 이민 가정이었던 우리는 안식처가 되어준 나라의 역사와 문화에 대해 아무런 사전 지식도, 애착도 없었다. 하지만 몽고메리의 작품을 읽으면서 나는 캐나다 사람이 되었다. 맞다, 이 소설에 등장하는 것은 캐나다의 특정 지역, 그러니까 주로 프린스에드워드섬에 국한되지만, 그런데도 그 독특하고 세심한 묘사들은 놀랍도록 큰 위안이 되었고 마음 편히 받아들일 수 있었다.

몽고메리가 바라보는 가족 사이의 다툼, 보수당과 자유당의 차이, 그리고 예쁜 퍼프소매에 대한 통찰력을 통해 나는 내 것으로 삼기로 마음먹은 과거와 한 세계 안에 자리를 잡고 들어갔다.

모든 위대한 문학은 독자에게 이 같은 역할을 한다. 《전쟁과 평화》를 읽으면 우리는 전장이 어떤 곳인지, 전쟁이 왜 일어나는지를 이해하게 된다. 우리 앞에 펼쳐지는 세계는 그 안의 이야기를 우리가 어느 정도 경험했다 하더라도 우리가 묘사할 수 있는 세계가 아니다. 이해와 인식과 연민이라는 더 커다란 세계가 위대한 글에서 등장한다. 몽고메리는 그런 세계를, 아니 그 이상을 창조하여 20세기 내내 그녀의 책을 읽는 모든 독자에게 보여줬다.

몽고메리가 재능 있고 개성 넘치는 인물이었다는 사실은 새삼 말할 필요도 없다. 하지만 작은 시골 마을이 캐나다 전체를 대표할 수 있었던 배경이 무엇인지, 몽고메리가 보여주는 깊은 이해는 경이로울 따름이다.

앤 시리즈의 마지막 편인 《잉글사이드의 릴라》를 읽으면서 나는 제1차 세계대전에서 캐나다가 어떤 역할을 했는지 처음 알게 됐다. 앤의 두 아들인 젬과 월터의 이야기를 통해 어떤 희생이 있었는지 이해했다. 고향에 남아 있던 사람들이 그 지명도 발음하기 어려운 이국땅에서 치러지는 이 전쟁을 어떻게 바라봤는지에 대해서는 앤의 충직한 가정부 수전의 반응으로 이해할 수 있었다.

나는 이 모든 것을 나 자신의 역사로 받아들였고, 그 점을 언제나 한없이 고맙게 생각한다. 몽고메리에게서 배운 모든 것이 내게는 훗날 역사 수업에서 배운 어떤 내용보다 더 귀중했다. 나에게 몽고메리는 시골에서 시작하여 상황을 타고 세계 무대를 누빈다는 게 어떤 의미인지 누구보다 깊이 이해하는 작가이다. 나는 몽고메리의 작품이 꾸준히 사랑받는 이유를 잘 안다. 나 역시 그 이야기들을 한시도 잊은 적이 없으니까. 나는 몽고메리의 소설을 "유치한 것"이라 생각해본 적이 없다. 내 옆에서 치운 적도 없다. 나는 지금까지도 몽고메리를 사랑한다.

26대 캐나다 총독
에이드리엔 클라크슨Adrienne Clarkson
PC, CC, CMM, CD

L. M. 몽고메리와 빨강 머리 앤

루시 모드 몽고메리(1874-1942)의 소설《빨강 머리 앤》은 많은 사랑을 받는 고전이 되어 세계에서 5천만 권 이상이 팔렸고, 백 년이 넘도록 꾸준히 발간되어왔다. 이런 지속적인 성공의 열쇠는 몽고메리가 마음으로 썼다는 데 있을 것이다. 이미 정기간행물에 단편소설 300여 편과 시 200여 편을 발표하며 작가로서 성공적인 길을 걷고 있던 몽고메리는 평생의 꿈을 실현하고자 자신이 사랑하는 풍경들과 친숙한 사건들을 채워 담은 장편소설을 한 편 쓰기로 결심했다. 이 소설은 여러 출판사에서 거듭 거절당한 끝에 마침내 보스턴의 L. C. 페이지 컴퍼니에서 1908년에 출판됐고, 곧바로 큰 호평을 받았다.

몽고메리는 프린스에드워드섬의 조그만 시골 마을에서 태어났는데 지금은 뉴런던이라 불리는 곳이다. 어머니인 클라라 울너 맥닐Clara Woolner Macneill은 몽고메리가 태어난 지 이십일 개월이 되었을 때 결핵으로 세상을 떠났다. 그 뒤로 몽고메리는 프린스에드워드섬의 캐번디시에서 외조부모와 함께 살았고, 아버지인 휴 존 몽고메리Hugh John Montgomery는 서쪽 지역으로 이주하여 새 삶을 살았다. 프린스에드워드섬에서 몽고메리는 삼십육 년 동안 살면서 공부하고, 글을 쓰고, 학생들을 가르치고, 할머니를 돌봤다. 그 후 삼십일 년 동안은 장로교 목사였던 남편 이완 맥도널드Ewan Macdonald와 온타리오에 살면서 두 아들을 키웠고 한 아이를 떠나보냈다. 프린스에드워드섬은 몽고메리가 쓴 장편소설 20편 중 19편의 무대일 뿐만 아니라, 단편소설 500여 편과 시 500여 편이 탄생하는 데 영감을 준 곳이었다. 몽고메리는《빨강 머리 앤》으로 세계적인 명성을 얻었고 미국, 캐나다, 영국 등에서 평생을 유명 인사로 지냈다. 백여 년이 지난 오늘날, 몽고메리의 작품들은 전 세계 수십여 개의 외국어로 번역되어 독자들과 만나고 있다.

친구들에게 '모드'라는 이름으로 알려진 몽고메리는 평생 색채를 좋아했다.《빨강 머리 앤》도 색깔로 가득하다. 몽고메리가 지닌 많은 열정, 예컨대 마음이 통하는 친구, 자연의 아름다움, 낭만, 시, 단어, 패션은 주인공 앤 셜리의 열정이 되었다. 몽고메리가 보았던 일상의 세계는 생생한 공간이었고, 연민뿐만 아니라 웃음도 가득 넘쳐흐르는 곳이었다. 몽고메리는 상상의 세계를 자유로이 날아다닐 수 있었지만 현실 세계에 굳건히 뿌리를 내리고 있었다. 마찬가지로 앤 셜리 역시 연애소설의 주인공이 되기를 꿈꾸면서도 일상의 삶에 도취되고, 사과나무 가지와 저녁노을의 아름다움에 넋을 잃는다.

몽고메리는《빨강 머리 앤》을 사랑하는 프린스에드워드섬의 북부 해안으로 데려왔고, 자신에게 가장 특별한 의미를 지닌 꿈의 공간 두 곳을 앤에게 주었다. 하나는 나무와 들판이 보이는 혼자만의 침실이고, 다른 하나는 나뭇가지를 푸른 지붕 삼아 굽이도는 붉은 숲길인 '연인의 오솔길'이었다. 이 소설 속에 시를 쓰듯 묘사한 자연의 모습들은 몽고메리 자신이 방에서 창밖 풍경을 바라보고 초록 아치의 길을 거닐던 경험에서 우러나왔다. 몽고메리는 앤에게 친구와 파티, 예쁜 옷과 비밀을 사랑하는 자신의 모습까지 물려줬다. 소설 안에서 덩실거리는 활력은 몽고메리의 초기 편지와 일기, 그리고 여러 매체와 간행물에서 기념할 만한 글과 모아둠 직한 기사를 오려 붙인 스크랩북에 넘치던 그것이다.

　　몽고메리는 일찍이 만들어둔 스크랩북을 참고하여 1905년에《빨강 머리 앤》을 집필했다. 퍼프소매도 스크랩북에서 볼 수 있고, (몽고메리가 가장 좋아하는 풍경이자 표현 가운데 하나였던) '길모퉁이'나 정식 꽃다발과 숲에서 꺾어 만든 꽃다발의 흔적들, (몽고메리 본인이 프린스오브웨일스 대학Prince of Wales College에서 보낸 행복한 시절에서 떠올린) 퀸스 학교에서의 즐거운 생활, 어린 시절의 비밀들, 감상적인 시, 우스개 이야기들도 마찬가지다. 여러 장면, 대화, 사건, 이야기가 서로 연관을 주고받으면서 바라보고, 존재하고, 상상하는 방법들을 제시한다. 단편적인 일상 가운데에서 삶의 양식이 드러나고 이야기의 줄거리가 만들어진다. 스크랩북에는 기억들이 저장되어 있어서 들춰볼 때마다 다시금 새로운 삶을 엮어냈다. 앤을 상상하기 위해 몽고메리는 자기 과거 속으로 들어가 온몸을 담갔던 것이다.

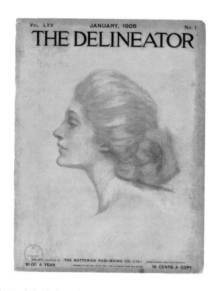

잡지 《딜리니에이터》 1905년 1월 호 표지에 실린 조지 깁스의 초상화로, 《빨강 머리 앤》 초판본 표지 그림으로 사용됐다.

프린스에드워드섬 스크랩북

루시 모드 몽고메리가 보기에 가장 벅차고 아름다운 모습은 무지개 빛깔의 춤이었다고 한다. 하얀 옷을 입고 춤추는 사람들을 색색의 불빛이 반짝반짝 물들이는 광경이었다. 춤을 보면서 몽고메리는 그 강렬한 색들과 예술적인 자유로움을 만끽하기만 한 것이 아니라 수집해 간직하고 싶었는지도 모른다. 몽고메리는 스크랩북에 특별한 순간들을 담아서 간직했고, 그 이미지와 색채를 통해 여러 생각을 파고들며 그림을 구상할 수 있었다. 여러 매체의 자료들을 조합하는 콜라주에서 시간의 순서는 문제가 아니다. 밝고 선명한 조각들은 은유를 드러내고, 층층이 쌓인 이야기를 암시하며, 느낌을 전달한다. 개인적인 스크랩북, 특히 몽고메리가 고군분투하던 젊은 작가 시절에 완성한 프린스에드워드섬 스크랩북 두 권에서 알 수 있는 것은, 몽고메리가 기억과 이미지를 좋아했고 시간이 지난 뒤에는 사건들을 재구성한 콜라주를 만들고 극적인 요소와 역설적인 상황을 더하며 더욱 다채로운 이야기를 만들어냈다는 사실이다. 이렇게 하면서 몽고메리는 스크랩북 안에서 작가로서의 삶을 지켜보는 관중도 만들어냈다.

몽고메리는 스크랩북을 두 종류로 만들어 관리했다. 하나는 자신이 (또는 다른 사람이) 발표한 단편소설, 시, 기사를 오려 붙이고 나중에는 자기 장편소설에 대한 서평까지 모아둔 스크랩북이었다. 다른 하나는 개인적인 스크랩북으로 기념할 만한 물건들, 주로 자신과 다른 사람들의 사진, 우편엽서, 고양이 털, 견본으로 쓰는 천 조각, 잡지에 실린 그림, 눌러서 말린 꽃 등으로 채운 것이었다. 이런 개인적인 스크랩북은 여섯 권이 있는데, 두 권은 프린스에드워드섬에서 살 때 만들었고, 나머지 네 권은 결혼 후 온타리오에서 생활하면서 만든 것이었다. 몽고메리가 쓴 일기를 보면 그 전에 만든 스크랩북도 있었지만, 몽고메리는 초창기 일기를 없앴듯이 그 스크랩북도 없애버렸다. 몽고메리는 평생 동안 몇 개나 되는 상자와 작은 가방에 소중히 여기는 보물들과 비밀들을 넣어서 간직하다가 주기적으로 분류하여 스크랩북을 채웠고, 때때로 그때 쓰지 않고 남은 것은 태워 없애곤 했다.

프린스에드워드섬 시절에 만든 스크랩북 두 권은 여섯 권의 개인적인 스크랩북 가운데에서 특히 색채가 풍부하고 생동감이 넘친다. 그 안에는 몽고메리의 젊은 시절과 낙천적인 성격이 잘 드러나 있다. 몽고메리는 시간을 아까워하지 않고 스크랩북을 정리했다. 그 스크랩북에 가득 채워진 뜻깊은 기억들에서 아마도 몽고메리는 윌리엄 워즈워스William Wordsworth가 말한 "시간의 점spots of time"을 떠올렸을 것이다. 그렇게 담아낸 순간들은 말로는 다 포착할 수 없을 만큼 생생하고 선명하다.

몽고메리의 어깨 너머로 스크랩북을 읽고 있자면 19세기와 20세기 초 캐나다 시골 마을의 일상이 생생하게 되살아난다. 교회와 학교는 마을의 사교 중심지였다. 프린스에드워드섬이든 서스캐처원의 프린스앨버트든 마찬가지였다. 교사와 목사는 존경받는 지도자였다. 마을 전체가 좋은 일을 하다가 떠나는 목사나 교사에게 경의를 표했다. 지역의 문학 단체와 학교의 발표회는 모든 세대를 아우르는 중요한 행사였다. 종교 부흥회도 많은 사람이 고대하는 사교 행사였다. 잡지와 신문같이 특별한 읽을거리는 넓은 세상의 모습을 실어다 주었다. 유행과 취미와 멀리 떨어진 곳에서 대립하고 논쟁하는 뉴스까지 사진과 함께 알려줬다. 신문에는 친근한 이웃들의 세상살이 소식도 실렸다. 기차는 마을과 다른 도시들을 연결했다. 몽고메리는 무도회 드레스와 값비싼 공단과 레이스를 보며 탄식했다. 몽고메리와 친구들 사이에는 우아한 품격을 지키기 위한 그들만의 약속이 있었다. 그것은 바로 예쁜 이름표였다. 훗날 몽고메리가 일기에 적은 것처럼 "이름은 가느다란 손에 들린 화려한 꽃다발 아래에 감추었다. (…) 유행을 따르고 싶은 사람은 누구나 이런 이름표를 한 통씩 구하여 친구들과 교환했다". 전통 춤을 추는 댄스파티도 있고, 말이 끄는 썰매 타기도 있고, 기부 물품을 바구니에 담아 전시하는 바구니 경매와 교회에서 가는 소풍도 있었다. 몽고메리의 젊은 시절은 스크랩북에 고스란히 담겼고, 훗날 앤의 삶으로 되살아났다.

스크랩북은 살아 있는 기록이다. 몽고메리는 몇 년에 걸쳐 자료를 모으고 첨삭하며 스크랩북을 만들었고, 스크랩북 자료를 가져와서 친필로 쓰는 일기에 삽화를 넣기도 했다. 몽고메리는 일기도 이런 식으로, 개개의 사건이 삶이라는 보다 큰 줄거리에 들어맞도록 다시 썼다. 외부의 시선을 극도로 꺼리는 사람이었던 몽고메리는 무심한 눈길이 닿지 않도록 가장 고통스럽고 가장 상처받기 쉬운 부분을 보호했다. 어쩌면 이런 이유에서 이완 맥도널드와의 약혼이나 《빨강 머리 앤》과 관련된 글처럼 그 삶에서 가장 중요한 몇 가지 사건의 뚜렷한 흔적을 스크랩북에서 찾아볼 수 없는 것인지 모른다. 보어 전쟁Boer War(1899-1902)도 사진은 찾아볼 수 없지만, 전쟁이 시작되자 몽고메리는 캐나다의 참전에 강한 관심을 보이며 전시에 발간된 잡지들에서 프린스에드워드섬 출신 군인들의 사진과 유니언잭으로 장식된 프린스에드워드섬의 거리 사진을 오려두기도 했다. 스크랩북 안에서 어떤 표지와 양식을 찾아낸다면 몽고메리의 개인적 삶과 그를 둘러싼 세계에 관한 실마리를 밝힐 수도 있을 것이다. 그 스크랩북들은 자세히 읽어볼 가치가 있다.

몽고메리는 두 차례에 걸쳐 스크랩북 관련 항목들을 일기에 길게 적었는데 1905년 7월 30일과 1926년 11월 22일 일기가 그것이다. 1905년 여름, 몽고메리는 즐겁게 《빨강 머리 앤》을 써 내려가다가 블루 스크랩북을 들춰보며 향수에 젖어 이렇게 적었다. "스크랩북을 보면서 여러 번 웃었다. 그만큼 한숨도 쉬었지만!" 1926년 말, 몽고메리는 세계적으로 유명한 작가가 되었지만, 소송 문제에 남편의 정신 질환까지 재발하여 근심이 그칠 날이 없었다. 오래전 블루 스크랩북과 레드 스크랩북에 담아둔 여러 재미있는 이야기는 잊은 채 "최근 내 스크랩북은 저 유쾌한 신랑과 신부의 아이들이 결혼한다는 소식으로 가득하다!"라고 한탄하면서도 "고서의 마력이 나를 사로잡아서 한동안 그 마력에서 헤어 나오지 못했다"라고 고백했다.

마찬가지로, 오늘날 독자들 역시 스크랩북의 마력에 사로잡힐 것이다. 그 안에 선명하게 포착된 순간들, 그 시대의 정취, 생생한 무지개 빛깔의 춤에서 삶을 창조하고 상상하는 한 작가의 열정을 고스란히 느끼고 경험할 수 있을 것이기 때문이다.

스크랩북을 편집하며

 이 책은 루시 모드 몽고메리가 프린스에드워드섬에서 만든 스크랩북 두 권, 즉 블루 스크랩북과 레드 스크랩북에 실린 글과 이미지를 추려서 담아낸 것이다. 이 스크랩북들은 루시모드몽고메리생가재단Lucy Maud Montgomery Birthplace Trust의 소유이며 현재 연방미술전시관Confederation Centre Art Gallery에서 보관하고 있다. 매년 여름이면 스크랩북 일부를 프린스에드워드섬의 뉴런던에 위치한 몽고메리 생가에서 전시한다. 여기에 나는 주석과 해설을 달아 스크랩북 내용들이 몽고메리의 삶과 당시 사회라는 맥락 안에서 읽히도록 했다. 이 세부적인 작업을 위해 기존에 출판된 자료는 물론 미발표된 자료까지 샅샅이 조사했고, 당시에 발간된 정기간행물과 책, 몇몇 학자의 학술 자료들까지 검토했다.

몽고메리는 이름의 철자나 날짜를 정확히 옮기는 데 별로 관심이 없었고, 스크랩북 내용들도 시간 순서대로 철저하게 정리하지는 않았다. 옛날식 달력을 사용하여 보다 최근의 사건들을 기록하고, 기념품들은 자그마한 흰 카드에 날짜를 덧붙이거나 시구를 인용하기도 하고, 해당 사건과 관련된 대화 일부를 첨부하여 보관하는 방식을 좋아했지만, 이따금 날짜 자체를 잘못 적을 때도 있었다. 수십 년이나 시간이 차이 나는 이미지들을 특정하여 한데 뒤섞기도 했다. 1930년대의 기념사진이 1890년대의 수집품들 사이에 붙어 있는 식이다. 이렇게 없어지거나 앞뒤가 뒤바뀐 이유를 지금은 설명하기 힘들지만 그 덕분에 남겨진 이야기들은 훨씬 흥미진진해진다. 몽고메리가 언제 어떤 지면을 구성했는지는 알지 못하지만, 풀 자국과 찢어진 가장자리를 보아 기존 자료를 떼어내고 그 자리에 다른 것을 풀로 붙였다고 짐작할 수 있다.

몽고메리는 성인이 되어서는 줄곧 일기를 꾸미고 다듬었다. 뭔가를 보거나 생각이 떠오르면 급하게 메모해뒀다가 나중에 여유가 있을 때 더 적절한 단어와 표현을 찾아 제대로 기록했다. 스크랩북도 그렇게 했을 것이다. 나중에 봤을 때 그 부분이 재미없게 느껴지거나, 로라 프리처드 애그뉴Laura Pritchard Agnew의 결혼 기념품처럼 다른 곳에 안전하게 보관하고 싶을 때는 자료를 떼어냈다.

이처럼 스크랩북을 다듬으며 어떤 자료를 떼어내어 다른 곳으로 옮기는 습관에 대해서 흥미로운 의문이 제기된다. 앤을 구상하는 데 반영했다고 몽고메리가 훗날 밝혔던 사진도 원래는 스크랩북에 보관되어 있었을까? 몇 년 뒤 몽고메리는 《빨강 머리 앤》을 쓸 당시에 미국 잡지에서 오려낸 정체불명의 여성 사진을 옆에 지니고 있었다고 일기장에서 밝혔다. 현재 이 여성은 구릿빛 머리카락을 지닌 모델 에벌린 네즈빗Evelyn Nesbit(1884-1967)으로 밝혀졌는데, 1906년에 백만장자 남편인 해리 소Harry Thaw가 그의 전 연인이었던 부유한 스탠퍼드 화이트Stanford White를 살해한 사건으로 재판을 받게 되면서 유명해졌다. 젊고 아름다운 네즈빗은 19세기 말에 많은 예술가의 모델로 활약했다. 특히 미국 화가 찰스 데이나 깁슨Charles

잡지에서 오려낸 에벌린 네즈빗의 사진으로, 몽고메리는 여기에서 영감을 받아 앤의 이미지를 떠올렸다.

Dana Gibson에게 많은 영감을 주었다. 깁슨이 창시한 깁슨 걸 룩은 1890년대 말부터 제1차 세계대전까지 크게 유행한 여성 패션으로, 잘록한 허리에 윤기 흐르는 머리카락을 이마 위로 높이 빗어 올리거나 둥글게 부풀린 머리 모양, 불손하고 독립적인 분위기를 풍기지만 우아한 여성스러움을 놓치지 않는 것이 특징이었다. 깁슨 걸은 교육 수준이 높은 여성상을 제시했지만 여성 참정권론자는 아니었다. 이 스타일은 서구 패션계 전반에 걸쳐 재현됐고, 1908년에 발간된 《빨강 머리 앤》 초판본 표지의 초상화에도 영향을 미쳤다. 삽화가 조지 깁스George Gibbs의 '앤' 초상화는 실제로 1905년 1월 호 《딜리니에이터The Delineator》에 표지 삽화로 실렸으며, 같은 때에 몽고메리는 소설을 쓰기 위해 준비하고 있었다. 참으로 역설적이게도 훗날 불미스러운 사건으로 퇴색되긴 했어도 네즈빗의 사진은 몽고메리에게 앤의 이미지를 떠올리게 해줬고, 깁슨 걸 스타일에 영향을 받은 화가의 삽화가 초판본 표지의 앤이 된 것이다. 몽고메리는 잡지에서 오려낸 네즈빗의 사진을 스크랩북에 보관했다가 떼어내어 곁에 두고서 소설을 썼을까? 확실히 몽고메리가 스크랩북에 남긴 (당시 이스트먼 코닥Eastman Kodak 광고에 실린 코닥 걸의 사진 같은) 다수의 유행 스타일 이미지는 깁슨 걸의 영향을 보여준다.

생전에도 몽고메리는 스크랩북이 조금씩 손상되는 것을 걱정했다. 그 이후로 스크랩북은 여러 차례 사람들 앞에 공개되고 전시되어 이제는 스크랩북 표지를 건드릴 때마다 자료가 하나씩 떨어지거나 손상될 지경이다. 이 책을 집필하는 동안에도 말린 꽃과 잎들이 바스러졌고 예쁜 이름표는 수작업으로 꿰맨 지면의 가장자리에 간신히 매달려 있었다. 이제 스크랩북은 디지털 화면으로 전시되는데, 관리인들은 오랜 세파를 견디고 살아남은 자료를 복원해 보존할 방법들을 찾고 있다. 내 바람은 스크랩북 내용을 현재 상태로라도 기록하여 스크랩북을 보존하는 한편, 몽고메리가 사랑해 마지않았던 프린스에드워드섬에서 보낸 삶의 흥미진진한 일상을 그의 많은 팬과 나누고자 하는 것이다.

　블루 스크랩북은 대략 1893년부터 1897년까지의 시간을 담고 있지만, 마지막에 가면 1920년대에 오려낸 글과 1930년대의 사진도 실려 있다. 레드 스크랩북은 1896년에 (샐리 워드Sally Ward의 이미지와 함께) 시작하는 것 같지만, 거의 곧장 1902~1903년으로 넘어가 몽고메리 자신과 1903년 전반기에 맥닐가에 하숙한 교사 노라 리퍼지Nora Lefurgey의 익살스러운 행위들을 보여준다. 레드 스크랩북은 1910년 초를 마지막으로 끝이 나고, 온타리오 스크랩북들이 1910년 가을부터 시작되는데, 이때는 몽고메리가 《빨강 머리 앤》의 열혈 팬인 캐나다 총독 그레이 백작을 만난 때였다.

　블루 스크랩북과 레드 스크랩북에는 몽고메리가 학생으로서 학교에 다니고, 교사가 되어 아이들을 가르치며 작가로서 고군분투하다 《빨강 머리 앤》으로 명성을 얻게 된 시절의 삶과 상상력에 관한 이야기가 담겨 있다.

– 엘리자베스 롤린스 에펄리

　공개된 몽고메리의 일기나 수첩에서 인용한 구절들은 모두 메리 루비오Mary Rubio와 엘리자베스 워터스턴Elizabeth Waterston이 총 다섯 권으로 편집한 《루시 모드 몽고메리 일기선집The Selected Journals of L. M. Montgomery》(옥스퍼드대학교출판부)에서 발췌했다. 공개되지 않은 일기는 겔프 대학교 문서보관실University of Guelph Archives의 도움을 받아 인용했다. 몽고메리와 노라 리퍼지가 같이 작성한 '비밀' 일기는 아이린 가멜Irene Gammel이 편집하여 《루시 모드 몽고메리의 비밀스러운 삶The Intimate Life of L. M. Montgomery》(토론토대학교출판부)으로 출판했다. 우리는 몽고메리가 만든 스크랩북의 순서를 그대로 따랐고, 블루 스크랩북과 레드 스크랩북 각각의 앞표지 안쪽과 1쪽부터 시작하여 그 순서에 따라 쪽 번호를 매겼다.

블루 스크랩북The Blue Scrapbook은 대략 1893년부터 1897년까지 루시 모드 몽고메리가 열여덟 살에서 스물두 살이 될 때까지의 기록을 담고 있다. 이 시기에 몽고메리는 샬럿타운에 있는 프린스오브웨일스 대학에서 1급 교사 자격증을 취득했고, 시와 단편소설을 발표하여 첫 원고료를 받았으며, 프린스에드워드섬에 있는 세 학교에서 학생들을 가르쳤다. 핼리팩스에 위치한 달하우지 대학에서 일 년 동안 공부도 했다. 연애를 하면서 사랑에 빠지고, 그 사랑에서 빠져나와 작가가 되고자 하는 포부에 몰두하기도 했다. 이 스크랩북에는 몽고메리가 서스캐처원에서 학교에 다니던 시절(1890-1891)과 그때 아버지를 찾아갔던 일이 자주 언급된다. 실제로 어린 시절과 관련해 오리거나 가져온 글과 물건이 있는가 하면, 한편으로 수년 동안 스크랩북을 꾸민 뒤에 덧붙인 자료들에는 몽고메리가 오십 대에 들어선 1930년대의 것까지 있다.

블루 스크랩북은 어린 성년의 활기와 실험, 향수, 고양이, 익살스럽고 경망한 행동, 선남선녀로 가득하다. 몽고메리는 일기에 불만을 늘어놓았지만, 초기 스크랩북에서는 슬픔과 실망을 감추는 다채로운 콜라주 빛깔로 호기심 어린 시선을 차단했다.

블루 스크랩북과 레드 스크랩북을 관통하는 한 가지 매혹적인 주제는 특히 거침없는 앤 셜리의 팬들을 사로잡는 요소로서, 바로 여성성 그 자체이다. 그리고 19세기 말의 젊은 여성에게 패션과 감성이란 무엇을 의미했는가 하는 것이다. 젊은 몽고메리는 역사 속 아름다운 여성의 이미지를 모아서 1890년대 광고에 등장하는 여자들이나 그들이 입은 유행 스타일의 옷과 나란히 놓았다. 이마 위로 한껏 쓸어 올려 풍성하게 부풀린 머리 모양, 잘록한 개미허리, 주름을 넣어 부풀린 퍼프소매 드레스, 우아하고 여유로워 보이는 분위기 등이 몽고메리 시대에 신여성과 깁슨 걸과 코닥 걸에 관한 논쟁의 중심에 있었다. 자연의 아름다움은 물론 패션도 사랑하는 젊은 여성으로서 몽고메리는 캐번디시 우체국을 통해 넓은 세상에서 맥닐가의 부엌까지 배달되어 손에 받아 쥔 잡지들을 보면서, 그리고 작은 도시인 캐번디시 안에서도 흥미로운 것도, 알고 싶은 것도 정말 많았다.

블루 스크랩북을 읽는다는 것은 마음껏 창의적인 활동을 펼치는 몽고메리를 눈결로 엿보는 것과 같다. 모든 이미지에는 기억과 의미가 가득 담겨 있다. 이미지와 관련된 이야기를 밝혀내는 작업은 추리소설의 단서를 판독하는 것과도 같다. 이런 추리를 통해 우리는《빨강 머리 앤》을 탄생시켜 한 세기 넘도록 세상에 독서의 즐거움을 선물한 작가의 재기발랄한 상상력을 다시 한 번 새롭게 평가하게 될 것이다.

The Blue Scrapbook

ALBUM

1893 to 1897

프린스에드워드섬에서 만든 첫 번째 스크랩북의 앞표지 안쪽은 루시 모드 몽고메리가 열여덟 인생에서 거둔 승리의 흔적이다. 그 성과를 더 높여《빨강 머리 앤》의 앤 셜리에게 부여한 승리이기도 하다. 1893년 7월 18일, 몽고메리는 주정부가 주최하는 까다로운 입학시험을 치러 응시자 264명 가운데 5등으로 합격했다. 이 시험에 합격한 덕분에 몽고메리는 샬럿타운에 있는 프린스 오브웨일스 대학에 진학하여 교사가 되기 위한 공부를 할 수 있었다.

구두 버클 캐번디시의 교사인 설리나 로빈슨Selena Robinson의 도움을 받아 젊은 몽고메리는 대학입학시험을 준비했다. 비슷한 또래였던 두 사람은 친구가 되었고, 같은 시기에 스크랩북을 만들기 시작했다. 설리나는 몽고메리에게 작은 편자 모양의 구두 버클을 행운의 상징으로 주었다. "노래일 수도 있고, 설교일 수도 있네"라는 문장은 몽고메리가 좋아한 시인 로버트 번스 Robert Burns의 〈젊은 친구에게 보내는 편지Epistle to a Young Friend〉에서 인용한 시구로, 나이 많은 친구가 세상에 막 나가려는 어린 친구에게 보내는 충고의 말이다.

장갑 장갑을 펼치면 달력과 함께 W. G. P라는 머리글자가 나타난다. 윌리 G. 프리처드Willie G. Pritchard와 그의 여동생 로라Laura가 몽고메리와 친구가 된 것은 몽고메리가 아버지와 새어머니를 찾아 서스캐처원으로 갔던 1890~1891년 사이, 학생 시절이었다. 붉은 머리에 회녹색 눈동자로 늘 웃었던 윌리는 1897년에 갑자기 세상을 떠날 때까지 몽고메리의 반지를 끼고 있었다. 앤 셜리와 가장 절친한 친구 다이애나 배리의 모델로 보이

는 로라는 몽고메리와 평생의 "단짝 친구"였다. 몽고메리는 달력에 76개의 "꼬리 달린 점"을 표기하여 행복한 날을 기념했다(블루 스크랩북 39쪽 참고). 블루 스크랩북의 마지막 장에서 윌리와 여동생 로라는 꽃과 사진, 오려 붙인 글들로 추억된다.

예쁜 달력 이 달력에도 점들로 표시되어 있지만, 두 달력 어디에도 몽고메리의 생일인 11월 30일을 특별한 날로 표시하지 않았다.《젊은이의 벗Youth's Companion》은 좋은 잡지로 여겨졌고, 1896년 몽고메리는 이 잡지에 자작시 〈어부 아가씨들Fisher Lassies〉을 기고하여 원고료 12달러를 받고 무척 신나 했다.

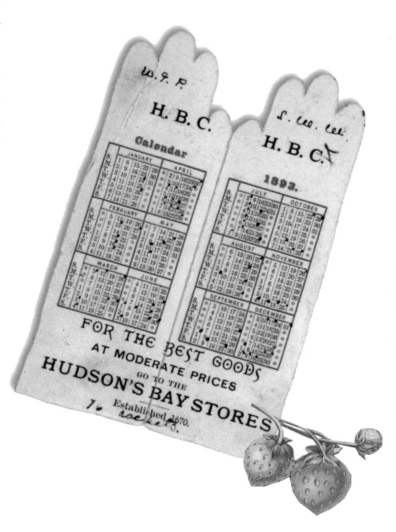

THE
DAINTY CALENDAR
for
1894

Presented by
The Youth's Companion.
BOSTON, MASS.

July 18
1893.

Good Luck

"Perhaps it may
turn out a song
Perhaps turn
out a sermon"
Burns.

루시 모드 몽고메리는 프린스오브웨일스 대학에서 2년제 교사 양성 프로그램을 1년 속성으로 신청하고, 1급 교사 과정을 선택하여 이 프로그램에 입학하는 데 필요한 시험에 합격했다. 앤 셜리도 똑같은 과정을 걷는다. 프린스오브웨일스 대학은 프린스에드워드섬의 주도인 샬럿타운에 위치하여 앤이 다닌 퀸스 학교의 모델이 되었다. 몽고메리가 프린스오브웨일스 대학 시절에 자신이 했던 공부를 사랑하고 "꼬리 달린 점"을 무척 좋아했다는 사실은 스크랩북에 잘 드러나 있고, 앤의 이야기에서도 다시 기억된다. 프린스오브웨일스 대학 졸업식에서 몽고메리는 윌리엄 셰익스피어William Shakespeare의 《베니스의 상인The Merchant of Venice》에 나오는 여주인공 포샤를 다룬 수필을 낭독했는데, 샬럿타운 일간지 《가디언Guardian》에서 이를 극찬했다. 오페라하우스의 무대에 앉아서 몽고메리는 자신이 써준 고별사를 짐 스티븐슨 Jim Stevenson이 읽는 소리를 기분 좋게 들었다. 프린스오브웨일스 대학은 1969년에 세인트던스턴 대학Saint Dunstan's University과 합병하여 프린스에드워드아일랜드 대학교University of Prince Edward Island가 되었다.

기사 1894년 6월 9일, 《가디언》지는 몽고메리가 쓴 수필 〈포샤Portia〉를 일컬어 문학의 보석이라 칭했다. "완벽에 가까운 예술적 구문"으로 "그날 저녁의 '백미'"였다고 평가했다.

프로그램 몽고메리는 프린스오브웨일스 대학의 상징색인 빨간색과 파란색을 졸업식 프로그램에 붙여뒀다.

꽃 몽고메리는 졸업식에서 꽂았던 팬지를 간직했다. 리본 아래에는 "우리는 헤어지지만 영원히 헤어지는 것은 아니다"라고 적혀 있다.

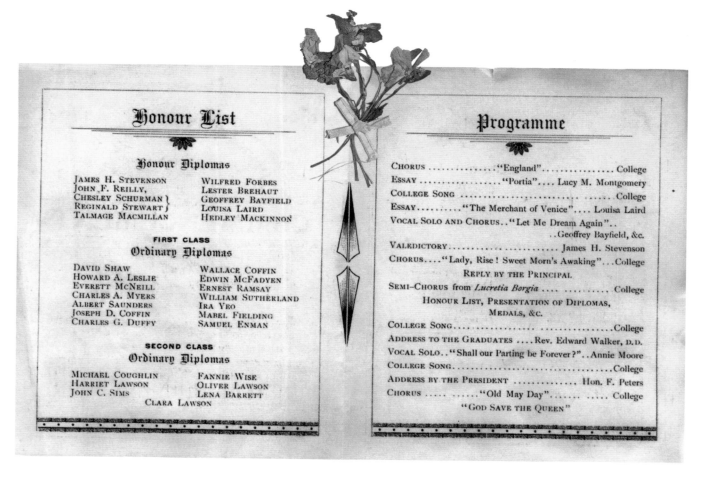

Pleasant Evening of Speech and Song.

...ier Peters Announces That a ...w College Worthy of the Prov- ince Will be Built.

...vernor Howlan certainly spoke with... ...mark when he said that the sight ...assembled Prince of Wales stud- ...—"maidens fair and manly youths" ...hey appeared on the platform ... Temple Opera House last evening ... sight the sister provinces of the ...should have seen. It was the Col- ...onvocation night; and the students ...in the garb and mood of a high ...al.

...program was unique among the ...f fare served at functions such as ...True, it followed the hoary, ortho- ...custom of reserving the greatest ...for the finale, but it placed the best ...most attractive features first. There is ...om to doubt that the *pièce de resistance* ...evening was Miss Lucy Montgomery's ...on "Portia." It was a characteri- ...such as might have come from ...ge Elliott in her 'teens. It was not ...a subtle, analytical study; it was a ...y gem. Miss Montgomery began with ...iri Portia in maiden meditation bus- ...ee; bound by the mystery of the ...n of lead and silver and gold, "the ...y, graceful heiress of a long past ...

...phrases of almost perfect art, Miss ...gomery praised the beauty of the ...an type of heart and mind and soul. ...cially heart; for that was where the ...anity lay, was it not? And Portia, ...a little touch of human frailty now ...hen endeared herself to every heart." ...ue, this sweet, strong heroine of ...eespeare's greatest thought was, to ... the suitor of her choice, "a perfect ...el of maidenly delicacy and womanly ..." But it was in her capacity as the ...sessor of a magnificent intellect" ...Portia won the young essayist's most ...usiastic words of praise. To say that ...Montgomery in this analysis did ...ice to Portia's intellectual worth ...seem a strong statement and undue ...e; but it is simple truth.

...ss Louisa Laird, too, proved beyond ...l her mastery of the sense and her ap- ...iation of the dramatic power of the ...popular of Shakespeare's plots if not ...greatest of his plays. Her essay on ..."Merchant of Venice" was a resume ...e plot rather than a study of the ...I was necessarily, therefore, less ...nal than that of Miss Montgomery, ...it showed none the less that power of ...pretation which Shakespearean clubs ...e the *sine qua non* of admission to ...charmed and charming circles.

...e valedictory by Mr. J. H. Steven- ...began as most of its predecessors ...cities have done, by uttering the ...nt of the parting class. But before it ...hed, it made practical suggestions and ex- ...sed other thoughts of such value as won ...praise of the principal of the P. of W. ...the Premier of the Province. It said ...example, that the students of the Col... ...were "cribbed, cabined and confine'd' ...ack of sufficient elbow-room, or words ...at effect, vigorous yet not inelegant. ...n it recounted the glories of the ...ball Club, the *Times* and the Debat... ...ciety, the professors one and all, and ...of the other institutions which the

1860 — 1894

Prince of Wales College

COMMENCEMENT

Friday, June 8th, 1894

AT 8 O'CLOCK, P. M.

"boys" hold in deep and, as it were, pro- prietary love. Whereat the aforesaid boys filled the house with loud and lusty cheers. And when the valedictorian closed with the conventional but intensely earnest appeal to the class, girls as well as boys, to re- member their Alma Mater in the days of their youth and forever, the male mem- bers of the class cheered again and in chorus inquired as the nature of the ailment of Mr. Stevenson to which came the stentorian reply, "he's all right, oh, yes you bet."

Prof. Anderson made a very character- istic, which is to say, a very happy, whole- some response. He was proud of the graduates of the Prince of Wales 'Uni- versity." The word "University" was prophetic. He had a right to be proud of the Prince of Wales students.

He likened their diligence and energy to the radii of a circle, representing the extent of human knowledge. As the radii increased the circumference length- ened, the area grew and the infinity of the unexplored darkness outside the circle became, if that were possible, less infinite. At all events the area of knowledge grew and the world was brighter and better.

Nor should the search for knowledge cease with college life, even with these alumni who entered upon careers of "business." It were apostasy for them to turn away from the goddess of truth, to sell themselves to the hideous god of mammon. That was the gist of the Principal's speech, emphasized by grace-

...ful gestures peculiarly his own, and ...u created by the plaudits of the boys.

Rev. Dr. Edward Walker gave a prac- tical and a really valuable address. He urged particularly a more systematic and assiduous study of English literature. Grammar was not enough. The power to express one's own thought was by far a greater desideratum than the power to analyze the sentences of others.

Mr. Stevenson's eloquent suggestion as to the need of more room in the "Alma Mater" was its text. Mr. Peters thanked Mr. Stevenson for that happy utterance. The overcrowding of the college was a disgrace. It was an outrageous disgrace. It endangered the bloom of health that made the beauty of the young ladies of that class.

Premier Peters' speech was more than a mere congratulatory address. It was some- what of a political pronouncement.

Education, he said, had the most im- portant bearing on the social and polit- ical welfare of the people. While he had any charge of the conduct of public affairs in this province, popular education would never be neglected. It was hardly possible to waste public money for this purpose so long as the results were commensurate with the ex- penditure, however great it be. And what he had heard this evening proved the adequacy of the results. Therefore, he hoped that in the near future the College, as it now stood, would be swept away and a building worthy of the pro-

...vince erected in its stead... ...ment was regarded as worthy of ... than the common kind of applause. Three cheers and a tiger was its meed.

Governor Howlan's speech was greeted with equal enthusiasm. He had re- viewed the History of the school. He knew it when it was the Central Academy, then as the Prince of Wales College and he hoped before his term of office as Governor expired to know it as the University of the Province. The class of 94 should be worthy of their Alma Mater; but he impressed upon them that only by persistent effort could they reach positions that would maintain the reputation of the Prince of Wales as students as they were now known in almost every land. Then, as true men and women they must be true to each other, and they would find as he had found, that they would never lack a friend as long as their classmates lived.

"Old May Day", the last of a goodly list of choruses and songs, and the national hymn closed the convocation.

Following is a list of the winners of diplomas and prizes:

HONOR DIPLOMAS.

James H. Stevenson, New Glasgow, 95. John F. Reilly, Summerside, 94. Chesley Schurman, Summerside, 90. Reginald Stewart, Charlottetown, 90. Talmage Macmillan, New Haven, 88. Wilfred Forbes, Vernon River, 86. Lester Brehaut, Murray Harbor, 86. Geoffrey Bayfield, Charlottetown, 83. Louise Laird, Charlottetown, 81. Hedley Mackinnon, Charlottetown, 78.

FIRST-CLASS ORDINARY DIPLOMAS.

David Shaw, Covehead, 94. Howard A. Leslie, Souris, 93. Everett Macneill, Lower Montague, 92. Charles A. Myers, Charlottetown, 89. Albert Saunders, Summerside, 88. ...D Coffin, Charlottetown, 87. Charles G. Duffy, Shamrock, 86. Wallace Coffin, Mount Stewart, 86. Edwin McFadyen, Tignish, 83. Ernest Ramsay, Hamilton, 81. William Sutherland, Sea View, 81. Ira J. Yeo, Charlottetown, 78. Samuel Eaman, Pownal, 76. Mabel Fielding, Alberton, 75.

SECOND-CLASS ORDINARY DIPLOMAS.

Michael Coughlan, Hope River, 72. Harriet Lawson, Charlottetown, 70. John C. Sims, French River, 68. Fannie Wise, Milton, 68. Oliver Lawson, Charlottetown, 65. Lena Barrett, Charlottetown, 63. Clara Lawson, Charlottetown, 61.

MEDAL WINNERS.

Governor-General's Silver Medal—Jas. H. Stevenson.

Governor-General's Bronze Medal, for Teaching and School Management—Ethel Connors, North Bedeque.

Medal awarded by Mr. Miller for the best kept set of books in the class of Book-keeping—John A. McPhee.

The judges of book-keeping were J. W. S. Lewis, R. H. Jenkins and John Con- nolly. In awarding the medal they de- sired honorable mention to be made of the work of Kenneth Graham, Ella J. Stavert and Jessie Stavert.

Basket Ball match on Thursday. Come one! Come all!! and shout for College.

We notice that the barque "Maud M." is now being towed into Shaw's wharf.— Prince Street School Times.

We are pleased to learn that one of our young lady students has just recover- ed from a severe attack of inflammat... and is now able to attend concerts an...

Worn at P. W. College Commencement Masonic Opera House Friday June 8th 1894

"Farewell to Alma Mater."

"...e past... at forever"

여학생의 진취적인 마음과 우애는 경쾌한 콜라주로 엮여서 루시 모드 몽고메리가 프린스오브웨일스 대학과 프린스앨버트에서 보낸 나날이 어땠는지 짐작하게 한다.

1890년부터 1894년까지를 기념하는 물건들은 백합에 둘러싸인 채 머리는 보석으로 장식하고 눈을 별처럼 반짝이는 젊은 여성의 삽화를 중심에 두고 그 둘레에 놓여 있다. 몽고메리는 여성의 삽화 위에 배船 이미지와 "많은 즐거움Many Pleasures"이라고 적힌 명함을 붙였는데, 그 삽화와 아래에 있는 시를 연결시키려는 의도인 듯하다. 네 귀퉁이의 글들은 행복한 시절을 보여준다.

왼쪽 위 몽고메리는 1894년 부활절 휴가를 프린스오브웨일스 대학 친구인 메리 캠벨Mary Campbell과 함께 즐겁게 보냈다. 1894년 3월 29일에 몽고메리는 프린스에드워드섬의 헌터 강에서 열린 교회 발표회에서 〈늙은 정착민의 이야기The Old Settler's Story〉를 암송했다.

오른쪽 위 케이트 맥그레거Kate McGregor와 T. S. 존스T. S. Jones의 명함은 프린스앨버트에서 학교에 다니던 시절의 것이다. 두 명함 옆에 붙인 들꽃도 그때의 것이다.

오른쪽 아래 몽고메리와 메리는 샬럿타운 시내로 저녁 산책을 나갈 때면 프린스 스트리트에 있는 "유명한 가로등"을 자주 지나가곤 했다. 나무 조각 밑에 "좋은 친구 중의 으뜸," "오, 휘파람을 불면 내가 당신에게 달려갈게요"라고 적혀 있다. 몽고메리가 쓴 '에밀리' 시리즈에서 에밀리 버드 스타가 테디 켄트에 대해 말할 때 인용한 번스의 시구이다. 1894년 4월 7일, 몽고메리와 메리는 그 가로등 옆 모퉁이에서 스튜어트 심슨Stuart Simpson과 짐 스티븐슨을 만났다. 이후에 두 청년은 피츠로이 스트리트 187번지에 있는 맥밀런가에서 함께 하숙한다. 시의 운율에서 강강약과 강약약을 뜻하는 "스폰디Spondee와 닥틸Dactyl"은 발음의 박자감이 맞아떨어지는 심슨과 스티븐슨을 가리키는 것일 수 있다.

왼쪽 아래 1894년 6월 15일 금요일은 "자유의 기념비적인 날", 즉 시험이 끝난 날이었다. 타버린 성냥개비는 지금은 사라지고 없지만, 메리와 함께 학교 시험지를 태우는 의식에 쓴 것이었다. "사인조"에 들어가는 사람은 메리 캠벨, 아이다 매키천Ida McEachern, 넬 맥그래스Nell McGrath, 몽고메리였다.

오른쪽 가운데 "내일 검은색으로 염색하겠다"라는 알 수 없는 글귀와 함께 붙어 있는 흰 모직 조각은 몽고메리가 처음으로 집까지 정식 에스코트를 받은 날 밤에 걸쳤던 하얀 사각 숄에서 잘라낸 것이다.

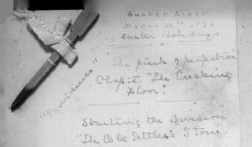

Hunter River
March 25th 1894
Easter Holidays
"The pink of perfection"
Chap. I. "The Creaking Floor"
"Pandidas"
Starting the Division
"The Old Settler's Story"

Saskatchewan.
Prairie.

Miss Kate McGregor.

Mr. and Mrs. T. S. J.

H. PRICE WEBBER had a splendid audience at the Masonic Opera House last night. It was a crowded house. "Jessie Brown or the Relief of Lucknow" was presented. The play is a spirited one and the acting was excellent. Frequent bursts of applause were heard. Edwina Grey as Jessie Brown was of course the star and all the others did their parts well. The audience was much pleased with the play. This afternoon at 2 o'clock a matinee performance will be given, viz. Tobin's Comedy of "The Honeymoon." The windows will be darkened and the hall will be lighted by electricity during this performance. Price to all parts in the hall 25 cents. Tonight "Arrah-na-Pogue" will be presented and this will be the last appearance here of the Company.

Four Happy Hearts.

TWO MARRIAGES—CONTRACTING PARTIES WELL KNOWN IN CHARLOTTETOWN.

[WHEAR—MURCHIESON.]

(Daily Sept 5)

This morning, as the GUARDIAN goes to press, Mr. John F Whear, Attorney-at-Law, of this city, leads to Hymen's Alter, Miss Florrie Murchison, formerly of Point Prim, but now one of the most popular young ladies of Charlottetown. The happy event takes place at the residence of Capt. Alex. Cameron, uncle of the bride, the officiating Clergyman being the Rev. T. F. Fullerton. The fair bride is attired in navy blue broad cloth, trimmed with blue and gold surah silk, blue hat to match, and carrying a beautiful white bouquet. She is attended by Miss Matilda Wyatt, and Miss Whear, sister of the groom. The bridesmaids wear pearl grey crepon with silver irridescent trimmings, hats to match, and carrying pink bouquets. The groom is supported by his brother, Mr. Louis G. Whear. The wedding presents are both numerous and costly—that of Messrs James Paton & Co, being a handsome mahogany case, containing half a dozen silver fish knives and forks, while her fellow employes presented a very beautiful mirror. After partaking of a sumptuous breakfast the happy couple will take the morning press for St. John and other Maritime centres, not omitting the historical Blomidon and other points of interest in the Land of Evangeline. The GUARDIAN extends congratulations.

JOHNSON—LYMAN.

We may assume that X equals Y; multiplying both sides by Y, XY equals Y²; and of course XY equals Then adding X² to both sides, XY equals X²—Y². Using X—Y as X(X—Y) equals (X+Y) (X—Y) cancelling out X—Y we have equals X+Y equals 2X, since X equals Dividing both sides by X, one equals

How She Heeded His Words member dear," said the father as he sent his young most pitied daughter away to school, "that all my hopes centered on you. Remember your struggles for intellectual acy, your triumphs, your defe your temptations, that a good rather to be chosen than great "I will, father," replied the girl, and the train bore her away will it be believed that three later that girl married a man with the villainous name of Gandersh

---

MY SHIP.

One day I watched a white-winged ship
  Sweep out beyond the harbor-bar ;
She bore from me my dearest hope,
  And sailed toward the evening star.

Long months have passed ; but ne'er again
  In evening's hush, or morning's glow,
Her gleaming sails mine eyes have seen —
  The ship I love, and long for so.

I think she drifted on, and on,
  And far beyond the evening star,
And through the happy "Golden Gate" ;
  And furled her sails within the bar.

Friday 1894
June 15th
Landmark of freedom
In memory of "the quartette"
"Caramels Stars"
"No matter where o'er the world we roam
We'll remember each other
for age and aye"

"That famous limp-post
Car Concert"
"Corner Corner Corner"
The "Fatal Spot"
The grand rallying place
My heart is in Prince Street
My heart is not here
"Beauties"
Evening

명함 존 A. 머스터드John A. Mustard는 프린스앨버트에서 몽고메리를 가르친 선생님이었다. 그는 몽고메리에게 관심을 보이며 귀찮게 하고 청혼도 했다. 이름 뒤로 보이는 꽃을 통해 장미 꽃다발을 받은 시기를 넌지시 말하는 것 같다. 몽고메리는 꽃다발을 받아주기는커녕 머스터드와 함께 걷는 동안에 꽃을 마구 잡아 뜯어 길가에 뿌려버렸다.

자작나무 껍질 "네 껍질을 나에게 주렴, 오 자작나무야"라는 헨리 워즈워스 롱펠로Henry Wadsworth Longfellow의 시구를 인용한 이 나무껍질은 1893년 6월에 친구이자 교사인 셀리나 로빈슨과 연인의 오솔길로 나섰던 황금빛 나들이를 기념하는 것이다.

말린 꽃으로 장식한 카드들 1894년 6월의 카드에 덧붙인 라일락과 이름 모를 꽃은 프린스오브웨일스 대학에서 발견한 것이다. 머리글자 A, F, I, M, L, M, M은 프린스오브웨일스 친구들인 애니 무어Annie Moore, 패니 와이즈Fanny Wise, 아이다 매키천, 메리 캠벨, 루시 모드 몽고메리를 가리키는 것으로 보인다.

'모의재판' 기사 이 기사에서는 하코트Harcourt 교수의 수업 시간에 벌어진 "중대한 학칙 위반"을 언급하는데, 1894년 3월 8일에 학생들이 서로 땅콩을 던지며 수업을 방해한 사건을 말한다. 몽고메리는 이 사건을 재미있는 이야기로 만들어 프린스오브웨일스 대학 교지인 《칼리지 레코드The College Record》에 〈2학년 교실 쥐의 일기 중에서〉라는 제목으로 기고했다.

달에 사는 여인 초승달은 몽고메리가 늘 좋아하는 이미지였다. 《빨강 머리 앤》을 쓰던 중인 1905년 8월 23일, 몽고메리는 스코틀랜드의 펜팔 친구 조지 보이드 맥밀런George Boyd MacMillan에게 이런 편지를 보냈다.

요전 밤에 시를 한 편 봤어. 혼자 산책을 하러 나갔지. 8월의 저녁은 고요하고 황금빛이 내려앉고 이슬도 없었어. 언덕 꼭대기에 올라서 빙 둘러보는데 영원히 기억 속에 간직해야 할 것이 눈에 들어왔어. 가문비나무 두 그루가 검은 손을 꼭 맞잡고 있었는데, 그 위로 아치처럼 펼쳐지며 은빛으로 물든 황혼의 하늘이 보였지. 바로 그 아치 안에 붉은 금빛 쪽배 같은 초승달이 떠 있는 거야. 나는 하늘을 바라보면서 그런 광경을 볼 수 있는 세상에 살고 있다는 데 하느님께 감사드렸어. 천국에는 초승달이 없을까? 황혼은? 아, 아니야. 분명히 있을 거야!

White lilacs.
Charlottetown.

"In lilac time
The noons are still
At night we hear
The whippoorwill"

P. W. College.
June. 1894.

Remember me when far away
And I'll remember you.
A. E. I. M.

—As will be seen in another column, some of our mathematicians have proved conclusively that one equals two. One of our students recently made a practical application of this grand truth. He owed a fellow-student two cents, and paid him in full with one.

THE MOCK TRIAL is degenerating into a farce. The evidence for the prosecution has been entirely too long; and much valuable time is consumed, without any practical benefit to the average student, except, perhaps, in developing his natural talent for noise and disorder. In the language of Byron, "we feel the fulness of satiety." Give the defence a chance.

UNDOUBTEDLY a gross breach of discipline has been committed in Mr. Harcourt's room. Many of the students are justly indignant at the base manner in which several of the most guilty sneaked out of the affair, leaving the innocent to pay for the damage.

IN THE PORTRAIT GALLERY
BY MAY LENNOX

GRANDFATHER looks from the paneled wall
    At grandmother hanging across the hall,
In the ripened glow of her stately grace;
And a frown comes over his shadowed face
As he says: "The world has grown askew,
My dear, since we were young—we two.

"Nothing that was is the same to-day;
Old-time fancies are cast away;
All our scruples are laughed to scorn;
All our customs are quite out-worn;
Each is seeking for something new—
We were content with the old—we two."

Into the shade of the grim old room,
Steal two forms through the twilight's gloom,
Grandfather's eyes are sharp to see,
And a deep voice utters tenderly:
"For aye will I love, and love but you,
And we'll follow love to the end—we two."

Grandfather's face has lost its frown,
And his eyes grown softer gaze gently down
On the pair who naught of his watching know,
And grandmother smiles and whispers low:
"One thing goes on as it used to do—
In the days when we were young—we two."

As ye sow so
shall ye reap.

most
extraordinary.

Scrap of desk
Dr. Anderson's room
P. W. C.
1893 — 94.

"The path of learning is no royal road"

PERSONALS.

It is with sorrow that we hear of the death of Mrs. Ramsay of Hamilton, the mother of Mr. E. H. Ramsay '95. We are sure we speak the sentiments of his college mates when we say that Mr. Ramsay has our deepest sympathy.

Island students abroad have, as usual, been very successful. Mr. W. S. Ferguson, of P. W. C. '93, took best general standing in arts for the Maritime Provinces at McGill. The other Island men at McGill, among whom may be mentioned Messrs. Geo. D. Mckinnon, Charlottetown; Geo. McLeod, Uigg; R. H. Rogers, Alberton, acquitted themselves very creditably. At Dalhousie, Brehaut of Murray Harbour is a tie with Logan of Pictou for the medal. In the Freshman Class Mr. R. L. Coffin, Charlottetown, leads in Latin, and takes high place in other subjects.

J. A. Mustard

While this short
greeting I indite
pray God grant
you prospects
bright.

루시 모드 몽고메리는 프린스오브웨일스 대학 시절의 기념품을 모아서 좋았던 추억과 학업의 성취를 자축했다. 카드와 거기에 덧붙인 글귀를 보면 몽고메리가 얼마나 열정적이고 극적으로 일상에 임했는지 알 수 있다.

4쪽 1905년 《빨강 머리 앤》을 쓸 당시, 몽고메리는 일기에 이 전단지가 태어나서 처음으로 '오페라'를 보고 받아 온 것이라고 적었다. 몽고메리는 1894년 12월 오페라하우스에서 헤들리 번튼Hedley Buntain과 함께 이 무대를 두 번 관람했다. 1893년 10월 22일(1894년으로 날짜가 잘못 표기되어 있다), 몽고메리의 하숙집 주인인 맥밀런 부인은 연락선을 타고서 프린스에드워드섬의 사우스포트로 놀러 가자고 했지만, 여자아이들을 '사우스포트'라는 이름의 연락선에 태우는 바람에 항구를 가로질러 로키포인트라는 곳으로 가게 됐다. 이런 실수를 할 때면 몽고메리는 재미있게 살을 붙이고 이야기를 꾸며서 그 사건을 기억했다. 4쪽 아래에 있는 카드는 어느 토요일 밤에 '맥밀런 호텔Hotel de McMillan'에서 메리 캠벨과 함께 침대 밑판을 부수고는 깨진 조각들을 숨긴 뒤에 그 괴상망측한 사건을 모두 4장으로 이루어진 한 편의 이야기로 만들려고 짤막하게 적어둔 기록이다. 과장된 정서가 담긴 〈휴고 경의 선택Sir Hugo's Choice〉 같은 시를 봤다면 어린 앤 셜리는 마음을 홀딱 빼앗겼을 것이다.

5쪽 이 지면에 오려 붙인 기사에는 주정부 대학입학시험의 합격자 명단이 실려 있다. 몽고메리가 264명 가운데 5등으로 합격한 그 시험이다. 메리 캠벨과 몽고메리의 사촌인 스텔라 캠벨Stella Campbell은 상당히 낮은 성적으로 합격했다. 패션과 관련된 그림들은 단순히 예쁜 장식으로 붙여둔 것이 아니다. 이 그림들은 몽고메리가 '여성' 자체, 그리고 여성이 세상에서 차지하는 위치를 분석했음을 시사한다.

7쪽 몽고메리는 꽃을 통해 프린스오브웨일스 대학의 앤더슨Anderson 박사와 작별한 일을 얘기하고 있으며, 1894년 교사자격시험 프로그램을 보관하고(지원자들은 대학을 졸업한 뒤에 교사자격시험에 응시할 수 있었다), 프린스에드워드섬의 신조 "Parva sub ingenti(강자의 보호를 받는 약자)"가 적힌 상징물을 풀로 붙여놓았다. 오른쪽 위에 있는 멋진 옷차림의 여인은 몽고메리가 앤의 이미지를 떠올리는 데 영감을 주었던 에벌린 네즈빗의 사진을 연상시킨다(13쪽 '스크랩북을 편집하며').

8쪽 1893년 입학시험공고와 설명이 달린 시험 시간표 사이에 작은 카드를 붙여서 보관했는데, 이것은 재미있는 사건이 있었음을 암시하며 아마도 셜리나 로빈슨과 시험에 관련된 것으로 보인다. 현창과 배는 앞에서 봤던 배 이미지를 떠올리게 한다(블루 스크랩북 2쪽).

9쪽 길게 오려 붙인 기사를 통해 몽고메리는 네 과목, 즉 영어, 영문학, 농업, 학사 운영에서 1등을 한 사실을 자랑스럽게 강조하면서도 얌전한 아가씨가 시선을 돌리는 그림으로 재미있는 대비를 보여준다(학사 운영 과목에서 1등을 했다는 내용은 블루 스크랩북 10쪽으로 이어지는 신문 기사에 언급된다). 이 기사의 앞부분에 소개된 프로그램을 보면 몽고메리가 포샤를 주제로 수필을 낭독했다는 사실도 알 수 있다(블루 스크랩북 1쪽).

Mary J. Campbell

Alex. MacNeill Esq
Cavendish

Moss
from old French fort–
Rocky Point
P.E. Island

October 22nd 1894

"Did you ever get left?"

"They who reach the top boys
First must climb the hill."

"What's in a name?"

SIR HUGO'S CHOICE.

BY JAMES JEFFREY ROCHE.

It is better to die, since death comes surely,
In the full noontide of an honored name,
Than to lie at the end of years obscurely,
A handful of dust in a shroud of shame.

Sir Hugo lived in the ages golden,
Warder of Aisne and Picardy:
He lived and died, and his deeds are told in
The Book immortal of Chivalrie:

How he won the love of a prince's daughter—
A poor knight he with a stainless sword—
Whereat Count Rolf, who had vainly sought her,
Swore death should sit at the bridal board.

'A braggart's threat, for a brave man's scorning!'
And Hugo laughed at his rival's ire,
But couriers twain, on the bridal morning,
To his castle gate came with tidings dire.

'The first a-faint and with armor riven:
In peril sore have I left thy bride.—
False Rolf waylaid us. For love and Heaven!
Sir Hugo, quick to the rescue ride!'

Stout Hugo muttered a word unholy;
He sprang to horse and he flashed his brand,
But a hand was laid on his bridle slowly,
And a herald spoke: 'By the king's command

'This to Picardy's trusty warder:—
France calls first for his loyal sword,
The Flemish spears are across the border,
And all is lost if they win the ford.'

Sir Hugo paused, and his face was ashen,
His white lips trembled in silent prayer—

God's pity soften the spirit's passion
When the crucifixion of Love is there!

What need to tell of the message spoken?
Of the hand that shook as he poised his lance?
And the look that told of his brave heart broken,
As he bade them follow, 'For God and France!'

On Cambray's field next morn they found him,
'Mid a mighty swath of foemen dead;
Her snow-white scarf he had bound around him
With his loyal blood was baptized red.

It is all writ down in the book of Glory,
On crimson pages of blood and strife,
With scanty thought for the simple story
Of duty dearer than love or life.

Only a note obscure, appended
By warrior scribe or monk perchance,
Saith: 'The good knight's ladye was sore offended
That he would not die for her but France.'

Did the ladye live to lament her lover?
Or did roystering Rolf prove a better mate?
I have searched the records over and over,
But nought discover to tell her fate.

And I read the moral.—A brave endeavor
To do thy duty, whate'er its worth,
Is better than life with love forever—
And love is the sweetest thing on earth.

LOVE IS REALLY BLIND, AFTER ALL.

SHE—"How I love to sit in your lap and have your big manly arms about me!"
HE—"My little darling!"

THE ORGAN.

Oh that ancient College Organ
With its yellow-tinted keys,
With no tone at all to speak of
Getting lesser by degrees.
Ten successive generations
Patiently have thumped away,
Hoping ever,—always vainly—
They at last would make it play.
How they practise with their fingers.
Then they try it with a thumb;
And at last they never mind it,
For the poor old thing is dumb.

—*Ulysses Webster.*

THIS EVENING

For the first time here by this Company, the Beautiful Irish Comedy Drama, by Dion Boucicault, entitled ;

ARRAH-NA-POGUE

—OR—

The Wicklow Wedding

ARRAH-MEELISH, (Arrah-na-Pogue)	EDWINA GREY
Shaun, the post, a Wicklow Carman	C. H. STEVENS
Michael Feeney, a process-server	W. H. BEDELL
Major Coffin, commanding the detachment of troops at Wicklow	J. McMILLAN
Hon. Ailsa Craigg, chief secretary of State for Ireland	J. INGRAHAM
Beamish McGoul, an outlawed patriot	W. R. NOBLE
Oiney Farrell, a friend of Shaun's	F. H. HILL
Col. Bagnal O'Grady, the O'Grady	H. PRICE WEBBER
Lanty Louchlin	ROSE LILLEY
Nora McTaggerty	ISABEL CLIFTON
Fanny Powers, of Cabinteely, in love with Beamish	LOTTIE CARMEN
Katie Welsh	LOUISE CLIFTON

ACT I. The Wicklow Wedding. The Arrest.
ACT II. The Trial. The Sentence.
ACT III. The Escape. The Denouement.

PRICES TO SUIT THE TIMES.

Admission 25 cts., Reserved Seats, 35 cts.

Doors Open at 7.15. Commences at 8 o'clock.

RESERVED SEATS ON SALE AT USUAL PLACES

Positively Last Night.

JOHN COOMBS, Steam Printer, Queen Street, Charlottetown.

Hotel de McMillan
chapters
I Awful catastrophe
II Gathering up fragments
III Almond Candy.
IV Concealment
Sequel
"Unknown grave".
'You've done it now Mary'.
Broken slats versus irate landladies

Saturday 14th April 1894

A fat-al secret.

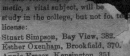

Prince of Wales College and Normal School.

MATRICULATION EXAMINATION, JULY, 1893.

The result of the recent examination for entrance to the Prince of Wales College and Normal School will be found below. The number of marks attainable was 650; necessary to pass, 325. Of the 264 candidates who presented themselves for examination 118 were successful, as follows:

Annie Moore, Crapaud, 491.
J Samuel Willis, Kingston, 490.
E N M Hunter, Alberton, 477.
Innis Fraser, Miscouche, 471.
Lucy Maud Montgomery, Cavendish, 470.
Nellie McGrath, Tignish, 465.
W S Lea, Victoria, 460.
Lawrence J Curran, Victoria Cross, 451.
Faustina McIver, Kinkora, 450.
Edward Laird, North Bedeque, 441.
Allen Matthews, Alberton, 437.
Cyrus McMillan, Wood Islands West, 437.
P S Duffy, Emerald, 435.
William J Haberline, Murray Harbor South, 431.
Minnie McKay, Clifton, 430.
Patrick Campbell, Souris, 429.
James A Campbell, Montague, 426.
Mary J O'Connor, Tignish, 426.
William McCheyne Robertson, Marshfield, 422.
Ethel Dutcher, Orwell, 415.
Susie Bentley, Kensington, 418.
Reginald P Smith, Emerald, 413.
Elios L L Clerc, Wellington Station, 410.
Ellen Taylor, Ch'town, 409.
Annie J McLean, New Dominion, 408.
Ada McLeod, Eldon, 407.
Bessie Haslam, Springfield, 403.
Winfield Matheson, Ch'town, 402.
Ethelbert McDuff, Kingston, 402.
Owen L Horne, Milton, 399.
Lizzie Kirwin, Tignish, 394.
Eliza Rodgerson, Piaquid, 390.
Alice B Kelly, Kinkora, 390.
Agnes McWilliams, Hope River, 389.
Arthur Campbell, Souris, 389.
Mary Campbell, Darlington, 386.
Ida B Scott, Warren Grove, 382.
Birdie Leard, Victoria, 377.
Minnie Hennessy, Kensington, 376.
Arthur Trainor, Ch'town, 372.
Clara Fleming, North Rustico, 369.
Colin C Ferguson, Marshfield, 367.
Nellie Hodgson, Ch'town, 366.
Joseph S DesRoches, Wheatley River, 366.
Katie McFarlane, Sea Cow Head, 363.
Charles C Richards, Ch'town, 363.
Erin Gallant, New Glasgow, 362.
Jennie Leard, North Carleton, 362.
George Cameron, West Royalty, 357.
Maggie C McDonald, Kinkora, 354.
Josephine E Dwan, Fortune Road, 353.
Jay Cameron, Souris, 352.
Geo H Jardine, Mt Stewart, 351.
Lucetta McInnis, St Peters Bay, 351.
Flora McPhee, Gray's Road, 350.
Mirtle McGregor, Ch'town, 368.
Ella Campbell, Park Corner, 346.
James, Ch'town, 345.
A Todd, Bradalbane, 345.
Thomas McLeod, Georgetown, 344.
Cowan, Murray Harbor South, 342.
Stevenson, Warren Grove, 341.
William E Campbell, Union Road, 341.
Benjamin L Mellish, Victoria Cross, 338.
Beers, Ch'town, 336.
McKenna, Rennie's Road, 334.
Pigott, Mt. Stewart, 332.
Stavert, Kensington, 332.
Stavert, Kensington, 329.
B Connors, North Bedeque, 329.
Read, Summerside, 328.
Rose Stewart, Ch'town, 326.
McKenzie, Ch'town, 325.
Emyvale, 325.

Albert Lynch

metic, a vital subject, will be study in the college, but not for teach license:

Stuart Simpson, Bay View, 382.
Esther Oxenham, Brookfield, 370.
Annie Fraser, Kensington, 351.
Agnes B Sharkey, Corraville, 341.
Walter Curtis, Milton, 336.
Ella Matthew, Souris, 335.

The following candidates, unsuccessful in the senior examination, passed the junior:

Nora Reid, Ch'town, 261.
Emmanuel Arsenault, Abram's Village, 247.
A D McArthur, New Dominion, 246.
Katie Monaghan, Treugh, 244.
Wallace Ellis, Mill Cove, 243.
Willie Coombs, Ch'town, 242.
Fenton T. Aitken, Lower Montague, 242.
Alma Robertson, Ch'town, 242.
Charles Kennedy, Bradalbane, 241.
Bessie McKinnon, Souris, 240
John Callaghan, Emyvale, 233
Cecil Stewart, Ch'town, 232
J Stewart McNevin, Rocky Point, 230
Katie B McLean, Culloden, 2
Maggie McDonald, Souris, 229
Norman Campbell, Darlington, 228
Donald M C H Crawford, Wood Is North, 226
Edith Finlayson, Ch'town, 226
Percy Crosby, Marshfied, 225
Hugh McEachern, Rock Barra, 225
Junior examination—Number of marks attainable, 450; necessary to pass, 225:
Jemima McPhail, Argyle Shore, 281
Alexander Martin, Eldon, 278
Marianne Cummings, Hunter River, 257.
A J Myers, Ch'town, 257
Louis H Douglas, Mt Stewart, 252
Maurice McDonald, Kelly's Cross, 2
Adeline Arsenault, Tignish, 246
Agnes Arsenault, Abram's Village, 23
Clement F Flood, Kelly's Cross, 237
Oscar W Roberts, Murray Harbor N 227
Peter Morrison, Georgetown, 227
James A Rodd, Brackley, 226.
The following having previously pass the junior examination have been succe ful in the senior:
Enoch Mugford, Ch'town, 144
Minnie Shea, Kensington, 137
Katie McMurdo, Kensington, 133

PARENT AND OFFSPRING.

Mamma—What are you playing with Essie?
Essie—A caterpillar an' two little kitten-pillars.

GRANDFATHER CLOCK.

"Yes, my boy, it's over a hundred years old, and goes for eight days without winding."
"And how long does it

블루 스크랩북 5쪽

Nor do we often find any thing more genuinely, passionately tender than this from " Interludes :"

"Good night! I have to say good night
To such a host of peerless things!
Good night unto that fragile hand
All queenly with its weight of rings;
Good night to fond, uplifted eyes,
Good night to chestnut braids of hair,
Good night unto the perfect mouth,
And all the sweetness nestled there—
The snowy hand detains me, then
I'll have to say good night again."

But there will come a time, my love,
When, if I read our stars aright,
I shall not linger by this porch
With my adieus. Till then good night!
You wish the time were now? And I—
You do not blush to wish it so?
You would have blushed yourself to death
To own so much a year ago—
What, both these snowy hands! ah, then
I'll have to say good night again.

THE WEAKER SEX.

She'd been a belle all winter long—the queen, in fact, of all.
She'd been to all the coaching meets ; had danced at every ball.
No function of society had this fair maiden missed,
Her name was certain to be found on every social list.

When summer came she went away to get a needed rest,
And to the hills she hied herself, because they pleased her best,
And this is how she took her ease, this lovely city belle,
And this is how she ' rested' in that little mountain dell :

She walked each day a dozen miles 'twixt break-fast-time and one ;
She bowled five games of tenpins ere the lunch-hour was begun ;
She played five sets of tennis, and she took a horseback ride,
And then a row upon the lake this worn-out maiden tried.

She dressed for dinner after six ; and when the meal was o'er
She promenaded up and down the hotel corridor,
Until at nine the orchestra began its evening task,
And then she danced the hours through with any one who'd ask.

She danced the waltz with Billy Jones ; she danc-ed the York with me ;
She tripped the polka with a boy whose age was ten and three ;
And when the men were all worn out and ready for repose,
This lovely belle was just as fresh as any budding rose.

And as I watched this maiden when the day at last was done,
I deemed her the most wonderful of wonders 'neath the sun.
Her kind of 'rest' would take a man—the strong-est man I know—
And but a single week of it would surely lay him low.

And so I asked this question, which this maid brought to my mind,
As I sat wrapped in wonderment at her and all her kind ;
Why is it that these girls can do the things that make men wrecks,
And yet be called by all mankind at large 'The Weaker Sex?'

COURTSHIP IN CHURCH.

A YOUNG gentleman happening to sit in church in a pew adjoining one in which sat a young lady, for whom he conceived a sudden and violent passion, was desirous of entering into a courtship on the spot; but the place not suiting a formal declaration, the exigency of the case suggested the following plan : He politely handed his fair neighbor a Bible (open) with a pin stuck in the following text: Second Epistle of John, verse fifth— " And now I beseech thee, lady, not as though I wrote a new commandment unto thee, but that which we had from the beginning, that we love one another." She returned it, point-ing to the second chapter of Ruth, verse tenth —"Then she fell on her face, and bowed her-self to the ground, and said unto him, " Why have I found grace in thine eyes, that thou shouldst take knowledge of me, seeing that I am a stranger?'" He returned the book, pointing to the thirteenth verse of the Third Epistle of John—" Having many things to write unto you, I would not write with paper and ink, but I trust to come unto you, and speak face to face, that our joy may be full." From the above interview a marriage took place the ensuing week.

HARVARD
BRONCHIAL
SYRUP

PARVA SUB INGENTI

Souvenir of Mr.
Anderson's Room.
P. W. College
1893 – 94.
"Professors who led us thro'
learning's dark maze
And examined us with
classical knowledge."

PROVINCIAL EXAMINATIONS

JUNIOR EXAMINATION

FOR

ENTRANCE TO THE NORMAL SCHOOL

COMMENCING ON THE

FIRST TUESDAY IN JULY

1894

This examination will be held at the following local centres :—Charlottetown, Summerside, Mont-ague, Souris, and Alberton.

Subjects for Examination :

ENGLISH—Parsing and Analysis from Goldsmith's Traveller, Reading, Composition, and Literature from page 1 of the Sixth Reader to page 200. (The candidates' papers on this subject will be examined as an exercise in dictation).

HISTORY.— British and Canadian History, as in Schmitz' History of England, and Calkin's His-tory of British America. British, from the beginning of the Tudor Period to the end of the Brunswick. Canadian History from Chapter 17 to the end.

블루 스크랩북 7쪽

Education office
Charlottetown June 1893

On July 4th you will be expected to
present yourself at Charlottetown
for the Senior & Junior Examination
your number will be   3 2
D. J. McLeod
Chief Supt of Education

California Grass

In Memoriam
of
"The Saturdayite"

"A friend in need is a friend indeed
Was not made to mourn"

ON THE ROAD.

We were out on the road that moonlight night,
Willie and I sitting side by side:
The little bay mare stepped gayly and light,
It was such a beaut'ful night for a ride.

We passed Nell Howe in the phæton with
Paul
(She madly loved Willie, and that I knew);
Sweet lover-like words in my ear he let fall,
And vowed we would ever, yes, ever be true.

The little bay mare would be mine, he said,
And I would reign queen of his heart for
aye;
Then he kissed me good night, while the stars
overhead
Shone bright, and the full moon flooded the
sky.

"Tis a whole year ago, oh alas and alack!
We quarreled and parted—a so'ry affair;
Paul and I, best of friends, in the phæton lean
back,
While Nell, Willie's wife, drives the little
bay mare.

Prince of Wales College
July 6. 4
1893

_ Time - Table _
of
Matriculation Examination into
Prince of Wales College and Normal School —
July 1893.

Tuesday July 4th
10 - 1 - - - - - English. done
2.30 - 5 - - - - History done

Wednesday July 5th
9 - 12 - - - - - Arithmetic done
2 - 4.30 - - - Geography & Agriculture
done

Thursday July 6th
9 - 12 - - - Geometry & Algebra done
2 - 4.30 - - Latin. done

Hurrah! Hurrah!! Hurrah!!!

블루 스크랩북 8쪽

Commencement Exercises This Evening at the Masonic Opera House.

Programme of Exercises---Honor List of the Year---Names of Those Who Won Prizes.

Prince of Wales College "Commencement" will be held this evening at the Masonic Opera House, beginning at 8 o'clock. Premier Peters will occupy the chair. The programme prepared for the occasion is as follows:

PROGRAMME.

Chorus—"England "...............College
Essay—" Portia "...Lucy M. Montgomery
College Song....................College
Essay—" The Merchant of Venice "...
...............................Louise Laird
Vocal Solo and Chorus—"Let Me Dream Again "..Geoffrey Bayfield, etc
Valedictory............James H. Stevenson
Chorus—"Lady, Rise! Sweet Morn's Awaking "...................College
Reply by the Principal.
Semi Chorus from Lucretia Borgia....
...............................College
Honor List, Presentation of Diplomas, Medals, &c.
College Song....................College
Address to the Graduates............
...............Rev. Edward Walker, D. D.
Vocal Solo—"Shall Our Parting be Forever?"................Annie Moore
College Song....................College
Address by the President—Hon. F. Peters
Chorus—"Old May Day "..........College
"God Save the Queen."

The diplomas and prizes of the year have been awarded to the following young ladies and young gentlemen:

GRADUATING DIPLOMAS.

HONOR DIPLOMAS.

James H Stevenson, New Glasgow, 95.
John F Reilly, Summerside, 94.
Chesley Schurman, Summerside, 90.
Reginald Stewart, Charlottetown, 90.
Talmage McMillan, New Haven, 88.
Wilfred Forbes, Vernon River, 86.
Lester Brehaut, Murray Harbor, 86.
Geoffrey Bayfield, Charlottetown, 83.
Louise Laird, Charlottetown, 81.
Hedley McKinnon, Charlottetown, 78.

FIRST-CLASS ORDINARY DIPLOMAS.

David Shaw, Covehead, 94.
Howard A Leslie, Souris, 93.
Everett McNeill, Lower Montague, 92.
Charles A Myers, Charlottetown, 89.
Albert Saunders, Summerside, 88.
Joseph D Coffin, Charlottetown, 87.
Charles G Duffy, Shamrock, 86.
Wallace Coffin, Mount Stewart, 86.
Edwin McFadyen, Tignish, 83.
Ernest Ramsay, Hamilton, 81.
William Sutherland, Sea View, 81.
Ira J Yeo, Charlottetown, 78.
Samuel Enman, Pownal, 76.
Mabel Fielding, Alberton, 75.

SECOND-CLASS ORDINARY DIPLOMAS.

Michael Coughlan, Hope River, 72.
Harriet Lawson, Charlottetown, 70.
John C Sims, French River, 68.
Fannie Wise, Milton, 68.
Oliver Lawson, Charlottetown, 65.
Lena Barrett, Charlottetown, 63.
Clara Lawson, Charlottetown, 61.

MEDALS.

Governor-General's Silver Medal—James H Stevenson.

Governor-General's Bronze Medal, for Teaching and School Management—Ethel Connors, North Bedeque.

Medal awarded by Mr. Miller for the best-kept set of books in the class of Bookkeeping John A. McPhee.

The judges of bookkeeping were John S. Lewis, R. H. Jenkins and John Connolly. In awarding the medal, they desired honorable mention to be made of the work of Kenneth Graham, Ella J. Stavert and Jessie Stavert.

THIRD YEAR.

Note.—Those students who have gained 75 per cent, or over, of the attainable number of marks are placed in the first rank; those from 60 to 74 in the second rank.

Latin, Horace and Livy—first rank : J H Stevenson and Chesley Schurman, equal; L Macmillan; J Reilly and Reginald Stewart, equal; W Forbes, L Brehaut, H McKinnon, Louise Laird and Norman Hunter, Alberton, equal; Geoffrey Bayfield.

Latin Composition—first rank : J

"Hood's Sarsaparilla Calendar 1894"

"SWEET SIXTEEN."

COPYRIGHTED, C. I. HOOD & CO., LOWELL, MASS.

Stevenson, J Reilly, T R MacMillan and C Schurman, equal; R Stewart, W Forbes; second rank : L Brehaut, H McKinnon, G Bayfield, Louise Laird.

Greek—Homer and Herodotus—first rank : J H Stevenson, R Stewart, J F Reilly, C Schurman, L R McMillan, W Forbes, L Brehaut, equal; second rank : H McKinnon.

Greek Composition—first rank : J H Stevenson, W Forbes, R Stewart, J F Reilly, C Schurman, L Brehaut; second rank : L R McMillan, H McKinnon.

Higher Algebra—first rank : J F Reilly, R Stewart, C Schurman, equal; J Stevenson, L McMillan, equal; L Brehaut, W Forbes, G Bayfield, equal; second rank : H McKinnon.

Geometry, conic sections, &c — first rank : J H Stevenson, R Stewart, J F Reilly, equal; C Schurman, L Brehaut, L R McMillan, W Forbes, equal; Louisa Laird; second rank : H McKinnon, G Bayfield.

English, Childe Harold, &c—first rank : J F Reilly, R Stewart, H McKinnon, equal; J Stevenson, W Forbes, equal; Louise Laird, L McMillan, G Bayfield, equal; L Brehaut.

English Literature—first rank : Louisa Laird, R Stewart, equal; J H Stevenson, J Reilly, L Brehaut, H McKinnon, G Bayfield, equal; W Forbes.

French, Chateaubriand, "Aventures du dernier Abencerage," &c—first rank : J Stevenson, C Schurman, R Stewart, equal; Louise Laird, W Forbes, L Brehaut, L McMillan, equal; H McKinnon, J Rielly, equal; G Bayfield.

Chemistry—first rank : J Rielly, J H Stevenson, W Forbes, C Schurman, L Brehaut, equal; L. McMillan, Louise Laird, R. Stewart, G. Bayfield; second rank : H. McKinnon.

History of Rome, first rank—J. H. Stevenson, J. F. Reilly, C. Schurman, L. McMillan, G. Bayfield, R. Stewart, L. Brehaut, W. Forbes, H. McKinnon; second rank : L McMillan.

SECOND YEAR.

Latin, Virgil & Cicero—1, David Shaw; 2, Howard Leslie, Albert Saunders and Norman Hunter, equal; 3, Everett McNeil; 4, Charles Myers; 5, Edwin McFadyen......

Latin Composition—1, Howard Leslie; 2, David Shaw; 3, Stuart Willis, Kingston; 4, Everett McNeill; 5, Joseph Coffin; 7, Albert Saund......

Greek Grammar and Xenophon—1, David Shaw......ward Leslie; 3, S Willis; 4, Stuart Simpson, Bay View; 5, Edwin McFadyen; 6, William Sutherland.

Greek Composition—1, N Hunter; 2, S Willis, E. McFadyen and Ernest Ramsay, equal; 3, D Shaw and H. Leslie, equal; 4, Matthias Smith, Kelly's Cross, and Ethelbert McDuff, Kingston.

English, "The Merchant of Venice," &c—1, Lucy M Montgomery; 2, Charles Myers, David Shaw and Charles Duffy, equal; 3, Everett McNeill and Michael Coughlan, equal; 4, Annie Moore, Crapaud, and Wallace Coffin, equal; 5, Nellie McGrath.

English Literature—1, Lucy Maud Montgomery; 2, Samuel Willis and Albert Saunders, equal; 3, Charles Duffy and David Shaw, equal; 4, Howard Leslie, Charles Myers and Everett McNeill, equal.

French, "Racine's Iphigenie," etc—1, David Shaw; 2, Charles Duffy; 3, Everett McNeil and Jos Coffin, equal; 4, Wallace Coffin; 5, Chas Myers and Howard Leslie, equal.

Geometry—1, Chas Myers, 2, H Leslie, Matthias Smith and C Duffy, equal; 3, Stuart Simpson, Chester Houston, Wallace Coffin and Everett McNeill, equal; 4, W Sutherland; 5, E McFayden.

Algebra—1, D Shaw, C Myers and N Hunter, equal; 2, S Willis; 3, H Leslie and E Ramsay, equal; 4, Annie Moore; 5, Oliver Bock and Everett McNeill, equal.

Trigonometry—1, Matthias Smith; 2, D Shaw, C Duffy, S Willis and E McDuff, equal; 3, C Myers; 4, C Schurman; 5, A Saunders, F Dougherty and Wallace Coffin; 6, Everett McNeill and H Leslie, equal.

Chemistry—1, C Myers; 2, E McNeill; 3, D Shaw and Joseph Coffin, equal; 4, C Duffy; 5, H Leslie and E Ramsay, equal.

Physiology—1, C Duffy; 2, D Shaw; 3, M Smith; 4, O Lawson; 5, S Willis.

Horticulture—1, D Shaw, E McNeill, C Duffy and J Fraser; 2, E Ramsay; 3, J Sims; 4, H Leslie and J Howatt.

History of Rome—1, H Leslie and E McNeil; 2, N Hunter and T Willis, equal; 3, S Simpson, D Shaw and C Myers, equal; 4, A Saunders.

Agriculture—1, Lucy M Montgomery; 2, Matthias Smith; 3, Bessie ...field.

FIRST Y...

Flora McPhee, Gray's Road; 2, Grace Dutcher, Souris, Mary McGregor, Gray's Road, equal; 4, Ellen Taylor, Ch'town; 5, Owen Horne, Milton.

Latin Composition—1, Ellen Taylor; 2, Edna Laird, North Bedeque; 3, Lillian Robertson; 4, Flora McPhee, Grace Dutcher, equal.

English, Milton's Paradise Lost, etc—1, Ellen Taylor; 2, Lillian Robertson; 3, Flora McPhee; 4, Thomas Driscoll, Mount Herbert, Edna Laird, Ethel Connors, North Bedeque.

French—1, Nellie Hodgson, Ch'town; 2, Flora McPhee; 3, Mary Jost, Ch'town; 4, Blanche Smallwood, Ch'town; 5, Ellen Taylor, Walter Curtis, Milton.

Bookkeeping—1, Katie McMurdo; 2, L B Mellish, Thomas Driscoll, Jenny Laird, equal.

Geometry—1, Grace Dutcher; 2, Lester Mellish, Union Road, George McLeod, Milton; 3, W. Curtis; 4, T. Driscoll, O. Horne equal; 5, James Todd, Bradalbane.

Algebra—1, Hattie McFarlane, Sea Cow Head; 2, L. Mellish; 3, T. Driscoll; 4, James Todd, George McLeod equal.

Arithmetic—1, Grace Dutcher, Patrick Campbell, Souris, T. Driscoll, L. Mellish equal; 2, O. Horne, Kenneth Graham, Bradalbane; 3, Hattie McFarlane; 4, W. Curtis.

Chemistry—1, Lillian Robertson; 2, Flora McPhee; 3, O Horne, Mary McGregor equal; 4, Peter L. Duffy, Emerald; 5, Edna Laird; 6, Ella Stavert, N. Bedeque.

Physiology—1, Peter Duffy; 2, Lillian Robertson, T. Driscoll, John McPhee, Bayfield, equal; 3, Charles C. Richards, Charlottetown; 4, O. Horne; 5, Edna Laird.

Physical Geography—1, James Campbell, Montague; 2, Lillian Robertson; 3, O. Horne; 4, Patrick Campbell; 5, W. Curtis, Hattie McFarlane equal.

Physics—1, Hattie McFarlane, P. Campbell equel; 2, Mary McGregor; 3, Kate McMurdo, Elytha Reid, S'Side, Annie McLean, New Dominion equal.

Agriculture—1, Katie McMurdo, Wilmot Valley; 2, L Driscoll, Elytha Reid and John McPhee, equal; 3, J Campbell; 4, Flora McPhee; 5, Grace Dutcher and G McLeod, equal.

History of England—1, P Campbell; 2, O Horne; 3, W Matheson, Ch'town; 4, Peter Duffy and J. McPhee, equal; 5, John Campbell and Lillian Robertson.

SECOND DIVISION.

Latin—1, William Robertson, Marshfield, and Cora White, North River, equal; 2, Annie McMillan, Wood Islands, and Colin Ferguson, Tulloch, equal; 3, Ellen Rodgerson. Pisquid; 4, Lawrence Curran, Victoria Cross.

Latin Composition—1, W Robertson and Josephine Dwan, equal; 2, Faustina McIver, Kinkora; 3, Esther Oxenham, Brookfield, and Annie McMillan, equal; 4, Agnes Sharkey, Corraville and Ellen Rodgerson, equal.

English—1, W Robertson; 2, Annie McMillan and Cora White, equal; 3, Esther Oxenham and Ellen Rodgerson, equal; 4, Maggie James and Willie Myers, Ch'town, equal.

French—1, Lizzie Kirwan, Tignish; 2, Esther Oxenham; 3, Clara Flemming, North Rustico; 4, Mary Campbell, Darlington; Ida B. Scott, Warren Grove; Annie Hennessey and Annie McMillan.

Geometry—1, W Robertson; 2, Ellen Rogerson, Lawrence Curran, Cora White, equal; 3, Colin Ferguson; 4, Esther Oxenham.

Algebra—1, W Robertson; 2, Ellen Rogerson; 3, Ida McEachern, Summerside; 4, Mary Campbell; 5, Colin Ferguson.

Arithmetic—1, W Robertson; 2, Annie McMillan, Colin Ferguson, Esther Oxenham, equal; 3, Ellen Rogerson, Percy Crosby, Marshfield, equal; 4, Cora White, Mary Campbell, equal.

Chemistry—1, Annie McMillan; 2, Cora White, Esther Oxenham, equal; 3, Ellen Rogerson, L Curran, equal; 4, W Robertson.

Physiology—1, Thomas Trainor, Kingston; 2, Annie McMillan, L Curran, equal; 3, Ellen Rogerson; 4, Cora White; 5, Bessie McKinnon, Souris; 6, W Robertson, W Myers, equal.

Physical Geography—1, Cora White; 2, Ellen Rogerson; 3, Percy Crosby, Wallace Ellis, Millcove, equal; 4, W Myers; 5, Colin Ferguson.

Physics—1, Annie McMillan, Josephine Dwan, equal; 2, Regina Smith, Emerald; 3, Esther Oxenham; 4, Thomas Trainor; 5, W Robertson.

Agriculture—1, Esther Oxenham; 2, Cora White, Ellen Rogerson, equal; Annie Macmillan, W Robertson...

아래 페이지들에서 루시 모드 몽고메리는 프린스앨버트 시절과 프린스오브웨일스 대학 시절을 하나로 묶었다. "마음이 통하는 친구들"과 대화하며 상상 놀이를 펼친 것이다.

10쪽 꽃들은 몽고메리가 프린스앨버트에서 로라, 윌리 프리처드 남매와 즐겨 표현하던 언어 가운데 하나였다. 프린스앨버트 세인트존스 연극클럽의 프로그램은 꽃을 잘라 그 테두리를 장식하고 누군가가 "그의 작은 눈을 보라"라고 적은 흰 카드를 덧댄 위에 말린 풀을 붙여놓았는데, 이 풀은 블루 스크랩북의 앞표지 안쪽, 윌리의 머리글자가 적힌 달력 옆에 붙여둔 말린 풀과 같은 것이다. 그 프로그램은 연극 〈우리의 장병들Our Boys〉을 공연하기 위해 만든 것으로, 이 연극에서 윌리는 마종馬從인 켐스터 역할을 맡았다. 이 지면에서 몽고메리는 윌리를 짐 스티븐슨과 대면시켰다(스티븐슨도 앤 셜리의 연인인 길버트 블라이드의 모델이었을지 모른다). 스티븐슨은 졸업식에서 고별사를 낭독했고 그 고별사는 몽고메리가 써준 것이었다.

12쪽 오른쪽에 잘라 붙인 짧막한 기사가 프린스앨버트에 전해졌을 때 몽고메리의 아버지는 물론 프린스앨버트에서 만났던 몽고메리의 친구들도 틀림없이 마음이 뿌듯했을 것이다. 아몬드 꽃은 캐번디시에서 몽고메리를 가르친 교사 해티 고든Hattie Gordon이 오리건주 포틀랜드에서 보낸 것으로 보인다. 6월 15일 시험이 끝난 날, 몽고메리는 신나서 써놓은 메모 옆에 찬란하게 빛나는 천사의 자리를 마련했다.

13쪽 몽고메리가 이런 철로 사진을 기념으로 모은 것은 1930년에 서스캐처원으로 로라 프리처드 애그뉴를 만나러 갈 때였던 것 같다. 로라에게 나눠줄 자료들을 스크랩북에서 떼어내고 그 자리를 철로 사진으로 대신하려 한 듯하다. 몽고메리는 자신이 관객 앞에서 뭔가를 암송한 것과 관련해 기사들을 오려서 수집했고, 1894년 1월 8일 윈슬로 홀Winsloe Hall 발표회에서 사용한 종이꽃도 보관했다. 멋진 시와 재미있는 이야기 몇 편이 색으로 물들인 깃털, 메리 캠벨과 함께 참석한 부흥회 입장권과 나란히 자리를 잡았다. 몽고메리는 일기에 이렇게 적었다. "유명한 전도사 B. 페이 밀스B. Faye Mills가 참석해 여기서 집회를 여니 이곳은 흥분의 도가니에 빠진 듯했다. (…) 밀스 씨는 연사처럼 보이지 않았지만 강한 자석 같은 뭔가를 가진 사람이었다. 아이다는 그들의 표현에 따르면 '회심했다'. 나는 이 표현이 너무 싫다! 메리 캠벨도 홀딱 빠졌을 것 같다." 프린스오브웨일스 대학의 새 교지 《칼리지 레코드》 4월 호에는 몽고메리의 촌극 〈정해진 법칙The Usual Way〉 기사가 실렸다(레드 스크랩북 42쪽).

...tory of England—1, Corin Ferguson;
2, Ellen Rogerson; 3, Annie Hennessy; 4,
Cora White; 5, Thomas Trainor.

Book Keeping — Jessie Stavert, Wilmont Valley; Lester Mellish, Jennie Leard, North Carleton; Annie McLean; Hattie McFarlane; Ella Stavert, Kelvin Grove; Katie McMurdo, T. Driscoll.

Essays—Louise Leard and Lucy M. Montgomery.

School Management—1, Lucy M. Montgomery, David Shaw, equal; 2, Ida McEachern, Stuart Simpson, Nellie McGrath, Tignish, equal; 3, Howard Leslie, Lawrence Curran, Thomas Trainor, equal; 4, Anna Roberson, Annie McMillan, equal;

Teaching—Ethel Connors; Annie Clark, Bay View; Mary Smith, Roseneath; Ellen Taylor; Lucy M. Montgomery; Edward Ryan, Johnston's River; Walter Curtis.

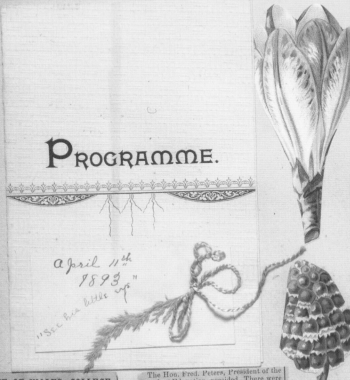

PROGRAMME.

April 11th 1893

"See his little eye"

PRINCE OF WALES COLLEGE.

Commencement Exercises Last Evening.

The Valedictory and Dr. Anderson's Reply.

Music and Essays by the Pupils.

The Important Address of Rev. Dr. Walker, D. D.

Speeches by His Honor the Lieutenant-Governor and the Premier.

A New College Building Promised.

The Prince of Wales College commencement exercises in the Opera House last evening were well attended, and the greatest interest was taken in the proceedings. The programme prepared for the occasion was carried out in a manner which reflected credit on all concerned.

The Hon. Fred. Peters, President of the Board of Education, presided. There were also on the platform His Honor the Lieutenant-Governor, the Superintendent of Education, Rev. Dr. Walker, Hon. Donald Farquharson, Hon. Angus McMillan, and Dr. Anderson and the teaching staff of the College. The pupils occupied seats on the stage, and a more intelligent-looking company of young ladies and gentlemen it would be hard to find anywhere.

Professor Earle presided at the piano and led the musical exercises, the different numbers being well executed considering the short period in which the pupils have been under the instruction of the Professor. Mr. James Hyndman assisted with his violin, playing with his usual skill.

Miss Annie Moore appeared for the first time as a soloist. She possesses a fine voice, which she will do well to cultivate fully.

The essay on "Portia," by Miss Montgomery, was well written and clearly and distinctly read. Miss Laird's subject was "The Merchant of Venice." Her paper was also well written, and it was capitally read by Dr. Anderson. We regret that space will not admit of their publication in full to-day. But we shall try to find room for them in a future issue. The valedictorian was Mr. James H. Stevenson, "the best scholar in the school,"...

Prince of Wales College Commencement.

BRILLIANT GATHERING

IN THE OPERA HOUSE.

THE CLOSING EXERCISES.

Graduation Day of the most important educational institution, (not yet university), in this province is numbered with the past, but joyous recollections will linger in the memories of the staff and students throughout a life time. It is a good thing to be a P E Islander.

Never has a more animated, more intellectual or more inspiring picture been seen on any stage in this Island, than that beheld by the large and select audience assembled last night. Lieut Governor, Premier, Judge and Mayor, all were there honoring and being honored.

On the platform, besides the chairman, Premier Peters, were Lieut Governor Howlan, who gracefully awarded the diplomas, the Hons. Angus McMillan, Donald Farquharson, Prof D J MacLeod, Chief Superintendent of Education, Dr. Anderson, the famed Principal of the Prince of Wales College, and its staff of Professors as follows, namely:—Messrs. Caven, Harcourt, Robertson Shaw and Miller. The students were arranged on the stage, the young ladies in the front row and centre, while the young men were grouped on either side.

The numbers on the pretty souvenir programme were rendered in true college style under the skilful direction of Prof. Earle, who presided at the piano and was publicly and warmly thanked at the conclusion of the exercises by Dr. Anderson.

The two essays read we hoped to have published in full to-day, but owing to the length of Rev Dr Walker's excellent address to the graduates, we will have to defer their publication until Monday. Miss Lucy Maud Montgomery's analysis of Portia was of a high order. In well rounded periods she described the noble characteristics of mind and heart which make this heroine of Shakespeare one of the most admired of all the creations of his genius. We must add also that the essay was read with good effect.

Miss Louisa Laird's resume of the plot in the Merchant of Venice showed a good deal of power of condensation. The chief points were seized, and spiritedly epitomized.

When the Valedictory number on the programme was announced, Mr. James H. Stevenson, the winner of the medal stepped forward, and after the loud and prolonged cheering had ceased, read in excellent form and with suggestive emphasis the following

VALEDICTORY

Another year in the annals of the Prince of Wales College has rolled by and once again its students assemble here to welcome with pleasure those who have so kindly come to witness our commencement exercises. This is an hour when joy and happiness and and kindly feeling should pervade every heart, when every petty annoyance or disappointment of the past year should be forgotten, and everyone clasp hands in friendly affection, for to-night many of us must part to meet no more fellow students and classmates.

Some in higher colleges will steadily strive to reach that far off shining goal where fame holds out her laurel crown; while some will bid farewell to college life to-night, and plunge at once into the busy world — a thereto...

...wrest from the world influence and fortune ever to be won by industry and perseverance. But whatever part we may pursue, whatever pleasures await us in after life, no memory will be so dear to our hearts as that of our college course. A tie of common fellowship will forever bind those who have wandered together through classic mazes or wrestled with mathematical mysteries at P. W. College.

A larger number of students than ever before have attended our college this session, and lack of accommodation has been the greatest drawback to satisfactory work. It is earnestly to be hoped that the powers that be will see fit at no distant day to provide us with a more commodious building. But notwithstanding this, the past year has been one of steady progress. All the various branches of the curriculum have been well sustained, and drawing has been added under the the able instruction of Prof Shaw.

But the College year has not been one of wholly unrelieved toil. Pleasant, and we also hope profitable, recreation was afforded by the Debating Society, where our budding orators displayed their powers, and by the football contests where strength and activity of body as well as of mind were promoted. A new departure has been witnessed by the publication of a monthly newspaper by some enterprising students. This bright little periodical is devoted to the interests of the College and has formed a pleasurable feature in the history of the year.

And as regards our Professors, what can we say but what has been said again and again by students who have gone out from this our college, encouraged and strengthened by their hearty assistance and sympathy. None of us will ever forget the instruction and advice of our energetic and esteemed Principal, Dr. Anderson. The recollection of Prof. Caven's genial humor will ever bring a smile to our faces and a hearty remembrance to our hearts. Prof. Harcourt, our teacher of science, has interested all and opened to our view many of the wonders of the natural world. Profs. Shaw and Robertson have taken the chairs formerly occupied by Profs. Robinson and West. It is superfluous to speak of the splendid work they have accomplished in their various departments; suffice it to say, that deserved success has crowned their efforts. Among the athletes of the college, Prof. Shaw will be gratefully remembered for the interest he has displayed in their sports. Prof. Miller and Arsenault have officiated in their several branches to the satisfaction of the students and all concerned. Owing to Mr Lloyd's departure from the province we had no instructor in music until late in the term, when Prof Earle commenced an enthusiastic and successful course of instruction, and the hours spent with him have been enjoyed, and will long be remembered by us all. We take this opportunity of extending our heartiest thanks to our friends in Ch'town, who have done so much to make our sojourn among them pleasant.

And now, dear fellow students, we turn to each other for a last farewell. Let each and all of us take this as a sacred trust through life to keep the reputation of our *Alma Mater* unsullied, to reflect honor on the teachers to whom we owe so much, and to help our fellow men to higher planes of thought and action. Let us take the sublime yet simple motto as our own: "*Ich Dien*—I serve." And let us serve—not ignoble ends, petty factions and the darker passions of human nature, but rather acknowledge as our masters only the noblest thoughts and motives, the highest aspirations and the kindliest feelings between man and man. Such a servitude would be glorious indeed. Once more, friends, professors, classmates, we bid you all farewell, and yet to the end of time we will be students, for what is the world, but one great college, where we must all learn the deepest lessons of human life. Let us then,

"Go forth prepared in every clime
To love and help each other,
And know that they who counsel strife,
Would bid us strike a brother."

블루 스크랩북 10쪽

No 5 Lucy Maud Montgomery
P. W. College
1893 - 94.
September 5th - June 8th
Monday. June 11th
Begun!

Time Table
of
Examination for Teachers' Licenses, June 1894.

Monday June 11th

	Class I		Class II
9 - 12	English	done. all.	English
1.30 - 3.30	History	done all.	History
3.45 - 5.45	Agriculture	Done Some	Agriculture

Two days over.

Tuesday. June 12th

	Class I		Class II
9 - 12	Geometry	Done. 6 out of 8	Geometry
1.30 - 3.30	French	done Some.	French
3.45 - 5.45	Scientific Temperance	done	Scientific Temp.

One step nearer freedom.

Wednesday, June 13th

	Class I		Class II
9 - 11.30	Latin	done all.	Latin
1.30 - 3.30	English Literature	done not	Physics
3.45 - 5.45	School Management	done all	School Management

Light ahead.

Thursday, June 14th

	Class I		Class II
9 - 11.30	Greek	done all	Geography
1.30 - 3.30	Chemistry	done some	Chemistry
3.45 - 5.45	Algebra	done some	Algebra

Almost there.

Friday. June 15th

	Class I		Class II
9 - 11.30	Trigonometry	done	Arithmetic
	Optional English	done	

At last.

"Hail, Freedom hail! Sweet Liberty".
All finished.
20 minutes to twelve.
Friday Morning
10

Concert
or
basket Social
Winsloe Hall
Jan 8 /89.

"Let him have
it then"

"And it was cold
Oh it was cold.
35°-20°. Amen!"

Devotion.

Wednesday
June 20 th
1894.

"Dreams of
childhood"

"Under
the old
birch trees"

"Luck and Happiness"

"Rest cometh after
toil"

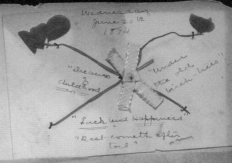

CONCERT AND BASKET SOCIAL.

Concert and Basket Social.—Quite a number of people from the city drove up to Winsloe yesterday afternoon to "take in" the concert and basket social for the benefit of the hall at that place. The Choir of the First Methodist Church, assisted by some of our local talent rendered a programme of choruses and songs in a most pleasing manner. The songs were received with much applause by those present. Particularly good were the recitations by Miss Montgomery and the vocal selections by Messrs. Bremner and F. deC. Davies and Master Chas. Earle. In his selection, "The Cork Leg," Mr. Bremner fairly "brought down the house," as also did Master "Tod," by his capital rendition of "Sarah Jane." Both were encored. The second part of the entertainment consisted of the sale of baskets, which were rapidly bought up by the young men, some thirty being disposed of, bringing from $1 to $4 per basket. Messrs. L. E. Prowse, E. H. Norton and Sheriff Horne were the auctioneers. This brought the proceeding to a close. All were well pleased with the capital manner in which the entire proceedings were carried out.

Concert at Winsloe.

A very large audience assembled in the Winsloe Hall last night to listen to a concert given by the Choir of the First Methodist Church and their friends. The programme was a good one and faithfully carried out. The selections by the choir were fine. Messrs. Cooke, Lewis, and Davies' solos were well rendered. Master Charles Earle's "Good Bye Susan Jane," and Mr. Bremner's "Cork Leg," brought down the house. Miss Montgomery's Recitations were splendidly given. The good people of Winsloe are to be congratulated upon being the owners of such a beautiful Hall capable of seating we understand 300 people. The choir and friends are loud in their praise of the kindness shown them by the committee, and thoroughly appreciate their kindness. The baskets, which realized good prices, were auctioned off by Messrs. L E Prowse, Sheriff Horne and E H Norton,—each of whom seemed to know his business thoroughly. Mr John T Holman's beautiful residence was open to receive the guests. It looked splendid—lit up from top to bottom. The Charlottetonians say "Long live Mr and Mrs J T Holman." They will not forget their kindness for some time to come.

DOROTHY: A DISAPPOINTMENT
By Charles B. Going

Her hair is soft—the brown that glows
With sudden little glints of gold;
Her rounded cheek, faint flushing shows,
Like apple buds that half unfold.

Her throat is full and round and white—
The sweet head poised so daintily;
She reads a note; I wish I might
Address her, too, "Dear Dorothy."

Ah, Dorothy, so very dear!
With clear sweet eyes of tender brown
And, close above the small pink ear,
The dark hair rippling gently down.

Dear Dorothy, so very fair!
My thoughts outrace the rushing train
To build strange castles in the air,
With Dorothy for chatelaine.

How sad when pleasures born of hope
Are born so late so soon to die!
She drops her letter's envelope
Addressed to—Mrs. Arthur Why!

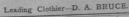

Leading Clothier—D. A. BRUCE.

The College Record

"Non Collegio sed vitæ discimus."

VOL. I.   P. W. COLLEGE, CHARLOTTETOWN. APRIL, 1894.   NO. 3.

The College Record.

The Record will be published monthly during the remainder of the term.

Subscription price 25 cents, in advance. Single copies 10 cents.

Editors—E. N. M. Hunter, H. McKinnon.

Business Manager—T. R. MacMillan.

Address all communications to

Business Manager,
P. W. College,
Charlottetown.

MOUSTACHE EXAMINATION.

Passed—
    Daniel Chowen.

Honorable Mention—
    Thomas James.
    Howard Leslie.

POMPADOUR EXAMINATION.

First Class—
    Reginald Stewart.
    Frederick Miller.

Passed—
    Hedley McKinnon.
    Charles Myers.

Honorable Mention—
    Wallace Coffin.
    Samuel Willis.

Jan / Feb / March / April / May / June / July / Aug / Sept / Oct / Nov / Dec calendar 1892

COMPLIMENTS OF .
W. B. ROBERTSON,
Dealer in FARM SEEDS AND IMPLEMENTS.

GOOD REASON FOR CRYING.

Among the early lawyers of Missouri were Judge James C—— and Gen. John C——, brothers, both excellent lawyers and splendid advocates. Gen. John, when occasion required, closed his argument to the jury bathed in tears himself, with most of the jury and audience weeping, too.

One day he and Judge James were trying a case, James prosecuting and John defending. James made his speech, a strong one for his side of the case, and ended with telling the jury:

"Gentlemen, my brother John will next address you on the other side of the case; and I want to caution you, he will cry and try to make you cry. He does it in all his cases."

Gen. John then spoke to the jury, making one of the very best of his pathetic appeals, causing jury and audience to forget James's admonition; and as tears were freely flowing, John, with great drops rolling down his cheeks, said to the jury:

"My brother Jim told you I would cry; I am crying; and, gentlemen of the jury, if you had such a darned mean brother as Jim, you would cry, too."

John's client was acquitted.

ADMIT TWO
DOORS OP N 3 00 P M

THE LAST DAY, SUNDAY, 3.30, P. M.

REV. B. FAY MILLS

AT FIRST METHODIST CHURCH

Owing to the crowds, this ticket must not be used by any church member, unless accompanied by one who is not.

블루 스크랩북 13쪽

블루 스크랩북 14쪽의 맨 위에 있는 꽃 이름표 뒷면에는 각각 설리나 로빈슨(왼쪽), L. M. 몽고메리(가운데), 몽고메리의 사촌인 루시 맥닐Lucie McNeill(오른쪽)의 이름이 찍혀 있다. 잡지 사진에 보이는 글 쓰는 공간은 캐번디시에 있는 외가에서 몽고메리 자신이 글을 쓰던 공간(아래)과 매우 흡사하다.

1891년 6월 30일, 몽고메리와 메리 스토벨Mary Stovel은 프린스앨버트에서 린지까지 마차를 몰고 가서 옛 학교 친구가 그곳 시골 학교에서 발표회를 열 수 있도록 도와줬다. 몽고메리는 그곳을 오가는 길에 봤던 꽃들에 대해 일기에 이렇게 적었다. "너른 들판은 이제 들장미로 온통 붉게 물들었고, 우리는 멋진 길을 달렸다. 우리는 (…) 마차를 몰아서 통나무 교사校舍에 도착했다. 눈부시게 아름다워 정신이 혼미해지는 광경이었다. 사방에 무성한 포플러 나뭇가지와 들장미와 오렌지색 나리꽃이 천지를 뒤덮었다." 그때는 아직 몽고메리에게 카메라가 없어서 그 풍경을 사진에 담을 수 없었다.

"LET THERE BE KITTENS."—"Who makes the kittens, Jackie?" "Why, God makes them, Ethel. He doesn't make them as he does babies, one by one, but He just says, 'Let there be kittens,' and there are kittens."

A TOUCH OF NATURE
By Madeline S. Bridges

FATHER (winding the clock): "Time to lock up now. It's nearly ten o'clock."

Mother: "Oh, don't hurry, father."

Father: "Don't hurry? We ought to be asleep by this time, considering we've got to be at the haying by sun-up to-morrow. Are the boys in bed?"

Mother: "They've gone up-stairs."

Father: "Well then, I'll close the——"

Mother: "Ida hain't come in yet."

Father: "Hain't come in? Why?"

Mother: "Oh, she's at the gate. She's been down to singing-class."

Father: "Well, why doesn't she——"

Mother: "Sh—sh—they'll hear you. There's a young man with her."

Father: "A young man? Who?"

Mother: "Isaac Penn came up with her."

Father: "I should think her brothers would be company enough."

Mother (dryly): "Should you?"

Father: "And if a young man does walk up with her he needn't stand three hours at the gate."

Mother: "He hasn't been there ten minutes."

Father (severely): "He has no business to be there any minutes. Why doesn't he know enough to say good-night and go?"

Mother: "Ephram, wasn't there ever a young fellow that used to walk home with me from singing, and hang over the gate till all hours, especially a night like this?"

Father: "That was different. You were woman big."

Mother: "Ida's woman big. She's nineteen past."

Father: "Ida's nothing but a child."

Mother: "Well, she's a whole year older than I was, when you——"

Father (hastily): And, besides, er—ah—I was dead in love."

Mother (quietly): "How do you know that Isaac hain't?"

Father: "Isaac Penn in love with Ida? Sho! The boy hasn't a vote yet."

Mother: "He's got a heart, though. You had your first vote the year we were married—just remember that."

Father: "Mother, I'm surprised at you putting up with such nonsense about Ida. Time enough for her to keep company five years from now."

Mother (approvingly): "Of course it is, and it's time enough now, if the right one comes along. Isaac is good and steady."

Father (firmly): "Well, I won't have it, that's all. Call her in. It's bedtime."

Mother: "Ephram, you don't suppose I would do such a thing as that?"

Father (with sternness): "Neelie, it's your duty."

Mother (with spirit): "It isn't my duty to insult my daughter. My mother never did it to me."

Father (half smiling): "She never had to; you wouldn't let me stay so long."

Mother: "Oh, I wouldn't let you stay——"

Father: "And no sensible fellow would want to stay."

Mother: "You were a sensible fellow, Ephram."

Father: "Now, mother."

Mother (with decision): "But you were; every one said so."

Father: "I couldn't be sensible with Neelie; you just turned my head."

Mother (softly): "Well, they were pleasant times. I love to remember them."

Father: "Ye-es. I don't know as any one ever had a pleasanter courtship."

Mother: "But you were mighty jealous."

Father (musingly): "Was I? I suppose I was. I know there seemed to be always some one trying to cut me out."

Mother: "Do you remember the night at Lucy Crumm's wedding, when you sat and sulked all evening in a corner."

Father: "And that big student fellow from New Haven was shinning up to you? But I walked home with you, after all."

Mother: "I guess you did! And how you scolded. We stood at the gate till the moon rose—the little silver half moon."

Father: "And you cried, and we made it all up."

Mother: "And the next day you wrote me a letter"—(the gate clicks)—"oh, there comes Ida."

(Enter Ida, smiling, radiant.)

Ida: "It's the loveliest night! Just a sin to go to bed."

Father (smiling, also): "Well, Ida, dismissed your company, have you?"

Ida (demurely): "Isaac? Oh, yes."

Father: "What a shame to send him off so early."

Mother: "Ida knows what to do."

Father: "But Isaac don't. I'm blest if any girl could hustle me like that when I was Isaac's age!"

With food of love to thee

Forget Not the Old Folks at Home
BY LOUISE S. UPHAM

Afar from the scenes your young hearts loved
Atar from the homestead's shade
O, active women and busy men,
Your toiling feet have strayed;
But whether you strive in the public mart,
Or by firesides of your own,
O, never forget the home of your youth,
And the couple who wait alone.

Their cups are not brimming o'er with joys,
Their hands are not full of flowers;
They live in life's silvering, autumn years,
And dwell in life's solemn hours.
When, together, they struggled up life's fair hill,
Child-voices made music sweet
In their happy home, while their hearts kept time
To the patter of little feet.

But now, adown the shadowy side
They wearily move, and slow;
And their eyes grow dim, when, with faltering tones,
They speak of the "long ago."
They gave their youth, they gave their strength,
That their children might attain
To station, or wealth, or heights of fame,
That never were theirs, to gain.

And now by the lonely hearth they wait,
Whose years are almost done,
Like shocks of corn that are whitening fast
In the mellow, autumn sun;
And the Benjamin-cup, in their burdened sacks,
The joy of all priceless joys,
Is the clasping hand and the yearning heart
And the love of their "girls and boys."

So, never forget the dear "old folks,"
And the blessings far away;
Far, farther off from their peace and rest,
Your feet each year will stray;
And, by and by, when the turf is pressed
O'er their graves, you will long, in vain,
For the loving smile and the welcoming kiss
That will never be yours again.

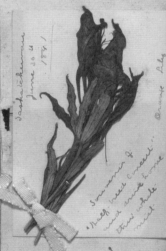

KISSES.

There's a great deal of bliss in a lingering kiss,
And oceans of solid rapture;
There are lots of fun in a stolen one—
If you're clever about the capture.

The cutest trick in a kiss that's quick
Is to put it where it belongs;
To see that it goes below the nose
And knocks at the gate of songs.

A kiss that is cold may do for the old,
Or miss with a near relation;
But one like that is a work—that's flat—
Of supererogation.

If you're going to kiss, be sure of this—
That the girl has got some heart in her;
I wouldn't give a dare for the full of a barn
Of kisses without a partner.

The point of this rhyme is to take your time;
Kiss slowly, and do it neatly;
If you do the thing right, and are halfway bright
You can win her sweet heart completely.

여기에 루시 모드 몽고메리는 프린스에드워드 섬의 비더포드에서 첫 교편을 잡고 행복했던 처음 몇 달 동안을 장난기 가득하게 요약해뒀다. 몽고메리는 이곳에서 1894년부터 1895년까지 학생들을 가르쳤다. 귀퉁이를 차지한 기사 세 편은 결혼 소식이고, 네 번째 기사(오른쪽 아래)는 루 디스턴트 Lou Dystant와 관련된 내용으로, 그는 몽고메리에게 반한 그 지역의 청년이다. 가운데 놓은 것은 캐번디시와의 작별 인사라 할 수 있다. 캐번디시는 훗날 몽고메리가 소설 속에서 앤의 에이번리로 재탄생시킨 마을이다. 꽃은 번영을 의미하고, 촌극의 개요를 적은 카드들이 작은 꽃다발처럼 가운데 꽃다발을 둘러싸고 있다.

1894년 7월 26일 목요일, 캐번디시에 있던 몽고메리는 비더포드 학교의 교사로 합격했다는 소식을 받았다(오른쪽 아래 카드). 같은 날 서부에 나가 있던 로라 프리처드에게서 편지를 받았는데, 곧 앤드루 애그뉴와 약혼한다는 소식을 넌지시 알리는 내용이었다. 몽고메리는 "삼총사trio"인 펜시Pensie, 루시 맥닐과 함께 로라의 새로운 인생과 오랜 우정을 축하했다.

7월 28일(가운데 카드)에 펜시와 루시는 새벽 5시에 몽고메리를 마차에 태워 헌터 강 기차역까지 배웅했다. 비더포드의 엘러슬리 기차역에서 베이필드 윌리엄스 Bayfield Williams(가운데 위 카드)와 약혼녀 이디스 잉글랜드 Edith England를 마주쳤다. 훗날 두 사람은 몽고메리와 친구가 되어 수십 년 후 스크랩북에 등장한다.

몽고메리는 8월에 열린 파티와 무도회에 즐겁게 참석했다(1894년 8월 9일과 8월 16일, 왼쪽과 오른쪽 가운데 카드). 방학을 맞아 고향에 돌아온 베이필드 윌리엄스와 그의 동생 아서를 축하하기 위해 열린 파티였다. 몽고메리는 춤추는 것을 아주 좋아했다.

1894년 10월 19일, 몽고메리는 찰리 매켄지Charley McKenzie가 캐번디시에서 주최한 파티에서 밤새 춤을 추었다(오른쪽 위 카드). 찰리 K. 해리스Charley K. Harris의 감상적인 노래 〈무도회가 끝난 후After the Ball Is Over〉는 1890년대 대중음악계 최고의 히트곡이었다.

가이 포크스Guy Fawkes의 날(1605년 11월 5일, 영국 국회의사당 폭파와 국왕 제임스 1세 시해를 의도한 화약 음모 사건이 무산되고 가담자인 가이 포크스가 체포된 것을 기념하는 날 – 옮긴이)인 1894년 11월 5일 밤, 몽고메리는 엘러슬리의 한 사교 파티에서 루이스 디스턴트를 만났고(가운데 위 카드, 몽고메리는 그를 '루Lew 또는 Lou'라고 적었다), 그는 몽고메리에게 데이트를 청했다. 11월 15일에 루는 몽고메리와 자기 누이인 세이디Sadie를 타인밸리 사교 파티에 데려갔다(왼쪽 아래 카드). 몽고메리가 그를 거절한 뒤에도 루는 계속 시를 보냈다.

1894년 12월 28일, 몽고메리는 첫 번째 학교 시험을 성공적으로 치른 후에 꽃으로 자축했다(왼쪽 위 카드, 연도가 1895년으로 잘못 표기되어 있다). 시험은 구두시험으로 공개적으로 치러졌으며, 마을의 큰 행사여서 연설과 상품도 준비됐다.

몽고메리는 그해를 마무리하며 또 한 번 환희를 맛봤다. 12월 29일에 열린 타인밸리 발표회에서 몽고메리는 연극처럼 각색한 대담 두 편에 출연했고, 살구색 주름 종이로 장식한 자신의 바구니가 경매에서 최고가로 팔렸다는 사실을 알게 됐다(아래 가운데 카드). 바구니를 산 사람은 몽고메리에게 푹 빠져 있던 루 디스턴트였다. 주로 파이 같은 먹을거리를 채워 넣은 장식 바구니를 경매에 부쳐 마련한 기금은 마을 사업을 위해 사용됐는데, 이때 경매 기금은 비더포드에 새로운 마을 회관을 짓기 위한 것이었다.

E. Bayfield Williams

THE young people of Bedeque held a concert and sale of fancy baskets at Tyne Valley on Saturday last the 29th ult. I was in aid of a new Hall to be erected in Bideford and was very successful in all respects. It is difficult to find in any country place a better array of dramatic talent. In the drama "Cinderella" Mr. S J. Ellis as the Prince, Miss Edith England as Cinderella, and Misses Maud Montgomery and Maud Hayes as Lucretia and Arabella respectively, were exceptionally good. Miss Montgomery, who recited the "Old Sailors' Story" proved herself to be an accomplished elocutionist and Miss England sang 'That Melody Divine' splendidly. But not only dramatically but also financially, as the neat sum of $25 was realized, which was considered very good especially as the evening was very disagreeable.

여기에 실린 몇 가지 이야기에서는 연애와 결혼에 관한 생각이 드러난다. 루시 모드 몽고메리는 〈이중주The Duet〉라는 재미있는 시 아래에 삼촌인 리앤더Leander가 세 번째 부인이 될 여자와 약혼했다는 기사를 배치했다. 다소 우울한 〈무도회 후에After the Ball〉라는 시의 제목은 큰 인기를 끌었던 노래 〈무도회가 끝난 후〉를 의도적으로 연상시키려는 배치

인 듯한데, 몽고메리도 앞쪽에서 이 노래를 인용한 바 있다. 꽃다발은 1890년 몽고메리가 어릴 때 외할아버지와 프린스앨버트로 가던 길에 꺾은 것으로, 뜻밖에 마주친 행복한 순간을 의미한다. 아버지는 리자이나에서 두 사람을 맞아 프린스앨버트까지 동행했다.

구혼자

모순적인 일이지만, 열 번도 넘는 청혼을 받으면서 열정적인 사랑을 천명했던 여인은 결국 열렬히 사랑하지도 않는 남자와 결혼했다. 1906년 10월의 어느 날, 목사인 이완 맥도널드의 청혼을 남몰래 받아들인 서른두 살의 몽고메리는 그날 일기장에 이렇게 적었다. "완벽하고도 황홀한 행복 같은, 뜨겁게 사랑하는 남자와 결혼할 때 비로소 찾아오는 감정을 나는 더 이상 바라지 않았다." 몽고메리는 허먼 리어드Herman Leard를 만났던 스물세 살에 그런 황홀한 행복을 느꼈지만 두 사람 다 서로 다른 상대와 약혼했고, 몽고메리는 지적인 면에서나 미래에 대한 포부에서나 허먼을 자신에게 걸맞은 상대로 여기지 않았다. 허먼과의 이루어지지 않은 사랑은 그 후 몽고메리의 삶에서 열정의 기준이 되었고, 1909년 올리버 맥닐Oliver Macneill에게 육체적으로 끌리는 감정을 이 기준에 견주어 가늠했다.

몽고메리가 첫사랑이라 말하는 순간은 십 대 초반에 찾아왔고, 그 상대였던 네이트 록하트Nate Lockhart는 아카디아 대학Acadia University에 입학한 뒤에도 한참 동안 몽고메리에게 편지를 보냈다. 열여섯 살에 아버지를 찾아가 프린스앨버트에서 지낼 때는 이름을 밝히지 않은 남자아이에게서 크리스마스 선물을 받았다. 단짝 친구의 오빠였던 윌리 프리처드의 관심은 기꺼이 받아들였지만, 자기 선생이었던 존 A. 머스터드의 구혼은 외면했다. 캐번디시에서는 적어도 세 청년, 잭 레어드Jack Laird, 헨리 맥루어Henry McLure, 알렉 맥닐Alec Macneill이 몽고메리에게 구애했고, 교사 생활을 하는 동안에는 렘 매클라우드Lem Mcleod와 루 디스턴트가 청혼했다. 에드윈 심프슨Edwin Simpson의 청혼을 받아들여 사랑 없는 약혼을 한 상태에서 허먼과도 밀회를 즐겼다. 벨몬트의 심프슨 가족이 느꼈을 참담함을 생각해보라. 몽고메리는 에드윈의 청혼을 거절했다가 받아들였고, 다시 거절했다. 에드윈의 동생 풀턴Fulton도 몽고메리에게 집착하게 됐는데, 몽고메리는 에드윈의 또 다른 동생 앨프Alf와도 마차를 몰고 나가 데이트를 했다.

이완 맥도널드가 캐번디시에 온 1903년 즈음, 몽고메리는 "몽고메리 집안의 열정적인 피와 맥닐 집안의 청교도적인 양심" 사이의 갈등으로 지쳐 있었던지, 낙천적인 성격답게 배경과 포부의 편안한 조화를 선택했다.

With the Christmas greetings of The Editor

A DUET.

BARITONE—Now we're engaged, if you have
    brothers,
    By that I mean the men whom
      you've refused,
    They must be on a footing with the
      others;
    I won't have any mild endear-
      ments used,
      Now we're engaged.

SOPRANO—If you had any sister and I knew it,
    I mean a girl who said she'd be
      your sister,
    She should be taught how not to do it,
    And comprehend that you can
      quite resist her,
      Now we're engaged.

BARITONE—As if I wished to look at other beau-
    ties,
      Now you are mine.
SOPRANO—   As though I cared for men
    Compared to you! I hope I know my
      duties;
    Of course we used to flirt, but that
      was then;
      Now we're engaged.

BARITONE—Who was the man with topcoat lined
    with sable?
SOPRANO—   Who was the girl with bonnet
      trimmed with pink?
BARITONE—I would inform you, but I am unable,
SOPRANO—   I'd tell his name, but really I can't
      think,
      Now we're engaged.

BARITONE—Now no more lingering in conserva-
    tories,
    Under dim colored lights and
      tropic bowers.
SOPRANO—Now no more reading sentimental
    stories
    To girls and giving them bonbons
      and flowers;
      Now we're engaged.

BARITONE—I shall not tolerate the least flirta-
    tion,
    I warn you fairly.
SOPRANO—Please don't be enraged;
    But might we sometimes take a
      brief vacation.
      Now we're engaged!
        —*Yankee Blade.*

The engagement is announced of the
Rev. L. G. Macneill, the eloquent and
able pastor of St. Andrew's church, to
Miss Mary Kennedy, daughter of Ald.
James Kennedy of Summer street.

After the Ball.

They sat and combed their beautiful hair,
  Their long, bright tresses, one by one,
As they laughed and talked in the chamber
    there,
  After the revel was done.

Idly they talked of waltz and quadrille;
  Idly they talked, like other girls,
Who over the fire, when all is still,
  Comb out their braids and curls.

Robe of satin and Brussels lace,
  Knots of flowers and ribbons, too,
Scattered about in every place,
  For the revel is through.

And Maud and Madge in robes of white,
  The prettiest nightgowns under the sun,
Stockingless, slipperless, sit in the night,
  For the revel is done.

Sit and comb their beautiful hair,
  Those wonderful waves of brown and gold,
Till the fire is out in the chamber there
  And the little bare feet are cold.

Then out of the gathering winter chill,
  All out of the bitter St. Agnes weather,
While the fire is out and the house is still,
  Maud and Madge together—

Maud and Madge in robes of white,
  The prettiest nightgowns under the sun,
Curtained away from the chilly night,
  After the revel is done,

Float along in a splendid dream
  To a golden gittern's tinkling tune,
While a thousand lusters shimmering stream
  In a palace's grand saloon.

...ing of jewels and flutter of laces,
  ...l odors sweeter than musk,

Men and women with beautiful faces
  And eyes of tropical dusk—

And one face shining out like a star,
  One face haunting the dreams of each,
And one voice sweeter than others are,
  Breaking into silvery speech—

Telling, through lips of bearded bloom,
  An old, old story over again,
As down the royal bannered room,
  To the golden gittern's strain,

Two and two they dreamily walk,
  While an unseen spirit walks beside,
And, all unheard in the lover's talk,
  He claimeth one for a bride.

O Maud and Madge, dream on together,
  With never a pang of jealous fear!
For, ere the bitter St. Agnes weather
  Shall whiten another year—

Robed for the bridal and robed for the tomb,
  Braided brown hair a... ...den tress,
There'll be only one of y... ...eft for the bloom
  Of the bearded lips to press—

Only one for the bridal pearls,
  The robe of satin and Brussels lace,
Only one to blush through her curls
  At the sight of a lover's face.

O beautiful Madge in your bridal white
  For you the revel has just begun,
But for her who sleeps in your arms tonight
  The revel of life is done.

But, robed and crowned with your saintly
    bliss,
  Queen of heaven and bride of the sun,
O beautiful Maud, you'll ...ever miss
  The kisses another ha... ...n.
          —Nora Perry.

18쪽 거의 정확히 삼 년이라는 시간이 차이 나는 두 꽃다발은 고등학생에서 교사로 몽고메리의 전진을 자축하는 것이다. 1891년 8월 26일은 프린스앨버트에서 보낸 마지막 날이었다. 몽고메리와 로라는 에글링턴 빌라Eglinton Villa(아버지가 자기 집안과 에글링턴 백작가의 연관성을 강조하기 위해 선택한 이름이다) 밖에 있는 정원에서 눈물을 훔치며 페튜니아, 목서초, 스위트피 등을 꺾어 꽃다발을 만든 다음 기념으로 서로 맞바꿔 가졌다. 1894년 8월 8일, 몽고메리는 비더포드에서 활기찬 사교 생활을 즐기고 있었다. 인디언 아일랜드로 떠난 소풍은 윌리엄 부부가 방학 중인 두 아들 베이필드와 아서를 위해 개최한 일련의 파티 중 하나였다. "엘러슬리 노트Elerslie Notes"라는 제목의 기사는 "훌륭한 교사라는 사실을 입증했다"라고 말하여 몽고메리를 기쁘게 했다.

19쪽 작가는 로맨스라는 단어를 다룰 줄 안다. 프랑스의 유명한 매춘부로 카미유라고도 불린 마리 뒤플레시스Marie Duplessis(1824-1847)는 아름답고 재치 넘치는 것으로 유명했다. 뒤플레시스의 때 이른 비극적 죽음은 소설과 연극, 오페라(주세페 베르디의《라 트라비아타》)와 영화에도 영감을 주었다. 앤 셜리가 알았다면 가슴 시린 뒤플레시스의 이야기에 열광했을 것이다. 재미있는 사건의 기억은 데이지에 담겨 있다. 1893년 6월 16일 저녁, 몽고메리가 프린스오브웨일스 대학입학시험을 치르기 며칠 전에, 몽고메리와 셜리나 로빈슨, 그리고 잭 레어드는 자물쇠로 잠긴 학교 건물을 실수로 창문까지 깨가며 장난삼아 억지로 밀고 들어갔다.

20쪽 여기에는 1891년부터 1895년까지 매해의 기념품을 모아놓았다. 1895년, 몽고메리는 비더포드에서 즐거웠던 교직 생활을 그만두고 일 년 과정으로 영문학을 공부하기 위해 달하우지로 떠났다. 몽고메리는 앤 셜리에게도 똑같이 즐거운 가르침의 경험을 주었고, 핼리팩스에서 대학교를 다닌 일 년의 경험을 확장하여 앤이 킹스포트의 레드먼드 대학이라는 가상의 학교에서 4년제 학사 학위를 받도록 했다. 잡지에서 오려낸 서스캐처원 강(서스캐처원에서 생활할 때 몽고메리에게 중요한 장소였다) 사진 위에 붙여둔 초대장은 1891년 4월 8일에 있었던 결혼식 초대장으로, 몽고메리 새어머니의 숙모인 메리 매켄지Mary McKenzie와 사이러스 스토벨Cyrus Stovel이 그 결혼식의 주인공이었다. 왼쪽 아래의 흰 카드와 함께 붙인 타버린 성냥은 1892년 12월 19일에 사용한 것으로, 그날 몽고메리는 캐번디시의 옛 학교로 돌아와 프린스오브웨일스 대학입학시험을 준비하기 시작했다. 그 카드에 적힌 글귀는 다음과 같다. "반쯤은 미소 지은 얼굴로, 반쯤은 한숨을 쉬며, 그대는 사색하네. 즐거웠던 과거를. 오, 그대가 아직 선택할 수 있다면 그 즐거웠던 시간이 지속되기를 바라겠는가." 이 지면의 가운데를 차지한 기사는 1895년 2월의 부고로, 몽고메리가 좋아한 삼촌인 존 몽고메리의 사망 소식이다. 편자 모양의 꽃 장식은 스크랩북 앞부분에서 프린스오브웨일스 대학 생활의 행운을 기원했던 1893년의 편자 장식처럼 달하우지 대학의 상징색을 둘러싸고 있다.

THE FIRST SONG-SPARROW.

Sunshine set to music!
  Hear the sparrow sing!
In his note is freshness
  Of the new-born Spring;
In his trill delicious
  Summer overflows—
Whiteness of the lily,
  Sweetness of the rose.

Splendor of the sunrise,
  Fragrance of the breeze,
Crystal of the brooklet
  Trickling under trees,
Over moss and pebbles,
  Hark! you have them all
Prophesied and chanted
  In the sparrow's call.

Pilgrim of the tree-tops,
  Burdened with a song
That he drops among us
  As he flies along,
Promises and blessings
  Scattering at our feet,
Till we sing together,
  "Oh, but life is sweet!"

Listen! the song-sparrow!
  Spirit or a bird!
Simple joy of singing
  In his song is heard.
Somewhere, far in glory,
  Love our life has kissed;
He resounds the rapture,—
  Heavenly optimist!

Resurrection-singer!
  Gladness of the year!
In thine Easter-carol
  Bringing heavens so near
That we scarcely know it
  From the earth apart;
Sing immortal summer
  To the wintry heart!

Waft us down faith's message
  From behind the sky,
Till our aspirations
  With thee sing and fly!
"God is good forever!
  Nothing shall go wrong!"
Sunshine set to music—
  'Tis the sparrow's song!—*Lucy Larcom.*
[Written in 1889.]

BASHFUL.

JOHN—"Sallie, ef I was to ask you if you'd marry me, do you think you Ca ... yes?"

SALLIE—"I—er—I guess so."

JOHN—"Wa-al, ef I ever git over this 'ere darn bashfulness I'll ask ye ... o' these times."

Ellerslie Notes.

... Division is in a flourishing condition. ... Williams, our Worthy Patriarch, is ... n of push and ability and under his ... ection we prophecy success for our ...

... our young people have not lost their ... old fashioned dance. Quite a num- ... ones met at the house of James ... Bideford, a few nights ago and were ... by the sweet strains of music from the ... ngus Currie until the "wee sma' ours." ... ple of Bideford have decided to build ... Church. It will be built upon the ... joining the beautiful grounds of the ... parsonage, and the frame, which was ... four years ago, will be used.

... stees of the Bideford School have at ... eded in getting a teacher. Miss M, ... ery is the one selected and is proving ... ood teacher.

... Congregation assembled at the Meth- ... on Sunday evening, the 12th inst., ... ev. J. Dystant, a former resident of the ... ach. His text was Luke 17: 14. The ... as well delivered, very impressive and ... ed to with rapt attention.
OBSERVER.

My thoughts are with you this Christmastide.

Thought with thought is fondly meeting,
While our hearts with love are beating.

ABOUT twenty guests assembled at the residence of Mr Alexander McLeod, Valleyfield Dec 5, 1893 to witness the marriage of his second daughter Margaret Anna Bella, to Mr William Ramsay of Park Corner. The ceremony was performed by Rev D B McLeod M A of Orwell, assisted by the Rev J M McLeod M A of Kensington, brother of the bride. The contracting parties were supported by Dr J Martin of Montague, and Miss Lizzie P McLeod sister of the bride. Both bride and bridesmaid were simply and beautifully dressed in white. An elegant supper was served and all did ample justice to the good things prepared. The remainder of the evening was very pleasantly spent in conversation and singing. Mr Charles R McLeod of Orwell presided at the organ in his usual happy manner. At a late hour—or rather an early hour—the delighted guests returned to their homes. The happy couple will make their home at Park Corner.—COM

Jake was on his knees by Marthy, trying to get her boot off. She was squirming like an eel, shrieking and declaring that he should-n't touch her; her leg was broken, she knew it was, and he was a brute to hurt her so, instead of going for a doctor. Well, it didn't take me long to tell Tom I was alive, and then I staggered over to Marthy and sat down beside her, and tried to help Jake get off her boot. We did it at last, and found she had a sprained ankle and

NO BONES WERE BROKEN,

and the question was how to get her home. The colt was lamed, and the carriage wrecked. Jake was a big fellow, and said he would carry her; and Tom said he'd spell him if he gave out. They tried it. She screamed so when Jake picked her up that he nearly dropped her. She said it hurt her so to let it hang she couldn't endure it, and he must put her down at once. He didn't do it, on the instant, and she seized his hair with one hand, and pulled till she shook his head so he must have been dizzy. She was wild with pain, and too hysterical to know what she was doing. But he put her down after the hair-pulling, you may be sure, and then she sat on a heap of stones with the tears rolling down the side of her nose, while we stood round

AND SHE SCOLDED US

like so many primary-school children, de-claring that we were cruel, and did not know anything. Then suddenly she cried out: "'Look there! Here you've been mur-dering me, when, if you'd had a spark of sense you might have got me most home by this time!' She pointed to an old wheel barrow that had been left by the side of the road. Tom went and got it, and Jake put her in— and they wheeled her home. She cried all the way. The rusty old barrow squeaked like a pig being killed, and whenever there was a jounce she screamed in unison with it. I walked behind on Tom's arm, white and trembling, and thoroughly wet from the water he had flung over me when I fainted, and with my skirt half out of the gathers, and my hat mussed, and scratches all over my face. That was the way we went down the village street, and I never was so mortified in my life. But there was a runaway, and a faint, and a sprained ankle all together—and it ought to have been romantic!"

Friday:
"Sleeves to the dimpled elbow."
"Just look at the win-dow."
"Never mind the window." 1893.

June 16th
"Go out and circumnavi-gate the premises."
"Is it fire or fore ordination or — what?"
good night so be it.

NOT ROMANTIC.

STORY OF A SPRAINED ANKLE.

It is Not so Easy to Carry a Young Woman Home as it Looks in a Novel.

"Some things are romantic in novels," said little Miss Drusilla, pensively, "that somehow don't turn out that way in real life. For instance, in a story, when there has been a sprained ankle, or a faint, the young man 'supports the heroine's fainting form,' and 'chafes her delicate hand,' and 'bathes her lily temples,' or something of that sort, but he never drops water on her gown, or spoils her best bonnet ribbons. If she sprains her ankle, why, he 'cuts the lacing of a fairy shoe,' and does not seem to find it any particular trouble to carry her home a mile or two. But in real life—well! —did I ever tell you how Marthy Gates and I went to ride with the two Hicks boys when we were young? That was a case in point. It ought to have been romantic, but it wasn't. They took us to ride, Marthy and me. The roan colt that drew us in our two-seated waggon was as frisky as a kitten, and Jake, who was driving, was too much taken up with Marthy (she wore a pink bonnet and gray gown, and looked as pretty as a rose) to be attending to the spirited animal properly. So when a hare jumped up under the colt's nose, it bolted, took the bit between its teeth, and tore along at a furious rate before we hardly knew what was happening. There wasn't anything to do but sit still and hold on. The

ROAD WAS FAIRLY LEVEL

till we got to Stony Brook Hill. There we hoped the colt would get over his fright. But he didn't. He started down the hill with the sparks flying under his heels, and the stones rolling, and Jake pulling back and shouting, 'Whoa!' like a wild Indian. Just as we reached the bridge at the bottom he stumbled, pitched forward in a heap, and out we all went into the road. Neither of the boys was hurt. But when I came to myself Tom was wringing his hands and

with my compliments 1890

With best Christmas Wishes.

I have nothing so much at heart as your happiness both in this world and the next

MORE POTATO.

RENAN had a great contempt for mere words, however eloquent. One evening he met, at a sort of literary dinner, Caro, the philosopher beloved of fine ladies. His elo-quent assertions did not seem to interest the sage. In the midst of one of his most sonorous periods Renan at-tempted to make himself heard. But all the ladies were intensely interested; they would not have their pleasure spoiled. "In a moment, M. Renan; we will listen to you in your turn." He bowed submissively. Toward the end of dinner, Caro, out of breath, stopped with a rhetorical emphasis. At once everyone turned toward the illustrious scholar, hoping that he would enter the lists, and the hostess, with an encouraging smile, said: "Now, M. Renan"— "I am afraid, dear lady, that I am now a little behindhand." "No, no!" "I wanted to ask for a little more potato."

"MARIE DUPLESSIS"
[From the only portrait known to exist.]

r & Mrs McFage

est the pleasu

e mo

VIEW ON THE SASKATCHEWAN.

Hamilton's

Assorted

Cream

BONBONS

Gathered to their Fathers.

THE subject of this notice was born at the family home on the 4th day of January, A.D., 1843, and was the third son of the late James T. Montgomery, and one of a family of ten, four sons and six daughters, all of whom survive him—he was nephew of the late Senator Montgomery of Park Corner, and grandson of the Hon. Donald Montgomery, a native of Argyleshire, Scotland, who emigrated to this Island and settled with his parents in Malpeque about the year 1770—and who was the leading magistrate and a representative of Prince County in the House of Assembly for over a quarter of a century and up till the time of his death, when he was succeeded by his son Donald, the late senator. He was married to Miss Perman of New England, by whom he had a family of sixteen, nine sons and seven daughters. The homestead descended to James T., the fifth son and father, who was born in March 1800 and died in June 1871, leaving a widow and 10 children, the homestead again descending to John M. It now descends to the fifth generation in uninterrupted succession. John married in March 1882, Mary Emily, youngest daughter of Alexander McNeill, Esq., of Cavendish, who survives him with a family of five small children. He was a man of robust constitution, and enjoyed almost perfect health all through his life—until about the middle of November last when he had a attack of paralysis which slightly affected his speech and some time afterwards his right hand. Notwithstanding the close attention of the family physician, Dr. Kier, who visited him nearly every day, and by his well-known skill and long experience, supplemented by several of the most prominent physicians Drs. Taylor and McLeod of Charlottetown, Carruthers of Alberton, and McNeill of Kensington, who held consultations on his case on the different occasions—all their efforts proved unavailing as the slow but steady march of the disease manifested that death had marked him for its own. During a long illness under the most excruciating suffering he retained all his faculties to a most surprising degree—he bore it all with the most Christian fortitude and patience that surprised all who saw him—he seemed to rally on Friday and to continue better on Saturday and Sabbath and peacefully passed away at 5 o'clock on Monday, the 18th inst., so composed that the immediate attendants could hardly tell what moment the spirit fled. Mr. Montgomery was a member of the Presbyterian Church at Malpeque—a prominent and useful citizen and an ardent temperance worker and reformer. He was for a term of years usher of the black rod. For four years he represented the 3rd district of Prince County in the House of Assembly. He made an excellent representative and was a great favorite with the masses of the people. Every year it was his custom to hold meetings through the district to meet his constituents and to attend to the local wants. He was an honest and faithful and sagacious public servant. More than that he had a firmness and determination that would not stoop to promote party purposes when he felt his party was in the wrong. This was specially manifested when biennial sessions were proposed as a means of curtailing expenditure. He and one or two others on that occasion took strong grounds against the party and proposed and insisted upon the amalgamation bill instead of biennial sessions. The result proved the soundness of his judgment and the wisdom of his choice. To John M. Montgomery above all other men this province owes a permanent debt of gratitude. Notwithstanding the state of the roads there were over 100 sleighs in the funeral procession. The pall-bearers were Hon. John Yeo, M.P., George Ramsay, Esq., William McN. Simpson, Esq., Robt. Crozier, Esq., Robt. Stewart, Esq., and Geo. Bearsto, Esq. The funeral services at the house and grave were conducted by Rev. W. P. Archibald of Cavendish. The floral tributes contributed by lady friends in the settlement were artistic and beautiful. No man in recent years in this province has passed away more highly respected or more deeply and widely mourned.

A FASHIONABLE PRAYER.

Give me an eye to others' failings blind—
Miss Smith's new bonnet's quite a fright behind!

Wake in me charity for the suffering poor—
There comes that contribution plate once more!

Take from my soul all feelings covetous—
I'll have a shawl like that, or make a fuss!

Let love for all my kind my spirit stir—
Save Mrs. Jones—I'll never speak to her!

Let me in truth's fair pages take delight—
I'll read that other novel through to-night.

Make me contented with my earthly state—
I wish I'd married rich. But it's too late!

Give me a heart of faith in all my kind—
Miss Brown's as big a hypocrite as you'll find!

Help me to see myself as others see—
This dress is quite becoming unto me!

Let me act out no falsehood, I appeal—
I wonder if they think these curls are real!

Make my heart of humility the fount—
How glad I am our pew's so near the front!

Fill me with patience and strength to wait—
I know he'll preach until our dinner's late!

Take from my heart each grain of self-conceit—
I'm sure the gentleman must think me sweet!

Let saintly wisdom be my daily food—
I wonder what we'll have for dinner good!

Let not my feet ache in the road to light—
Nobody knows how these shoes pinch and bite.

In this world teach me to deserve the next—
Church out! Charles, do you recollect the text?

Bideford Breathings.

The Debating Society of East Bideford is a rapidly growing institution, and deserves credit for its great progress. The young people take a very active interest in the meetings, which are well attended every Saturday night, in spite of blizzards and snow banks. The meeting of Feb. 9th was specially interesting, the subject for discussion being, "Which could we do without with the less inconvenience, wood or iron?" It was hotly contested and resulted in a majority of six for those that upheld that iron is more useful than wood. After the debate was closed, Mr. Preston Ellis favored the meeting with an amusing song of his own composition which was loudly applauded. Mr. Bruce Hayes, ambitious of emulating the proceeding production, then sang an extempore song, in which he made so many personal illusions that he was frequently interrupted by storms of applause. The subject of debate next night is, "Which is the most benefit...

루시 모드 몽고메리는 모험과 로맨스를 기리면서 자료들은 모두 간직했다가 훗날 소설에 담아냈다.

이 지면에서는 최소한 세 번의 여행 이야기를 회상한다.

눌러 말린 카네이션은 기적 같은 날이었던 1890년 8월 11일을 기념한 것이다. 이날 몽고메리는 외할아버지와 함께 서스캐처원의 프린스앨버트로 아버지 휴 존 몽고메리를 만나러 가는 긴 기차 여행을 시작했다. 늙은 상원의원은 오랜 정치적 동지인 존 A. 맥도널드John A. Macdonald 경이 기차로 프린스에드워드섬을 여행하고 있다는 소식을 듣고는 여행 중에 잠시 들러 자신들과 동승하자는 전보를 친구에게 보냈다. 그렇게 야심 찬 미래의 작가이자 훗날 캐나다를 대표하는 고전 소설을 쓰게 되는 열다섯 살 소녀는, 첫 기찻길에 오르며 캐나다 초대 총리 내외와 함께 캐나다 횡단 여행을 시작했다. 몽고메리는 그날의 만남을 다음과 같이 일기에 기록했다.

나는 정말이지 캐나다 총리를 만나게 된다는 생각에 너무나 흥분했다. 특별 열차가 도착하고 할아버지를 따라 기차에 오르자, 다음 순간 그 위대한 분이 있었다. 그분은 정말 다정했는데, 그분과 영부인 사이에 앉으라고 나에게 손짓하셨다. 나는 얌전히 앉아 곁눈으로 두 분을 열심히 살펴봤다.

존 경은 정정해 보이는 할아버지였고, 미남은 아니지만 상냥한 얼굴이었다. 영부인은 매우 위엄 있고 우아한 분으로, 은빛 머리카락이 굉장히 아름다웠다. 하지만 예쁜 얼굴은 아니었고, 옷차림도 내 생각에는 볼품없었다.

전에는 기차를 타본 적이 없지만 첫 기차 여행은 정말 아주 즐거웠다.

프랭크 K. 로체스터Frank K. Rochester(명함)는 그로부터 일 년 후, 몽고메리가 프린스앨버트에서 캐번디시로 돌아오는 기차에 오를 때 배웅 나온 사람들 가운데 하나였다. 1895년 6월 17일 월요일은 몽고메리가 비더포드에서 교사로 보낸 마지막 주의 첫날이다(눌러 말린 꽃 묶음 옆에 보이는 15일이라는 날짜는 잘못 적은 것이다).

우리를 가만히 쳐다보는 고양이는 네덜란드 화가 헨리에트 론네르 크닙Henriette Ronner-Knip(1821-1909)이 그린 〈밴조〉로, 1891년 론네르 크닙의 작품에 대한 리뷰와 함께 인쇄된 것이다. 이 네덜란드 화가는 고양이와 한가로운 실내와 풍경을 즐겨 그린 것으로 유명하다. 몽고메리는 고양이를 무척 좋아해서 론네르 크닙의 고양이 그림을 스크랩북 삽화로 많이 사용했다. 한 예로 레드 스크랩북 35쪽이 그렇다. 몽고메리가 소설《블루 캐슬The Blue Castle》(1926)에 등장하는 고양이들 중 한 마리의 이름을 지을 때 이 밴조 그림이 영향을 줬을지도 모른다.

IN PRAISE OF CATS.

Cat-fancying and the cult of the cat have made rapid and popular progress during the last few years. We have cat shows, cat societies, and cat clubs (which have nothing to do with "The Kitcat"), and lastly we have Mrs. Graham R. Tomson's dainty little Anthology of Cats† and Mr. Spielmann's gorgeous volume in praise of Madame Ronner and her cat pictures.‡ All these phenomena would seem to suggest that long ages of neglect, ill-treatment, and absolute cruelty have passed and are done with, and that Shylock's "harmless, necessary cat" is gaining general favour, not merely as a creature given to us by Providence for the destruction of rats and mice and the consumption of kitchen scraps, but as an animal fitted by beauty and intelligence, devotion and courage to be the companion and pet of mankind.

Mrs. Tomson very properly says in her preface or "foreword" that her anthology "needs neither excuse nor justification." In these days of anthologies it was inevitable, considering the fresh vogue of the cat, that it should occur to some one to ask, "Why should not a selection be made of what poets have said and sung concerning the mysterious and suspected beast?" It is fortunate for the cat and for the reader that Mrs. Tomson should have been prompted to make the selection: she has the necessary sympathy with cats, and she has herself written graceful verses on her favourites. It is no reproach to her that, in spite of her industry in research and her taste in selection, the result should be comparatively disappointing. For, though the poets have written a tolerable deal about cats, very few of them have set down aught of consequence. It must be sorrowfully admitted that in the past not even poets have fully understood and appreciated the cat: they have usually dwelt on her common or garden characteristics—her irresponsible grace and playfulness as a kitten, the secrecy of her ways, the mystery of her look when grown up, and the persecuted life she leads in maturity. Even Mrs. Tomson

one must be feline one's self." But to be feline is not enough, for the cat will surrender her secret to no one, painter nor poet, who does not love her much and who does not study her with unremitting attention. The artists who have succeeded in rendering the cat may be counted on the fingers of one hand—the Japanese Hokusai, the Swiss Mind, the English Burbank, the French Lambert, and the Dutch Madame Ronner—and the greatest of these, the one who has succeeded absolutely and all round, is the last, the lady. Has not Champfleury well said "one must be feline one's self"? The pictures of the industrious Madame Ronner are more than a liberal education in cat life and character—they must be to many a revelation of these. Moreover, the technique, the manipulation of the paint, is a superb achievement, and thus Madame Ronner's work gives the supremest delight both to those who are ignorant of art and to those who know what art should be. She represents for preference the most pleasing sides of cat life and character—the simple and amazed gamesomeness of the kitten and the demure satisfaction and anxiety of the cat; the frank mischief infusing the splendid orbs of "Banjo" and the elegant sentiment suffusing the liquid eyes of "Sans Souci"; but, however she sets her cats before us, whether asleep or awake, at rest or in action, all are graceful with the singular feline grace, and all are true—how delightfully true one only perceives by comparing them with the *felidæ* of other artists who have essayed to compass the portrayal of the cat. Mr. Spielmann, in his monograph, has much to say of both critical and biographical interest concerning Madame Ronner, but to artists no item will be of more interest than that about her method of work. "She does not stay to draw her outlines and then proceed to fill them in; she adopts the higher method of regarding in the first instance the object to be painted purely as masses of light and shade." The result is that both the form and the fur of cats and kittens (Madame Ronner prefers the long-haired varieties) are rendered in the most masterly manner, as may be judged from the numerous photogravures with which the work is adorned. The volume is published simultaneously in England, France, and Holland in celebration of Madame Ronner's seventieth birthday; and many a lover of cats would give untold wealth to possess it.

J. MacLaren Cobban.

MADAME RONNER'S "BANJO."

seems mainly fascinated with her "sombre, sea-green gaze inscrutable"; and though Cowper (in his "Colubriad"), the neglected Joanna Baillie (who in her heyday was compared to Shakspere's self), and Wordsworth have written with a certain charm about kittens, they have but expressed at tedious length—Wordsworth has even made the kitten minister to his moral improvement!—what the schoolboy more successfully said in a few words of prose: "A kitten is an animal that is remarkable for rushing like mad at nothing whatever, and generally stopping before it gets there." Mrs. Tomson gives Gray's delightful "Elegy on the Death of a Favourite Cat drowned in a Tub of Gold Fishes," Calverley's "Sad Memories," Dr. Garnett's pretty little "Marigold," and (in her preface) Matthew Arnold's admirable elegy on "Poor Mathias"; yet, on the whole, one is compelled to the conclusion that our English poets have not sufficiently studied the cat before writing about her. Besides the Scots "Auld Bawthren's Song" (which, with its burden of "Three threads and a thrum," is perfect of its kind), the best home productions are those in the section called "Children's Cats"—a section which Mrs. Tomson might have made a little more of. We miss, for instance, "I love little pussy, her coat is so warm," "Three little kittens, one stormy night," and "The old black cat." It is to the French, however, that we must go for the most sympathetic verses about the cat, and especially to the Romanticists of 1830 and their successors. From these—from Baudelaire, from Joseph Boulmier, and (to be quite up to date) from Paul Verlaine—Mrs. Tomson has culled choice examples.

It is remarkable that where the poets have mostly failed the painters have failed too. Where the great masters (as Mr. Spielmann says in his excellent monograph on Madame Ronner) have attempted the painting of a cat, "they have [...] egregiously." The cat's great friend

이 페이지는 루시 모드 몽고메리가 어떻게 스크랩북을 이용하여 훗날 소설에 사용할 보석 같은 소재들을 모아두는지 그 좋은 예를 보여준다. 몽고메리는 C. 로런 후퍼C. Lauron Hooper의 〈세상에 입맞춤이 생겼을 때When Kissing Came into the World〉를 읽고 큰 감명을 받은 나머지, 그 글을 차용하여 1902년 3월 31일 핼리팩스 일간지《데일리 에코Daily Echo》에 칼럼을 기고했고(이 칼럼은 '신시아Cynthia'라는 필명으로 실렸는데, 여기에는 몽고메리가 여러 다른 신문에서 오려낸 기사 내용과 더불어 순간적인 장면들을 허구적으로 창작하여 논평한 글들이 같이 들어가 있다), 나중에 이 글을 고치고 다듬어 네 번째 소설인《스토리 걸The Story Girl》(1911)에 인용했다. 이 책은 프린스에드워드섬에서 쓴 마지막 소설이 되었는데, 그러는 사이에도 블루 스크랩북과 레드 스크랩북은 계속 편집해나갔다.《스토리 걸》18장에서 몽고메리는 스토리 걸을 통해 후퍼의 이야기(세부적인 묘사와 등장인물들의 이름을 바꾸어)를 전하는데 그 부분을 찾아보면 이렇다. "그런데 입맞춤에 대해 말하면 요전에 올리비아 아주머니의 스크랩북에서 봤던 이야기가 생각나요. 들어보실래요? '입맞춤은 어떻게 생겨

났을까'라는 이야기예요."

두 친척의 결혼 소식을 알리는 기사와 결혼 청첩장이 후퍼의 이야기 양옆을 차지하고 있다(왼쪽 위의 짤막한 기사는 몽고메리와 존스턴Johnstone의 자필 결혼식 초대장 뒷면에 붙인 것이다). 1894년 7월 17일에 작성된 이 카드에는 하얀 공단 조각과 함께 짧은 대화와 인용구가 적혀 있는데, 그 결혼에 이루지 못한 로맨스가 있음을 짐작하게 한다. 카드 오른쪽에 몽고메리는 이렇게 적었다. "'L씨, M양이에요.' '알고 있어요.' '아아!!!'" 그즈음 몽고메리는 프린스오브웨일스 대학 과정을 마치고 캐번디시에 있는 집으로 돌아와 교사 자리를 구하는 글을 쓰는 데 열중해 있었다. 그날 저녁, 몽고메리는 매기Maggie와 체슬리 클라크Chesley Clark와 함께 외출했는데, 낮에는 (모드 캐번디시Maud Cavendish라는 필명으로 쓴) 자기 단편소설 〈생강 쿠키 굽기A Baking of Gingersnaps〉가 토론토의《레이디 저널Ladies' Journal》에 채택됐다는 소식을 들은 터였다. 카드 아래쪽에 적은 인용문은 1892년에 발표한 자작시 〈1883년 마르코폴로 호의 침몰The Wreck of the Marco Polo, 1883〉에서 가져온 것이다.

MARRIED.

At the home of the bride, on the 8th inst., by Rev J M McLeod, James T Montgomery, Park Corner, to Mrs Eliza R Johnstone, Clifton.

WHEN KISSING CAME INTO THE WORLD

By C. Lauron Hoo...

NO one has ever been able to improve the wheelbarrow. It was perfect when first invented. Since the days of Aristotle the science of logic has remained practically unchanged, for that eminent Greek established it in its perfection at the outset. The first epoch is still better than all that have followed it, nor can any one ever learn to write such poetry better than did Homer, for he reached the utmost perfection of the art at a bound. So, also, those who discovered—or invented—kissing did their work so well that no one has been able to improve it to this day. It may seem strange that there was ever a time when kissing was unknown among men and women, but such is the case. For many thousands of years our ancestors lived in profound ignorance of the blissful, kissful art, and it was only after the process of evolution had gone so far as to rid man entirely of the characteristics of his tailed ancestors, and there grew in him those higher sentiments and emotions which the poets have been singing to us since the days of Sappho, that kissing came into vogue. I have delved deeply for many years into the ancient writings of Oriental peoples and have at last discovered the exact manner and place—though the time is somewhat doubtful—in which kissing began.

MOST things began in Greece. At least many of the best things of life did, and kissing is among the number. The account of its beginning is carefully and accurately narrated in the old writings which I have mentioned, and I will endeavor to repeat it as best I can, knowing that I cannot, with our strong and vigorous English speech, reproduce the soft and tuneful flow of the Greek tongue. It would be well if I could, for much of the charm of the account is in the very musical sound of the language in which it was first told, and indeed the account needs this charm, for it is not a story in the true meaning of that word, a story with an unexpected and surprising end, but only a little incident which terminated just as any one would expect. So wholly unremarkable was it that only one man in all Greece thought it worthy to be written down and preserved. But thanks to him and his posterity, who carefully kept it, it has at last come into my possession. And as I shall now tell it to you in good faith you must know that every word of it is true.

KISTHENES was a shepherd in that part of Greece known as Bœotia. He lived with his father in a little village named Thebes, which in after years became a great walled city, the most powerful one in all Greece, about and in which occurred some of the events that have been handed down to us in the tragedies of Sophocles. Here lived Kisthenes until he grew to be a young man—a very handsome one, too, the writing ...

... and his shepherd's crook in his hand, he turned his face to the north. After many days he came into Thessaly, another province of Greece. Here he entered into the employ of a man named Dryades, who had many sheep to pasture. Each day Kisthenes led the sheep up the slopes of Mt. Pelion, and let them graze while he played on a pipe. In the distance he could see the Ægean glistening in the sun, the same Ægean upon which the baby Perseus was sent adrift, the same Ægean upon which Agamemnon's fleets sailed to Troy, the same Ægean (to speak of more authentic events) which Xerxes caused to be whipped because its waves broke his bridge of boats. Now Dryades had a daughter named Eurybia, beautiful in form and face, gentle in nature, and skilled in all the accomplishments known to young ladies at that time. Very naturally she and Kisthenes became acquainted, and as she was just as high as his heart and seemed to think very much of him, and as he thought equally as much of her, he hoped some time to have flocks of his own and a little cottage for her to live in with him. Sometimes Eurybia in her rambles over the mountain slopes would meet Kisthenes—by chance of course—with his flock. On such occasions they would talk together with such pleasure that the sun would sink behind them and stretch old Pelion's shadow to the Ægean before they knew that it was time to lead the sheep home. At other times Eurybia, filled with maidenly shyness, would loiter just out of sight among the rocks or in the groves near where her lover pastured his flocks, and listen to the melodies that floated dreamily from his pipe.

And he, knowing in some mysterious way that she was near, would pour forth such dulcet strains that even the sheep would raise their heads to listen.

BUT Kisthenes at length persuaded Eurybia to be less coy and to come out on the mountain every day. They soon became so well acquainted and addressed each other so often that they really hadn't time to pronounce their long names, so Eurybia came to call Kisthenes merely Kiss, and Kisthenes called Eurybia merely Rib. This latter fact is of peculiar significance; for though Kisthenes and Eurybia, young heathens that they were, had never heard that Eve, their first mother was made from a rib of Adam, their first father, yet he—Kisthenes, not Adam—called his sweetheart by the name of the very thing of which the first of her sex was made. Let this carry what proof it may. One day, in wandering over old Pelion within sound of her lover's mellow pipe, Eurybia found a very beautiful little stone in the edge of a mountain stream. She sat down on a rock to examine it. It was scarcely as large as a pea and had very ragged edges. As she turned it round and round in the sunlight she was surprised and delighted to see it flash every color she knew. "The rainbow, the rainbow," she exclaimed, and was about to carry it to Kisthenes when she heard a clatter of hoofs and a snort behind her. Turning she saw a being whom all her life she had prayed the gods she might never meet. It was the great god Pan. There he stood, horns, coarse, hairy ... goat legs and all. Eurybia had often ...

woods, but thought the notes discordant, enamored as she was by the music of her lover's pipe, and now she trembled as she looked at the terrible creature before her.

"Give me the stone," said Pan, holding out his hand.

"But," faltered the quaking Eurybia, "I want it for Kisthenes."

"Bah! Who's Kisthenes? I want it for one of my wood nymphs," said the god, advancing with a menacing step; but before he could reach the girl she was running screaming up the mountain.

SHE heard the clatter of the god's cloven hoofs behind her, heard his hoarse, angry bellowing, and was so terrified that only the thought that Kisthenes would be her protector prevented her from fainting on the spot. In less than a minute she rushed into her lover's arms. Her sudden coming, followed by the terrible roaring god, set the sheep flying, and Kisthenes, brave as he was, trembled like the young lamb in his flock.

Nevertheless he addressed the god humble language, beseeching him to ... away, and promising that on the next ... rificial day he should receive a double of ... ing. Grunting and muttering to hims... Pan clattered away over the mountain, ... he always granted the fervent praye... honest shepherds.

"Now, Rib, tell me what all this is abo... said Kisthenes, and Eurybia told him ... simple tale of her meeting with Pan.

"But," said he, when she had finis... "where is the stone thou wast going ... bring to me? By Jupiter, I fear that in ... fright thou hast thrown it away."

Kisthenes, however, was mistaken. Eurybia had put the jewel in her mo... and she now thrust it out between her ... where it glistened and flashed every c... of the sunlight.

"Take it," she whispered.

Now Kisthenes had both his arms aro... Eurybia, and both Eurybia's arms ... held close to her side by the strong ... brace of Kisthenes, so how could e... have a hand to remove the stone from ... maiden's lips?

Kisthenes solved the problem. On... genius could have conceived the idea ... came into his head at that moment. ... curred to him to take the stone from ... rybia's lips with his own.

Bending over, his face came near ... Nearer and nearer until their lips tou... and then—well, Kisthenes forgot all a... the stone, for such a series of thrills and tremors scampered and scurried over his frame that he not only forgot the stone, but the sheep, the pipe, the mountain, the sea, the sky, the earth, everything in fact but the bliss of that one moment. And Eurybia. She had forgotten the stone, the sheep, the pipe, the mountain, the sea, the sky, the earth, even Pan himself in the bliss of that one moment. And not that one moment alone was this new ecstasy enjoyed, for in fulfillment of Kisthenes' desire and the tender yearning in Eurybia's limpid eyes, again and again their lips met in blissful osculation.

It was something new. Never before had anything like this been discovered by mortal man. Kisthenes and Eurybia, feeling themselves the originators of the delight, and thinking on that account they should have the exclusive right to it, and further, as there was no patent office in those days where inventors could be assured no one would trespass on their rights, these two selfish lovers, I say, determined to keep their secret to themselves.

BUT alas! alas! the secret got out, as secrets are said to when entrusted to women. Forgetting her agreement, Eurybia told a friend of hers, a little Miss Leda, who lived down by the sea. Little Miss Leda, being somewhat coquettish, had two lovers, Magon and Nesides, both of whom she taught this new thing which Eurybia, in honor of her lover, called a "kiss." Now Magon had another sweetheart in a town in Epirus, and on his first visit to her he taught her this new thing called a kiss. Nesides had two other sweethearts west of old Pelion, and to them the secret, as well as its practical workings, was soon confided. One of these young ladies soon jilted Nesides, and as he wearied of the other shortly after this, they both found other lovers to whom they communicated the blissful discovery. From that time it spread, until kissing was not onl... known in Epirus and Thessaly, but ... Thebes, where Kisthenes had spent his b... hood, and in all Greece, and in all th... world. It is told of an Athenian statesma... that, learning of the art of kissing while i... the market-place, he kissed fourteen shop ... girls on the way home that he might be i... practice to show his wife just how it wa... done. At least kissing has become uni... versal, having spread from earth to th... heavens, for who does not know how ofte... our novelists say the sun was kissing th... and roofs of some city, or even ... hair of some fair girl? Now when ... the old rascal whom we have looked u... to and even worshiped in the centuries gone by, is up to such tricks, how can you know, ladies, whom to trust?

Be it known, finally, that Kisthenes and Eurybia were afterward married, and in all their long life Kiss never kissed any woman but his "own dear Rib," as he called her, for he was as true-hearted a fellow as ever bore a shepherd's crook. Their bodies have these many hundred years reposed in old Pelion's side and their names are known to but a few, but their discovery is known wherever men and women have gone over the great earth, and it is still sweetening the joys of life, lessening its sorrows, increasing its love, decreasing its hate, as I hope it may until the day after the end of time.

A
Song of Spring
Leaves of green, violets fair,
Song of lark and black bird trill,
Summer rain and fragrant air!
When I in these measures sing,
Needst thou some greater thing
The Spring tides praise to fill?

WEDDING BELLS.

Rev. Mr. Macneill and Miss Kennedy Married—Robertson-Holly.

A quiet but none the less interesting event took place at 12.30 on Thursday at the residence of Ald. James Kennedy on Summer street, when his only daughter, Mary Gray Kennedy, was united in marriage to Rev. L. G. Macneill, pastor of St. Andrew's Presbyterian church. Only the near relatives of the bride and groom were present. Rev. Dr. Bruce tied the nuptial knot. The bride was charmingly attired in a handsome bluish grey travelling costume of Avon cloth, with a jacket to match, and a brown straw hat, daintily trimmed with forget-me-nots. She carried a large bouquet of bridal roses. She was attended by little Miss Flo. Bullock as a maid of honor. She looked very pretty in a dress of cream-colored surah and a large white leghorn hat. Immediately after the ceremony the bridal party and guests partook of a sumptuous repast, after which Mr. and Mrs. Macneill took the C. P. R. train for Halifax. A large number of friends were at the station to bid them good bye. From Halifax they will take the steamer Vancouver for England. They will go direct from there to Paris and travel as far as Vienna. They will be absent until August. The bride received ma... beautiful presents. Her father's gift was a substantial cheque and a silver tea service. Her mother's gift was an elegant Japanese tea service. The Boys' Association of St. Andrew's church presented their pastor with a fine engraving. The groom presented the maid of honor with a gold link bracelet.

Mr. and Mrs. Co...

"The moon peeped down between the wondrous laced waves of royal forest-green"

Tuesday July 17 1894

"Is the post-office shut"? "Ms L. this is Miss M." "I know it is" alas!

"The gentle wavelets rippled in the ... the stars peeped slyly thro' the yellow haze".

루시 모드 몽고메리는 자신의 과거와 현재에서 여러 장면과 사람을 불러내어 대화를 꾸며냈다. 훗날 앤 셜리에게도 열정적으로 과거와 대화하는 비슷한 취미를 주었다.

25쪽 몽고메리는 편자 모양의 장식을 오려내어 옛날 스타일의 잡지 삽화를 에워쌌다. 그 아래에는 1893년 프린스오브웨일스 대학에 입학하기 직전에 세상을 떠난 사랑하는 친할아버지에 관한 기사를 붙였다. 그 아래에 이름 철자를 잘못 쓴 카드에는 날짜도 잘못 표기한 듯하다. 1895년에 몽고메리는 비더포드가 아니라 핼리팩스에 있었다. 눌러놓은 장미꽃은 비더포드에서 시험과 발표회를 잘 치른 기념으로 붙여둔 듯한데(블루 스크랩북 15쪽), 화려한 카드로 덮은 곳 아래에 몽고메리가 좋아한 캐번디시 교사 해티 L. 고든Hattie L. Gordon의 이름이 있는 것을 보면 거의 확실해 보인다. 어린 두 소녀를 그린 삽화는 확실히 몽고메리가 고를 만한 것이다. 실제로 몽고메리는 겨울이면 빛이 부족하여 고통스러웠다.

26쪽 마지막 프랑스 황후인 외제니 드 몽티조Eugenie de Montijo(1826-1920)는 수십 년 동안 영국에서 유배 생활을 하면서 프랑스 제2제정과 고인이 된 남편, 아들을 기리는 기념비를 세웠다. 머리에 후광이 빛나는 인물과 외제니 황후가 사교 활동과 가벼운 연애를 기념하며 삼각형으로 배치해놓은 카드의 중심을 차지했다. 서스캐처원으로 소풍을 떠난 1891년 7월의 어느 날, 윌리 프리처드는 "순결과 아름다움"이 그 특징이라면서 데이지와 전동싸리를 몽고메리의 드레스에 꽂아줬다. 왼쪽 아래의 데이지 꽃은 비더포드 학교의 가을 방학 동안 캐번디시로 돌아와 클라크 남매, 잭 레어드와 함께 신나게 보내던 때에, 렘 매클라우드가 파크 코너에서 몽고메리에게 청혼한 지 정확히 이틀 후에 꺾은 것이다(블루 스크랩북 33쪽). 몽고메리가 루이스 디스턴트를 만난 것은 1894년 11월이었는데, 오른쪽 카드를 보면 루가 12월에 이미 몽고메리에게 빠져 있었음을 알 수 있다. 카드에 적힌 머리글자는 세이디 디스턴트, 루시 모드 몽고메리, 루 디스턴트, 이스트 비더포드 발표회, 프린스에드워드섬을 뜻한다. 왼쪽에는 외할아버지의 부고 기사와 그에 관한 감상적 시가 있는데, 앞쪽에 실린 친할아버지에 관한 기사와 한 쌍을 이룬다.

27쪽 눈길을 사로잡는 화관을 쓰고 토가를 입은 여인은 보닛을 주제로 한 시와 클레오파트라의 "문학적 호기심" 사이에서 시각적인 연결 고리를 만들어낸다. 웰링턴 넬슨Wellington Nelson은 동생 데이비드David와 함께 맥닐가에서 삼 년 동안 하숙하면서 몽고메리와 같이 캐번디시 학교에 다녔는데, 알록달록한 꽃 그림 카드 아래에 그의 이름이 적혀 있다. 캐번디시의 기념품은 지금은 사라지고 없지만 1892년 6월에 몽고메리가 상상했던 것과 관련 있을지 모른다. 몽고메리가 학교 밖에서 펜시와 비밀을 주고받다가 해티 고든 선생님이 어둠 속에서 모든 말을 엿듣고 있었다는 사실을 알게 된 게 그때였기 때문이다. 1892년 6월 1일, 몽고메리는 프린스에드워드섬의 파크 코너를 방문하여 사촌인 스텔라 캠벨과 함께 과수원에서 네잎 클로버를 찾아다녔다. 이때 몽고메리는 에드윈 심프슨을 처음 만났다. 에드윈과 렘 매클라우드는 서로 몽고메리의 관심을 끌기 위해 경쟁했다.

Better be born lucky than rich.

"Three is company in this case."

...the circle. Bideford

THE SHADOW.

The sun's in a cloud,
　The morning is dreary,
The way is too long,
　The feet are too weary.
The friend is not kind,
　And smiles are not shining,
The roses and robins
　Are paling and pining,
That hour is the saddest
　From May day to Yule
When little Dolores
　Is going to school.

What is the reason? She turns from the light,
And walks in her shadow from morning till night.

They Did Not Try.

Three men-of-war ships, Dutch, French, and English, while anchored in port, were contending with each other for the best display of seamanship, so the captain of each vessel determined to send aloft an active sailor to perform some deed of grace and daring. The Dutch captain sent a Dutchman, the French a Frenchman and the English an Irishman. The Dutchman stood on the top of the mainmast with his arm extended. The Frenchman then went aloft and extended both arms.

Now, the Irishman thought if he could stand on the top of the mainmast with a leg and an arm extended he would be declared the most daring sailor. Nimbly he clambered aloft untill he reached the highest point. Thence he carefully balanced himself upon both feet, extending his right hand with a graceful motion. Then he threw out his left leg untill in a line with his right arm. In doing this he ingloriously lost his balance and fell from the masthead, crashing through the rigging toward the deck.

The various ropes against which his body came in contact broke his fall, and his velocity was not too great to prevent his grasping a rope attached to the mainyard. To this he hung for two seconds, then dropped lightly to the deck, landing safely on his feet. Folding his arms triumphantly, as if fall and all were in the programme, he glanced toward the rival ships and joyously exclaimed, "There, ye frog ating and sausage-stuffed furriners, bate that it you can!"

WHERE IS IT?

The sun is the brightest,
　The morn is the clearest,
The burden is lightest,
　The friend is the dearest,
The flowers are all waking,
　The way is not long,
The birds are all breaking
　At once into song.
That hour is the gladdest
　From May day to Yule,
When little Allegra
　Is going to school.

What is the secret? Wherever you find her,
The shadow of little Allegra's behind her.

MARY A. LATHBURY.

Reminiscences of the Late Senator Montgomery.

The Ottawa Citizen contains a letter signed P.E.I., who is evidently resident at the capital, giving some interesting reminiscences of the late Senator Montgomery. Among other things he says:

It is not absolutely correct to speak of the late Senator's "continuous service" as a parliamentarian. There was one General Assembly or parliament of Prince Edward Island of which he was not a member. I refer to the 21st, which was convened in Charlottetown on 17th February, 1859, prorogued two days later and followed immediately by dissolution. There had been a general election in the summer of 1858, at which Mr. Montgomery was defeated by Mr. John Ramsay. When the Legislature met, Mr. Ramsay declined to take the oath of qualification, while parties were so equally divided that it was found impossible to elect a speaker. After waiting two days, the Lieut. Governor, Sir Dominick Daly, prorogued the Legislature, and forthwith dissolved the House. At the new general election Mr. Montgomery was successful, and upon the opening of the session, on 12th April, 1859, was elected Speaker of the House Assembly. Thus, although he missed one parliament, he was yet a representative of the people in every year from the time he was first elected in 1838.

One other reminiscence: In company with a friend, I was talking to Senator Montgomery during the session of 1892, when he showed us a photograph of a venerable lady, living in London, England. Said he. "I have just received this photograph—she is a cousin of mine. Last year I sent her my photograph and she has sent me hers in exchange. I have not seen her for 80 years." And the old gentleman spoke as unconcernedly as though it had been only ten years instead of four score.

"SUMMER."—JOHN SCOTT, R.I.

"In the heart of a rose"

Dec. 28th 1895.

Lucie M. Montgomery
Bideford
P.E.I.

At a meeting of this Society held on the above date the following resolution was unanimously adopted:—

Whereas, It hath pleased God in His Providence to remove from our midst by death our late sister, Mary J. Cameron;

Therefore Resolved, That we, the members of Rising Star Division, do hereby place on record our appreciation of her worth as a member of our Society, and further, we would desire to convey to the bereaved parents and surviving brothers and sisters our sincere and heartfelt sorrow with them in the loss of a dutiful daughter and loving and affectionate sister, and as we erase her name from the roll of our Society on earth, we would sincerely cherish the hope that it may be recorded in the Lamb's Book of Life;

It was further resolved, that we drape our charter in mourning for thirty days.

Signed on behalf of the Division: Newton McLeod, W. P.; Louisa Crosby, R. S.; Emma J. Smith, Florence Orr, A. Simpson.

Friday July 24 1891

"Innocence and Beauty"

Maidens Lake Pointe Saskatchewan.

"Here is a summer day on purple hills. Compare with daisies and..."

Most wives will end their story with:
  "Ah well, men are but human,"
I long to tell the secret of
  A truly happy woman.

Through all the sunshine-lighted years,
  Lived now in retrospection,
My husband's words brought never tears,
  Nor caused a sad reflection.

Whate'er the burdens of the day,
  Unflinching, calm and steady,
To bear his part—the larger half—
  I always find him ready.

House-cleaning season brings no frown,
  No scream, pointed keenly;
Through carpets up, and tacks head down
  He makes his way serenely.

Our evenings pass in converse sweet,
  Or quiet contemplation,
We never disagree except
  To "keep up conversation."

And dewy morn of radiant June,
  Fair moonlight of September,
April with bird and brook atune,
  Stern, pitiless December—

Each seems to my adoring eyes
  Some new grace to discover,
For he unchanging through the years,
  Is still my tender lover.

So life no shadows holds, though we
  Have reached the side that's shady;
My husband? Oh! a dream is he,
  And I'm a maiden lady.

ELEANOR M. DENNY, in the *Ladies' Home Journal.*

WHEN GRANDPA WAS A LITTLE BOY.

BY MALCOLM DOUGLAS.

"When grandpa was a little boy about your age," said he,
To the curly-headed youngster who had climbed upon his knee,
"So studious was he at school, he never failed to pass;
And out of three he always stood the second in his class—"
"But if no more were in it, you were next to foot, like me!"
"Why, bless you, grandpa never thought of that before!" said he.

"When grandpa was a little boy about your age," said he,
"He very seldom spent his pretty pennies foolishly;
No toy or candy store was there for miles and miles about,
And, with his books, straight home he'd go the moment school was out—"
"But if there had been one, you might have spent them all, like me!" said he.
"Why, bless you, grandpa never thought of that before!" said he.

"When grandpa was a little boy about your age," said he,
"He never stayed up later than an hour after tea;
It wasn't good for little boys at all, his mother said;
And so, when it was early, she would march him off to bed—"
"But if she hadn't, maybe you'd have stayed up late, like me!"
"Why, bless you, grandpa never thought of that before!" said he.

"When grandpa was a little boy about your age," said he,
"In summer he went barefoot, and was happy as could be;
And all the neighbors round about agreed he was a lad
Who was as good as he could be except when he was bad—"
"But, 'ceptin' going barefoot, you were very much like me."
"Why, bless you, grandpa's often thought of that before!" said he.
  —*St. Nicholas.*

Milking-time.

"I TELL you, Kate, that Lovejoy cow
  Is worth her weight in gold;
She gives a good eight quarts o' milk,
  And isn't yet five year old.

"I see young White a-comin' now;
  He wants her, I know that.
Be careful, girl, you're spillin' it!
  An' save some for the cat.

"Good evenin', Richard, step right in;"
  "I guess I couldn't, sir,
I've just come down"—"I know it, Dick,
  You've took a shine to her.

"She's kind an' gentle as a lamb,
  Jest where I go she follers;
And though it's cheap I'll let her go;
  She's your'n for thirty dollars.

"You'll know her clear across the farm,
  By them two milk white stars;
You needn't drive her home at night,
  But jest le' down the bars.

"Then, when you've own'd her, say a month,
  And learnt her, as it were,
I'll bet,—why, what's the matter, Dick?"
  "'Taint her I want,—it's—*her!*"

"What? not the girl! well, I'll be bless'd!—
  There, Kate, don't drop that pan.
You've took me mightily aback,
  But then a man's a man.

"She's your'n, my boy, but one word more;
  Kate's gentle as a dove;
She'll foller you the whole world round,
  For nothin' else but love.

"But never try to drive the lass;
  Her natur's like her ma's.
I've allus found it worked the best,
  To jest le' down the bars."
    PHILIP MORSE.

EUGENIE, EMPRESS OF FRANCE

"Procrastination is the thief of time."

Oct. 24. Banks of seaweed versus unfortunate youths.

"Two is company three is a crowd."

"Two school-teachers are too many for a crowd of six."

"Good-night × 11 = 6 pl. J. Wednesday October 24 1894"

"Jingle bells, jingle bells, jingle all the way"

"Gaily over the moonlit snow"

"That's to be continued."

"Distance lends enchantment to the view"

"Lover's Lane"

S. D. R. M. M. L. D. E. B. C. P. S. I.

East Bideford, Tuesday Dec. 11 1894

HER BONNET.

BY MARY E. WILKINS.

When meeting bells began to toll,
   When pious folks began to pass,
She deftly tied her bonnet on,
   The little sober meeting lass,
All in her neat, white-curtained room, before her tiny
      looking-glass.

So nice'y round her lady cheeks
   She smoothed her bands of glossy hair,
And innocently wondered if
   Her bonnet did not make her fair;
Then sternly chid her foolish heart for harboring such
      fancies there.

So square she tied the satin strings,
   And set the bows beneath her chin;
Then smiled to see how sweet she looked;
   Then thought her vanity a sin,
And she must put such thoughts away before the ser-
      mon should begin.

But, sitting 'neath the preached word,
   Demurely, in her father's pew,
She thought about her bonnet still,
   Yes, all the parson's sermon thro',
About its pretty bows and buds, which better than the
      text she knew.

Yet, sitting there with peaceful face,
   The reflex of her simple soul,
She looked to be a very saint—
   And maybe was one on the whole—
Only that her pretty bonnet kept away the aureole.

A LITERARY CURIOSITY.

The two following poems, either of
which might have inspired the other,
have long been favorites with the lovers of poety of both continents. We
have no knowledge when the one by
Thomas S. Collins was written, but
that by General William Lytle was
written on the eve of the battle of
Chickamauga, where General Lytle was
killed. The late Colonel Realf, poet,
author and soldier, has placed upon
record the peculiar circumstances under
which the poem was written, which
briefly amount to the fact that on the
night preceding the battle referred to,
General Lytle read the poem, which
was then in an unfinished state, to
Col. Realf, at the same time telling
him that he had a premonition that
he would never live to finish it. Col.
Realf laughed at his friend, and ral-
lied him upon his superstition, but ack-
nowledged afterward that he himself
became so thrilled with unnatural fear
that he besried the general to finish
the piece before he slept, that such a
fine work might not be lost to the
world. When Col. Realf next saw his
friend he lay cold in death among
the heaps of slain. Then he thought of
the poem, and searching the pocket
where he had seen him place it, he
drew it forth and forwarded it to General Lytle's friends.
The lines by Thomas S. Collins were
written first and are probably the best,
but readers can judge for themselves.

CLEOPATRA DYING.

Sinks the sun below the desert,
   Golden glows the sluggish Nile;
Purple flame crowns Sphynx and tem-
      ple.
   Lights up every ancient pile,
Where the old gods now are sleeping;
   Isis and Osiris great!
Guard me help me, give me courage
   Like a queen to meet my fate.
"I am dying, Egypt, dying!"
   Let the Caesar's army come—
I will cheat him of his glory,
   Though beyond the Styx I roam.

chain he drag this beauty with him,
   While the crowd his triumph sings?
No, no, never! I will show him
   What lies in the blood of kings.
Though he hold the golden sceptre,
   Rule the Pharaoh's sunny land,
Where o'd Nilus rolls resistless,
   Through the sweeps of silvery sand,
He shall never say I met him
   Fawning abject like a slave—
I will foil him, though to do it
   I must cross the Stygian wave.
Oh, my hero, sleeping, sleeping—
   Shall I meet you on the shore
Of Plutonian shadows? Shall we
   In death meet, and love once more?
See, I follow in your footsteps—
   Scorn the Caesar and his might;
For your love, I will leap boldly
   Into the realms of death and night.
Down below the desert sinking,
   Fades Apollo's brilliant car,
And from out the distant azure
   Breaks the bright gleam of a star;
Venus, Queen of Love and Beauty,
   Welcomes me to death's embrace.
Dying free, proud and triumphant!
   The last sovereign of my race.
Dying! dying! I am coming,
   Oh, my hero, to your arms;
You will welcome me, I know it—
   Guard me from all rude alarms.
Hark, I hear the legions coming.
   Hear their cries of triumph swell;
But, proud Caesar, dead, I scorn you,
   Egypt—Antony—farewell!
      —Thomas S. Collins.

ANTHONY AND CLEOPATRA.

I am dying, Egypt, dying!
   Ebbs the crimson life tide fast,
And the dark Plutonian shadows
   Gather on the evening blast.
Let thine arm, O, Queen, support me,
   Hush thy sobs and bow thine ear,
Listen to the great heart secrets
   Thou, and thou alone, must hear.
Though my scarred and veteran legions
   Bear their eagles high no more,
And my wrecked and scattered galleys
   Strew dark Actium's fatal shore;
Though no glittering guards surround
      me,
   Prompt to do their master's will,
I must perish like a Roman—
   Die the great Triumvir still!
Let not Caesar's servile minions

Mock the lion thus laid low;
   'Twas no foeman's arm that struck him
   'Twas his own that dealt the blow—
His, who pillowed on thy bosom
   Turned aside from glory's ray—
His, who drunk with thy caresses,
   Madly threw a world away.
Should the base plebeian rabble
   Dare assail my fame at Rome,
Where the noble spouse, Octavia,
   Weeps within her widowed home,
Seek her! Say the Gods have told me—
   Altars, augurs, circling wings—
That her blood with mine commingled,
   Yet shall mount the throne of kings!
As for thee, star-eyed Egyptian!
   Glorious sorceress of the Nile!
Light the path to Stygian horrors
   With the splendor of thy smile.
Give to Caesar crowns and arches,
   Let his brow the laurel twine,
I can scorn the Senate's triumphs,
   Triumphing in love like thine.
I am dying, Egypt, dying;
   Hark! the insulting foeman's cry!
They are coming! Quick, my falchion!
   Let me front them ere I die.
Ah! no more amid the battle
   Shall my heart exulting swell;
Isis and Osiris guard thee—
   Cleopatra—Rome—farewell!
      Gen. Wm. H. Lytle.

Linkletter Road Notes.

The Literary Society of this place is a rapidly growing institution. The members take
quite a lively interest in the meetings, which
are well attended every Friday evening. There
is always a well filled programme consisting of
readings, recitations and dialogues, after which
a debate is brought on.
Our school is doing good work under the
management of our efficient teacher Miss Fyfe.
Miss Lulu M. Gamble arrived home on
Saturday from Bideford where she has been
attending school during the fall and winter.
Mr. and Mrs. Ed. Bell, who have been
visiting their many friends on Linkletter Road,
returned to their home in Cape Traverse on
Friday last.
Messrs. J. W. Everett and Edwin Clark ar
having large quantities of hay pressed.

Mr & Mrs Wm. McKenzie

request the pleasure of your company at the

Marriage of their neice

Mary McRae

to

Hugh J. Montgomery

On Tuesday morning, April 5th, 1887.

Ceremony in Presbyterian Church at 10.30.

28쪽 확대 몽고메리의 아버지인 휴 존 몽고메리와 메리 맥레이Mary McRae의 결혼 청첩장이다. 몽고메리는 청첩장 아래 "실수"라는 제목의 짧은 이야기를 붙였는데, 이 제목으로 보아 아버지의 선택을 지적하려 한 것이 틀림없다. 몽고메리는 새어머니와 사이가 좋지 못했다.

29쪽 확대 이 페이지의 가운데 아래에 놓인 카드에서 날짜를 정확히 읽기는 어렵지만 1893년 6월 28일로 보인다(그런데 화요일이 아니라 수요일이었다). 말린 꽃과 시구는 프린스오브웨일스 대학입학시험을 앞두고 캐번디시 학교를 마칠 때 수없이 주고받은 작별 인사 가운데 하나이다. 여기서 보이는 장미는 캐번디시를 떠나서 비더포드로 학생들을 가르치러 갈 때 작별을 기념했던 장미를 떠올리게 한다(블루 스크랩북 15쪽).

30쪽 확대 1890년에서 1891년까지 몽고메리가 서스캐처원의 프린스앨버트에서 학생으로 학교에 다니는 동안, 고등학교 수업은 과거에 로열 호텔Royal Hotel이었던 건물에서 진행됐다.

꿈과 꿈같은 사건들이 프린스앨버트, 캐번디시, 프린스오브웨일스 대학, 비더포드의 나날을 연결시킨다. 스크랩북은 좋은 시절을 두드러져 보이게 하고 슬픔은 지우거나 누그러뜨린다.

33쪽 가운데에 초승달이라 잘못 이름 붙인 그믐달은 실패한 로맨스를 의미하는 듯하다. 그믐달 옆으로, 루시 모드 몽고메리는 렘 매클라우드에게 청혼을 받고서 거절했던 1894년 어느 일요일 저녁을 기념했다. 모직천으로 작은 장미를 만들어 그날 밤 자신이 앉았던 소파 쿠션을 장식했다. 시구는 존 G. 휘티어John Greenleaf Whittier의 〈모드 멀러Maud Muller〉라는 시에서 인용한 것으로, 늙은 남녀가 서로와 결혼하지 않은 것을 각자 회고하며 한탄하는 내용이다. 모직 장미 아래에 덧붙인 네모난 격자무늬 천은 몽고메리가 마음껏 즐겼던 비더포드 파티와 관련된 것이다(블루 스크랩북 15쪽). 벌판의 해바라기는 1890년 서부 여행길에 꺾었던 것으로, 역시 다른 곳에서 즐겁게 보낸 시간들을 떠올려주는 기념물일 것이다.

34쪽 낭만적인 〈자라Zara〉 이야기의 배경은 스페인 그레나다이다. 몽고메리는 워싱턴 어빙Washington Irving의 흥미진진한 소설 《알함브라The Alhambra》 때문에 그레나다를 무척 좋아했다. 오른쪽 아래 카드에 길게 쓴 수수께끼 같은 머리글자(L. D. M. C. M. S. M. H. R. M. C.)에는 1892년에 프레더리카 캠벨Frederica Campbell과 몽고메리가 프레더리카의 검고 노란 점박이 새끼 고양이 카리시마에게 길게 붙여준 이름 "미뇨네트 카리시마 몽고메리 캠벨Mignonette Carissima Montgomery Campbell"이 포함되어 있다. 알렉 맥닐(과의 반갑지 않은 로맨스)을 피하기 위해 몽고메리는 1893년 7월 20일 기도회를 마치고 체슬리 클라크와 함께 마차를 타고 집으로 돌아왔는데 깨진 창문, 유클리드 기하학, 달빛과 관련된 어떤 일이 벌어졌다. 아마 몽고메리는 6월 16일 저녁에도 이처럼 유리창을 깨뜨린 적이 있다는 것을 떠올렸을 것이다(블루

스크랩북 19쪽). 비더포드 소식을 기고하는 지역 신문 칼럼에서는 앞 페이지의 카드에 언급했던 1894년 8월 8일 레녹스 섬 나들이, 그리고 교사로서 몽고메리가 이룬 "위업"을 다루었다.

35쪽 몽고메리는 프린스오브웨일스 대학에서의 '영웅적 행위'에 대한 재미있는 기사를 이 페이지의 가운데에 놓고, 뒤이어 핼리팩스 여학교Halifax Ladies' College 사진을 배치했다. 이후 1895년부터 1896년까지 이 학교에서 기숙하면서 달하우지 대학에 다니게 된다. 이들 두 대학과 관련한 자료 양옆에는 할머니에 관한 시 두 편을 실었다. 한 편은 할머니가 손주들에게 "삶이란 양말"과 같아서 뜨개질하듯 삶을 만들어가야 한다고 설명하는 내용이고, 다른 시는 어린 남자아이가 할머니를 도와 하는 일마다 불평을 늘어놓지만 결국 할머니가 한없이 베푼 사랑과 지지를 회고하며 끝난다. 외할머니는 (외할아버지와 달리) 몽고메리가 프린스오브웨일스 대학에 진학할 때나 달하우지 대학에 들어갈 때나 그 용감한 도전을 모두 지지했다. 몽고메리는 비더포드 칼럼에서 "우리의 인기 선생님"으로 언급되어 기뻤다.

1892년에 데버루Devereux 부인의 영국 초상화를 그린 사람은 프레더릭 구달Frederick Goodall(1822-1904)이다. 몽고메리는 유명한 여성이나, 옷차림과 자세가 남다른 세련된 여성의 사진을 취미처럼 수집했다. 어린 앤 셜리가 이상형으로 간직한 아름다움이 이런 모습이었을까?

A Skating Lesson

We spoke in sentences condensed,
   Yet said enough.
Sometimes I wildly bumped against
   Her furry muff.

Sometimes her lovely weight half hurled
   Me from my feet,
Nor would I miss for all the world
   This onslaught sweet.

Sometimes with both dear hands she clung
   In dire alarm;
Again, quite calm, she merely hung
   Upon my arm.

Oh, moonlight night! oh, silvery ring
   Of skaters' steel!
With fingers locked we glide and swing,
   We carol and reel.

I feel her skirt that flutters warm
   Against my knees,
I turn and twist her pliant form
   With graceful ease.

Last—kneeling, draw the straps apart
   From ankle neat;
My gloves are in her lap—my heart
   Is at her feet.

   *   *   *   *

A half-forgotten memory—
   Yet, at a word
How clearly it comes back to me!
   Just now I heard

My eldest-born, my handsome Claude,
   (Oh, smile of fate!)
Coaxing her lovely daughter Maud
   To learn to skate!
         M. S. BRIDGES.

FARCE

'My Turn Next.'

DRAMATIS PERSONÆ.

"Taraxicum Twitters" (Apothecary) T. N. CAMPBELL.

"Tim Bolus," (Apothecary's Assistant) MR. GRAY.

"Tom Trap." (Commercial Traveller) J. F. BETTS, M.L.A.

"Farmer Wheatear" (Farmer) MR. PAVIER.

"Lydia," (Mrs. Taraxicum Twitters) MISS PRITCHARD.

"Cicely," (Mrs. Twitters Sister) MISS F. A. REID.

"Peggy," (Housekeeper to Mr. Twitters) MISS CLARKE.

A Schoolroom Idyl.

How plainly I remember all!
   The desks, deep-scored and blackened,
The row of blackboards 'round the wall,
   The hum that never slackened;
And, framed about by map and chart,
   And casts of dusty plaster,
That wisest head and warmest heart,
   The kindly old schoolmaster!

I see the sunny corner nook
   His blue-eyed daughter sat in,
A rosy, fair-haired girl, who took
   With us her French and Latin.
How longingly I watched the hours
   For Ollendorf and Cæsar!
And how I fought with Tony Powers
   The day he tried to tease her!

And when, one day, it took the "Next!"
   To stay some Gallic slaughter,
Because I quite forgot the text
   In smiling at his daughter.
And she and I were "kept till four
   To study, after closing.
We stopped the clock an hour or more
   While he, poor man, was dozing!

And there he sits, with bended head,
   O'er some old volume poring
Or so he thinks; if truth be said
   He's fast asleep and snoring),
And where the shaded lamplight plays
   Across the cradle's rocking,
My schoolmate of the olden days,
   Sits, mending baby's stocking.
CHARLES B. GOING, in the *Ladies' Home
Journal.*

THE NEW MOON.

"Of all sad words of tongue
  or pen
The saddest are, it might
  have been" *Whittier*

"Here there was laughing
of old"
     Swinburne.

"Compliments"

"Farewell, a word that
has been
And yet again must be."

So ends the first lesson.

Sunday,
September 21st
1884

"In India a woman's—"

Gathered
Sunday
Aug. 17th
1890

Prairie
Sunflower

Winnipeg
Manitoba
Can.

Badge of "The Wanderers"

Lennox Island "Home
of the Micmac"

"I'll wear it
as long as it
will wear
there"

Search for water
Blueberry festival
Indian fiddler

To the house
Indians where
potato and mills

Wednesday
Aug. 5th
1854

AN ODE TO SPRING.

"Oh, beautiful, budding, verdant Spring,"
   So sang a poet of renown;
But he, himself, alone was *green*,
   For the snow lay deep on the ground.

"All hail!" he cried, "thou beautiful
     Spring,"
   And it did just as he said;
And the hail came down from the
     Heavenly King,
   And hit him and knocked him dead.

We give this warning to 'poets of Spring,'
   Who write when the snow's on the
     ground,
Be careful about the words you use,
   Or when Spring comes you won't be
     found.
         U. G. H——E

Joy and all good things attend your CHRISTMASTIDE.

ZARA.

"A silvery veil of pure moonlight
Is glancing over the quiet water,
And oh ! 'tis beautiful and bright
As the soft smile of Selim's daughter.

"Sleep, moonlight ! sleep upon the wave,
And hush to rest each rising billow,
Then dwell within the mountain cave,
Where this fond breast is Zara's pillow.

" Shine on, thou blessed moon ! brighter still,
Oh, shine thus ever night and morrow ;
For day-break mantling o'er the hill,
But wakes my love to fear and sorrow."

'Twas thus the Spanish youth beguiled
The rising fears of Selim's daughter ;
And on their loves the pale moon smiled,
Unweeting of the morrow's slaughter.

Alas ! too early rose that morn,
On harnessed knight and fierce soldada—
Alas ! too soon the Moorish horn
And tambour rang in Old Grenada.

The dew yet bathes the dreaming flower,
The mist yet lingers in the valley,
When Selim and his Zegris' power
From port and postern sternly sally.

Marry ! it was a gallant sight
To see the plain with armour glancing,
As on to Alpuxara's height
Proud Selim's chivalry were prancing.

The knights dismount ; on foot they climb
The rugged steeps of Alpuxara ;
In fateful and unhappy time,
Proud Selim found his long-lost Zara.

They sleep—in sleep they smile and dream
Of happy days they ne'er shall number ;
Their lips breath sounds—their spirits seem
To hold communion while they slumber.

A moment gazed the stern old Moor,
A scant tear in his eye did gather,
For as he gazed, she muttered o'er
A blessing on her cruel father.

The hand that grasped the crooked blade,
Relaxed its gripe, then clutched it stronger,
The tear that that dark eye hath shed
On the swart cheek is seen no longer.

'Tis past !—the bloody deed is done,
A father's hand had sealed the slaughter !
Yet in Grenada many a one
Bewails the fate of Selim's daughter.

And many a Moorish damsel hath
Made pilgrimage to Alpuxara ;
And breathed her vows, where Selim's wrath
O'ertook the Spanish youth and Zara.

—:O:—

Bideford Notes.

On Wednesday last a small party of
our young folk paid a visit to Lennox Island, the home of the Micmacs. They
sailed from Bideford wharf in the pleasure
boat "Discipline" and after landing and
enjoying an excellent lunch they repaired
to Mr. Thomas Abram's house and
indulged in a rustic dance in which both
Micmac and pale-face enjoyed themselves.
The music furnished by Messrs Abram
and Prospere was excellent and showed
that those gentlemen are masters of the
violin.

Harvesting has been begun here, and
although the the oats are only fair, the
wheat crop is good.

A new Episcopal church is about being
started here and when completed will add
greatly to the beauty of our already
beautiful village.

Our young friend, Mr. John Dystant,
preached an excellent sermon in the
Methodist church on Sunday last. We
are glad to note the success of this
estimable young man and hope for its
continuance.

Our school is doing grand work under
the guiding hand of Miss Lucy M.
Montgomery, who, although only a few
weeks in charge, is fast becoming very
popular with both scholars and rate-
payers.

Com.

Carissima
"Park Corner".
1892

L. D. M. C. M. . M. H. R. M. C.

THE HON. MRS. DEVEREUX.—F. GOODALL, R.A.

courage of Horatius. His assailants have got the advantage; they surround him on all sides. Overpowered with numbers he is forced to give up the contest and is driven from the field, yet not till he had shown by his valour that some of the blood of the knights of Arthur's Round Table still courses in the veins of the Celt. Although we can only mourn for his defeat, it is no more than we could have expected from the unequal contest, and let us hope that his name may be inscribed by worthier hands than ours among the Great Ones of History.

N. O. T.

CLEMATIS.

LIFE A STOCKING.

The supper is over, the hearth is swept,
And in the wood-fire's glow
The children cluster to hear a tale
Of that time so long ago,

When grandma's hair was golden brown,
And the warm blood came and went
O'er the face that was scarcely sweeter then
Than now in its rich content.

The face is wrinkled and careworn now,
And the golden hair is gray,
But the light that shone in the young girl's eye
Has never gone away.

And her needles catch the fire's bright light
As in and out they go,
With the clicking music that grandma loves,
Shaping the stocking-toe.

And the waiting children love it too,
For they know the stocking's song
Brings many a tale to grandma's mind,
Which they shall hear ere long.

But it brings no story of olden time
To grandma's heart to night;
Only a sermon, quaint and short,
Is sung by the needles bright.

"Life is a stocking," grandma says,
"And yours is just begun;
But I am knitting the toe of mine,
And my work is almost done.

"With merry hearts we begin to knit,
And the ribbing is almost play;
Some are gay-colored, and some are white,
And some are ashen-gray;

"But most are made of many a hue,
With many a stitch set wrong,
And many a row to be sadly ripped
Ere the whole is fair and strong.

"There are long plain spaces without a break,
That in youth are hard to bear,
And many a weary tear is dropped
As we fashion the heel with care.

"But the saddest, happiest time is that
Which we court, and yet would shun,
When our heavenly Father breaks the thread
And says that our work is done."

The children come to say "Good-night"
With tears in their bright young eyes,
While in grandma's lap with a broken thread,
The finished stocking lies.

HEROISM.

Peace has so long reigned supreme throughout the world that we sometimes come to doubt the authenticity of history that treats of startling conflicts, heroic deeds and such like seemingly fabulous performances. But these events were localized in the recent collision witnessed on the campus of the Prince of Wales College, when one individual was seen to contend against a multitude of "the most cruel of animals." While we are moved by his heroic conduct, we cannot but reprimand the action of the number of young men who witnessed the scene and with that wanton spirit, which forms such a marked feature of students everywhere, exhausted themselves with laughter at the perilous situation of their fellow-being. No voice was raised to urge them on, no one was found to lead the band. Alas! "the day of chivalry is past." Meanwhile the battle thickens; the multitude rush on "with the prodigal exuberance of early youth," but retreat with the instability of savages. Step by step he is driven back; now he gains some advantage, but it is only momentary. The attack is renewed again and again. Still he fights with the

WHAT ONE BOY THINKS

A stitch is always dropping in the everlasting knitting,
And the needles that I threaded, no, you couldn't count to-day;
And I've hunted for the glasses till I thought my head was splitting,
When there upon her forehead as calm as clocks they lay.

I've read to her till I was hoarse the Psalms and the Epistles,
When the other boys were burning tar-barrels down the street;
And I've stayed and learned my verses when I heard their willow whistles,
And I've stayed and said my chapter with fire in both my feet.

And I've had to walk beside her when she went to evening meeting,
When I wanted to be racing, to be kicking, to be off;
And I've waited while she gave the folks a word or two of greeting,
First on one foot and the other and 'most strangled with a cough.

"You can talk of Young America," I say, "till you are scarlet,
It's Old America that has the inside of the track!"
Then she raps me with her thimble and calls me a young yarlet,
And then she looks so woe-begone I have to take it back.

But! There always is a peppermint or a penny in her pocket—
There never was a pocket that was half so big and deep—
And she lets the candle in my room burn 'way down to the socket,
While she stews and putters round about till I am sound asleep.

There's always somebody at home when every one is scattering;
She spreads the jam upon your bread in a way to make you grow;
She always take's a fellow's side when every one is battering;
And when I tear my jacket, I know just where to go!

And when I've been in swimming after father said I shouldn't,
And mother has her slipper off according to the rule,
It sounds as sweet as silver, the voice that says "I would'nt;
The boy that won't go swimming such a day would be a fool!"

Sometimes there's something in her voice as if she gave a blessing,
And I look at her a moment and I keep still as a mouse—
And who is she by this time there is no need of guessing;
For there's nothing like a grandmother to have about the house!

—*Harriet Prescott Spofford.*

Bideford Notes.

The beautiful waters of Goodwood river are now dotted with boats whose occupants are obtaining for the markets the bivalves for which the place is noted. The oysters are very scarce and the price consequently very high.

The talk of the day in society circles, is the prospective entrance into the ranks of matrimony of some of our *sage* young folk. We hope the summer villas of Bideford will all be occupied by them next season.

The people of this place of every denomination hear with pleasure that the term of residence of the Methodist ministers has been extended by the General Conference, as the work on the new church would be greatly retarded by the removal of our present pastor.

Our sportsmen are mercilessly slaughtering the partridge since the season began, and judging by the numbers bagged they must be exceedingly plentiful.

Social gatherings are now the order of the day, or rather of the evening, and many enjoyable evenings are thus passed by our young folk.

Our popular teacher, Miss Montgomery, is at present spending her vacation at her home in Cavendish.

We are glad to see again among us our old friend, Mr. Thomas McDougall, who has just returned from his sojourn in the land of Uncle Sam.

37쪽 토머스 로런스Thomas Lawrence가 1827년에 그린 필 부인Julia Peel의 초상화는 구달이 그린 데버루 부인의 초상화처럼 아름다운 여인의 세련된 옷차림과 귀족 같은 자태를 잘 보여준다. 몽고메리는 필 부인을 보고서 잡지《펀치Punch》에서 소설처럼 꾸며 쓴 정치판의 귀부인들을 떠올린 듯하다. 자전소설 '에밀리' 시리즈에서 몽고메리 자신이라 할 수 있는 에밀리는 종종 자신이 똑 부러지고 정치적으로 사리 분별에 밝은 트레바니언 부인이라고 상상한다.

공개되지 않은 일기에 따르면, 몽고메리와 루시는 1895년 5월 29일에 클라크 가족의 집까지 걸어갔다. 그동안 귀신 이야기와 귀신 놀이에 빠져든 모양이었다. 확실히 두 사람이 걸어간 길은 야생 벚나무와 사과나무 꽃이 둔갑한 세상이었을 것이다. 루 디스턴트의 명함도 분명히 다른 기념품들과 함께 보관되어 있다.

38쪽 비더포드 목사관을 기념하는 나뭇조각들은 문, 계단, 벽, 벤치에서 떼어낸 것인데, 그 위에는 "1895년 4월 14일, '검은 밤'의 부활주일"을 기념하는 기다란 나뭇조각이 하나 더 있다. 성토요일에는 비가 내리고 어두워서 이스티Estey 부인은 저녁 예배를 마치고 자신과 몽고메리를 집까지 데려다준 루 디스턴트를 자고 가라고 붙잡았다. 동네 청년들도 루를 애먹일 생각으로 그 집에서 벗어나기 어렵도록 출입구들을 통나무로 막아버렸다.

39쪽 1890년 달력에 쾌활하게 표시된 "꼬리 달린 점"들은 몽고메리가 비더포드에서 지내는 동안의 빽빽한 사교 일정을 어떻게 생각했는지 잘 보여주는 듯하다. 1895년 6월 26일 수요일은 반휴일이어서 마지막 댄스 파티가 열렸고, 이날 몽고메리와 친구인 모드 헤이즈Maud Hayes는 자선을 목적으로 재봉봉사회 바자회에서 레모네이드와 사탕을 팔았다.

JULIA, LADY PEEL.

FROM THE PICTURE BY SIR THOMAS LAWRENCE, IN THE VICTORIAN EXHIBITION.

By permission of Messrs. Graves, Pall Mall.

Lady Katherine

POLITICS AND POLITENESS.

(*Punch.*)

Dear Mr. Punch,—I see that the Duke of Argyll, when he received the freedom of the Burgh of Paisley, the other day, told the following interesting story :—

'I was going once to call on a lady in London, and when the door was opened and the servant announced my name, I saw the lady advancing to the door with a look of absolute consternation on her face. I could not conceive what had happened, and thought I had entered her room at some inconvenient moment, but, on looking over her shoulder, I perceived Mr. and Mrs. Gladstone sitting at the tea-table, and she evidently thought that there would be some great explosion when we met. She was greatly gratified when nothing of the kind occurred, and we enjoyed a cup of tea as greatly as we had ever done in our lives.'

Now, my dear Mr. Punch, I have great sympathy with ' the Lady,' and think (with her) the meeting, as described by his Grace of Argyll, was mild in the extreme. If something out of the common had taken place, it would have been far more satisfactory. To make my meaning plainer, I give roughly (in dramatic form) what should have happened to have made the action worthy of the occasion.

Scene—A drawing-room. Lady entertaining Mr. and Mrs. G. at tea. A loud knock heard without.

Mrs. G. (greatly agitated.)—Oh dear, I am sure it is he !

Mr. G. (with calm dignity.)—Do not fear—if he appears, I shall know how to deal with him.

Lady (pale, but calm.)—Nay, my good, kind friends, believe me, you shall not suffer from the indiscretion of the servant.

Mrs. G. (pushing her husband into a cupboard.) Nay, William, for my sake ! And now to conceal myself, so that he may not suspect his presence by my proximity. [Hides behind the curtains.

The Duke of Argyll (breaking open the door, and entering hurriedly)—And now, madam, where is my hated foe ? I have tracked him to this house. It is useless to attempt to conceal him

The Lady (laughing uneasily)—Nay, your Grace, you are too facetious ! Trace the Premier here ! Next you will be saying that he and his good lady were taking tea with me.

The Duke (suspiciously)—And, no doubt, so they were ! This empty cup, that half-devoured muffin—to whom do they belong ?

The Lady (with forced gaiety)—Might I not have entertained Mr. and Mrs. Joseph Chamberlain, my Lord Duke ?

The Duke (aside)—Can I believe her ? (Aloud.) But if it is as you say, I will send away my clansmen who throng the street without. (Opens window and calls.)—Gang a waddy Caller Herring ! They will now depart. (A sneeze heard off) What was that ?

The Lady (terrified)—I fancy it was the wind— the cold wind—and now, believe me, Mr. Gladstone will abandon home rule.

Mr. G. (suddenly appearing)—Never ! I tell you to your face that you are a traitor ! [Sneezes, and hurriedly closes the window.

The Duke (savagely)—That sneeze shall be your last ! [Takes up a knife lying on the table.

Mr. G. (repeating the action)—I am ready, Sir !

Mrs. G. (rushing between them)—Oh, William ! Do not fight !

The Lady (falling on her knees)—I prithee stay !

Mr. G.—Never ! May the better man win !

The Duke—So be it ! [The scene closes in upon a desperate duel. Curtain.

There, Mr. Punch !—What do you think of that ? Still, perhaps, under the circumstances of the case, it is better as it is.

Yours most truly,

ONE WHO NEVER PAID TWOPENCE FOR MANNERS.

Wednesday,
May 29th 1889.

"which gate
is the terminus"

Shortly rooms
vs.
Haunting ghosts.

"The orchards hung out their sweet-
white screen
In the time of blossoming"

1889.

Sir Hyslant.

TWILIGHT.

COURTSHIP AT THE CHURN
By S. K. BOURNE

He—O leave that hateful churning!
   For your company I'm yearning!
   How reluctantly I'm turning
      To the woods and fields away!

She—Pray do not stand and tease, sir!
   Go as quickly as you please, sir!
   Do not wait at all for me, sir,
      I must stay and churn to-day.
   Hark! I have begun already,
   And the cream says "Flap a-tap,"
   And my arm is strong and steady,
      "Flap a-tap, a-tap, a-tap."

He—Will it take you all the day, dear?
   Can I help you if I stay, dear?
   Come and welcome back the May, dear,
      Welcome back the lovely spring!

She—Oh, I fear 'twill be too late, sir,
   And too long for you to wait, sir,
   Bet.er seek some other mate, sir.
      I've no time to laugh and sing!
   See! how rapidly I'm turning!
   And the cream says "Flop a-top;"
   Oh, I love the work of churning!
      "Flop a-top, a-top, a-top!"

He—Dear, you know how I adore you;
   How my heart is longing for you,
   Since the time when first I saw you
      Full of girlish life and joy!

She—Do not speak of trifles now, sir;
   Say good-bye, and make your bow, sir.
   Sentiment I can't allow, sir,
      Work must all my mind employ.
   Hark! I do believe I hear it!
   For the cream says "Flump a-tump,"
   And the butter sure is near it!
      "Flump a-tump, a-tump, a-tump!"

He—Your indifference is killing!
   And your answers, hard and chilling,
   Show too well a heart unwilling;
      I will leave you to your churn!

She—Really now, 'twas all in fun, dear;
   See, my work is almost done, dear;
   And my heart is fairly won, dear,
      Take it for your own!
   Yes, my heart is in a flutter!
   For the cream says "Swish a-wish!"
   And—Hurra! there comes the butter!
      "Swish a-wish, a-wish, a-wish!"

cy—The lines which you refer to are as follows:
Married in white, you have chosen all right.
Married in gray, you will go far away.
Married in black, you will wish yourself back.
Married in red, you will wish yourself dead.
Married in green, ashamed to be seen.
Married in blue, he will always be true.
Married in yellow, ashamed of your fellow.
Married in brown, you will live out of town.
Married in pink, your spirits will sink.

STARTLING HISTORICAL FACTS.

The following examples of schoolgirl erudition are not from the recent great examinations, but from some papers at a girls' school of some standing in the Eastern districts. The funny thing about them is the complete mastery of isolated facts, with the ability to mate them properly. It reminds one of the yokel who said he knew his letters all right, but 'never could put them together.' Here are the extracts:—

The cotton famine was when the grass was so scarce that the sheep had nowhere to go for food, and there was no wool for the people to make clothes with.

The Indian Mutiny was when the people all had to be mutinied, and all the husbands and wives and children had to be mutinied, because the Indians were very cross if one was left out.

The American war was a very civil war, the people had hardly anything to eat. The war lasted for seven years, there was scarcely a shoe in the camp. People were all starved to death, the king escaped to England, then he went to France.

The battle of Waterloo was fought because the Americans did not want the tea and they threw it into the water. Then they said they did not want to be taxicated so they fought the battle of Waterloo.

The Jacobites were people who lived in huts and they took 300 men and those who lapped like a dog were taken.

[French translation].—Sickness is a strange thing in the interior of a peasant.

Walpole was the man who fought the battle of Waterloo. Having beaten the French he died in the moment of victory.—'Cape Mercury.'

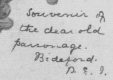

"Block Night".
Easter Sunday
April 14th
1895.

Toms

Souvenir of
the dear old
parsonage.
Bideford.
D. E. I.

AUGUST

Now August brings the holidays
 To gladden us once more,
And tempt us to her wooded hills
 And rugged, rock-bound shore;
While scented breeze from field and
 lane
 Steals softly through the air,
And low, sweet notes the happy birds
 Are piping everywhere.

Or on a mossy bank we lean
 With fishing-rod held fast,
In hope that some unwary trout
 Will take the bait at last;
Or in the surf we boldly plunge
 When waves are rolling high,
Or drowse beside the lapping tide
 To hear its lullaby;

Now all of us may freely choose
 The way we love the best,
Of all that nature offers us,
 In these long days of rest.
The river gaily beckons us
 To float adown the stream
And drift away the idle hours
 Along a fairy dream.

Or wander by the winding shore
 In nooks we love so well,
To search for gleaming ocean weed
 Or gaily tinted shell.
For young and old in childish mood
 These simple sports enjoy,
Which August brings with lavish hand
 To every girl and boy.

LUCY COMINS

The Masons of Port Hill.

THE brethren of Alexandra Lodge of A.F. and A.M. met at their Lodge Room, Port Hill, on the 27th ult., being St. John's Day, and installed the following officers for the ensuing year: Hugh Montgomery, W.M.; J. W. Brown, S.W.; Harry Williams, J.W.; John Maynard, sr., Treas.; Rev. H. Harper, Sec'y; Past Grand Master Yeo, Chaplain; Hugh A. McDonald, S. D.; Robert Hayes, J. D.; Wm. Woolridge, I. G.; Edward Gorrill, S. S.; W. W. McDonald J. S.; Dr. McLaughlin, Marshall; Norman McPhail, Tyler. After the installation an excellent supper followed. It is needless to say the repast was prepared in splendid style and did grand credit to the committee who had the affair in charge. The gentlemen who composed the committee are experienced hands at such work, but on this occasion they more than surpassed themselves, for the tables fairly groaned under the weight of the good things provided. Several toasts (drunk in cold water) were happily proposed and felicitously responded to. A most interesting address appropriate to the occasion was given by the Rev. Henry Harper. It was listened to with keen attention and at its close the appreciation of the audience was manifested by enthusiastic applause. We must not forget to mention that the festive board was graced by the presence of a number of ladies, and this was one of the pleasing features of the entertainment. During the evening some of them favored the company with recitations and songs all of which were heartily enjoyed. Where all did so well it may seem invidious to particularize, but the recitations given by Miss Montgomery, teacher at Bideford school, were so well rendered as to deserve special mention. Miss Bennett of Port Hill, also recited very nicely. After spending a most enjoyable evening the proceedings were closed by singing "God Save the Queen." The unfavorable weather prevented many members of the Mystic Tie residing at a long distance from Port Hill, from being present. Their company was greatly missed, but they were not forgotten for the toast "Absent Brethren" was duly honored both in words and song. Long may Alexandria Lodge live to give such pleasant entertainments as was the one of last Thursday evening.—[Com.

1890

<table>
<tr><td colspan="7">January.</td></tr>
<tr><td>S</td><td>M</td><td>T</td><td>W</td><td>T</td><td>F</td><td>S</td></tr>
<tr><td></td><td></td><td></td><td>1</td><td>2</td><td>3</td><td>4</td></tr>
<tr><td>5</td><td>6</td><td>7</td><td>8</td><td>9</td><td>10</td><td>11</td></tr>
<tr><td>12</td><td>13</td><td>14</td><td>15</td><td>16</td><td>17</td><td>18</td></tr>
<tr><td>19</td><td>20</td><td>21</td><td>22</td><td>23</td><td>24</td><td>25</td></tr>
<tr><td>26</td><td>27</td><td>28</td><td>29</td><td>30</td><td>31</td><td></td></tr>
</table>

(1890 calendar with months January through December)

DREADFUL ENCOUNTER.

It is hard for people who are not superstitious—or who think they are not—to understand the mental condition of persons who believe in ghosts, and are continually in fear because of some ridiculous "sign." In Yorkshire, England, according to the Rev. S. Baring-Gould, there is much dread of the Kirk-Grim, so called, an imaginary evil spirit in the shape of a huge black dog with eyes like saucers. He is said to haunt church lanes, and according to the popular belief, whoever sees him must die within the year.

On a stormy night in November Mr. Baring-Gould was out, holding over his head a big umbrella that had a handle of white bone. A sudden gust whisked the umbrella out of his hand, and away it went out of sight in the thick darkness and the storm.

That same evening a friend of the clergyman was walking down a lonely church lane, between hedges and fields, with no house near. Suddenly his feet and even his very breath were arrested by the sight of a great black creature which occupied the middle of the way directly before him, shaking itself impatiently, moving forward with a start, then bounding to one side, then running to the other.

No saucer eyes could be seen, but the creature had a white nose which, to the horrified traveller, seemed lit up with a supernatural radiance. Being a man of intelligence, however, he would not admit to himself that he was confronted by the Kirk-Grim. It must be a huge Newfoundland dog, he said to himself. So he addressed it in broad Yorkshire:

"Sith'ere, lass, don't be troublesome. There's a bonny dog, let me pass. I've no stick. I win't hurt thee. Come, lass, let me by."

At that moment a blast swept up the lane. The dog, monster, Kirk-Grim, whatever it was, made a leap upon the man, who screamed with terror. He felt the creature's claws in him, and he grasped—an umbrella!

Wednesday.
June 26th
1890

"Last dance
Bideford.
Eyes looked love
to eyes that
spake again."

515 L. M.
516 L. M.
467 L. M.

Bideford Breathings.

The farmers in this vicinity are busy at present getting out their years supply of wood. Messrs. John Williams & Sons have taken a contract of repairing the public wharf. As they are experienced hands we anticipate a speedy and substantial work. This place is soon to be supplied with a long felt want in the way of a new public hall. The shareholders held a meeting in the office of Mr. J. W. Richards on the 27 ult. and decided to erect it at once. There is already almost $300 subscribed. Our debating society is still in a prosperous condition.

BLUFF & CO.

40쪽 펼쳐놓은 시간표 밑으로 보이지 않는 글은 유진 필드Eugene Field(1850-1895)의 단편소설 〈콩키 스타일스 Conky Stiles〉로, 매사에 성경 구절을 인용하는 어느 젊은 이에 관한 이야기다. 몽고메리는 이 이야기가 비더포드 에 있는 감리교 목사관에서의 하숙 생활 마감을 기념하 기에 적합하다고 생각했던 것 같다. 1895년 5월 10일, 몽고메리는 이스티 부인과 함께 우체국에 다녀왔다. 캐 번디시에서 봄방학을 보내고 돌아온 뒤에는 "우체국" 에서 하숙했다. 의욕 넘치고 헌신적인 선생님이었던 몽 고메리는 복잡한 수업 시간표를 만들어 비더포드 학교 에 다니는 여러 학년의 아이들 수십 명을 가르쳤다.

41쪽 루 디스턴트는 1895년 6월 30일에 몽고메리에게 청혼했다. 몽고메리는 그가 거절당한 뒤 벌인 소동에 넌더리가 났는지 어느 정도 경멸 조로, 1894년 렘 매클 라우드의 청혼을 거절하고 실었던 휘틀러의 〈모드 멀 러〉 시구를 이곳에 그대로 인용했다(블루 스크랩북 33쪽). 세 가지 사랑 이야기는 디스턴트의 청혼에 아이러니한 배경이 된다. 아름답기로 유명했던 해밀턴 부인Emma Hamilton은 넬슨 제독Horatio Nelson의 헌신적인 정부였다. 두 편의 시는 서로 완전히 다른 사랑을 얘기한다. 애들 레이드 앤 프록터Adelaide Anne Procter의 시(왼쪽 아래에서 시 작한다)는 금세 잊고 마는 남자의 얄팍한 사랑을 말하고, 롱펠로의 시(오른쪽 아래)는 생을 초월하여 지속되는 한 남자의 변함없는 사랑을 노래한다.

42쪽 1895년 6월 28일 비더포 드 학교에서 치른 "시험 시간표 Programme Examination"가 맨 위에 접혀 있다. 학생 스물한 명의 공연 과 학생들의 연설 뒤에 학교 운영 회와 관계자들이 적절한 감사 인 사를 하고 나면 모두 함께 국가 國歌인 〈신이여, 여왕을 지켜 주소서 God Save the Queen〉

를 합창했다. 다시 학생들이 연설을 시작하고 "우리의 현재 또는 미래의 안녕. 부족하나마 이것으로 인사를 대신하겠습니다. 비더포드 학교 학생 일동" 같은 말로 끝이 났다. 흥미롭게도 몽고메리는 이 지면에다가 어 린 시절 첫사랑이었던 네이트 록하트의 졸업 이야기를 꺼내면서 비더포드 교사로서 자신의 "졸업"을 언급했 다(오른쪽 아래). 에밀리 도널슨Emily Donelson은 아내를 잃 은 삼촌이자 미국의 제7대 대통령인 앤드루 잭슨Andrew Jackson을 위해 한동안 영부인 역할을 대신했다.

43쪽 "여성의 고등교육"을 다룬 만화는 몽고메리의 다 음 도전, 즉 달하우지 대학 진학을 언급한 것이다. 카드 는 헤이즈 씨의 "아늑한 거실"에 모인 젊은이들과의 마 지막 만남을 기념한다. "2차"는 "신입 회원들이 돌아간 후 점심식사"였다고 몽고메리의 미공개 일기에 적혀 있다.

44쪽 실제로 일어난 극적인 사건이 여백에 짤막한 메 모로 적혀 있다. 1895년 6월 6일, 몽고메리는 비더포드 에서 가르친 어느 학생의 집에서 식사를 했다. 그리고 일기에 그 상황을 눈에 보일 듯 생생하게 기록했다. 먹 지 못할 음식이며 그 밖의 모든 일을. 몽고메리는 박식 함을 증명하듯 그 집안의 가장에게 파피루스는 신문을 뜻하는 라틴어라고 말해줬다.

Time-Table.

[From Jan. 1st 1895 to May 3rd 1895].

Bideford School. No6.
L. M. Montgomery
Teacher

Hour.	Monday & Wednesday.	Hour.	Tuesday & Thursday.
10–10.10	Bible reading Roll Call	10.–10.10	Bible reading. Roll Call
10.10–10.20	First Primer Class	10.10–10.20	First Primer Class.
10.20–10.30	First Grammar Class	10.20–10.30	First History Class.
10.30–10.45	Second Gram. Class	10.30–10.45	Second History Class
10.45–11	Second Class.	10.45–11	Third Geog. Class. Second Class
11–11.30	Arithmetic 2nd Prim.	11–11.10	First Primer Class.
11.30–11.40	Arithmetic Classes.	11.10–11.30	Dictation for VI. V + IV.
11.40–12	Junior Latin Class.	11.30–11.40	Arithmetic and Algebra
12.–12.45	Dinner Hour.	11.40–12	Junior French.
12.45–1	First Primer Class	12.–12.45	Dinner Hour.
1–1.15	Fifth Class	12.45–1	First Primer Class.
1.15–1.30	Fourth Class.	1–1.15	Sixth Class.
1.30–1.45	Third + Second Classes	1.15–1.30	Second Geography class.
1.45–1.55	Writing class.	1.30–1.40	First Geography class
	Second Primer	1.—2	Third + Second Primer
2.15–2.30	Arithmetic.	2.10–2.30	Junior Geometry Class.
2.30–2.40	Arithmetic Classes.	2.30–2.40	Arithmetic Classes Tables.
2.40–3	Writing. Roll Call	2.40–3	Writing. Roll Call
3.—3.30			
3.—3.30	Senior Latin + Cæsar.	3.—3.30	Senior Geometry
3.30–3.45	Senior English	3.30—4	Senior French
3.45—4	Senior Can. History		

Wednesday.		Thursday	
11–11.10	Second Primer	11–11.10	Second Primer
11.10–11.30	Canadian History	11.10–11.30	Arithmetic and Algebra
3.45—4	Senior Hygiene	11.30–11.40	Arithmetic Classes.

Friday.

1.55–2.05	Junior Agriculture
2.05–2.15	Unit Drill
2.40–3	Recitations
3.—3.40	Senior Latin + Cæsar
3.40—4	Senior Agriculture

1st Monday. Bring Composition

2nd Week Bring drawn Map

All lessons must be prepared at Home.

Lucy. M. Montgomery. Teacher

Friday May 10th 1896

From a reproduction in carbon, by James L. Breece.
PORTRAIT OF LADY HAMILTON, BY ROMNEY.

The Lime-trees' shade at evening
  Is spreading broad and wide ;
Beneath their fragrant arches,
  Pace slowly, side by side,
In low and tender converse,
  A Bridegroom and his Bride.

The night is calm and stilly,
  No other sound is there
Except their happy voices :
  What is that cold bleak air
That passes through the Lime-trees,
  And stirs the Bridegroom's hair ?

While one low cry of anguish,
  Like the last dying wail
Of some dumb, hunted creature,
  Is borne upon the gale :—
Why does the Bridegroom shudder
  And turn so deathly pale ?

* * * * *

Near Purgatory's entrance
  The radiant Angels wait ;
It was the great St. Michael
  Who closed that gloomy gate
When the poor wandering spirit
  Came back to meet her fate.

"Pass on," thus spoke the Angel :
  "Heaven's joy is deep and vast ;
Pass on, pass on, poor Spirit,
  For Heaven is yours at last ;
In that one minute's anguish
  Your thousand years have passed."
          ADELAIDE ANNE PROCTER.

THE STORY OF THE FAITHFUL SOUL.

FOUNDED ON AN OLD FRENCH LEGEND.

THE fettered Spirits linger
  In purgatorial pain,
With penal fires effacing
  Their last faint earthly stain,
Which Life's imperfect sorrow
  Had tried to cleanse in vain.

Yet, on each feast of Mary
  Their sorrow finds release,
For the Great Archangel Michael
  Comes down and bids it cease ;
And the name of these brief respites
  Is called "Our Lady's Peace."

Yet once—so runs the Legend—
  When the Archangel came
And all these holy spirits
  Rejoiced at Mary's name ;
One voice alone was wailing,
  Still wailing on the same.

And though a great Te Deum
  The happy echoes woke,
This one discordant wailing
  Through the sweet voices broke :
So when St. Michael questioned
  Thus the poor spirit spoke :—

"I am not cold or thankless,
  Although I still complain ;
I prize our Lady's blessing
  Although it comes in vain
To still my bitter anguish,
  Or quench my ceaseless pain.

"On earth a heart that loved me,
  Still lives and mourns me there,
And the shadow of his anguish
  Is more than I can bear ;
All the torment that I suffer
  Is the thought of his despair.

"The evening of my bridal
  Death took my Life away ;
Not all Love's passionate pleading
  Could gain an hour's delay.
And he I left has suffered
  A whole year since that day,
"If I could only see him,—
  If I could only go
And speak one word of comfort
  And solace,—then, I know
He would endure with patience,
  And strive against his woe."

Thus the Archangel answered :—
  "Your time of pain is brief,
And soon the peace of Heaven
  Will give you full relief ;
Yet if his earthly comfort
  So much outweighs your grief,

"Then through a special mercy
  I offer you this grace,—
You may seek him who mourns you
  And look upon his face,
And speak to him of comfort
  For one short minute's space.

"But when that time is ended,
  Return here, and remain
A thousand years in torment,
  A thousand years in pain :
Thus dearly must you purchase
  The comfort he will gain."

L. Dystant

REPRESENTING
The Halifax Confectionery and
Baking Co. (Ltd.)
HALIFAX, N. S.

J. A. M. wrote me a few weeks a,
concerning a poem by Longfellow that w
not published until after his death, with th
request that I publish the lines. Here
the poem referred to :

Alone I walk the peopled city,
  Where each seems happy with his own ;
Oh ! friends, I ask not for your pity—
  I walk alone.

No more for me yon lake rejoices,
  Though moved by loving airs of June
Oh ! birds, your sweet and piping voices
  Are out of tune.

In vain for me the elm tree arches
  Its plumes in many a feathery spray ;
In vain the evening's starry marches
  And sunlit day.

In vain your beauty, summer flowers ;
  Ye cannot greet these cordial eyes ;
They gaze on other fields than ours—
  On other skies.

The gold is rifled from the coffer,
  The blade is stolen from the sheath ;
Life has but one more boon to offer,
  And that is Death.

Yet well I know the voice of duty,
  And, therefore, life and health must crave,
Though she who gave the world its beauty
  Is in her grave.

I live, O love one ! for the living
  Who drew their earliest life from thee,
And wait until with glad thanksgiving
  I shall be free.

For life to me is as a station
  Wherein apart a traveller stands—
One absent long from home and nation,
  In other lands ;

And I, as he who stands and listens,
  Amid the twilight's chill and gloom,
To hear, approaching in the distance,
  The train for home.

For death shall bring another mating
  Beyond the shadows of the tomb,
On yonder shore a bride is waiting
  Until I come.

In yonder field are children playing,
  And there—oh ! vision of delight !—
I see the child and mother straying
  In robes of white.

Thou, then, the longing heart that breakest,
  Stealing the treasures one by one,
I'll call Thee blessed when thou makest
  The parted—one.

12. Dialogue "The Grown Up Land" U. Cannon & M. McKenzie
14 Reading "Summer" — Master Frank Grant
15 Speech — Master Amos McKay.
16. Recitation "Little Christel" Miss Bertie Hayes.
17 Recitation "What A Boy Can Do" Master Claud Williams
18 Reading "Ellerslie" — Master Clifford Hayes.
19. Recitation "Willies Breeches" Master Ray Gorrill
20 Recitation "How to Lighten Troubles" Miss Bebie Williams
21 Closing Speech — Miss Bertie Ellis

Address

Dear and Respected Teacher

Having heard of your intention of leaving us we as
scholars cannot allow this
opportunity to pass without
expressing to you how deeply
we regret to hear of your
departure.

We heartily thank you
for the justice you have
given to us, You have left
nothing undone that would
tend in any way to expan

"THE BEAUTIFUL MRS. DONELSON"

LEGEND OF THE ORANGE BLOSSOM

Like all familiar customs whose origin is lost in antiquity, the wearing of orange blossoms at a wedding is accounted for in various ways. Among other stories is the following pretty legend from Spain:

An African prince presented a Spanish king with a magnificent orange tree, whose creamy waxy blossoms and wonderful fragrance excited the admiration of the whole court. Many begged in vain for a branch of the plant, but a foreign ambassador was tormented by the desire to introduce so great a curiosity to his native land. He used every possible means, fair or foul, to accomplish his purpose, but all his efforts coming to naught, he gave up in despair.

The fair daughter of the court gardener was loved by a young artisan, but lacked the dot which the family considered necessary in a bride. One day chancing to break off a spray of orange blossoms, the gardener thoughtlessly gave it to his daughter.

Seeing the coveted prize in the girl's hair, the wily ambassador offered her a sum suffi-

cient for the desired dowry, provided she gave him the branch and said nothing about it. Her marriage was soon celebrated, an[d] on her way to the altar, in grateful remembrance of the source of all her happiness she secretly broke off another bit of the lucky tree to adorn her hair.

Whether the poor court gardener lost his head in consequence of the daughter's treachery the legend does not state, but many lands now know the wonderful tree, and ever since that wedding day orange blossoms have been considered a fitting adornment for a bride.

Two Cavendish Graduates at Wolfville.

WOLFVILLE, N. S., June 5.—[Special]—Two Islanders graduated from Acadia today with honors. They were Nathan J. Lockhart of Cavendish, honors in English and Malcolm W. A. McLean, Cavendish, honors in Classics,

WHAT THE HIGHER EDUCATION OF WOMEN IS COMING TO.

Miss Brentwood (*Vassar '94, at home on vacation*)—"Don't wait breakfast for us, auntie. We'll be down as soon as we're through the morning calisthenics."

WHY SANTA CLAUS' BEARD IS WHITE

A Legend: By M. A. Bird

DURING the babyhood of Santa Claus—long, long ago—while still many good and worthy folk believed wood-sprites lived in the holes of trees, witches in caves, and dwarfs deep down under earth, there lived in far Germany, on one of the lesser mountains of the Harz, a miner, with his wife and seven children.

Deep down in the bosom of the mountains was the mine. Here the father had worked each day from morn to night to feed, even scantily, his wife and children. At last came a season of great dearth. The miner fell sick. Sadly his wife hung out of sight his leather work-suit.

The cold winter with its cruel grasp stole down from the mountain-tops; still the miner lay sick; still the dearth of food throughout the little town; nowhere a mouthful to spare. The birds in the trees lived and were merry. Must the little children starve? Who had done it? "I tell you, it's the Gübich, king of dwarfs, who spoiled the crops last year. I know his pranks, curse him," said the oldest of the miners. "Who in summer steals all the raspberries and strawberries? He never eats aught else, and has lived like a prince, in his rocky cavern up there among the holy firs, ever since the old giant threw these mountains out of his shoe because the bit of sand hurt him. I tell you, the Gübich can make us sick with a glance, touch or breath. Save me from going near his home! Yet they say the cones off his trees are good to eat, and can be made into wondrous pretty things which sell well in the town below us. Starve or touch them? Starve, I say!"

"Dear husband," said the patient wife, "thou knowest the holy firs; I go to gather their cones. I will sell them and buy thee food which will make thee well. Children, care for thy father while I am gone."

Quickly throwing a shawl over her head and taking a basket on her arm, out into the gathering coldness of the coming night stepped the mother. The wind shook the alders at the cottage door until they nodded and peeped at the windows. It roughly rattled the dried foliage of the stately oaks, whose sacredness to the gods the elements were thought to respect, and then died away among the pines in a soft, sad music, that brought tears to the mother's eyes. It was like the moan the bairns made for bread. The tears broke into a sob; half-blinded, with bent head, she reached the edge of the holy forest.

Pityingly, out from his bed of clouds, the setting sun glanced warm and tender. He shot his parting rays among the firs, and filled their deep shadows with a cheerful glow. Suddenly, into the marked pathway of his light, stepped a little man with snowy beard, who gravely doffed his leathern cap and waited for the sad mother to reach him.

"Good woman, what ail'st thou? Why so sad?" broke upon her startled ear.

"Oh, sir, I mean no harm. My children starve; my husband never again will be well. I cannot see them ask each day for bread and give them none. I go to gather cones. Do let me pass and fill my basket."

"I would harm thee not, my friend," said the little man. "And knowest thou where the best cones can be found? Follow this path a hundred feet, and there they can be gathered with"—but the mother was on her way. A knowing look, a caress of his white beard, a sniff of the perfumed forest air, and the little man had vanished.

With glad feet the mother hurried on. Not a sound but the dropping of the cones broke the stillness of the forest. Faster and thicker they seemed to fall at each onward step. A perfect storm of cones. They dropped upon her head; they fell at her feet; they pelted her shoulders; they filled her basket. Frightened, the poor woman turned and fled, glancing neither to the right or left. Heavier and heavier the basket grew. Breathless and exhausted she reached her cottage door.

The mother entered and quickly barred the door. "Husband, husband, think what has happened! On the edge of the holy forest I met a little man with snowy beard, who told me where to gather the best cones. I hurried to find them, but the farther I went the faster the cones fell from the firs. They came about my head as thick as snow-flakes in mid-winter, yet the trees shook not. I was afraid and did not stop to pick up one; but some fell in my basket, and here they are."

"Hist, wife! Look, look thou! They are pure silver. It's the Gübich thou hast met."

Down the basket dropped. Around it grouped the mother and children. True, there lay the cones, silver every one, gleaming in the fire-light as had the beard of the little man in the golden glow of the sun.

The morrow's sun had tipped the graceful firs with gold, when again the mother stood at the edge of the forest. In a moment the Gübich was before her. "Good-morrow, good soul! Found'st thou not beautiful cones yester-eve?" And a laugh rang through the forest. The mother struggled to speak. "Keep thy thanks, I wish them not" continued the Gübich. "Be thou only faithful to thy husband's words, and each cold December give to me and my dear firs a loving thought to keep our hearts warm. Now hie thee home."

Not more quickly speeds the wind than the mother home again; not more happy are the birds than were the hearts in the miner's home that day. By night, nowhere a hungry soul on the "beautiful Hirbichenstein."

Dear Santa Claus—ever since, thy beard's been white as snow!

Dear Christmas joy—ever since, madly the Harz maidens dance round the graceful firs.

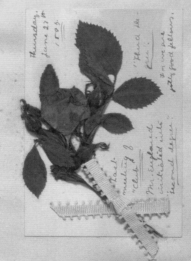

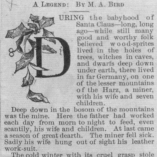

PRESBYTERIAN CHURCH.

Ba[se] Hits.

If one takes an interest in a paper is it necessary to *cleat* to the Business Manager?

Was the Sophy scared of the Dog or did he merely want to see what was on the other side of the fence?

Mr. J. H. S. has been removed to more commodious quarters three doors west of his old stand, where he is now prepared to welcome his friends.

FOUND—On Friday, April 6th, near Prince Street School, a beautiful *Pearl* probably purchased at Taylor's Jewelry Store. Owner can have the same by shooting the finder. Apply to H. L., P. W. C.

The three essentials to human happiness are said to be—Something to do, something to love, and something to hope for. If this be so we know some P. W. C. students who ought to be happy. (A sort of grim humor pervades the above remark).

We notice that a society whose initials are N. M. A. H. S. has been formed among the young Ladies for the purpose of encouraging Spring Poets. It is said that at the end of the term they will award a medal to the composer of the best poem on "The Absent One".

In the Barn.

O Jack, are you up in the hay-loft?
   I'm coming up there, too.
I'm tired of being a lady,
   I'd rather have fun with you.
There's company in the parlor,
   And mamma whispered to me,
"Now do be a lady, Pussie,
   And see how good you can be."

But, Jack, it was really dreadful!
   I couldn't sit still, you know,
And most likely the company wondered
   To see me fidgeting so.
But I heard you laughing and shouting,
   And I knew you were having fun,
And I looked at the clock and wondered
   How soon her call would be done.

But when they were busy talking,
   And didn't remember me,
I just slipped out as softly!
   And here I am, you see.
O Jack! it is awfully jolly
   Not to be grown-up folks;
They never have fun in the hay-loft,
   Laughing and telling jokes.

They can't go hunting for hen's eggs,
   Or swing on the old barn-door,
Or climp this steep old ladder,
   And jump, like us, to the floor.
To sit in a chair is horrid,
   To sit on a beam is fun,
And we don't care if we're sunburned,
   We aren't afraid of the sun.

Just fancy mamma or sister
   Rolling about in the hay!
It makes me laugh—because surely
   Their "trains" would be in the way.
I heard papa call me a "Tom-boy;"
   I'd rather be that, I declare,
Than to sit for another hour
   So still in a parlor chair.

Just think of the time I wasted,
   When I might have been here with you!
And it may have been another half hour
   Before her visit is through.
I'm sorry for mamma and sister,
   Long dresses, long manners and all!
And Jack, I'll be sorrier still, dear
   When you and "Pussie" grow tall.

비더포드에서 행복한 시간을 보낸 루시 모드 몽고메리는 이제 달하우지 대학에 진학하여 배링턴 스트리트에 위치한 핼리팩스 여학교에서 생활했다. 많은 작은 카드에 눌러 말린 꽃과 인용구를 가득 실었던 프린스오브웨일스 대학과 비더포드 시절은 알록달록 오려 붙인 그림들, 많은 시와 재미있는 이야기와 사건들이 대신하게 되는 듯하다.

49쪽 몽고메리는 핼리팩스에 있는 여학교에서 지낸 경험과 《데일리 에코》 직원으로 일한 시절(1901-1902)을 하나로 합쳤는지도 모른다. 1895년 11월 13일에 "홍역"이라고 적힌 작은 카드에 "모리스 스트리트"가 같이 쓰여 있는 것을 보면 그렇다. 몽고메리는 《데일리 에코》에서 일하던 시절에 처치 스트리트에서 살다가 나중에 모리스 스트리트로 거처를 옮겼다. 홍역에 걸린 것은 1895년 10월 말이었고, 최종적으로 병원에서 퇴원한 날짜가 11월 17일이었다. 화사한 튤립과 말린 꽃과 단풍잎에 둘러싸인 가운데 그림 속 아이는 생각에 잠겨 창밖을 내다보고 있는데, 아마도 그해 크리스마스 때 집에 가지 못했다는 사실을 언급하고자 한 듯하다. 헨리에트 론네르 크닙의 고양이 그림(레드 스크랩북 35쪽) 중 한 마리가 강아지에 관한 시 아래에 붙어 있다. 이 시는 강아지가 어린 주인을 충직하게 기다리지만 허망하게도 그 주인은 이미 죽었다는 내용이다. 다른 글 네 편도 재미있는 내용이지만, 〈소설 속 여주인공의 불평Plaint of the Heroine of Fiction〉은 장래의 소설가 몽고메리가 현대적 글쓰기를 살펴보면서도 보다 전통적인 이야기를, 이 지면에서도 분명히 드러나는 회환과 비애와 익살이 넘치는 이야기를 쓰기로 마음먹었다는 것을 넌지시 보여준다.

50쪽 맥길 대학McGill University의 휘장 조각이 〈이상The Ideal〉이라는 시 옆에 붙어 있다. 이 시는 앤 셜리가 아름다운 것을 볼 때마다 느낀, 그리고 에밀리 스타라면 "알프스 산길"을 따라가노라면 어딘가에 있을 영감이라 인정할 만한 소명에 대한 진지한 선언문이다(알프스 산길 이야기는 〈용담〉이라는 시에 나온다. 레드 스크랩북 23쪽). 휘장 위로는 1896년 기사에 눈길이 간다. 기사에 언급되는 두 사람의 이름 때문인데, 한 사람은 노먼 캠벨Norman Campbell(앞 페이지에 보관된 기사에서 언급됐는데, 프린스오브웨일스 대학 시절의 친구인 메리 캠벨의 마음씨 좋은 오빠이다)이고, 다른 한 사람은 에드윈 심프슨이다. 에드윈 심프슨은 몽고메리가 두 사람의 비밀 약혼을 깼을 때 몽고메리에게 너무나 큰 당혹감과 고통을 안겼다. "그대의 뜻이 이루어지리다"라는 글귀는 당시에 청혼을 거절당한 루 디스턴트가 보낸 것이었다. 몽고메리가 "작고 순수한 봉오리"인 자신에 대해 비꼬듯이 논평한 것을 시 옆에 배치한 풍자만화에서도 찾아볼 수 있을 것이다.

51쪽 앤 S. 스티븐슨Ann S. Stephens의 〈폴란드 소년The Polish Boy〉은 대중적으로 낭송되던 시였다. 애국심과 자기희생을 자아내는 장면을 묘사하여 앤 셜리라면 무척 좋아했을 시다. 자주색과 금색은 핼리팩스 여학교의 상징색으로, 그 후신인 암브레 아카데미Armbrae Academy에서도 그대로 사용하고 있다(1학년부터 12학년까지).

PLAINT OF THE HEROINE OF FICTION.

I once had lovely golden hair,
  Or raven hair—no matter which—
I was as good and sweet and fair
  As any angel in a niche.
Or, if I did a little wrong,
  It was to prove me human still;
My feelings were extremely strong,
  But I disciplined my will.

A change has come—and what a change!
  With awful problems I am vexed,
From crime to crime I reckless range,
  I know not what will happen next.
From frantic woe to frantic bliss,
  From frantic wrath to frantic glee—
I never wished to be like this!
  I can't make out what's come to me!

Gone are my gayety and cheer,
  Gone is my hero bold and true;
In my hysterical career
  I very often long for you!
Now me, all other woes above,
  My bitter destiny compels
To wed a man I do not love,
  Then fall in love with some one else.

Yet me how would you recognize,
  O Hero, if you met me now?
What scorn would lighten from your eyes
  And corrugate your manly brow!
The modern hero I have found,
  Upon the whole, I do not like;
He's either stupid or unsound,
  And if I were not worse I'd strike.

But I am worse—I never guessed
  How bad I could be till I tried,
Compelled too often to arrest
  My headlong course by suicide;
And though I cease from guilt and slang,
  A fresh reprieve I fain would beg—
For other authors seem to hang
  Theories on me like a peg.

Ah, yet I long a little share
  Of happiness and love to find;
Again I would be gay and fair,
  Loyal, and chivalrous, and kind!
Ah! do not bid me rant and rave
  Ah! do not bid me preach and bore;
Give back my Hero, true and brave,
  Whom I shall love forever more.
    —May Kendall, in Longman's Magazine.

THE LITTLE BROWN DOG AT THE DOOR.

Early and late you watch and wait,
  Little brown dog at the door,
For a quick footfall and a boyish call,
  For your master to come once more.
Eager to follow, through field and hollow,
  Wherever his feet may roam,
Content to stray, if he leads the way,
  Wherever he is, is home.

But you never hear the whistle clear,
  Nor the sound of the boyish call,
Nor the scamper of feet all bare and fleet
  Down through the shadowy hall;
Though long you wait at door and gate
  For your playfellow of old,
With his eyes so blue and his heart so true,
  And his hair like the sunshine's gold.

'Tis a year and a day since he went away
  To a country beyond our ken,
And those who go that way, we know,
  Never come back again.
Still early and late you watch and wait,
  Little brown dog at the door,
But the voice is still, and watch as you will,
  Your master comes no more.
          DOROTHY DEANE.

NORMAN CAMPBELL, President of our Debating Society, comes from Darlington. We cannot say of him that "he toiled not, neither did he spin," for he has been successful in securing first class honors. His "length" of admiration for the frailer sex has often been commented on, but it never interfered with his working hours! Norman was a regular attendant at the evening services at the Kiak.

"Maxelle" "Morris Str
Halifax
N.S.
November 10th
1895

MUTUAL CONFIDENCES : ... AL FRIENDS.

BY MARY CLARK HUNTI... N.

Said Miss Malvina Trotter to her neighbor Mrs. Potter,
  Together sitting on the porch one pleasant summer day,
"There's quite a startling story about young Mrs. Corey—
  Don't tell that I repeated it—or that's what people say.
"They quarreled with each other over one thing and another,
  Till her husband threw a cup of tea full in her face one day;
And vowing she would grieve him she now declares she'll leave him,
  Intends to sue for a divorce—or that's what people say."

"Do tell!" cried Mrs. Potter. "But I'm not surprised, Miss Trotter,
  I've thought they weren't quite happy. Now, don't you breathe a word
From me: but Deacon Draskitt stole a neighbor's bushel basket,
  And sold it for a quarter—or that is what I've heard.
"And his wife she is so cruel to that poor Pepita Buel,
  Whom she took from out the orphan's home! It actually occurred
That she called her 'lazy sinner,' made her go without her dinner,
  And whipped her, whipped her dreadfully—or that's what I have heard."

Thus Miss Malvina Trotter and her neighbor Mrs. Porter
  That livelong summer afternoon with converse sweet beguiled,
Till no matter what their station, not a shred of reputation
  Was left in all that goodly town to woman, man or child.
"Dear me," mused Mrs. Potter when Mrs. Malvina Trotter
  With many a lingering last "good-night" had homeward turned her way,
"It's positively inhuman for any decent woman
  To be forever talking about 'what people say.'"

Thought Miss Malvina Trotter as she left the house of Potter,
  "It's sad how many dreadful things have in this town occurred;
But worse than all together it puts in such high feather
  That gossip, Mrs. Potter, to tell 'what she has heard.'"

An Exchange of Syllables.

The Atlantic monthly tells of a young lady who, to her intense mortification, often reverses her vowels all unconscious of it even after speaking.

One summer evening she was sauntering with a friend towards the village post-office of the little town where they were staying. On the way they encountered an acquaintance with a handful of letters.

"Ah, good evening," she said in her peculiarly gracious, suave manner. "Are you strailing out for your mole!"

The mystified young woman made some inarticulate reply and passed on. As soon as the friend could recover her gravity, she gasped, "I suppose you intended to ask Miss May if she was strolling out for her mail?"

The same young lady was relating a sad story of various misfortunes which had overwhelmed a dear friend.

"Think," she concluded pathetically, "of losing husband, children, property, and home at one swell foop!" and a howl of laughter rent the roof.

CALLING IN THE COUNTRY

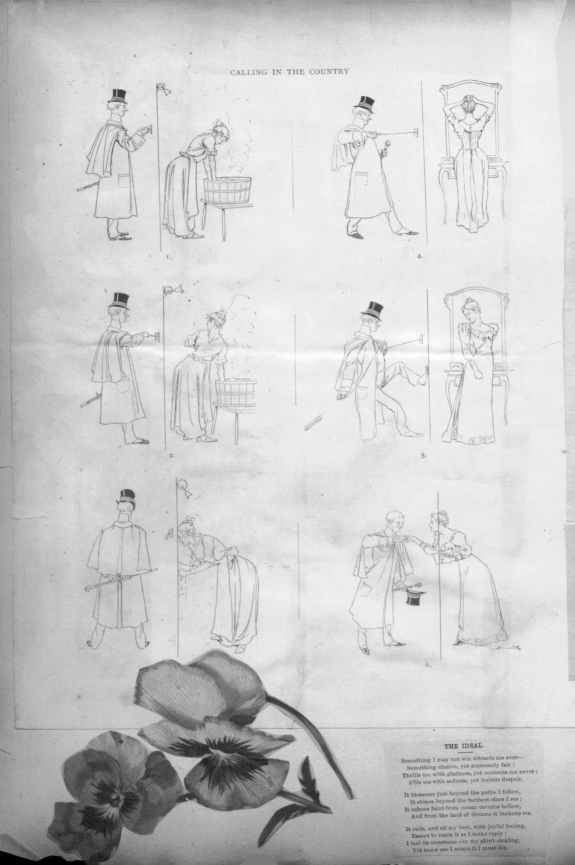

THE first number of the 1896 Prince
of Wales College Observer has just
been issued. The original matter as
well as the selections show unmistake-
able evidence of fine literary taste on
the part of the editors. The advertis-
ing patronage is very encouraging and
local topics are dealt with in an interesting manner. The staff of editors is
as follows : Edwin Simpson, Manager ;
Addison Anderson, Assistant Manager ;
Maggie James, Elsie McNeill, Montague Johnstone, Edwin Crockett, Norman A. Campbell, Parmenas McLeod,
Vivian Doran, Cyrus McMillan. William
McEwen, George Phillips ; H. Martin,
Business Manager. The Observer is
published monthly.

THE POLISH BOY.

Whence come those shrieks so wild and shrill,
    That cut, like blades of steel, the air,
Causing the creeping blood to chill
    With the sharp cadence of despair?

Again they come, as if a heart
    Were cleft in twain by one quick blow,
And every string had voice apart
    To utter its peculiar woe.

Whence came they? from yon temple, where
An altar, raised for private prayer,
Now forms the warrior's marble bed
Who Warsaw's gallant armies led.

The dim funereal tapers throw
A holy luster o'er his brow,
And burnish with their rays of light
The mass of curls that gather bright,
Above the haughty brow and eye
Of a young boy that's kneeling by.

What hand is that, whose icy press
    Clings to the dead with Death's own grasp,
But meets no answering caress?
    No thrilling fingers seek its clasp.
It is the hand of her whose cry
    Rang wildly, late, upon the air,
When the dead warrior met her eye
    Outstretched upon the altar there.

With pallid lip and stony brow
She murmurs forth her anguish now.
But hark! the tramp of heavy feet
Is heard along the bloody street;
Nearer and nearer yet they come,
With clanking eyes and noiseless drum.
Now whispered curses, low and deep
Around the holy temple creep;
The gate is burst, a ruffian band
Rush in and savagely demand,
With brutal voice and oath profane,
The startled boy for exile's chain.

The mother sprang with gesture wild,
And to her bosom clasped her child;
Then, with pale cheek and flashing eye,
Shouted with fearful energy,
" Back, ruffians, back! nor dare to tread
Too near the body of my dead;
Nor touch the living boy; I stand
Between him and your lawless band.
Take me, and bind these arms, these hands,
With Russia's heaviest iron bands,
And drag me to Siberia's wild
To perish, if 'twill save my child! "
" Peace, woman, peace! " the leader cried,
Tearing the pale boy from her side,
And in his ruffian grasp he bore
His victim to the temple door.
" One moment! " shrieked the mother ; " one !
Will land or gold redeem my son?
Take heritage, take name, take all,
But leave him free from Russian thrall!
Take these! " and her white arms and hands
She stripped of rings and diamond bands,
And tore from braids of long black hair
The gems that gleamed like starlight there;
Her cross of blazing rubies, last,
Down at the Russian's feet she cast.
He stooped to seize the glittering store;
Up springing from the marble floor,
The mother, with a cry of joy,
Snatched to her leaping heart the boy.
But no! the Russian's iron grasp
Again undid the mother's clasp.
Forward she fell, with one long cry
Of more than mortal agony.

But the brave child is roused at length,
    And breaking from the Russian's hold,
He stands, a giant in the strength
    Of his young spirit, fierce and bold.
Proudly he towers; his flashing eye,
    So blue, and yet so bright,
Seems kindled from the eternal sky,
    So brilliant is its light.
His curling lips and crimson cheeks
Foretell the thought before he speaks;
With a full voice of proud command
He turned upon the wondering band:
" Ye hold me not! no! no, nor can ;

This hour has made the boy a man.
I knelt before my slaughtered sire,
Nor felt one throb of vengeful ire;
I wept upon his marble brow,
Yes, wept! I was a child; but now
My noble mother, on her knee,
Hath done the work of years for me! "

He drew aside his broidered vest,
And there, like slumbering serpent's crest,
The jeweled haft of poniard bright
Glittered a moment on the sight.
" Ha! start ye back? Fool! coward! knave!
Think ye my noble father's glaive
Would drink the life blood of a slave?
The pearls that on the handle flame
Would blush to rubies in their shame;
The blade would quiver in thy breast

Ashamed of such ignoble rest.
No! thus I rend the tyrant's chain,
And fling him back a boy's disdain! "

A moment, and the funeral light
Flashed on the jeweled weapon bright;
Another, and his young heart's blood
Leaped to the floor, a crimson flood.
Quick to his mother's side he sprang,
And on the air his clear voice rang :
" Up, mother, up! I'm free! I'm free!
The choice was death or slavery.
Up, mother, up! Look on thy son!

His freedom is forever won ;
And now he waits one holy kiss
To bear his father home in bliss,
One last embrace, one blessing—one !
To prove thou knowest, approvest thy
What! silent yet? Canst thou not fee
My warm blood o'er my heart congeal
Speak, mother, speak! lift up thy hea
What! silent still? Then art thou de
——Great God, I thank thee! Mother,
Rejoice with thee,—and thus— to die.
One long, deep breath, and his pale l
Lay on his mother's bosom—dead.
                        —Ann S. Stephens.

She Identified Herself.

"You must be identified," brusquely exclaimed a San Francisco bank cashier the other day to a tall, hook-nosed woman in green, red and blue, who brought in a check at a time his window was crowded.

"Well, I—I—why—I—no, it can't be! Yes, it is, too. Ain't you Henry Smith?"

"That's my name, madam," he replied, coldly.

"And you don't know me, Hen? I've changed some, and so air you ; but I jist knowed I'd seen ye. You've got that same old cast in your left eye, your nose crooks a little to the left, an' you're a Smith all over. An' you don't know me? Don't know Salinda Spratt that you uster coax to become Salinda Smith? 'Member how you uster haul me to school on your sled and kiss me in the lane an' call me your little true love? 'Member how you cut up 'cause I give ye the mitten? Land! Hen, I could stand here all day talkin' over them old times! You kin identify me now, can't ye, Hen?"

"Hen" did so, but in a mood that almost produced apoplexy.—Wasp.

여기에서는 핼리팩스와 달하우지 시절을 중심으로 다루지만 캐번디시와 비더포드 이야기도 곁들여져 있다.

52쪽 왼쪽 위에 커다랗게 붙어 있던 기사나 이미지를 말끔하게 제거하고 사진으로 대체했다. 핼리팩스 여학교의 프로그램 안쪽을 보면 메이블 딕슨Mabel Dixon이 블루 스크랩북 51쪽에서 언급한 〈폴란드 소년〉을 낭송했다는 것을 알 수 있다. 1890년 달력에는 "꼬리 달린 점들"을 신나게 표시한 흔적이 전혀 없는 것으로 보아, 이 달력은 꽃 그림 때문에 보관한 듯하다. 몽고메리는 스코틀랜드와 아일랜드와 잉글랜드의 우스개 이야기도 몇 가지 모아뒀다. 아마도 켈트 문학을 공부하면서 그런 쪽으로 특히 더 마음이 끌렸던 것 같다. 가운데 기사에서 언급하는 아치볼드W. P. Archibald 목사는 캐번디시에서 십팔 년 동안 봉직한 뒤 1895년 말에 노바스코샤로 떠났다. "세미라미스에게"라는 기사는 루 디스턴트가 보낸 듯하다. 몽고메리는 1905년 일기에 그의 밑줄 긋는 습관을 경멸하며 이렇게 적었다. "루의 시적 취향은 지독히도 감상적이었고, 밑줄 그은 부분은 꼭 여학생 같았다. (⋯) 버사 클라크Bertha Clark와 내가 그 정신없는 종이쪽지를 보고 얼마나 비명을 질러댔는지!"

53쪽 1895년 8월, 몽고메리가 달하우지로 떠날 준비를 하는 동안 캐번디시에서 몽고메리를 가르친 선생님이자 친구였던 셜리나 로빈슨이 찾아왔다. 두 사람은 낮 동안에는 소풍도 가고 발표회도 즐겼다. 밤이 되면 이야기를 나누느라 시간 가는 줄 모른 채 성냥으로 불을 지펴가며 곧 달하우지로 떠날 시간을 두고 농담을

건네기도 했다. 가운데 아래에 놓인 기사는 1896년 1월 31일에 달하우지에서 여학생들이 남학생들을 위해 개최한 파티 관련 내용이다. 몽고메리는 손 글씨로 쓴 파티 프로그램을 블루 스크랩북 58쪽에 담았다. 미공개 일기에는 이렇게 적었다. "우리는 거의 두 주 동안 다른 건 생각하지도, 말하지도 않았다. 파티는 눈부시게 성공적이었다."

55쪽 〈당신You〉이라는 시는 몽고메리의 독자라면 관심을 가질 만하다. "번쩍A flash!"이라는 단어 때문에 그렇다. 여기서 "번쩍"은 영감을 주는 영혼의 극적인 등장을 가리킨다. '에밀리' 시리즈에서 몽고메리는 번쩍 비치는 섬광으로 영감을 은유하거나, 현실 세계 너머의 완벽한 세계를 엿보듯 순간적으로 지나가는 인식을 은유하곤 했다. 몽고메리는 집에 가지 못하고 멀리 학교에 떨어져 있어 슬픈 크리스마스가 되리라고 예상했지만 뜻밖에 즐거운 일이 벌어졌다. 오른쪽 카드는 핼리팩스 브런즈윅 스트리트 387번지에서 열린 신년 파티를 기념한 것이다. "러스티"는 몽고메리가 핼리팩스 시절의 경험을 담아 앤의 레드먼드 대학 생활을 그린 《레드먼드의 앤Anne of the Island》(1915)에서 까칠한 고양이로 등장했다. 성적표는 달하우지 대학이 아니라 프린스오브웨일스 대학에 재학하던 시절에 받은 것이다. 프랭크 앨리슨 커리어Frank Allison Currier는 '학문을 사랑하는 사람들Philomathic Society(《레드먼드의 앤》에서 지식인 모임으로 재현된다)'이라는 모임에서 강연한 강사였다. 몽고메리도 '학문을 사랑하는 사람들'에서 낭독해달라는 초청을 받았다(블루 스크랩북 66쪽).

An Englishman once boasted that he had been mistaken for a member of the Royal Family. A Scotchman, hearing this, replied that he had been addressed as the Duke of Argyle. Whereupon an Irishman said that he had been taken for a far greater person than either; for as he was walking along the street one day, a friend came up to him, exclaiming, "Holy Moses! is that you?"

BOASTING.

Three tailors were once boasting which could make the best suit for a man, one of the tailors being an Englishman, one a Scotchman, and the other an Irishman. The Englishman said he could make a suit for a man if I only just looked at him as he was going round a corner.' The Scotchman said, 'And I could make a suit for a man if I only saw his coat tails as he was going round the corner.' 'Faith,' said Pat, 'and I could make a suit for a man if I only saw the corner he went round.'

Rev. W. P. ARCHIBALD, of Cavendish, leaves Monday for his future home in Sunny Brae, N. S. At a meeting of the Cavendish Literary Society, a few evenings ago, Mr. Archibald was presented with an address, expressive of deep gratitude to him for the service he has so earnestly rendered in connection with that Society. It was signed by Messrs Walter Simpson, George R. McNeill and John Laird, in behalf of the Society, who wished to convey to Mrs. Archibald and family their kind regards and good wishes for their happiness and prosperity. Mr. Archibald replied in an address replete with good advice to the young, emphasizing the necessity of their storing their minds with the best literature and the best only.

HALIFAX LADIES' COLLEGE.

Elocution Recital

BY

MISS WHITESIDES' PUPILS,

TUESDAY, MARCH 24TH, 1896,

at 8 o'clock.

ACCOMPANIST. — MISS TILSLEY.

To Semiramis—"Some Day!"

BY CATHERINE ELLIOT.

I dreamed so dear a dream of you last night!
I thought I went to you and stood beside
Your chair. You took my hand in yours; looking
Up into my eyes you said: "There lies deep
Within stern fate's decree, a bond called
Love; 'tis marked 'A Whim.' There is within
That bond a living Light, called Hope. You
Understand?"—I thought your hand had wandered
To my arm, and, buffing with this mild caress
Unmeant, I bent above your head, my face
To make the softest pillow of your hair.
You moved not, nor one word spoke to break
The silent tumult in my heart, save
"Some day"—half in earnest, half in jest,
My cheek touched yours, and, resting so, my
Wild and fervid happiness, no chains could
Chain. "And then of course, your lips mine met?"
Ah, no! for a week, and more I was
Not standing there. Beyond the stillness of
The night, I heard a voice in sadness say:

"Instructions"

"Private coaching"

Cramming for degree.

"A free confession is good for the soul"

Are you ready for your examination?

[9 am].

August 13th 14th 1105

For the Companion.

A CANADIAN TWILIGHT.

I.

The white mists gather on marsh and fen,
And down by the river's edge
The tide is lapping the fibrous grass,
And the snarls of sea-green sedge.
Away in the west the sunset glow
Fades out of the cold grey sky;
And up from the reeds that bend and quake,
Comes the red-necked loon's weird cry—
"Oh-oo-whi-oo-who-wi, whi-oo—who-wi, whi-oo—
who-wi!"

II.

The fisher boats in the lonely bay
Are anchored serene and still;
A red light gleams like a far faint star
From the dim crest of the hill.
The wind through the high-limbed poplar trees
Is sweet as some quaint old tune,
Yet sadder, sweeter than crooning wind,
Pipes the single red-necked loon:
"Oh-oo-whi-oo-who-wi, whi-oo—who-wi, whi-oo—
who-wi!"

III.

From shadowless heights the night creeps down
And muffles the sounding shore;
The still white boats gleam spectral and thin,
And the red light shows no more.
Yet ever across the darkening world
Creeps the river's monotone,
And the pensive, plaintive murmuring
Of the red-necked loon alone:
"Oh-oo-whi-oo-who-wi, whi-oo—who-wi, whi-oo—
who-wi!"

JOSETTE GERTRUDE MENARD.

A MOST enjoyable reception was held in the Munro room on Friday, January 31st. The male students of the senior and junior classes in Arts were the guests of the ladies in the above mentioned faculty. Dr. and Mrs. Forrest welcomed the boys while Misses Baker and Hill, representing the ladies, handed each one a tastefully gotten up programme, which consisted of songs, piano and violin solos, topics for conversation, and a speech by our esteemed president. He was in good form, and his sentiments with regard to lady students, and "we girls," were heartily applauded. The introductory system was complete, the most bashful fellow there having at one time no less than three girls about him. Refreshments were served towards the last, and ample justice done to the good things provided. The singing of Auld Lang Syne and three cheers for the ladies, closed the pleasant entertainment which we hope is the forerunner of many more of a like nature. Now boys do your share to make the session of '95-'96 one never to be forgotten by the students in attendance.

He Thought One in the Family Enough.

"You love my daughter?" said the old man.

"Love her!" he exclaimed passionately, "why I would die for her! For one soft glance from those sweet eyes I would hurl myself from yonder cliff and perish, a bleeding, bruised mass, upon the rocks two hundred feet below!"

The old man shook his head.

"I'm something of a liar myse'f," he said, "and one is enough [for a] small family like mine."

A Woodland Song.

Clear and sweet and full of wierd, wild cadence
  The rich notes rose and fell,
And now it was a plaintive song of story
  Rang sobbing through the dell,
And now the glad trills of a nation's triumph
  That warriors love to tell.

And someone from a far-off country listening
  Thought of a sea-kissed shore,
Beyond whose stretch the swaying palm trees softly
  Echo the billows roar.
That night a white-winged vessel southward sailing
  Both bird and listener bore.

   *   *   *   *   *   *

A silvery note! Oh! never such glorious music
  As thrills the strange bird's song!
And eagerly a crowd of wondering people
  To the dim shadows throng.
They do not know of *home* that bird is singing
  Through hours sad and long.
                        L. R. BAKER.

YOU.

The chief want in life is somebody who
shall make us do the best we can.—Emerson.

A flash! You came into my life,
  And lo, adown the years,
Rainbows of promise stretched across
  The sky grown gray with tears;
By day you were my sun of gold,
  By night, my silver moon,
I could not from the Father's hands
  Have asked a greater boon.

Life's turbid stream grew calm and clear,
  The cold winds sank to rest,
Hand-clasped with you, no bitter pain
  Found dwelling in my breast;
I did not dread life's care and toil,
  Your love dispelled all gloom,
And now on graves of buried hopes
  The sweetest violets bloom.

My every breath and every thought
  Were pure because of you,
I had not dreamed that Heaven could be
  So close to mortal view;
My hands and feet were swift to do
  The good that near them lay,
And in my heart throughout the year
  The joy-bird sang each day.

A flash! You passed out of my life—
  No, no! Your spirit still
Is sun and moon and guiding star
  Through every cloud and ill;
As down the rain-bowed years I go
  You still are at my side,
And some day I shall stand with you
  Among the glorified.
              —Clarence Urmey.

FRANK ALLISON CURRIER, or as the local papers used to put it "The
Rev. F. A Currier," was one of the few theologues who were generally
popular and could enjoy a joke as well as anyone. Currier was a
popular pulpit preacher, his eloquent sermons drawing his fellow students
from other churches. Possessed of a striking presence, he was unusually
popular among his fair parishoners and others, and only a strong will like
his could have withstood Cupids' darts. As a sportsman he excels,
many a good fish story comes from his lips, and one of the articles he
exhibits with pride is an old blunder buss with which he shot "many a
moose." At present he is Arts' Librarian, and studies for M. A.

Eug 88
Lib 74
Hist 72
Lati 84
Gull 77
Frencl 68
Geome 57
Colplou 74
Chem 58
Diz 84
Asjinet 68
S. Tup. 88
Bch M 75
Leachg 76

1034

로 즈 하트윅 소프Rose Hartwick Thorpe의 〈오늘 밤에는 통행금지령을 울리지 마세요Curfew Must Not Ring To-Night〉는 두루 즐겨 암송하던 시다. 《빨강 머리 앤》 19장에서 앤은 같이 공부하는 프리시 앤드루스가 이 멋진 시를 암송하는 발표회에 가게 해달라고 마릴라에게 사정한다.

이 페이지에서는 꽤 큼직한 자료 두 개를 떼어내고 잡지에서 오린 사진들로 그 자리를 대신했다.

몽고메리가 《칼리지 옵서버College Observer》에 기고한 시 〈어느 날의 땅The Land of Some Day〉은 〈곧 가야 할 땅 Land of Pretty Soon〉에서 영감을 받은 듯하다. 파인힐 신학교Pine Hill Divinity Hall를 졸업하고 캐번디시에서 봉직한 아치볼드 목사에 대한 기사를 몽고메리는 파인힐에서 받은 초청장 바로 밑에 붙였다. 후일 파인힐 신학교 졸업생이자 캐번디시에서 봉직한 목사인 이완 맥도널드와 약혼하게 됐을 때, 몽고메리는 이 페이지를 들춰보며 틀림없이 크게 놀랐을 것이다.

초기의 문학적 성취

루시 모드 몽고메리는 개인사를 기록하는 스크랩북을, 문학적으로 이룬 성공을 자축하는 용도로 사용하지 않았다. 출판된 시, 단편소설, 수필(그리고 나중에는 평론까지) 등을 별도의 스크랩북들에 보관했는데 여기에 가장 먼저 실린 작품은 1890년에 최초로 발표한 시 〈르포스 곶Cape Leforce〉이다. 문학적으로 핼리팩스 학창 시절은 대단히 성공적이었다. 포부를 지닌 동료 학생들에게 초청받아 글과 생각을 함께 나누었다. 프린스오브웨일스 대학의 새로운 교지 《칼리지 옵서버》에도 시를 발표했다. 열심히 공부하면서도 시간을 내어 글을 쓰고 작품을 투고하여 시와 단편소설이 인기 잡지에 채택되곤 했는데 《골든 데이스Golden Days》, 《시카고 인터오션Chicago Inter-Ocean》, 《젊은이의 벗》, 《레이디 저널》, 《아메리칸 애그리컬처리스트American Agriculturist》 같은 잡지였다. 《핼리팩스 헤럴드Halifax Herald》의 편집자는 대학 특별판을 기획하여 "달하우지 여학생의 경험"을 써보라며 몽고메리를 초빙했다. 몽고메리가 일기에 적은 바에 따르면 핼리팩스 일간지 《이브닝 메일Evening Mail》이 주최한 공모전에서 자신이 1등을 차지해 상금 5달러를 받았는데, 몽고메리가 재치 있는 시로 응수한 공모전의 주제는 다음과 같았다고 한다. "일상적인 근심과 삶의 시련에 놓였을 때 남자와 여자 중 어느 쪽이 더 잘 인내할까?"

I.

Slowly England's sun was setting o'er the hill-
  tops far away,
Filling all the land with beauty at the close of
  one sad day ;
And the last rays kissed the forehead of a man
  and maiden fair,
He with footsteps slow and weary, she with
  sunny, floating hair ;
He with bowed head, sad and thoughtful, she
  with lips all cold and white,
Struggling to keep back the murmur, "Curfew
  must not ring to-night !"

II.

"Sexton," Bessie's white lips faltered, pointing
  to the prison old,
With its turrets tall and gloomy, with its walls
  dark, damp, and cold—
"I've a lover in that prison, doomed this very
  night to die
At the ringing of the Curfew, and no earthly
  help is nigh.
Cromwell will not come till sunset ;" and her
  face grew strangely white
As she breathed the husky whisper, "Curfew
  must not ring to-night !"

III.

"Bessie," calmly spoke the sexton—and his ac-
  cents pierced her heart
Like the piercing of an arrow, like a deadly
  poisoned dart—
"Long, long years I've rung the Curfew from
  that gloomy shadowed tower ;
Every evening, just at sunset, it has told the
  twilight hour ;
I have done my duty ever, tried to do it just
  and right,
Now I'm old, I still must do it ; Curfew, girl,
  must ring to-night !"

IV.

Wild her eyes and pale her features, stern and
  white her thoughtful brow,
And within her secret bosom Bessie made a
  solemn vow.
She had listened while the judges read, without
  a tear or sigh,
"At the ringing of the Curfew, Basil Under-
  wood must die."
And her breath came fast and faster, and her
  eyes grew large and bright,
As in undertone she murmured, "Curfew must
  not ring to-night !"

V.

With quick step she bounded forward, sprang
  within the old church-door,
Left the old man threading slowly paths he'd
  trod so oft before ;
Not one moment paused the maiden, but with
  eye and cheek aglow
Mounted up the gloomy tower, where the bell
  swung to and fro :
As she climbed the dusty ladder, on which fell
  no ray of light,
Up and up, her white lips saying, "Curfew shall
  not ring to-night.

VI.

She has reached the topmost ladder, o'er her
  hangs the great dark bell,
Awful is the gloom beneath her, like the pathway down to hell ;
Lo, the ponderous tongue is swinging, 'tis the
  hour of Curfew now,
And the sight has chilled her bosom, stopped her
  breath and paled her brow.
Shall she let it ring ? No, never ! Flash her
  eyes with sudden light,
And she springs and grasps it firmly : "Curfew
  shall not ring to-night !"

VII.

Out she swung, far out ; the city seemed a speck
  of light below ;
She 'twixt heaven and earth suspended as the
  bell swung to and fro ;
And the sexton at the bell-rope, old and deaf,
  heard not the bell,
But he thought it still was ringing fair young
  Basil's funeral knell.
Still the maiden clung more firmly, and, with
  trembling lips and white,
Said, to hush her heart's wild beating, "Curfew
  shall not ring to-night !"

VIII.

It was o'er ; the bell ceased swaying, and the
  maiden stepped once more
Firmly on the dark old ladder, where for hundred years before
Human foot had not been planted ; but the
  brave deed she had done
Should be told long ages after ;—often as the
  setting sun
Should illume the sky with beauty, aged sires,
  with heads of white,
Long should tell the little children, "Curfew
  did not ring that night."

IX.

O'er the distant hills came Cromwell ; Bessie
  sees him, and her brow,
Full of hope and full of gladness, has no anxious
  traces now.
At his feet she tells her story, shows her hands
  all bruised and torn ;
And her face so sweet and pleading, yet with
  sorrow pale and worn,
Touched his heart with sudden pity—lit his eye
  with misty light ;
"Go, your lover lives !" said Cromwell ; "Curfew shall not ring to-night !"
                    ROSE HARTWICK THORPE.

Miss Montgomery

*The Principal, Professors and Students
of the Presbyterian College request
the pleasure of your company at a
Conversazione,
in the College, on Friday evening, 27th March,
from 8.30 to 11.*

An answer is requested to the Secretary.

Pine Hill, Halifax.

WE come now to a famous, and to their time the largest class.
ARCHIBALD, WILLIAM P., divided with Scott the class prizes throughout
their course, only once, it was in their Junior year, did they share
honors with a third. With four others of his classmates, Archibald went
into the ministry, and after a course at Pine Hill was in 1875 settled in
Cavendish, P. E. I. There he remained till called to Sunny Brae, Pictou
Co., during the past autumn. His studies did not end with his leaving
College. He is still a student as was shown by his taking his B. D. from
his Alma Mater in Theology in 1887, and by the fact that his name was
mentioned for one of the recent vacancies on the staff of that Alma
Mater. Said one of his Island brethren to the writer only a few days
ago : "When Archibald came to the Island he was our worst preacher ;
when he left it he was our best." Thus P. E. I. finds its noblest use,
—as a training school for Pictou County.

LAND OF 'PRETTY SOON.'

I know of a land where the streets
  are paved
  With the things which we meant
    to achieve.
It is walled with the money we
  meant to have saved,
  And the pleasures for which we
    grieve.
The kind words unspoken, the pro-
  mises broken,
  And many a coveted boon
Are stowed away there in that land
  somewhere—
  The land of 'Pretty Soon.'

There are uncut jewels of possible
  fame
  Lying about in the dust,
And many a noble and lofty aim
  Covered with mould and rust ;
And Oh ! this place, while it seems
  so near,
  Is farther away than the moon,
Though our purpose is fair, yet we
  never get there—
  The land of 'Pretty Soon.'

The road that leads to that mystic
  land
  Is strewed with pitiful wrecks
And the ships that have sailed for
  its shining strand
  Bear skeletons on their decks.
It is farther at noon than it was at
  dawn,
  And farther at night than at noon ;
Oh, let us beware of that land down
  there—
  The land of 'Pretty Soon.'
                    —Exchange.

58쪽 1896년 1월 31일, 달하우지 여학생들이 남학생들을 위해 개최한 (위에 펼쳐져 있는) 파티 프로그램은 손으로 쓴 것이다. 〈오직 당신뿐Just You, Dear〉이라는 시는 또 루 디스턴트가 보낸 것일까? 그래서 청혼을 풍자한 만화 옆에 비정하게 배치했을까? 1895년 12월 12일 파티에서 가장 중요한 것은 몽고메리가 입은 의상이었다. 일기에 따르면 핼리팩스 여학생들이 몽고메리에게 "눈부시게 멋져" 보인다고 말했다.

60쪽 향수 어린 작품들로 유명한 유진 필드는 블루 스크랩북에 몇 차례 등장한다. 〈소꿉친구My Playmates〉는 핼리팩스에서 고향을 그리워하던 몽고메리가 옛 시절을 동경하는 마음을 적절히 보여주는 것 같다. 이 잡지의 삽화는 블루 스크랩북 27쪽에 실린 이미지의 슬픈 모습 같다. 프린스에드워드섬의 피스키드 출신인 J. A.

C. 로저슨J. A. C. Rodgerson은 1896년 달하우지 대학교 졸업반에 재학 중이었다. 몽고메리는 같은 반에 있던 사촌 머리 맥닐Murray Macneill을 통해 그를 만났을 것이다.

61쪽 에드윈 랜시어Edwin Landseer가 작업한 판화 〈골짜기의 군주Monarch of the Glen〉는 빅토리아 시대 가정집에서 흔히 볼 수 있었다. 파크 코너에 위치한 캠벨가도 그중 한 집이었다. 달하우지 대학  (다른 대학들과는 달리 대학 헌장으로 여학생들의 입학을 배제한 적이 없다)은 이제 재학생 수가 1만 5,000명을 넘어섰다.

"BEHOLD WHAT CHANGES
TIME CAN BRING!"
1795.

STUYVESANT LIVINGSTON'S
GREAT - GRANDFATHER.— Be
assured, Madame, that did language afford words to express
my happiness, this poor English of ours would glow, for a
moment with the fires of ancient
Greece. But I can only
thank you for your favorable
reply, and kissing your hand,
remain your most obedient
servant!

1895.

STUYVY (who understands more English than Greek).— You
WILL? O Emily! darling!

JUST YOU, DEAR!

If I could have my dearest wish fulfilled,
  And take my choice of all earth's treas-
    ures, too,
And ask from heaven whatso'er I willed
      I'd ask for you.

No man I'd envy, neither low nor high,
  Nor king in castle old or palace new;
I'd hold Golconda's mines less rich than I,
    If I had you.

Trial and privation, poverty and care,
  Undaunted I'd defy, nor future woo;
Having my wife, no jewels else I'd wear,
    If she were you.

Little I'd care how lovely she might be,
  How graced with every charm, how fond,
    how true;
E'en though perfection, she'd be naught to
  me
        Were she not you.

There is more charm for my true, loving
  heart
  In everything you think, or say, or do,
Than all the joys of heaven could e'er im-
  part,
        Because it's you.
            —St. Paul Pioneer Press.

Miss Montgomery.

The Officers and Members of the

Social Committee

of

Fort Massey Society of Christian Endeavor

invite you to a

Social Reception to be held at the Residence

of the Pastor, 97 Pleasant Street,

Thursday evening, at 8 o'clock.

Dec. 12
1895.

MY PLAYMATES.

The wind comes whispering to me of the
    country green and cool,
Of redwing blackbirds chattering beside a
    reedy pool;
It brings me soothing fancies of the home-
    stead on the hill,
And I hear the thrush's evening song and
    the robin's morning thrill;
So I fall to thinking tenderly of those I
    used to know
Where the sassafras and snakeroot and
    checkerberries grow.

What has become of Ezra Marsh who lived
    on Baker's hill?
And what's become of Noble Pratt whose
    father kept the mill?
And what's become of Lizzie Crum and
    Anastasia Snell,
And of Roxie Root who tended school in
    Boston for a spell?
They were the boys and they the girls who
    shared my youthful play;
They do not answer to my call! My play-
    mates, where are they?

What has become of Levi and his little
    brother Joe,
Who lived next door to where we lived
    some forty years ago?
I'd like to see the Newton boys and Quincy
    Adams Brown,
And Hepsy Hall and Ella Cowles who
    spelled the whole school down!
And Gracie Smith, the Cutler boys, Lean-
    der Snow and all
Who I am sure would answer if they only
    hear my call!

I'd like to see Bill Warner and the Conkey
    boys again,
And talk about the times we used to wish
    that we were men!
And one, I shall not name her, could I see
    her gentle face
And hear her girlish treble in this distant,
    lonely place!
The flowers and hopes of springtime, they
    perished long ago,
And the garden where they blossomed is
    white with winter snow.

O cottage 'neath the maples, have you
    seen those girls and boys
That but a little while ago made, oh! such
    pleasant noise?
O trees, and hills, and brooks, and lanes,
    and meadows, do you know
Where I shall find my little friends of forty
    years ago?
You see I'm old and weary, and I've trav-
    eled long and far;
I am looking for my playmates, I wonder
    where they are!
                —Eugene Field.

N. PRESCOTT-DAVIES.

THE GLEN."—AFTE

DALHOUSIE COLLEGE, HALIFAX, THE DOORS OF WHICH ARE WIDE
OPEN TO WOMEN.

63쪽 몽고메리가 진실한 사랑의 시 〈죽을 때까지Until Death〉를 스크랩북에 붙일 때 누구를 떠올렸을까 궁금하다. 몽고메리는 〈꽃의 사랑 이야기A Floral Love-Story〉로 자신이 이 첫 스크랩북 전반에 꽃을 폭넓게 사용한 이유를 유희하듯 논평한다. 꽃에 관한 이 시를 헨리에트 론네르 크닙이 그린 또 다른 고양이 그림 위에 덧붙여 자신이 변함없이 사랑하는 네 가지를 눈에 잘 띄도록 한 페이지에 모아놓았으니 바로 패션, 꽃, 시, 고양이다.

패션과 꽃

루시 모드 몽고메리가 패션과 꽃에 대해 평생 가졌던 관심은 색을 향한 사랑으로 연결된다. 몽고메리는 스코틀랜드 펜팔 친구인 조지 보이드 맥밀런에게 1905년(《빨강 머리 앤》을 집필할 때이다)에 이렇게 말했다. "나에게 색은 누군가에게 음악이 갖는 의미와 같아. 누구나 색을 좋아하지만, 나에게 색은 열정이야." 몽고메리의 일기와 편지, 시, 소설은 색에 대한 생생한 묘사로 가득하다. 《빨강 머리 앤》을 쓰다가 이 스크랩북을 다시 들췄을 때 몽고메리는 1905년에 다시 유행하기 시작한 1895년의 커다란 퍼프소매가 떠올랐다. 독자들이 《빨강 머리 앤》에서 가장 좋아하는 장면 중 하나가 앤이 초록 지붕 집에서 맞는 첫 번째 크리스마스다. 매슈 아저씨가 앤에게 퍼프소매 드레스라는 완벽한 선물을 주는 장면이다.

오, 정말로 아름다웠다. 아름답고 부드러운 갈색 글로리아 옷감에는 실크처럼 윤기가 흘렀다. 치마는 앙증맞은 프릴과 셔링 주름으로 장식되어 있었고, 허리에 정교하게 잡힌 핀턱 장식은 최신 유행 스타일이었으며, 목에는 얇은 레이스로 만든 작은 러플 주름 장식이 달려 있었다. 하지만 소매! 소매가 더없이 아름다웠다! 소맷동이 팔꿈치까지 길게 올라왔고, 그 위에 두 단으로 아름답게 부풀린 소매가 달려 있었다. 단이 나누어지는 곳에도 셔링 주름을 잡아서 갈색 실크 리본으로 나비 모양의 매듭을 지어놓았다.

맥밀런에게 색에 대한 사랑을 설명하면서 몽고메리는 이렇게 말했다. "내 탁자 위에 있는 노란 금영화를 바라볼 때마다 그 빛깔에 아찔할 정도로 즐거워." 그보다 한 달 전에는 일기에다 자신이 가꾸는 정원에 대해 열변을 토하면서 "더없이 향긋한 스위트피, 노란 금영화, 불꽃의 숨결 같은 한련화"를 꺾었다고 적었다. 몽고메리는 꽃말, 그러니까 꽃에 담긴 의미가 무엇인지 잘 알았고, 꽃들을 묶어서 하고 싶은 말을 전달하는 기술도 뛰어났다. 팬지가 스크랩북에 아주 많이 사용됐는데 팬지가 추억과 기념을 의미하기 때문이다. 정원을 가꾸는 데 열정적이었던 몽고메리는 1901년 일기에 이상적인 정원을 묘사했다. 조개껍데기나 갈풀로 가장자리를 두르고, 그 안에 진홍색, 감미로운 분홍색, 보라색, 주황색, 노란색, 흰색 꽃이 가득히 "전부 질서 속에서 무질서한 모습으로 자라나는" 한적하고 오래된 정원이었다.

UNTIL DEATH.

Make me no vows of constancy, my
  friend,
    To love me, though I die, the whole
    lifelong,
And love no other till thy days shall end—
    Nay, it were rash and wrong.

It would not make me sleep more peacefully
    That thou wert wasting all thy life in
    woe
For my poor sake.   What love thou hast
    for me
    Bestow it ere I go !

Carve not upon a stone when I am dead
    The praises which remorseful mourners
    give
To women's graves—a tardy recompense—
    But speak them while I live.

Heap not the heavy marble on my head
    To shut away the sunshine and the
    dew.
Let small blooms grow there, and let
    grasses wave,
    And raindrops filter through.

Thou wilt meet many fairer and more
  gay
    Than I ; but, trust me, thou canst nev-
    er find
One who will love and serve thee night
    and day
    With a more single mind.

Forget me when I die ! The violet
    Above my rest will blossom just as
    blue,
Nor miss thy tears—e'en Nature's self for-
    gets,
    But while I live be true !

A FLORAL LOVE-STORY

Fair (Marigold) a maiden was, (Sweet William) was
  her lover ;
Their path was twined with (Bittersweet), it did not
  run through (Clover).
The (Ladies' Tresses) raven were, her cheeks a
  lovely (Rose),
She wore fine (Lady's Slippers) to warm her small
  (Pink) toes.
Her (Poppy) was an (Elder), who had a (Mint) of
  gold,
An awful old (Snapdragon), to make one's blood run
  cold !
His temper was like (Sour Grass), his daughter's
  heart he wrung
With words both fierce and bitter—he had an
  (Adder's Tongue) !
The lover's hair was like the (Flax), of pure Germanic
  type ;
He wore a (Dutchman's Breeches), he smoked a
  (Dutchman's Pipe).
He sent (Marshmallows) by the pound, and choicest
  (Wintergreen) ;
She painted him (Forget-me-nots), the bluest ever
  seen !
He couldn't serenade her within the (Nightshade)
  dark,
For every (Thyme) he tried it her father's (Dogwood)
  bark !
And so he set a certain day to meet at (Four-
  o'clock),—
Her face was pale as (Snowdrops), e'en whiter than
  her frock.
The lover vowed he'd (Pine) and die if she should
  say him no,
And then he up and kissed her beneath the (Mistle-
  toe).
"My love will (Live-for-ever), my sweet, will you be
  true ?
Give me a little (Heartsease), say only 'I love
  (Yew)!'"
She faltered that for him alone she'd (Orange
  Blossoms) wear,—
Then swayed like supple (Willow), and tore her
  (Maidenhair) !
For (Madder) than a hornet before them stood her
  Pop,
Who swore he'd (Cane) the fellow until he made him
  (Hop) !
Oh, quickly up (Rosemary) ! She cried, "You'll
  (Rue) the day,
Most cruel father ! Haste, my dear, and (Lettuce)
  flee away !"
But that inhuman parent so plied his (Birch) rod
  there
He settled all flirtation between that hapless (Pear).
The youth a monastery sought, and donned a black
  (Monkshood) !
The maid ate (Poison Ivy), and died within a wood.

65쪽 몽고메리는 베이어드 테일러Bayard Taylor가 쓴 〈존 리드의 생각John Reed's Thoughts〉에서 매슈와 마릴라라는 등장인물을 생각해냈는지도 모른다. 매슈보다 자아 인식이 강하고 우울감이 높은 필자는 앤이 오기 전 매슈와 마릴라의 삶처럼 고루한 삶에 대해 묘사한다.

> 그리고 누이 제인과 나, 우리는
> 주장하고 양보하는 법을 배웠다.
> 누이는 마음대로 집을 다스리고
> 나는 헛간과 밭을 지배한다.
> 그렇게, 거의 삼십 년을! 마치
> 글로 쓰고 서명하고 인장이라도 찍은 것처럼.

1905년 일기에는 이 스크랩북에 실은 자료에 대해 기록하면서, 몽고메리는 이 사진이 걸을 때 치마를 어떻게 걷어 올려야 하는지 볼 수 있어서 재미있다며 이런 동작은 시간이 지나면 제2의 천성이 된다고 덧붙였다. 화려한 카드 밑에는 몽고메리의 사촌인 클라라 E. 캠벨Clara E. Campbell의 이름이 적혀 있다. '케이드Cade'라고도 불린 클라라는 젊을 때 미국 보스턴으로 이주해 일을 했고(당시 캐나다 연해주의 많은 주민이 그러했다) 그렇게 미국에 정착했다.

Albert Lynch

THE SLEEPING OF THE WIND

By Charles B. Going

great red moon was swinging
low in the purple east;
bins had ceased from singing;
noise of the day had ceased;
lden sunset islands
faded into the sky,
arm from the seas of silence
ind of sleep came by.

so balmy and resting
the treetop breathed a kiss,
drowsy wood-bird, nesting,
ped a wee note of bliss;
over fragrant thickets
ft as an owl could fly,
hispered to tiny crickets
vords of a lullaby.

owly the purple darkened,
whispering trees were still,
hush of the woodland harkened
crying whip-poor-will;
moon grew whiter, and by it
hadows lay dark and deep;
fields were empty and quiet,
e wind had fallen asleep.

JOHN REED'S THOUGHTS.

There's a mist on the meadow below; the berring-frogs chirp and
cry;
It's chill when the sun is down, and the sod is not yet dry;
The world is a lonely place, it seems, and I don't know why.

I see, as I lean on the fence, how wearily trudges Dan,
With the feel of the spring in his bones, like a weak and elderly man;
I've had it a many a time; but we must work when we can.

But day after day to toil, and ever from sun to sun,
Though up to the season's front and nothing be left undone,
Is ending at twelve, like a clock, and beginning again at one.

The frogs make a sorrowful noise, and yet it's the time they mate,
There's something comes with the spring, a lightness or else a
weight;
There's something comes with the spring, and it seems to me it's
fate.

It's the hankering after a life that you never have learned
to know;
It's the discontent with a life that is always thus and so;
It's the wondering what we are, and where we are going
to go.

My life is lucky enough, I fancy, to most men's eyes;
For the more a family grows, the oftener some one dies,
And it's now run on so long, it couldn't be otherwise.

And sister Jane and myself, we have learned to claim and
yield;
She rules in the house at will, and I in the barn and field;
So, nigh upon thirty years!—as if written and signed and
sealed.

I couldn't change if I would; I've lost the how and when;
One day my time will be up, and Jane be the mistress then;
For single women are tough, and live down the single men.

She kept me so to herself, she was always the stronger hand,
And my lot showed well enough when I looked around in
the land;
But I'm tired and sore at heart, and I don't quite understand.

I wonder how it had been if I'd taken what others need,
The plague, they say, of a wife, the care of a younger breed?
If Edith Pleasanton now were near me as Edith Reed!

Suppose that a son well grown were there in the place of
Dan,
And I felt myself in him as I was when my work began?
I should feel no older, sure, and certainly more a man!

A daughter, besides, in the house; nay, let there be two or
three!
We never can overdo the luck that can never be,
And what has come to the most might also have come to me.

I've thought, when a neighbor's wife or his child was carried
away,
That to have no loss was a gain; but now—I can hardly say;
He seems to possess them still, under the ridges of clay.

And share and share in a life is, somehow, a different thing
From property held by deed, and the riches that oft take
wing.
I feel so close in the breast—I think it must be the spring.

I'm drying up like a brook when the woods have been cleared
around;
You're sure it must always run, you are used to the sight and
sound,
But it shrinks till there's only left a stony rut in the ground.

There's nothing to do but to take the days as they come and go,
And not to worry with thoughts that nobody likes to show;
For people so seldom talk of the things they want to know.

There's times when the way is plain and everything nearly
right,
And then of a sudden you stand like a man with a clouded
sight—
A bush seems often a beast in the dusk of a falling night.

I must move; my joints are stiff, the weather is breeding rain,
And Dan is hurrying on with his plow-team up the lane.
I'll go to the village store, I'd rather not talk with Jane.

—Bayard Taylor.

달하우지 시절에 활동하고 성취한 일이 많이 기록되어 있다.

66쪽 찰스 맥도널드Charles Macdonald 총장 권한대행은 달하우지 대학의 중요한 후원자였던 조지 먼로George Munro의 사망을 추모하기 위해 개인적인 집회를 개최했다. 몽고메리의 사촌인 머리 맥닐은 많은 상을 받았다. 몽고메리가 달하우지 자료들과 나란히 배치한 네 가지 자료를 통해 다른 경험들을 엿볼 수 있다. 한 여자가 장미꽃 한가운데서 솟아 나오는 것처럼 만든 이미지가 있고, 연극에 출연하는 것처럼 의상을 차려입은 여자의 사진도 있다. 몽고메리는 또 1895년 '학문을 사랑하는 사람들' 모임에서 자료를 발표했던 가을밤에 관한 기사도 붙였고, 달하우지 시절을 끝낸 여름의 재미난 모험(1896년 6월 6~7일)에 관한 기억도 기록했다. 6월 6일에 몽고메리와 루시 맥닐은 마차를 몰고 달링턴으로 가서 메리 캠벨과 함께 이틀을 보냈다. 몽고메리는 미공개 일기장에 이렇게 적었다. "메리와 루시와 나는 같이 잤고, 메리가 늙은 게일 여자 말투를 흉내 내는 소리에 우리는 배꼽이 빠지도록 웃어댔다. 메리의 흉내는 거의 완벽했다." 몽고메리는 '학문을 사랑하는 사람들'에서 연설을 해달라는 초청을 받고 기뻤다. 이언 매클래런Ian Maclaren은 존 왓슨John Watson 박사(1850-1907)의 필명이다. 몽고메리는 스코틀랜드 사람들의 생활을 그린 왓슨 박사의 1894년작 베스트셀러 《아리따운 들장미 덤불 옆에서 Beside the Bonnie Brier Bush》에 감탄했을 것이다.

67쪽 몽고메리는 달하우지 시험지 위에 프린스오브웨일스 대학의 상징색을 풀로 붙이고, 시험지 상단에 진짜 마지막 시험을 끝냈다고 신난 듯이 적었다. "1884-1896"이라 적힌 연도는 캐번디시 선생님(프레이저 선생님) 밑에서 엄격하게 첫 시험을 치른 날짜와 달하우지에서 마지막 시험을 치른 날짜이다. 프린스오브웨일스 대학에 다니던 시절, 샬럿타운에서 몽고메리를 처음으로 오페라하우스에 데려갔던 헤들리 번튼(블루 스크랩북 4쪽)이 결혼을 하는데, 아이러니하게도 몽고메리는 그의 결혼 소식이 실린 기사 옆에 〈거지 학생The Beggar Student〉이라는 희가극 프로그램 안내지를 배치했다. 몽고메리는 〈빌리 테일러Billee Taylor〉를 핼리팩스 여학교 친구인 로티 섀퍼드Lottie Shatford와 함께 관람했지만 연극 자체는 마음에 들어 하지 않았다. "하지만 가까이 살아 있는 사람들은 아름답고, 볼 가치가 충분했다"라고 몽고메리의 미공개 일기는 말하고 있다.

68쪽 〈파우스트Faust〉 공연은 몽고메리에게 큰 감명을 남겼다(레드 스크랩북 53쪽도 참고). "웅장했다. 4막은 특히 악마와 마녀가 벌이는 향연 (…) 대단히 소름 끼쳤다. 처음부터 다시 보고 싶다. 이렇게 재미있는 공연은 처음이었다." 몽고메리가 1895년 11월 22일에 미공개 일기에 적은 내용이다. '종달새 엘렌'이라고도 알려진 엘렌 비치 요Ellen Beach Yaw는 1894년에 뉴욕에서 첫 무대에 올랐다. 엘렌은 D음을 높은 D음보다 높게 유지할 수 있었다고들 한다. 사촌인 버티 매킨타이어Bertie McIntyre가 에드윈 심프슨과 나란히 칭찬받는 프린스오브웨일스 대학 소식을 읽고는 얼마나 재미있었을까. 몽고메리도 심프슨과 약혼한 1897년에는 이 기사가 말하는 내용처럼 에드윈이 변호사가 될 것이라고 믿었다(그는 침례교 목사가 됐다).

CHARLES MACDONALD, M.A.
PROFESSOR OF MATHEMATICS, DALHOUSIE UNIVERSITY,

The Society met again on Nov. 29th. "Scotch Authors" we
topic of the evening. The first paper was on "Crockett," and was
by R. E. Crockett. He did full justice to himself and to his name
His character sketch was good, his history light and racy, his de
tions vivid and his quotations apt.

Miss Montgomery followed with a paper on "Ian McLaren.
was very well written, and was read with the enthusiasm the su
demanded. The writings of this author draw forth eulogy rather
criticism. Miss Montgomery's paper proved to be no exception t
rule, and many fine points were brought out.

Mr. F. S. Simpson, B. A., discussed "Barrie," and succeede
sustaining his former reputation as an essayist. He depicted Barri
his works both in his beauty and his weaknesses in language, tha
clear, forcible and sometimes humorous.

Messrs. Putnam, McKay, Milligan and Davidson took part
discussion which followed. After thanking the writers the S
adjourned.

CONVOCATION

OF

DALHOUSIE UNIVERSITY,

HALIFAX, N. S.

TO BE HELD ON

TUESDAY, 28th April, 1896.

PROF. C. MACDONALD, M. A., Acting President,
in the Chair.

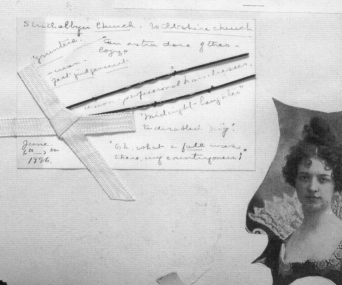

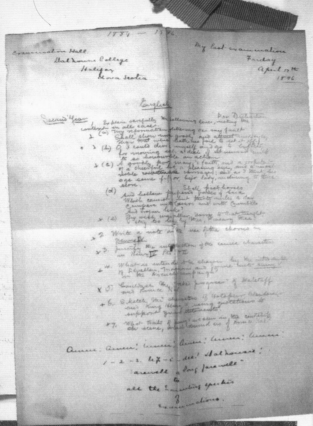

1884 — 1896

Examination Hall
Dalhousie College
Halifax
Nova Scotia

My last examination
Friday
April 19th
1896

English

Second Year

"Sincerity."

From a photograph by Ad. Braun & Co. (Braun, Clément Co., Successors) after the painting by Joseph ____

Orange Blossoms.

(Friday, Nov. 22.)

"Two hearts that beat as one" were united in the holy bonds of matrimony Wednesday night at the residence of Mrs. (Rev.) James Allan, Prince street. It was the marriage of her niece, Miss Mamie McDonald, daughter of James McDonald, Esq., of Chatham, N. B., to Mr. Hedley V. Buntain head book-keeper of the firm of Messrs. Peake Bros & Co. Next in importance in this event were the groom's sister, Miss Ella Buntain, who acted as bridesmaid, and Mr. James B. Allan who supported the groom. Rev. T. F. Fullerton solemnized the marriage vows.

The bride, who also wore a gorgeous bridal veil, was beautifully attired in an elegant suit of cream cashmere, daintily trimmed with lace and ribbons to match; while the bridesmaid's dress of cream crepon also trimmed with lace and ribbon made up a very pretty costume. Both the bride and the bridesmaid carried tasteful bouquets of beautiful flowers.

After the ceremony the guests repaired to the dining room, where stood a spacious table laden with the choicest viands. While the happy company still lingered around the festival board a number of toasts were drunk and were responded to by several gentlemen present, all of whom eulogized very highly the youthful couple who had just joined heart and hand.

After supper the wedding party repaired to Mr. Buntain's residence on Prince street where the festivities continued until a late hour. The time, however, passed all too quickly enlivened as it was by geniality, music and happy chat.

The popularity of the bride and groom was fully shown by the choice variety of magnificent presents which they received, among them being a beautiful marble clock from the groom's employer Mr. Handrahan, an elegant cake from Mrs. Handrahan and some handsome gifts from his fellow employes. The GUARDIAN joins with their many friends in wishing Mr. and Mrs. Buntain many years of wedded bliss.

Be joy for
ever near thee!

I've allus notissed fellers,
Hit's a risky thing to do
To kalkalate accordin'
To how things look to you.

The man 'at talks the nicest
Don't help you up the hill
The one 'at prays the loudest
Don't allus pay his bill.

Sometimes the biggest fishes
Bite the smallest kind o' baits;
An' mighty ugly wimmin
Can make the best o' mates.

The smartest lookin' feller
May be a reg'lar fool;
You're allus kicked the highest
By the meekest lookin' mule.

Academy of Music.
HALIFAX, N. S.

H. B. CLARKE, ... Lessee and Manager

Monday and Tuesday Evenings, April 6th and 7th, 1896.

THE
HUBERT WILKE COMIC OPERA COMPANY
Management..... W. S. HARKINS

The Beggar Student

Comic Opera in three acts and four scenes, by Millocker.

Stage Director .... Mr. Kirtland Calhoun

DISTRIBUTION OF CHARACTERS.

Symon, a Beggar Student .... Mr. Hubert Wilke
Janitzky, a Polish Nobleman .... Mr. Phillips Tomes
Gen. Ollendorf, Governor of Cracow ... Mr. Douglas Flint
Lieut. Poppenbring .... Miss Laura Pardee
Major Holtz .... Mr. Alex. Thompson
Capt. Schwantz .... Mr. Robt. Blake
Enterick, a Jailer .... Mr. Kirtland Calhoun
Puffke, his assistant .... Mr. E. G. Schaffer
Onifra, servant to the Countess ...... Mr. Jas H. Jones
Zitka, an Innkeeper .... Mr. Wm. Pullman
Burgomaster .... Mr. Bergh Morrison
Countess Palmettica .... Miss Sylvester Cornish
Laura ⎱ her daughters. ⎰ Miss Josephine Knapp
Bronistava ⎰ ⎱ Miss Celie Ellis
Rogemcil, a cousin .... Mr. A. E. Arnold
Eva, his wife .... Miss Flo Eckardt

SEE THIRD PAGE.

SYNOPSIS OF SCENES.

ACT I.—Scene 1. Courtyard of the Jail. Scene 2. The Fair at Cracow.
ACT II.—The Palace of the Countess Palmettica.
ACT III.—Gardens of the Palace.

Academy of Music.
HALIFAX, N. S.

H. B. CLARKE, ... Lessee and Manager

MONDAY EVENING, OCTOBER 21st, 1895.

Gilbert Opera Co.

Presenting Stephen's and Solomon's Nautical Comic Opera,

BILLEE TAYLOR,
OR, THE REWARD OF VIRTUE.
IN TWO ACTS.

Produced under the Personal Direction of JAMES GILBERT

CAST OF CHARACTERS:

Captain, the Hon. Felix Flapper, R. N., of H. M. S. "Thunderbomb," .... Hubert Dodd
Sir Mincing Lane, a self-made knight ... Elbert C. Cough
Billee Taylor, a virtuous gardener ..... Harry Nelson
Ben Barnacle, Bo'sn of H. M. S. Thunderbomb ... Thos. Callahan
Christopher Crab, an unfortunate villian ... Frank Edwards
Felix Gilhooley .... Frank Ranney
Phœbe Farleigh, a Southampton Maiden .. Miss Ethel Balch
Susan .... Miss Marie Zahn
Eliza Dabsey .... Miss Katherin Power
Arabella Lane, Sir Mincing Lane's daughter .... Miss Florence Gilbert
Charity Girls, Soldiers and Sailors of H. M. S. Thunderbomb by the Grand Chorus.

SYNOPSIS.

ACT I.—The Village Green of the village of Southampton.
ACT II.—Portsmouth Harbor.

SEE THIRD PAGE.

블루 스크랩북 67쪽

Ellen Beach Yaw.

SUMMER'S DONE.

Along the wayside and up the hill,
  The golden rod flames in the sun ;
The blue-eyed gentian nods good-bye
  To the sad little brooks that run.
And so the summer's done, said I,
    Summer's done !

In the yellowing woods the chesnut drop ;
  The squirrel gets galore ;
Though bright eyed lads and little maids,
  Rob him of half his store,
And so the summer's done, said I,
    Summer's done !

The maple in the swamp begins
  To flaunt in gold and red,
And in the elm the fire-bird's nest
  Swings empty overhead ;
And so the summer's done, said I,
    Summer's done !

The barberry hands her jewels out,
  And guards them with a thorn ;
The merry farmer boys cut down
  The poor old dried-up corn ;
And so the summer's done, said I,
    Summer's done !

The swallows and the bobolink,
  Are gone this many a day ;
But in the morning still you here
  The scolding swaggering jay !
And so the summer's done, said I,
    Summer's done !

A wonderful glory fills the air,
  And big and bright is the sun ;
A loving hand for the whole brown earth,
  A garment of beauty has spun ;
But for all that, summer's done, said I,
    Summer's done !

Miss Beatrice McIntyre is a Charlottetown lady, and is a brilliant student. In all her classes she has acquitted herself with credit.

Edwin Simpson, from Belmont, the Editor-in-Chief of the College Observer, has been a prominent factor in everything that tended to promote the interests of P. W. C. In debate he was a Hercules. Notwithstanding his many scruples, Ed. will, without doubt, be a star in the legal profession. He preferred spending his Sundays in the country.

Scene, Church Social—Mr. D-k-y having asked for more pie.
Young Lady—"Mr. D-k-y, you have eaten more pie than I have."
Mr. D.—"Well, what of that. You must remember you were eating pie before I was born. You might give a fellow a fair start."

A Song of the Camp-Fire.

Oh, the sparkle of the camp-fire on the sheltered
  woodland shore,
With the forest for a background, and the lake
  spread out before ;
While the frail canoes come tossing home to harbor
  in the bay,
And the star above the sunset marks the passing of
  the day !

As the summer night grows deeper, how the flame
  illumes the pines,
And its wavering reflection on the starlit water
  shines !
We have drawn a ring of magic in the wilderness
  and gloom,
And the darkness looms beyond it like the walls of
  some vast room.

Gathers now the twilight circle, each bronzed
  camper in his place,
While the laughter of the firelight meets the laughter on his face ;
And we sing the good old ballads, and the rolling
  college glees,
Till the owl, far up the mountain, hoots defiance in
  the trees.

Then the story and the laughter pass the merry
  circle round,
And the intervening silence thrills with many a
  woodland sound,
Now the weird and ghostly challenge of the solitary
  loon,
Now the whistle of a plover, journeying southward
  'neath the moon.

Ah ! the charm that hangs forever round the camp-
  fire's ruddy glow,
For the sage and for the savage, for the high and
  for the low !
There is something grand and godlike, being roofed
  with stars and skies,
And lulled solemnly to slumber by primeval lulla-
  bies.
          JAMES BUCKHAM.

블루 스크랩북의 마지막 몇 쪽은 시간 순서와는 전혀 상관없이 기록되어 있다. 루시 모드 몽고메리가 여러 해에 걸쳐 사건들을 재구성했다는 것을 보여준다.

69쪽 1896년 선교 프로그램과 달하우지 영어 교수였던 아치볼드 맥메컨Archibald MacMechan의 시에서 달하우지 시절이 떠오른다. 연기하듯 대담해 보이는 젊은 여성은 에벌린 네즈빗(13쪽 '스크랩북을 편집하며' 참고)과 무척 닮았다. 몽고메리는 그 이름 모를 모델의 사진을 옆에 두고《빨강 머리 앤》을 썼다. 남편이 1906년에 살인 혐의로 재판을 받는 동안, 네즈빗이 샴페인을 마신 상태로 빨간 벨벳 그네를 타고 현기증이 날 높이까지 올라가다가(화이트의 요구로) 의식을 잃은 사이에 스탠퍼드 화이트에게서 성폭행을 당했다는 말이 나돌았다. 네즈빗 자신이 특별 자문으로 직접 참여해 그녀의 인생을 얘기하는 영화〈빨간 벨벳 그네를 탄 여자The Girl in the Red Velvet Swing〉가 조앤 콜린스Joan Collins 주연으로 제작됐다. 양단으로 장식한 가로대는 후일 네즈빗의 상징이 된 빨간 벨벳 그네와 어떤 연관이라도 있는 걸까?

70쪽 이 페이지와 다음 페이지의 중심을 차지한 화려한 드레스는 1890년대 중반에서 말까지 유행하던 스타일이다. 포트힐 기사는 비더포드 시절을 연상시킨다. 낭독회 티켓 날짜는 몽고메리가 1891년에 캐번디시의 외삼촌 존 맥닐이 주최한 사교 모임에서 렘 매클라우드를 처음 만났던 날이다. 노래하는 울새 두 마리는 레드 스크랩북에 실린, 1903년 노라 리퍼지와 함께 만든 비밀 일기 중에서 "제이들jays"과 "롭인Rob-in"에 관련된 기록으로 보인다(레드 스크랩북 2~3쪽).

71쪽 달하우지 휘장이 두 페이지가 접히는 곳에 붙어 있다. 엄청나게 부풀린 드레스 소매를 보면서 1905년의 몽고메리는 일기에 1890년대 달하우지 여학생들이 한껏 부풀린 소매를 서로서로 외투 속에 "빽빽하게 밀어 넣어줘야" 했던 기억을 적었다. 알렉세나 맥그레거Alexena MacGregor는 로라와 몽고메리가 프린스앨버트에서 사귄 친구로, 몽고메리가 1930년에 찾아가 만나기도 했다. 알렉세나는 프레드 라이트Fred Wright와 결혼했는데, 몽고메리는 이 이름을 '앤' 시리즈에서 다이애나의 남편에게 준 듯하다. 1896년 6월 3일에 올린 로라 프리처드와 앤드루 애그뉴의 결혼식 소식을 전하는 기사가 있다. 1932년에 로라가 세상을 떠난 후, 몽고메리는 로라가 결혼식과 관련해 보냈던 기념물 몇 가지를 안전하게 보관하기 위해 직접 쓰는 일기장으로 옮겼다. 그 기념물들이 원래 있었던 곳이 이 지면인 것 같다. 말린 제라늄 뭉치와 "1897년 3월 28일 말페크"라고 적힌 글귀는 몽고메리가 벨몬트에서 보낸 몇 달을 기념한 것이라고 알려진, 유일하게 확실한 자료이다. 몽고메리와 앨프 심프슨은 마차를 타고 빙판길을 달려서 말페크에 사는 에밀리 숙모의 집으로 갔다. 공개되지 않은 일기에서는 몽고메리의 기쁜 마음이 읽히는 듯하다. "청명한 3월 저녁, 노을 지는 하늘 아래 꽁꽁 얼어붙은 빙판길에서 빙그르르 도는 것보다 더 신나는 일은 정말이지 없는 것 같다."〈어스름 속에서In The Gloaming〉라는 시는 렘 매클라우드나 루 디스턴트가 몽고메리에게 보냈을 법한 내용이지만, 몽고메리가 벨몬트에서 보낸 시간을 유일하게 직접적으로 언급한 이 지면에 그 시가 실린 것으로 보아, 오히려 에드윈 심프슨과 헤어지고 싶은 바람이나 허먼 리드와 헤어진 것을 뒤늦게 한탄하는 심경을 암시한다고 볼 수도 있다.

Missionary Meeting

(Jan 20th)

7. 3. 0 P. M.

"Four Phases of Missionary Work –

(a) Medical

R. Grierson. B.A

(b) Educational

Miss Montgomery

(c) Ladies' Work.

Miss Archibald.

(d) Evangelical –

R. L. Coffin

All are welcome

"The Valley of Lost Sunsets."

Behind that misty ridge the suns of many yesterdays were lying in a valley that must be all golden with their shining.
—From "Great-Grandmamma S..."

BEHIND the misty ridge of blue
   The suns of all the yesterdays
Fill all the valley hid from view
   With one transcendent golden blaze.
What other treasures harbour here,
   —Lost treasures that the past have blest?—
Perchance "the snows of yesteryear;"
   The birds that flew from last year's nest.

There where the gilded light is fed
   By suns of all the yesterdays,
The roses of lost summers shed
   Their scented petals o'er the ways,
'Mid sounds of all the brooks that purled,
   And whispering trees, and songs of birds;
Lost myriad voices that the world
   Made music to the heart's own words.

Here, too, their beauty re-illumed
   By suns of all the yesterdays,
Our lost illusions lie entombed
   In shimmering veils of sunset haze.
Those glints of Heaven that with us stayed
   When thence to Earth we newly stepped,
But doomed—ah me !—to fail and fade
   As slowly on through life we crept.

Here dallying in the golden beams
   Of suns of all the yesterdays
Are dreams that once were only dreams,
   And hopes fulfilled without delays.
Here life's lost morning breaks once more
   With bloom of lovely youth eterne,
And Time, from out his garnered store,
   Lets all our wasted hours return.

And here, maybe, we'll find erewhile,
   With suns of all the yesterdays,
Lost voices speak, lost faces smile,
   Lost eyes look back our loving gaze.
Old love will live, old hurts be healed,
   Old ills forgot in new-found good ;
And in that glorious light revealed
   Old errors will be understood.

Farewell, oh, sun ! that joins to-night
   The suns of all the yesterdays,
Merging your solitary light
   In their entirety.   The days
Are shortening now ; when done they be,
   I'll climb the ridge—that lies so far
I cannot reach it now—and see
   The "Valley where Lost Sunsets are."
                              H. M. WAITHMAN.

MY LADY OF DREAMS.

LAST Sabbath morn, I listen'd in the church ;
The organ whisper'd music soft and low,
Pierced thro' with half-hush'd wailings. And I seem'd
To hear silk draperies lightly near me sweep,
And feel the breath of some one moving by.
But vain in shadow and half gloom the search
For shape or vision. Veil'd to outward eye,
Soft as the sighings of a babe in sleep,
The gracious Presence came of one I know,
And long have lov'd. My lover's dream I dream'd,
With eyes wide open, in my carven stall.

Wavering the dim air down, the sweet sounds fell,
Gathering body of an airy form,
That to my side, a living likeness, stole,
And nestled in my arm, against my heart,
With tender trust a-tremble, shy and warm.
That moment's sweetness, tongue can never tell.

*   *   *   *   *

Thus, Best-Belovéd, Love is all in all,
And Love, the perfect music of thy soul,
And thy life, my life, tho' we breathe apart.

Saint's Day, '95.   ARCHIBALD MACMECHAN.

Just the Thing.

An English journal tells of an amusing rebuke administered to a sharp bargainer, one of those persons who always wish to get more than their money's worth. The offender in the present instance was a woman, who sent the following advertisement to a London paper:

"A lady in delicate health wishes to meet with a useful companion. She must be domestic, musical, an early riser, amiable, of good appearance, and have some experience in nursing. A total abstainer preferred. Comfortable home. No salary."

A few days afterward the advertiser received by express a basket labelled: "This side up—with care—perishable." On opening it she found a tabby cat, with a letter tied to its tail. It ran thus:

"MADAM.—In response to your advertisement, I am happy to furnish you with a very useful companion, which you will find exactly suited to your requirements. She is domestic, a good vocalist, an early riser, possesses an amiable disposition, and is considered handsome. She has had a great experience as a nurse, having brought up a large family. I need scarcely add that she is a total abstainer. As salary is no object to her, she will serve you faithfully in return for a comfortable home."

From Port Hill.

A session of the Grand Division, Sons of Temperance, was held in Port Hill Hall on the 26th ult., and as a report of which will, no doubt, be received from the usual quarter in due season, I will content myself at the present time by sending you an account of a public meeting held in the evening at which a programme, arranged by a committee appointed for that purpose, was creditably carried out. The meeting came to order, Bro. Anderson, G.W.P., in the chair, and he delivered the opening speech in his usual eloquent and pleasing style. He was followed by Bro. W. J. Montgomery who gave the address of Welcome, and the able manner in which he delivered it far exceeded the expectations of his fellow-members who selected him to perform that duty. Bro. Jas. Carruthers responded in a style characteristic of that gentleman, wit, humor, pathos and eloquence carefully arranged and resorted to in his speech with telling effect. "Sound the battle cry," was then rendered by the choir, Miss Katie Stewart, presiding at the organ, after which Bro. Wm. McNeil Simpson gave a very enthusiastic and effective temperance speech. Able and forceable addresses, in which those present were reminded of their duty to the present and future generations in regard to the plebiscite vote, were delivered in turn by Bros. Wright, A. Simpson and Arbing which were interspersed by choice selections from the choir, viz., "True hearted, whole hearted," "Marching on," "Good-bye, sweet day," "Evening bells," after which Bro. Arthur Simpson moved a vote of thanks be extended to the choir which was responded on their behalf by Bro. J. K. Ramsay. The thanks of the members of the Grand Division to the people of Port Hill for their kindness and hospitality was presented them by Bro. Jas. Carruthers, Bro. H. D. Dobie responded. The members of Port Hill Division who were identified with the musical part of the programme were assisted by Mr. Alfred Philips and Miss Annie Philips whose musical talents are of a high order, and noticeable among the queens of song who represented our sister divisions were Miss Nettie Miller of "Welcome" and Miss Matilda Boates and Miss Ella May McDonald of "Burns," who voices harmoniously mingled with the other voices of the choir. The meeting was concluded by the rendering of a praise anthem by the choir.
—[Com.

AN EGYPTIAN ADVERTISEMENT.

The story of the proposed trolley line from Cairo to the Pyramids, recalls another instance of modern enterprise. A certain tract society commissioned a painter to place religious texts on all available objects in Egypt.

He traced this question on one of the pyramids:

"Do you want to be saved?"

Another painter, in the interest of a quack medicine concern, came along and added beneath:

"If you do, take Blank's pills."

"If bards of old the truth have told
The sirens have raven hair.
But o'er the earth since art had birth
They paint the angels fair."

"Faith hope and charity"

ELOCUTION
❧ RECITAL ❧

ADMIT ½ ½ ONE.

Wednesday Oct. 13th 1891

Saturday.
Aug. 25th
1896

72쪽 사뭇 다른 분위기와 서로 다른 시대의 여성 세 명이 눈에 띈다. 세 여성은 로라 프리처드가 프린스앨버트의 집, 즉 로럴힐 팜Laurel Hill Farm에서 보낸 카드를 둘러싸고 있다. 그 카드를 보낸 날짜는 1896년 5월 17일이고, 이제는 희미해졌지만 이런 글귀를 읽을 수 있다. "'아, 달콤한 여름 저녁의 기억들 / 물결과 버드나무 길 위로 달빛이 비치고 / 별들도, 꽃들도, 이슬 맺힌 나뭇잎들도 떠오르네. / 그리고 그보다 더 소중한 미소와 목소리가 있었지.' '에덴의 마력은 결코 사라지지 않는다.'" 아래쪽 공고문은 잭 서덜랜드Jack Sutherland가 오타와로 직무차 떠났다는 소식을 전하는데, 몽고메리가 벨몬트에서 묵었던 방에도 그의 사진이 있었다. 에텐과 막달라 마리아는 잘생긴 잭을 잃은 아쉬움에 장난스럽게 가져다 붙인 것일까?

뒤표지 안쪽 프리처드와 애그뉴의 결혼식을 알리는 또 하나의 공고문으로 이 지면은 다시 로라와 윌에게 돌아간다. "1903년에 나는 신부였다"라고 적힌 이미지는 이 지면이나 스크랩북과 뚜렷한 관련이 없다. 1903년에 이완 맥도널드가 장로교 목사 자격을 얻어 캐번디시 목사로 부임했다. 캐나다국립철도 사진 세 장은 몽고메리가 1930년에 로라를 만나러 가는 길에 남긴 것이다. 1891년에 프린스앨버트를 떠나면서 몽고메리는 스위트피 등으로 만든 꽃다발을 로라와 교환했고(블루 스크랩북 18쪽), 이곳에 오려 붙인 스위트피 잡지 사진은 그때 주고받은 꽃다발을 추억할 마음이었던 것 같다. 꽃으로 올가미를 만들어 얼굴(영화배우 로레타 영Loretta Young일까?)에 씌운 이미지는 1930년대나 1940년대 초의 것으로, 1890년대의 것이 아니지만 미래는 과거에서 벗어날 수 없음을 장난스럽게 암시하는지도 모른다. 삼십구 년 만에 로라와 기쁘게 재회한 몽고메리는 1930년 10월 2일 일기에 이렇게 적었다. "그때 나는 사랑이 불멸이라는 것을 깨달았다."

스크랩북의 시작과 끝은 한결같이 이어지는 행복한 우정 이야기를 담고 있다. 윌리 프리처드의 달력이 블루 스크랩북의 첫 장을 장식했다면 그 여동생 로라 프리처드의 결혼식 이야기가 마지막 장을 수놓는다. 1930년, 몽고메리는 서스캐처원으로 로라 프리처드 애그뉴를 만나러 갔던 때를 여러 다양한 방법으로 회상했다.

이 스크랩북을 시작했던 것처럼 끝내기로 결심한 몽고메리는 반짝이는 순간이나 잔잔한 그리움이 이는 순간을 다루었고, 벨몬트에서 학생들을 가르치던 비참한 시기(1896-1897)의 기억들은 거의 지워버렸다. 1897년 4월에 몽고메리는 윌리가 세상을 떠났다는 소식을 듣고 큰 슬픔에 빠졌으며, 에드윈 심프슨의 청혼을 받아들인 뒤인 6월에는 더 참담해졌다. 블루 스크랩북이나 레드 스크랩북에서는 윌리의 죽음이나 아버지의 죽음(1900)을 다룬 시간을 전혀 찾아볼 수 없고, 에드윈 심프슨과 파혼한 뒤에 틀림없이 찾아왔을 고뇌에 대해서도 단 한 줄을 남기지 않았다. 그렇지만 레드 스크랩북에서는 그런 슬픔을 조금씩 드러내려 한 흔적을 볼 수 있다(레드 스크랩북 11~14쪽).

블루 스크랩북은 행복한 어린 시절과 젊은 시절을 기념하기 위해 만든 것이었다. 그리고 에이번리의 앤셜리에게 선물한 삶이기도 하다.

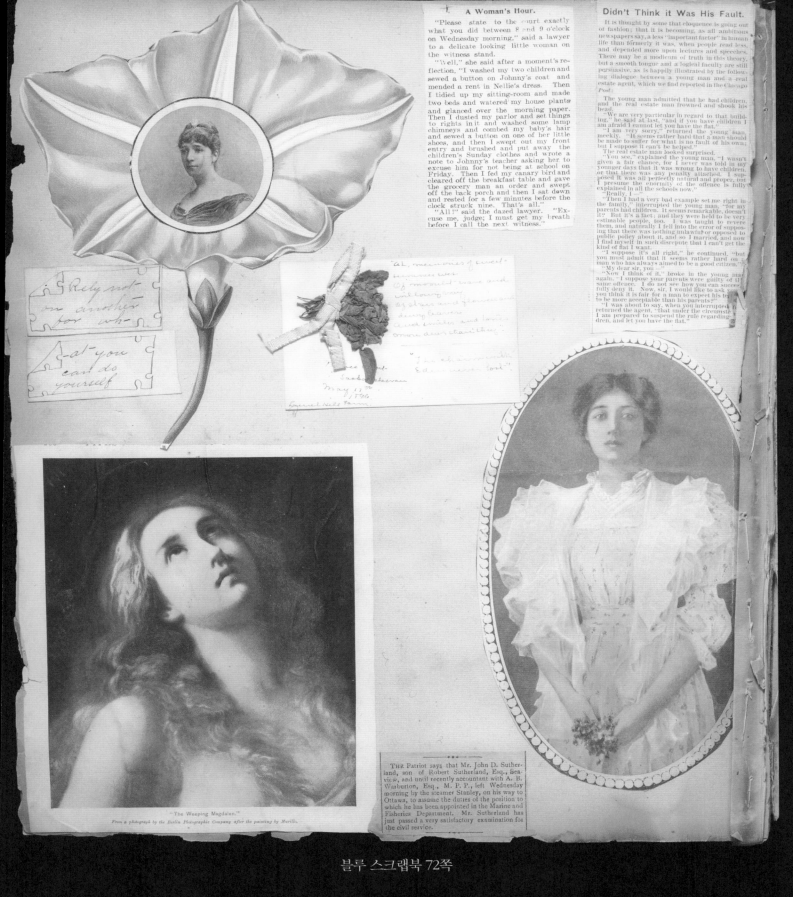

A Woman's Hour.

"Please state to the court exactly what you did between 8 and 9 o'clock on Wednesday morning," said a lawyer to a delicate looking little woman on the witness stand.

"Well," she said after a moment's reflection, "I washed my two children and sewed a button on Johnny's coat and mended a rent in Nellie's dress. Then I tidied up my sitting-room and made two beds and watered my house plants and glanced over the morning paper. Then I dusted my parlor and set things to rights in it and washed some lamp chimneys and combed my baby's hair and sewed a button on one of her little shoes, and then I swept out my front entry and brushed and put away the children's Sunday clothes and wrote a note to Johnny's teacher asking her to excuse him for not being at school on Friday. Then I fed my canary bird and cleared off the breakfast table and gave the grocery man an order and swept off the back porch and then I sat down and rested for a few minutes before the clock struck nine. That's all."

"All!" said the dazed lawyer. "Excuse me, judge; I must get my breath before I call the next witness."

Didn't Think it Was His Fault.

It is thought by some that eloquence is going out of fashion; that it is becoming, as all ambitious newspapers say, a less "important factor" in human life than formerly it was, when people read less, and depended more upon lectures and speeches. There may be a modicum of truth in this theory, but a smooth tongue and a logical faculty are still persuasive, as is happily illustrated by the following dialogue between a young man and a real estate agent, which we find reported in the Chicago Post:

The young man admitted that he had children, and the real estate man frowned and shook his head.

"We are very particular in regard to that building," he said at last, "and if you have children I am afraid I cannot let you have the flat."

"I am very sorry," returned the young man, meekly. "It seems rather hard that a man should be made to suffer for what is no fault of his own; but I suppose it can't be helped."

The real estate man looked surprised.

"You see," explained the young man, "I wasn't given a fair chance, for I never was told in my younger days that it was wrong to have children, or that there was any penalty attached. I supposed it was all perfectly natural and proper, but I presume the enormity of the offence is fully explained in all the schools now."

"Really, I—"

"Then I had a very bad example set me right in the family," interrupted the young man, "for my parents had children. It seems remarkable, doesn't it? But it's a fact; and they were held to be very estimable people, too. I was taught to revere them, and naturally I fell into the error of supposing that there was nothing unlawful or opposed to public policy about it, and so I married, and now I find myself in such disrepute that I can't get the kind of flat I want.

"I suppose it's all right," he continued, "but you must admit that it seems rather hard on a man who has always aimed to be a good citizen."

"My dear sir, you—"

"Now I think of it," broke in the young man again, "I suppose your parents were guilty of the same offence. I do not see how you can successfully deny it. Now, sir, I would like to ask you, you think it is fair for a man to expect his tenants to be more acceptable than his parents?"

"I was about to say, when you interrupted me," returned the agent, "that under the circumstances I am prepared to suspend the rule regarding children, and let you have the flat."

"Ah, memories of sweet summer time
Of moonlit wave and willowy way
Of stars and flowers and dewy leaves
And smiles and tones more dear than they"

"—free out Saskatchewan
May 17th 1896.
Laurel Hill Farm."

"In dreams with Eden never lost."

"The Weeping Magdalen."

From a photograph by the Berlin Photographic Company after the painting by Murillo.

The Patriot says that Mr. John D. Sutherland, son of Robert Sutherland, Esq., Seaview, and until recently accountant with A. B. Warburton, Esq., M. P. P., left Wednesday morning by the steamer Stanley, on his way to Ottawa, to assume the duties of the position to which he has been appointed in the Marine and Fisheries Department. Mr. Sutherland has just passed a very satisfactory examination for the civil service.

"I was a bride in 1903"

MARRIED.

AGNEW—PRITCHARD—At the residence of the bride's father, on Wednesday, June 3rd, by Rev. Mr. Lee, Laura, eldest daughter of R. J. Pritchard, to Andrew Agnew, of Prince Albert.

Winnipeg papers please copy.

블루 스크랩북의 뒤표지 안쪽

The Red Scrapbook

ALBUM

1890s to mid-1910

레드 스크랩북 표지에 있는 전화기 그림은 넓은 세계와의 소통을 암시하는 동시에 친밀감과 사적인 대화를 의미한다. 프린스에드워드섬의 전화국은 1885년에 설립됐고, 루시 모드 몽고메리는 그 새로운 발명품을 1892년 일기에 처음으로 언급했다. 캐번디시가 전화의 이점을 대중적으로 논하기 시작한 때는 1910년, 그러니까《빨강 머리 앤》이 출판되고 이 년이 지난 다음이었다.

벨몬트에서 교편을 잡고 우울하게 생활했던 시기(1896-1897)가 지나고 에드윈 심프슨과 짜증 나는 약혼을 한 뒤에 몽고메리는 프린스에드워드섬의 로어 비데크에서 학생들을 가르치면서 허먼 리어드와 비밀스런 사랑에 빠졌다. 1898년에 외할아버지가 돌아가시면서 몽고메리는 영원히 교직을 떠나 캐번디시로 돌아왔다. 1898년 3월부터 1911년 3월까지 몽고메리는 캐번디시에서 지내며 할머니를 돌보고, 글을 쓰고, 마을의 일과 교회 활동을 도우며, 우체국장의 조수로 일하기도 했다. 그리고 주로 책을 읽고 글을 발표하고 편지를 쓰면서 더 넓은 세상과 소통했다. 많은 친구가 캐번디시를 떠났고 결혼도 했다. 몽고메리는 딱 한 번 집을 떠나 오랫동안 체류한 적이 있는데, 1901년에서 1902년까지 열 달 동안 핼리팩스에서《데일리 에코》직원으로 일하던 때였다. 이따금 재미있는 일들을 만들어 다소 진지한 생활에 균형을 잡아줬다. 1903년에 몽고메리와 캐번디시 학교 교사였던 노라 리퍼지는 함께 익살스러운 비밀 일기를 쓰기 시작했고, 몽고메리는 그와 관련된 기념 자료들을 모두 스크랩북에 보관했다.

블루 스크랩북의 방식을 유지하여 선별한 사건만을 기록하고, 자료들은 당사자만 알아볼 수 있도록 언급하며, 시간의 순서는 엄격히 지키지 않았다. 몽고메리는 레드 스크랩북에서 자기 인생에 찾아온 두 번의 격변에 대해 한 번도 직접 언급하지 않았다. 장로교 목사인 이완 맥도널드와 비밀리에 약혼했고(아마도 비밀 약혼이어서 결혼하라는 압박을 받지 않았고, 그 덕분에 연로한 할머니 곁에 머물 수 있었을 것이다),《빨강 머리 앤》을 출판하여 엄청난 성공을 거두었다. 몽고메리는 첫 소설을 내고 곧바로 후속편인《에이번리의 앤》(1909)과 이어서《과수원의 킬메니》(1910)를 발표했다. 네 번째 소설인《스토리 걸》(1911)을 쓰던 중에 레드 스크랩북을 끝마쳤다. 이완 맥도널드에 대한 언급은 그의 활동을 전하는 신문 공고 몇 개뿐이지만, 그런 기사 몇 편을 익명으로 직접 썼을 수도 있다.《빨강 머리 앤》에 관한 언급은 짤막한 기사 한 편이 유일하다.

레드 스크랩북은 작가의 스크랩북으로, 개인적인 일화와 사진을 보관하고 그 안에서 작은 드라마나 대화가 만들어지도록 구성된다. 몽고메리는 이미지와 조각 기사를 이용하여 자기 내면의 삶을 지켜보는 일종의 관중과 사회를 창조했고, 그리하여 말로는 다 할 수 없는 시각적 배출구를 만들었다.

앞표지 안쪽에서는 켄터기 최고의 미인 샐리 워드Sally Ward(1827-1896)의 사진으로 몇 가지 주제를 선보인다. 패션으로 유명한 여성들, 성공한 "나쁜 여자(부유한 이혼녀 샐리 워드 로런스 헌트 암스트롱 다운스Sally Ward Lawrence Hunt Armstrong Downs는 명사 대우를 받았다)", 신중히 고른 시사 문제, 그리고 예쁜 얼굴의 유쾌한 힘이 그것이다.

GOOD NIGHT.

GOOD MORNING.

SALLY WARD, THE KENTUCKY BELLE.

Her Plea.—A priest asked a young man who had come to confess how he earned his living.

"I'm an acrowbat, your riverence."

The priest was nonplussed.

"I'll show ye what I mean in a brace of shakes," said the penitent, and in a moment was turning himself inside out in the approved acrobatic fashion.

An old woman, who had followed him to confession, looked on horrified.

"When it comes my turn, father," she gasped, "for the love of heaven don't put a penance on me like that; it 'ud be the death of me!"

PREFERRED THE OLD WAY.

Mrs. Bradbury was instructing the new cook, who was not only new, but as green as her own Emerald Isle. One morning the mistress went into the kitchen and found Katie weeping over a pan of onions.

"Oh, you're having a harder time than you need to have, Katie," said she. "Always peel onions under water."

"Indade, ma'am," said Katie, "I'm the last one to do that, askin' yer pardon. Me brother Mick was always divin' and pickin' up stones from the bottom. It's little he couldn't do under wather, if 'twas tyin' his shoes or writin' a letther; but me, I'm that unaisy in it I'd be gettin' me mouth full and drownin' entirely. So if ye plaze, ma'am, I'll pale thim the same ould way I've always been accustomed to, and dhry me tears afterwards."

He—"They say he flung himself at her feet."

She—"I heard she threw herself at his head."

A CRISIS IN THE SCHOOLROOM.

The inspector of schools in a country district, being in a hurry to catch a train, stood in the doorway and endeavored to give out dictation to Standard II. in the main room, and at the same time to give a sum to Standard V. in the schoolroom, jerking out the words a few at a time alternately.

This was the sum: "If a couple of fat ducks cost four dollars and a half, how many can be got for twenty-one dollars and thirty-five cents?"

And this was the other dictation: "Now as a lion prowling about in search," and so forth.

Naturally enough the poor children, unaccustomed to such hurried dictation, heard both, and were sadly mixed. One girl's dictation began: "Now a couple of ducks, prowling about in search of a lion who had lost four dollars and fifty cents."

And a small boy in the schoolroom vainly endeavored to solve the mysteries of this extraordinary sum:

"If seventy-two couples of fat lions cost four dollars and a half, how much prowling could be got for twenty-one dollars and thirty-five cents?"

몽고메리와 코닥 걸

루시 모드 몽고메리는 캐번디시 침실의 화장대 위에 코닥 걸 사진을 걸어놓았다. 경제활동을 하고, 사진에 매료되어 지내며, 넓은 세계로 원고를 송부하는 스스로를 몽고메리는 코닥 걸이라 생각했는지도 모른다. 코닥 걸은 젊고 소비력을 갖춘 여자들이 직접 사진을 찍도록 유도하기 위해 조지 이스트먼 George Eastman이 1980년대 초에 시작해 성공을 거둔 광고 캠페인의 모델이었다. 무심한 듯 한 팔로 안아 든 코닥 카메라는 세련된 의상과 여유로운 몸짓에 따라오는 패션 액세서리가 되었다. 코닥 걸은 독립적이고 자신만만하며 자기만의 취미를 손쉽게 추구하는 여자로 묘사됐다.

잡지와 책에 실린 사진에 매혹된, 시각 정보에 예민한 몽고메리는 1890년대에 처음 카메라를 구입했다. 몽고메리가 산 카메라는 아마 가로 10센티미터에 세로 12센티미터 정도 되는, 필름이 아니라 감광판을 사용하여 감광판 하나에 사진 한 장을 찍을 수 있는 벨로스 카메라였을 것이다. 몽고메리는 맥닐 가에 암실을 만들어 자신만의 사진을 현상했고 이를 즐겼다. 시골인 캐번디시에는 사진사가 흔하지 않았기 때문에 몽고메리는 공공 행사나 민간 행사 모두에 직접 촬영을 다녔다. 종종 특수하게 처리된 인화지에 저렴한 밀착 인화법으로 직접 청사진을 뽑아냈다. 레드 스크랩북의 청사진들에서는 캐번디시와 파크 코너의 몇몇 장소와 사람들을 볼 수 있다.《빨강 머리 앤》을 쓰기 시작할 즈음인 1905년에 몽고메리는 글과 사진에서 모두 이미지를 훌륭히 그려내는 작가로 성장해 있었다.

1911년, 결혼을 준비하면서 평생 꿈에 그리던 여행을 떠나 문학작품의 무대가 된 스코틀랜드와 잉글랜드 지역을 방문할 때 몽고메리는 즐거운 마음으로 새로운 코닥 카메라를 구입하여 스냅 사진 수십 롤을 찍을 수 있었다. 그 후로 몽고메리는 평생 동안 앨범과 상자를 사진들로 가득 채웠고, 나중에는 손으로 쓰는 일기에도 사진을 삽화처럼 이용했다. 몽고메리의 청사진 중 직접 찍고 인화한 "벽의 구멍 Hole in the Wall"이라는 작품은 뒤쪽에서 이곳으로 옮겨졌다(원래 있던 페이지는 레드 스크랩북에서 없었다). 몽고메리는 세상을 떠나면서 사진 2천여 장을 남겼고, 훌륭한 사진작가의 눈으로 바라본 형상과 빛, 그리고 그것들이 말하는 이야기가 담긴 소설 스무 권을 증거처럼 전해줬다.

BOARDING HOUSE GEOMETRY.

(1) All boarding houses are the same boarding house.

(2) Boarders in the same boarding house and on the same flat are equal to one another.

(3) A single room is that which has no parts and no magnitude.

(4) The landlady of a boarding house is a parallelogram; that is, an oblong, angular figure which cannot be described, but which is equal to any thing.

(5) A wrangle is the disinclination of two boarders to each other that meet together but are not on the same flat.

(6) All the other rooms being taken, a single room is said to be a double room.

POSTULATES AND PROPOSITIONS.

(1) A pie may be produced any number of times.

(2) The landlady may be reduced to her lowest terms by a series of propositions.

(3) A bee line may be made from any one boarding house to any other boarding house.

(4) The clothes of a boarding house bed, though produced ever so far both ways, will not meet.

(5) Any two meals at a boarding house are together less than one square meal.

(6) On the same bill and on the same side of it there shall be two charges for the same thing.

(7) If there be two boarders on the same flat, and the amount of side of the one be equal to the amount of side of the other, each to each, and the wrangle between one boarder and the land-lady be equal to the wrangle between the landlady and the other, then shall the weekly bills of the two boarders be equal also, each to each. For if not let one bill be the greater —then the other bill is less than it might have been—which is absurd.

** ** **

PRIMA FACIE EVIDENCE.

An English lord of the manor was returning home one night, when he found a country bumpkin standing by the kitchen door with a lantern in his hand.

"What are you doing here?" the lord asked, roughly.

"I've come a-coortin', sir," was the reply.

"A-courting? What do you mean by that?"

"I'm a follower o' Mary, the kitchen maid."

"Is it your habit to carry a lantern when you are on such errands?"

"Yes, sir."

"Nonsense!" retorted the master, angrily. "Don't talk such stuff to me! Be off with yourself! Courting with a lantern! When I was young I never used such a thing."

"No, sir," said the yokel, moving rapidly away, "Judgin' by the missus, I shouldn't think ye did."

❋ ❋

"You can say what you please, but it's a lucky thing for me that there are poets."

THE KODAK GIRL

Her Daily Food.

—"I love all that is beautiful in art and nature," she said, turning her dreamy eyes to his. "I revel in the green fields, the babbling brooks, and the little wayside flowers. I feast on the beauties of earth, and sky, and air; they are my daily life and food, and—"

"Maudie!" cried out the mother from the kitchen, not knowing that her daughter's beau was in the drawing room. "Maudie, whatever made you go and gobble up that big dish of mashed potatoes that was left over from dinner? I told you we wanted them warmed up for supper. If your appetite isn't enough to bankrupt your poor pa!"

A Puzzled Boy

A little boy was reading the story of a missionary having been eaten by cannibals.

"Papa," he asked, will the missionary go to Heaven?"

"Yes, my son," replied the father.

"And will the cannibals go there, too?'

"No," was the reply.

After thinking the matter over for some time the little fellow exclaimed :—

"Well, I don't see how the missionary can go to Heaven if the cannibals don't, when he's inside the cannibals."

A FATHER, fearing an earthquake in the region of his home, sent his two boys to a distant friend until the peril should be over. A few weeks after the father received this line from his friend: "Please take your boys home and send down the earthquake."

HE: "I saw our old neighbor, Mr. Skinner, to-day." She: "Did you? What is he doing now?" He: "He is interested in one of these wild-cat mining companies." She: "The idea! I never knew you had to mine for wild cats."—Exchange.

루시 모드 몽고메리가 학교 교사인 노라 리퍼지와 나눈 우정은 1898년부터 1911년까지 오랜 시간을 캐번디시에서 외할머니와 함께 지내는 동안에 활력소와도 같았다. 1902년에 스물여덟 살이었던 몽고메리는 핼리팩스 일간지 《데일리 에코》를 그만두고 집으로 돌아왔을 때 스물두 살의 노라가 마음이 통하는 친구라는 것을 알아봤다. 1903년 상반기 여섯 달 동안 맥닐가에서 함께 사는 동안, 두 사람은 재미있는 시간을 보내면서 익살스러운 일기도 나누어 썼다. 두 사람 모두 시와 소설을 무척 좋아했고, 인상적인 추억들이 있었다. 노라는 성격이 대담하여 몽고메리에게 1900년대 초반의 캐나다 시골에서 노처녀에게 기대할 법한 고루한 역할을 걷어차라고 재우쳤다.

캐번디시 문학회Cavendish Literary Society는 1886년 캐번디시에서 출범하여 수준 높은 토론과 강연과 낭송회 등을 열었다. 모임은 캐번디시 마을 회관에서 열렸는데, 이곳에 실린 청사진이 바로 몽고메리가 찍은 마을 회관의 모습이다(오른쪽 위). 몽고메리가 마을 회관에서 처음으로 사람들 앞에 서서 낭송을 한 것은 1889년으로, 해티 고든이 캐번디시 선생님으로 있을 때이다. 몽고메리는 여성으로서는 처음으로 문학회 임원으로 선출됐고, 1902년 이후에는 프로그램을 기획하는 위원회 멤버로 자주 활동했다. 이완 맥도널드는 캐번디시에서

목회를 하는 삼 년 동안(1903년 중반부터 1906년까지) 문학회 활동에 적극적이었고, 몽고메리와 함께 문학 프로그램과 아이디어를 기획했다. 1902년 가을과 1903년 겨울, 몽고메리는 문학회 활동을 이어가면서 노라와 함께 경쟁 아닌 경쟁을 벌이고 재미난 사건을 만들며 보냈는데, 젊은 청년들을 꾀어내어 눈길이나 진창길로 마차를 몰게 하곤 했다.

1902년 가을, 몽고메리는 오락 위원회Entertainment Committee에서 제레마이아 S. 클라크Jeremiah S. Clark와 조지 W. 심프슨George W. Simpson, 노라 리퍼지, 그리고 C. P. 윌슨 목사와 함께 위원으로 활동하면서 이 지면에 실린 프로그램을 만들었다. 이 지면 아래쪽, 오락 위원회의 불손한 회의록은 몽고메리가 작성한 것으로 익살을 이야기의 장으로 뒤바꾼다. 2월 6일, 초대 강사가 오지 않자, 위원들은 강연 주제를 모자에 모아 직접 뽑았다. "파Pa"는 아서 심프슨으로, 몽고메리는 그를 몹시 싫어했다. "제이들Jays"은 암호명으로 제임스 알렉산더 스튜어트James Alexander Stewart와 조 스튜어트Joe Stewart를 가리켰고, "롭인robbin(g)"은 제임스가 두 여자 가운데 한 명을 썰매에 태우고 남은 한 사람을 조에게 맡기는 것이었다. 부끄럼이 많은 제임스를 두고 몽고메리와 노라는 비밀 일기에서 모의 경쟁을 벌이곤 했다.

Friday. Nov. 28.
1902.

Entertainment Committee
meets.
J. S. Clarke B. A. in
the chair.
Chap. I. Two busy maidens.
Chap. II. A problem in division — of
candy.
Chap. III. "Suddenly I heard a
step something louder
than usual.
Chap. IV. A frantic exit.
Chap. V. "Hand me my collar".
Chap. VI. Apologies.
Chap. VII. J. C. proceeds to business
Chap. VIII. Micmac dictionary
To be continued.
"Say, you're locked up".
"Editor, editor, who's got an editor?"
Hands there are that are changed hands.
Wanted — a muddler!
"A man's a man although there's
nothing in him".

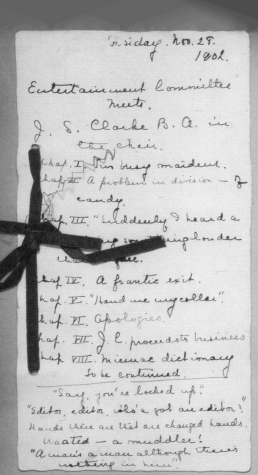

PROGRAMME

CAVENDISH LITERARY SOCIETY.

1902 -- 3.

Dec. 5th -- "The Indians of Canada." J. S. Clark.

Dec. 19th -- ....Christmas Entertainment.

Jan. 2nd -- Review of 1902 and outlook for 1903.

Arthur Simpson, Opener.

Jan. 16th -- Lecture ....Rev. E. P. Cald-

er.

Jan. 30th -- Debate -- "Trusts Are Justifiable."

Geo. Simpson Vs. Walter Simpson.

Feb. 6th -- "The Making of a Newspaper."

L. M. Montgomery.

Feb. 20th -- Newspaper Night. J. S. Clark, Editor.

L. M. Montgomery, Associate Editor.

Mar. 6th -- Lecture .... Rev. J. W. McConnell.

Mar. 20th -- "The Poets." .... N. Lefurgey

April 3rd -- "Chinese Gordon." ... Rev. E.P. Wilson.

Friday.
Dec 19.
1902
"Blessed are the disap-
pointed — for their turn
will come.
Rev. C. P. Wilson in
the chair.
"Is this for Indians?"
"Whispering angels".
"Gentle applause".
"Good long steps!"
"The interpretation thereof"
"One of the aborigines".
"A new departure".

Friday.
Jan. 2.
1903.
Rev. C. P. Wilson in
chair.
No minutes read and
approved.
Rev. Mr. Calder lect-
ures on the Fine Dollars
immigration".
There are lots of the fourth
class.
The president takes a
pain.
"First come, first served".
A chaperone.

Friday. Feb. 6.
Rev. C. P. Wilson
in chair.
Lecturer does not come.
Jerry passes round the hat.
Freddie prefers "Forty fives".
Howard stands "straight up".
Jerry discusses "pork".
"Pa" gets personal on
"Prohibition".
Two jays put their heads
together and make a robin (g).
A nose in the sleigh is
worth ten in conversation.

몽고메리와 노라가 같이 쓴 비밀 일기는 1903년 2월과 3월의 재미있는 회의록을 푸는 열쇠이다. 1903년 3월 20일 일기에는 세 명의 "제이들(제임스와 조, 그리고 제리 클라크Jerry Clark 까지)"이 전부 불참했지만, "롭인(로버트 A. 매켄지Robert A. MacKenzie)"은 참석했다고 적혀 있다.

몇 개월 동안의 사건들이 레드 스크랩북 3쪽 콜라주 안에 담겨 있다. "캐번디시 학교" 기사는 노라와의 작별 인사를 기록한 것으로, 그것은 몽고메리가 또다시 캐번디시에 가까운 친구 한 명 없이 혼자 남았다는 의미이다. 삼나무 잎은 오래전에 캐번디시를 떠난 해티 고든 선생님이 보낸 것이거나 최근 포틀랜드에서 결혼한 거티 무어Gertie Moore에게서 받은 것일 것이다(레드 스크랩북 5쪽, 잎사귀 밑에 오려 붙인 기사). 잡지에 실린 "르포스 곳" 사진은 몽고메리가 어렸을 때도 그런 모습이었을 것 같다. 암호명 "밤의 눈(꽃 위에 붙인 기사)"은 몽고메리가 비더포드에서 학생들을 가르치던 시절부터 데이지 윌리엄스Daisy Williams가 사용한 이름이었다. 당시 두 사람은 손 글씨를 분석 기관에 맡겨보기도 했다(레드 스크랩북 15쪽, 몽고메리의 "마음Psyche" 참고). 한 기사에는 메이블 심프슨Mable Simpson이 더 이상 캐번디시 장로교회에서 오르간을 연주하지 않을 것이라는 소식이 실렸다. 몽고메리가 오르간 연주자 자리를 대신 맡으면서 목사가 된 이완 맥도널드와 자주 만나게 됐고, 그는 장차 몽고메리의 남편이 된다.

마음이 통하는 영혼, 친구

성격이 다정하고 사교적인 데다가 사람들에게 우정이 쌓였다고 느끼도록 하는 재주가 있었지만 그런 루시 모드 몽고메리가 가장 깊이 애정을 갖는 상대는 일부 몇 명에 지나지 않았다. 몽고메리는 펜팔 친구였던 두 남자, 스코틀랜드의 조지 보이드 맥밀런과 앨버타주의 이프리엄 웨버Ephraim Weber를 마음이 통하는 영혼으로 꼽았을 것이다(112쪽 참고). 흥미로운 사실은 (자기 아이들을 제외하고는) 가장 강한 유대감을 발전시킨 상대는 전부 젊을 때, 《빨강 머리 앤》을 출판하고 유명해지기 전에 만난 사람들이라는 것이다. 프린스에드워드섬에서 만든 스크랩북 두 권과 캐번디시 시절에 쓴 초기 일기 및 편지들을 보면, 젊은 시절에 몽고메리가 서스캐처원의 프린스앨버트에서 지낼 때나 핼리팩스의 달하우지 대학과 《데일리 에코》 신문사에 있을 때, 또는 프린스에드워드섬에서 학교 친구들이나 문학회 회원들과도 얼마나 쉽게 관계를 맺고 즐겁게 우정을 쌓았는지 알 수 있다. 로라 프리처드 애그뉴와는 사십사 년 동안 소중한 친구 사이였다. 캐번디시의 머틀 맥닐 웹Myrtle Macneill Webb과도 평생 친구 관계를 유지했고, 머틀의 아이들은 몽고메리를 모두 "이모"라고 불렀다(웹 가족의 정원 파티에 대한 내용이 레드 스크랩북 52쪽에 실렸다). 노라 리퍼지와는 헤어진 지 이십사 년 만에 온타리오에서 반갑게 재회했다. 프린스에드워드섬의 사촌인 프레더리카 캠벨, 버티 매킨타이어와도 끈끈한 관계를 유지했다. 몽고메리가 프레더리카의 표현을 빌려서 나중에 앤 이야기에 쓴 것도 있는데, 앤이 마음 통하는 친구를 "요셉을 아는 사람들"이라고 정의한 바로 그것이다. 앤 셜리와 에밀리 스타의 중간 어디쯤에서, 몽고메리는 사람들과 편하게 지내는 자신만의 재능으로 소설 속 우정을 묘사하는 데 그토록 천재성을 발휘할 수 있었던 것이다.

February 27. 1913.

Rev. C. A. Wilson in
chair

Two (jays) get home from
funeral.

"Hold on" going up Davids
Hill.

The beloved disciple from
New Glasgow appears.

"A day in a newspaper
Office."

A quick despatch and
now for the ball.

March 6. 1913;

Father Pierce in the
chair. By Creon.

J. comes down like the
wolf on the fold.

And the headache evaporates
quickly and bold.

Theological ghosts

Telephone Poets

Who-a. Olive.

The voice(s) of the Press.

Three "J's" are too many
for one alphabet.

We "talk it over".

March. 20th 1903.

Father Pierce in chair.

Muddy knees.

A paper on Byron.

"My native land, good-night."

"His favorite poet."

The absence of all three
(blue) jays.

Never mind, we have a
Rob-in.

A good going sleigh.

Tennis wants to race.

Finis of Literary
1902 — 1903.

Night's Eve—Strength and firmness
of will is depicted in your writing. You
are energetic, even inclined to be domineering. You are shy, unassuming and
easily embarrassed. You are constant
and steady and a very reliable character.

Mr Ellis Bishop of this town was
married on Wednesday to Miss Fay
McKenzie of Cavendish by Rev. A. D.
Stirling of Cavendish at the bride's
home. In the evening a reception was
held at their home in Summerside.

Miss Mable Simpson the popular
teacher of Hope River is resigning to
take a course in the Halifax Ladies
College. She will probably be succeeded in the school by A. C. Cullen of Bay
View. Miss Simpson will be much missed in social circles and in the Presbyterian Church where she has been
organist for some time past.

CAVENDISH SCHOOL

On Friday, June 21st the semi-annual
examinations of Cavendish school was
held very successfully in the presence of
a number of visitors. The children acquitted themselves with honor and the
condition of the school reflects great
credit on the energetic and popular
teacher, Miss Nora LeFurgey.

At the close of the examination a
beautiful dressing case was presented to
Miss LeFurgey by her pupils, accompanied by the following address:—

DEAR AND RESPECTED TEACHER:

Having heard of your intention of
leaving us, we as scholars cannot allow
this opportunity to pass without expressing to you how deeply we regret to hear
of your departure.

During the two years in which you
have taught us you have labored most
earnestly and diligently for our welfare
and your kindness to and interest in us
have endeared you both to pupils in the
school and friends in the district. For
all that you have done for us we thank
you heartily and sincerely.

Our best wishes will go forth with
you in whatever new sphere of labor
your lot will be cast. We hope that
all the blessings of success, health and
happiness may be yours.

In conclusion we ask you to accept
the accompanying token of love and regard of your affectionate pupils signed
on behalf of the school.

ANNIE P. MACNEILL,
PEARL SIMPSON,
ERNEST CLARK,
AILEEN LAIRD,
LOTTIE MACNEILL,
CHARLIE M. MACKENZIE,
FAYE MACKENZIE,
JEAN LAIRD.

CAPE LEFORCE

A POOR ILLUSTRATION.

"I don't want to wear my old hat to
church," said eight-year-old Gladys,
"not even if it does rain. The trimming on that hat is all worn out,
mother."

"It's the best thing for you to wear
on a day like this," said her mother
firmly. "And you must remember
that it's the inside and not the outside—what is unseen, not what is
seen—that God looks at, my little girl."

"Yes'm," said Gladys eagerly. "I
do remember; but the lining of that
hat is worn even worse than the trimming is!"

The marriage of J. D. A. MacIntyre
at one time a resident of Sydney, to a
P. E. Island young lady, takes place
at Winnipeg next month. Mr. Mac-
Intyre is in the real estate business
in Edmonton.—Edmonton Ex.

"THE evidence," said the judge, "shows that
you threw a stone at this man."
"Sure," replied Mrs. O'Hoolihan, "an' the looks
av the man shows more than thot, yer honor. It
shows thot Oi hit him."—Chicago News.

사촌인 캠벨 가족이 살던 파크 코너의 캠벨가는 루시 모드 몽고메리에게 언제나 피난처였다. 프레더리카 캠벨(1883-1919)은 몽고메리에게 가장 소중한 친구이자 친척이었다. 레드 스크랩북 4쪽과 5쪽은 캠벨 가족과 그들이 살던 집이 주인공이다.

4쪽 가운데에 위치한 카드에 검은 그물 조각과 함께 1902년 11월 29일이라는 날짜가 적혀 있다. 노라는 1902년 11월 28일, 레드 스크랩북 2쪽에 언급한 문학회의 오락 위원회 모임이 끝난 뒤 몽고메리와 함께 밤을 보냈다. 다음 날에는 프레더리카도 찾아와 같이 지냈다. 몽고메리는 일기에 "평소 중요하게 생각했던 여러 주제를 토론했다"라고 적었다.

위쪽에 있는 청사진은 파크 코너에 있는 캠벨 가족의 집으로, 몽고메리는 이곳을 제2의 집으로 여겼고 1911년에 결혼식도 이 집에서 올렸다. 애니와 존 캠벨 부부는 마음씨 좋기로 유명했고, 식료품 창고는 유쾌한 사촌들이 장난을 일삼는 곳이었다. 클라라, 스텔라, 조지, 프레더리카는 몽고메리의 삶에서 매우 중요한 사람들이었다. 몽고메리는 1909년 메리 매킨타이어 Mary McIntyre 숙모의 부고 기사를 캠벨 가족의 기념 자료들 사이에 배치했다. 메리 숙모는 파크 코너에 살던 아버지 쪽 친척이었다. 몽고메리는 버티 매킨타이어와 특히 가깝게 지냈다. 화려한 이름 카드 밑에는 스텔라 캠벨, 클라라 캠벨, 이디스 J. 필먼Edith J. Pillman, 제임스 힐츠James Hiltz 부부의 이름이 쓰여 있다. 모두 파크 코너에 사는 사람들로, 몽고메리의 일기에 등장한다.

5쪽 청사진 속에 있는 캐번디시 침례교회는 몽고메리가 에드윈 심프슨의 청혼을 거절한 아픈 기억과 관련이 있다. 몽고메리는 1903년 10월 7일에 결혼하는 조지 캠벨의 청첩장을 붙여놓고(청첩장은 더 큰 봉투 안에 들어 있고, 위에 있는 봉투는 비어 있다), 결혼 기사를 에드윈과 관련된 자료 가까이에 배치하여 쓰라린 기억을 중화하려 한 것인지 모른다.

몽고메리가 1904년 4월에 처음 발표한 단편소설 〈아파트의 태니스Tannis of the Flats〉 관련 기사는 아마 프레더리카나 버티가 붙여뒀을 것이고, 4쪽에 실린 1903년 11월 호 《캐나다 잡지》의 〈에밀리의 남편Emily's Husband〉 기사도 마찬가지로 보인다. 왼쪽 위에 실린 재미있는 이야기는 몽고메리가 1901년 10월 12일 핼리팩스 신문 《데일리 에코》에 '신시아'라는 필명으로 기고한 칼럼에도 등장한다.

6쪽 여기에서는 몽고메리의 폭넓은 친구와 지인들을 볼 수 있다. 시 〈자장가Lullaby〉의 작가인 이프리엄 웨버는 1902년부터 새로 사귄 펜팔 친구였고, 앨마 S. 맥닐 Alma S. McNeill은 어린 시절의 친구이자 사촌이다. 루시 링컨 몽고메리Lucy Lincoln Montgomery는 펜팔 친구로, 그 자료가 초기 스크랩북들에 여기저기 등장한다. 애들레이드 존슨Adelaide Johnson(1859-1955)은 훗날 여성 인권 운동의 상징적 인물인 수전 B. 앤서니Susan B. Anthony, 엘리자베스 케이디 스탠턴Elizabeth Cady Stanton, 루크리셔 모트Lucretia Mott 등을 조각하여 세계적으로 유명해진 인물이다. 존슨은 《빨강 머리 앤》의 팬이었을까? 찰스 마실Charles Marcil은 자유당원인 퀘벡의 언론인으로, 1900년부터 1937년까지 하원의원을 지냈고 1909년에서 1911년까지는 하원의장을 역임했다.

On my friendship cordially

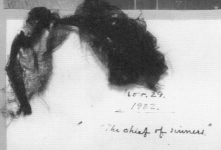

Nov. 29.
1902.

"The chief of sinners."

The Sanctity of Cats

A Sunday-school teacher in Carthage, Ill., has a class of little girls, and it is her custom to tell them each Sunday of one little incident that has happened in the week and request the children to quote a verse of scripture to illustrate the story. In this way she hopes to impress the usefulness of Biblical knowledge upon the little ones. One Sunday she told her class of a cruel boy who would catch cats and cut off their tails. "Now, can any little girl tell me of an appropriate verse?" she asked. There was a pause for a few moments, when one little girl arose and in a solemn voice said: "Whatsoever God has joined together let no man put asunder."—New York Tribune.

Miss Lucy M Montgomery has a cleverly written story in the Canadian Magazine for November. We congratulate this talented Island writer on the quality and quantity of the work she is doing with her pen.

The early hours of New Year's Day were saddened for many relatives and warm friends by the death of Mrs. McIntyre, of Brighton, who passed away at four o'clock, after a short illness. Mrs. McIntyre was a daughter of the late Hon. Senator Montgomery, a sister of the late Hugh John Montgomery of Prince Albert, Sask., and an aunt of Miss L. M. Montgomery, the Canadian author and poet. She leaves a bereaved husband and five young men and women. James McIntyre and Miss Laura McIntyre left distant Edmonton Friday and are now on their way home to pay the last tribute of filial love and duty, Miss Bertie McIntyre of the Model School and Mr. C. McIntyre of the Bank of Nova Scotia, in this city, were with their mother in her last hours here. Harry McIntyre of the Bank of Nova Scotia, Toronto, arrived home yesterday.

of the Cross Society

Abney.
LAIRD—STEWART—At Cavendish, on April 5th, by Rev. John Murray, Edwin Everett Laird to Elizabeth Cranston Stewart.

Accommodating

In one of Frank Sanborn's stories a gentleman requests release from his engagement. "I have been concealing something," he says to his fiancée. "The truth is, I am a somnambulist." "Oh, that needn't interfere," exclaimed the young woman. "I'm not particular. I was brought up a Baptist, but I'd just as soon change over to accommodate you."

A SIMPLE CHANGE.

The little daughter of the house watched the minister who was making a visit very closely, and finally sat down beside him and began to draw on her slate.

"What are you doing?" asked the clergyman.

"Making your picture," said the child.

The minister sat very still and the child worked away earnestly. Then she stopped and compared her work with the original, and shook her head.

"I don't like it much," she said. "Tain't a great deal like you. I guess I'll put a tail to it and call it a dog."—[Philadelphia Times.

A boy was asked to paraphrase the latter part of the Ballad of Lochinvar, which runs as follows:

"They'll have fleet steeds that follow," quoth young Lochinvar;
There was mounting 'mong Graemes of the Netherby clan,
Fosters, Fenwicks, and Musgraves, they rode and they ran,
There was racing and chasing on Canobie lea.

The unimaginative youth reflected awhile, and then wrote: "Loch left, followed by the whole gang."

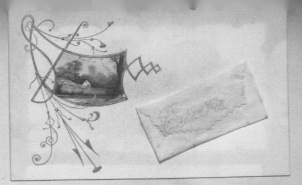

WEDDING BELLS

The home of Mr and Mrs John R Hooper, North Milton, was the scene of a very pretty wedding on Wednesday evening, 29th ult , when their only daughter, Miss Mary Elizabeth, was united in marriage to Mr Alexander C MacNeill of Cavendish. The nuptial knot was tied by the Venerable Archdeacon Reagh in the presence of the immediate friends of the contracting

The bride who was given away by her father, was attended by her cousins Miss Hattie Rodd of Winsloe, as bridesmaid and little Miss Verna Hooper of Ch'town, as flower girl, while the groom was supported by Mr Ernest Butman of South Rustico. The bridal gown was of grey broadcloth trimmed with white silk, while the bridesmaids were attired in figured muslin over white.

The bride was the recipient of many beautiful and costly presents. After the ceremony the company sat down to a bountiful wedding repast. The happy couple left for their future home at Cavendish on the following day with the best wishes of all who knew them.—Con.

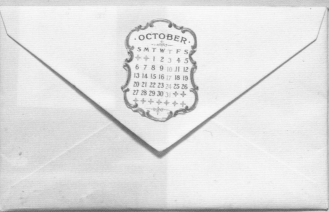

On the evening of Wednesday, October 7th the home of D. M. Johnstone of Long River was the scene of an extremely pretty wedding, when his sister Ella, was united in marriage to George L. Campbell of Park Corner. The rooms and stair case were lavishly decorated with ferns cut flowers and potted plants. At eight o'clock the strains of the wedding march played by Miss Stella Campbell, preceded the entrance of the bridal party. The Rev. Mr. Rattee of Malpeque performed the marriage ceremony in the presence of over one hundred guests. The bride was charmingly gowned in white silk, with trimmings of chiffon, applique and lace, with the bridal accessories of orange blossoms, veil and train, and carried a beautiful bouquet of roses and maiden hair fern. Miss Clara Campbell of Chestnut Hill, Mass., the sister of the groom, was bridesmaid and wore an extremely dainty dress of white point d'esprit with ornamentation of lace medallions. She carried a bouquet of lilies. Helen and Jean Johnstone, the little nieces of the bride made very charming flower girls, gowned in white organdy and lace, and carrying bouquets of chrysanthemums and carnations. Mr George McKay of Clifton supported the groom. After the newly-married pair had received the congratulations of their friends an elaborate supper was served. The next feature of the evening was the arrival of the charivariers who turned out from all quarters in striking costumes to do honor to the event. After their departure a pleasant evening of music and dancing was spent. The bride and groom received a large number of very beautiful presents among which may be mentioned a handsome set of sable furs, the groom's gift to the bride, and a substantial check from the bride's brother. The groom's gift to the bridesmaid was a very pretty crescent of pearls. On the following evening a reception was held at the home of the groom's parents, Mr and Mrs John Campbell of Park Corner. The spacious rooms of the old homestead were beautified by flowers and autumn leaves and thronged with guests the younger element of which kept time to the violin in the good old fashioned way. Supper was served in Mrs Campbell's well known bountiful style and at a late hour the guests wended their homeward way with hearty wishes for the welfare and happiness of the young couple through their whole future life.

Announcements have been received of the marriage of Miss Gertrude A. Moore to John D. Sheel of Portland, Oregon. The ceremony took place at Portland on April 4th. Miss Moore formerly belonged to Crapaud, but has been in the west for several years Mrs. H. J. Wright, Searletown, is a sister.

In the New York Criterion for August appears a very thrilling, illustrated story by L M Montgomery entitled "Tannis of the Flats." The PATRIOT hopes to be able to place it before its readers at an early date. By her talent as a poetess, and her ability as a prose writer, Miss Montgomery has made the productions of her pen welcome to the highest class publications both in Canada and the United States We hope and believe that she is within reach of fame as a writer.

THE marriage of Miss Margaret James daughter of Mr. T. C. James of this city, to Rev. George Millar of Alberton, takes place tomorrow morning at seven o'clock at the bride's home. Rev. T. F. Fullerton will officiate. After the ceremony Mr. and Mrs. Millar will leave by the 7.45 train for New Brunswick.

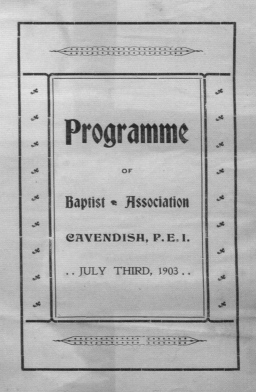

Programme

OF

Baptist • Association

CAVENDISH, P. E. I.

.. JULY THIRD, 1903 ..

"Ichabod."

CANDY

"Co-operating"

a Pearl & neck-lace.

Church going danclle

Adelaide Johnson requests the honour of your presence at an exhibition of her Portrait-busts and Medallions between the hours of noon and six p.m., from the eighth to tenth, January, nineteen nine. Studio and galleries, Five East Thirty-Sixth Street.

THE Presbyterian Church at Cavendish, tastefully decorated with flowers and ferns and autumn leaves, and filled with interested spectators, was the scene on Wednesday, September 23rd, 1903, at 10 a. m., of the marriage of Miss Mabel Simpson, of Mayfield, to Rev. Major H McIntosh, pastor of the Presbyterian Churches of West and Clyde Rivers The bride and bridesmaid, Miss Nora Lefurgey of Summerside, were becomingly dressed in white. The groom was ably supported by Rev R J Douglas of Little Harbour, Nova Scotia. The ceremony was performed by Rev Ewen McDonald assisted by Rev D B McLeod of Charlottetown. Mrs Cummings of Westville, N. S., sister of the bride, rendered appropriate music as the bridal party entered the church, and also on their retiring. Among the numerous and handsome presents was a gold watch from the bridegroom to the bride. The groom's gift to the bridesmaid was a beautiful pearl ring. After luncheon at the bride's mother's residence, the happy couple started on their wedding trip to Montreal and other Canadian cities.

A pleasing event took place yesterday afternoon at two o'clock at the residence of Rev. R. W. Stevenson, Kent Street, when Miss Maggie Warren daughter of T. A. Warren, North Rustico, was united in marriage to Russel McNeill of Cavendish. The ceremony was performed by Rev. W. R. Motley of Montague. The bride, who was unattended was becomingly attired in a suit of navy blue broadcloth with Persian velours trimmings and hat to match. After the ceremony the happy couple drove to their future home in Cavendish. The PATRIOT joins with their many friends in wishing them a long and happy journey through life.

THE LATE WILLIAM MONTGOMERY.

The recent death of William Montgomery removes one of Wakefield's oldest and most respected citizens. As briefly recorded in the ITEM, Mr. Montgomery died last Friday at the advanced age of 85 years. The funeral took place Monday at the late home of the deceased on Jordan avenue, Rev. Hugh A. Heath, pastor of the Baptist church, officiating. The pall bearers were Everett W. Eaton, Chester W. Eaton, Augustus D. Dimick and George H. Scovell. Undertaker Oliver Walton had charge. A profusion of floral offerings, sent by relatives and friends testified to the worthy character and esteem of the deceased. The burial was at Lakeside cemetery, in the family lot. George West of Byron st. sang "Pilgrims of the Night" at the services.

Mr. Montgomery was born in Scotland and came to America when 17 years of age with his father who was a cotton manufacturer. For many years Mr. Montgomery was engaged in the manufacturing of cotton in Biddeford, Me. and New York state. Later on, for a number of years he manufactured iron having foundries at Halifax, N. S. In 1880 Mr. Montgomery and family returned to the United States.

For some years Mr. Montgomery was in the employ of the Equitable Life Assurance society, but in recent years has lived in retirement, enjoying the blessings of a well spent and active life.

Mr. Montgomery's wife died in 1884. Three daughters and two sons survive the deceased. The daughters are Mrs. Mary G. Slocum, wife of President W. F. Slocum of Colorado college, Colorado Springs; Mrs. Margaret Goodale, wife of Gen Greenleaf A. Goodale of Wakefield, and Miss Lucy L. Montgomery of Wakefield. One of the sons is in northern Maine and the other resides in New York.

Mr. Montgomery was a Mason, having united with a Halifax lodge when a young man. He was a consistent member of the Congregational church and was a man of strict integrity and upright character.

HON. CHARLES MARCIL, M.P., THE NEW SPEAKER
OF THE HOUSE OF COMMONS

Many will be grieved to hear of ... death of Mrs. Rev. John Murray, ...ton, which occurred on Wednesday ...ght last, at the age of 63 years. ...a Murray had been in delicate ...alth for the past year but no fear ...as entertained of her death 'till a-...ut 24 hours before the call came. ...s Murray was a native of Halifax, ...ova Scotia, and leaves to mourn ...esides her husband, one daughter at ...ome and one son at Sydney.

OLD PRINCE OF WALES COLLEGE

Lullaby

"ROCK-A-BY, hush-a-by, baby, my sweet,
Pink little fingers and pink little feet;
Soft is your pillow, your cradle is white—
Rock-a-by, hush-a-by, baby, good-night."

Pure are your eyes as the dew on the gra...
Close them in slumber your spirit will pa...
O'er bridges of clouds like a pilgrim of lig...
And journey to Elfland in silken-winged f...

Go, soar to God's bosom, whence lately ...
came,
And tell him I love you, and bless his ...
name;
Dumb are your lips, but your spirit is fre...
So, thank him for sending an angel to me...

Rock-a-by, hush-a-by, baby, my love,
My darling, my fairy, my heavenly dove;
Dream till the dawn brings the glow of the
light—
Rock-a-by, hush-a-by, baby, good-night.
—Ephraim Weber.

Alma S. McNeill

Rev. J. E. Menancon,
Presby. Church Agent.

Pointe-aux-Trembles
Mission Schools.   (Near Montreal.)

문학을 사랑한 펜팔 친구들

문학은 루시 모드 몽고메리가 많은 사람과 연결되는 고리였다. 몽고메리는 캐번디시 문학회 회지에 더 넓은 세계에 있는 펜팔 친구들의 이름을 실었다. 마치 자기 문단의 폭이 얼마나 더 넓어지고 있는지를 암시하는 듯하다. 《빨강 머리 앤》을 출간한 후 몽고메리는 세계에서 편지를 받았다. 그중에는 새뮤얼 클레멘스Samuel Clemens(마크 트웨인)같이 유명한 작가도 있었다. 몽고메리가 스크랩북과 일기와 사진으로 찬양하고 발전시켰던 상상력은 앤 셜리를 비롯한 작품 속 여주인공들에게 돌아가 마침내 몽고메리의 문학적 공동체를 넓혀줬다.

캐번디시에서 보낸 초기에 몽고메리는 문학 이야기를 나누고 싶은 마음에 자기 세계가 넓어지기를 바라면서 몇몇 사람과 펜팔을 시작했다. 루시 링컨 몽고메리는 매사추세츠 웨이크필드 출신의 여성 작가로, 루시 모드 몽고메리와 자주 서신을 나누었고 몇 편의 글을 보내기도 했다. 몽고메리는 1910년 가을에 L. C. 페이지 출판사를 방문하러 보스턴에 갈 때 루시 링컨 몽고메리를 만나기도 했다. 1900년에는 버지니아에 사는 프랭크 먼로 베벌리Frank Monroe Beverley와도 편지로 친교를 맺으려고 노력했다. 몽고메리가 잡지에 발표한 시 〈숲에 내리는 비Rain in the Woods〉를 읽고 감동해 그가 먼저 편지를 보냈지만 두 사람의 교류는 오래가지 못했다. 그러나 프랭크는 몽고메리에게 필라델피아의 미리엄 지버Miriam Zieber를 소개했고, 미리엄은 1902년에 앨버타에서 교사로 일하던 이프리엄 웨버를, 1903년에는 스코틀랜드 저널리스트인 조지 보이드 맥밀런을 소개해줬다. 웨버는 토론하기를 좋아해서 몽고메리와 다투기도 했다. 웨버는 반전反戰을 지지했고 몽고메리는 아니었지만 두 사람의 우정은 제1차 세계대전을 이겨내고 지속됐다. 맥밀런은 고양이와 정원 가꾸기를 무척 좋아해서 몽고메리와 개인적인 이야기도 나누었다. 몽고메리는 거의 사십 년 동안 두 남자와 편지를 주고받았고, 1942년 세상을 떠나기 몇 달 전에야 두 사람 모두에게 작별의 글을 남겼다.

지금 우리는 전혀 알지 못하지만, 초기에는 서신으로 문학적 교감을 나눈 펜팔 친구가 더 많았을 것이다. 몽고메리는 웨버에게 아일랜드계 미국인 작가인 제럴드 칼턴Gerald Carlton에 대해 언급했고, 레드 스크랩북에 그의 명함과 관련 기사도 첨부했다. 핼리팩스 일간지 《데일리 에코》에서 같이 일했던 이디스 러셀Edith Russell에 대해서는 일기에 거의 언급하지 않았지만 이디스의 시 몇 편을 레드 스크랩북에 수집해놓았고, 1926년에는 이디스가 온타리오로 몽고메리를 방문한 것으로 보아, 두 사람이 꾸준히 편지를 주고받았다는 사실을 알 수 있다.

8-9쪽 몽고메리는 바느질 솜씨가 좋았다. 옷감 견본과 마음에 드는 옷 이미지를 보관했다(이 페이지와 다음 두 페이지의 견본 직물을 보라). 앤 셜리처럼 몽고메리는 패션을 좋아하고 새로운 의상을 즐겼다.

The Cavendish Literary Magazine

Published at Cavendish, Prince Edward Island

March. Nineteen Hundred and Three.

L.M.Montgomery.

Miss Miriam Zieber

Geo. B. MacMillan.

34 Castle Street,
Alloa, N. S.

여기에는 학교 교사인 노라 리퍼지와 함께 즐거운 시간을 보냈던 기억이 기록되어 있다. 가르치는 일과 학교에 대해 얘기할 때는 할 말이 더 많아졌다. 캐나다국립철도 사진조차 아마 루시모드 몽고메리가 1890년 서스캐처원 학창 시절부터 마음이 통하는 친구였던 로라 프리처드 애그뉴를 방문하러 1930년에 서부로 이동할 때 수집했을 것이다.

재담 액자 몽고메리와 노라는 둘 다 사진과 문학, 스크랩북 만들기를 좋아했다. 공들여 접은 "딱지 모양" 사각형에는 키플링Kipling과 여러 재담을 이용하여 노라의 청사진을 액자처럼 둘렀다.

시 〈학교에서 하는 키스The Smack in School〉는 수줍음은 많지만 훌쩍 커버린 남학생이 남녀 학생 60명이 공부하는 교실에서 요란하게 입맞춤하는 상황을 묘사한다. 몽고메리가 정확히 60명이라고 정한 이유는 첫 교직을 맡았던 프린스에드워드섬 비더포드 학교의 학생 수가 60명이었기 때문이다. 〈잘 가요, 행복한 날이여Good By, Sweet Day〉는 학교와 마을 모임에서 많이 부르던 유행가이다. 곡은 토머스 오닐Thomas O'neil이 작곡해 1880년에 발표했지만, 서정적인 가사를 쓴 사람은 실리아 댁스터Celia Thaxter였다.

카드 몽고메리와 노라는 같이 비밀 일기를 쓰면서 사랑에 빠진 캐번디시 청년들을 두고 얼마나 더 장난스러운 글을 쓸 수 있는지 서로 경쟁을 벌였다. 이 카드 안에 적힌 글을 보면 두 사람이 어떤 놀이를 했는지 알 수 있다. "한 명이면 키 큰 안내원, 둘은 동료, 셋이면 뭇사람."

사진과 그림 이 젊은 석공은 프레디 클라크Freddy Clark일 것이다. 몽고메리의 좋은 친구이자 비밀 일기에 자주 언급되는 사람이다. 1903년 4월 26일, 몽고메리와 노라는 "프레디의 채석장을 찾아보려는 막연한 생각"으로 산책을 나갔다가 우연히 늪지를 발견하고는 그곳을 모험하고 싶어졌다. 초승달은 몽고메리가 늘 좋아하는 이미지다(블루 스크랩북 3쪽도 참고).

꽃 1896년 9월, 프린스오브웨일스 대학 친구인 패니 와이즈Fanny Wise가 캐번디시 학교에 부임하여 몽고메리의 외삼촌 존 맥닐의 집에 하숙했다. 여기에 기록된 사건들은 패니와 관련 있는 것으로 보인다.

Greetings

The Smack in School

A district school not far away,
Mid Berkshire's hills, one Winter day
Was humming with its wonted noise
Of three-score mingled girls and boys.
Some few upon their tasks intent,
But more upon furtive mischief bent,
The while the master's downward look
Was fastened on a copy-book—
When suddenly, behind his back,
Rose sharp and clear a rousing smack,
As 'twas a battery of bliss
Let off in one tremendous kiss.
"What's that?" the startled master cries.
"That thir," a little imp replies;
"Wath William Willith, if you pleath,
I thaw him kith Thuthanna Peathe!"
With frown to make a statue thrill
The master thundered, "Hither Will!".
Like wretch o'ertaken in his track,
With stolen chattels on his back,
Will hung his head in tears and shame,
And to the awful presence came!
A great, green, bashful simpleton,
The but of all good-natured fun,
With smile suppressed and birch upraised
The threatener faltered, "I'm amazed
That you, my biggest pupil, should
Be guilty of an act so rude!
Before the whole set school, to boot;
What evil genius put you to't?"
"'Twas she, herself, sir," sobbed the lad,
"I didn't mean to be so bad,
But when Susanna shook her curls
And whispered I was 'fraid of girls,'
And dursn't kiss a baby's doll,"
I couldn't stand it, sir, at all,
But up and kisssed her on the spot!
I knew—boo-hoo—I ougbt to not,
But, somehow, from her looks—boo-hoo—
I thought she kind o' wished me to."

Sunday
Nov 4
1902

Cavendish
Starship Road

P. S.)

surely you
know this
thus

that is times

you think you
might."
Kipling

SEARCH
the Scriptures.

JOHN V. 39.

GOOD-BY, SWEET DAY.

GOOD-BY, sweet day, good-by!
 I have so loved thee, but I cannot
  hold thee,
Departing like a dream, the shadows
 fold thee;
Slowly thy perfect beauty fades away;
Good-by, sweet day!

Good-by, sweet day, good-by!
 Dear were thy golden hours of tranquil
  splendor,
 Sadly thou yieldest to the evening tender,
Who wert so fair from thy first morning
 ray!
Good-by, sweet day!

Good-by, sweet day, good-by!
 Thy glow and charm, thy smiles and
  tones and glances
 Vanish at last, and solemn night ad-
  vances.
Ah! couldst thou yet a little longer stay!
Good-by, sweet day!

Good-by, sweet day, good-by!
 All thy rich gifts my grateful heart re-
  members
 The while I watch thy sunset's smoul-
  dering embers
Die in the west beneath the twilight gray.
Good-by, sweet day!

Thursday
Sept 24
1896

"Will he bring
her back? Oh,
how nice"

레드 스크랩북 10쪽

날짜가 뒤죽박죽 섞이고 자료들로 빽빽하게 채워진 여기 세 페이지에는 마음 아픈 이야기 두 편이 담겨 있다. 하나는 에드윈 심프슨에 관한 이야기이고, 다른 하나는 허먼 리어드에 관한 이야기다. 안타깝게도 심프슨과 약혼하고 로어 비데크에서 학생들을 가르치면서 코닐리어스 리어드Cornelius Leard의 집에서 하숙하게 됐을 때(1897-1898) 루시 모드 몽고메리는 젊고 잘생긴 허먼과 뜨거운 사랑에 빠졌다. 캐번디시의 집으로 돌아온 몽고메리는 심프슨과의 약혼을 깨고 허먼을 향한 마음도 정리하기로 결심했다. 1898년 여름, 몽고메리는 비더포드로 여행을 떠났다가, 태평한 마음으로 학생들을 가르쳤던 과거의 공간들을 돌아보면서 에드윈과 허먼의 일로 겪은 마음의 고통 때문에 자신이 얼마나 달라졌는지 절감했다. 몽고메리는 비더포드에서 로어 비데크로 이동했다. 허먼을 향한 열정적 마음을 얼마나 철저히 억누르고 있는지 스스로를 시험하기 위해서였다. 허먼은 몽고메리에게 둘이서 산책을 가자고 청했다. 아마도 1898년 8월 26일이었을 것이다. 몽고메리는 거절했고, 나중에 1898년 10월 8일 일기에 만일 그를 따라나섰다면 어떻게 되었을까 의문을 품었다. "내 삶이 끝날 때까지 그 의문은 풀리지 않을 것이다"라고 몽고메리는 결론지었다. 나중에 알게 된 사실이지만, 허먼은 1899년에 갑작스럽게 세상을 떠났다. 몽고메리는 여전히 자신을 격려해주는 에드윈 심프슨 때문에 스스로를 자책했고, 그런 괴로운 마음을 안고 지내다가 1906년에 이완 맥도널드와 약혼했다.

11쪽 "최고재판소High Court"라는 제목이 에드윈 심프슨의 이름 바로 위에 붙은 손금 사진 옆으로 마치 심판 자체처럼 배치되어 있다. 이십 년 남짓 지난 1926년 11월 22일 일기에 몽고메리는 심프슨과 관련된 짤막한 기사에 대해 언급했다. "아무런 악의 없이 아주 흔한 기사이다. 하지만 내게는 그 뒤에 불편한 감정이 감춰져

있는 것처럼 느껴졌다." "최고재판소" 기사의 끝부분과 맨 위 왼쪽 귀퉁이에 붙인 우울한 기사는 보어전쟁(1899-1902)에 관한 것이다. 이 전쟁에서 캐나다는 병사 277명을 잃었고, 그중 다수가 피의 일요일이라 불리는 파르데베르그 전투the Battle of Paardeberg에서 사망했다(1900).

13쪽 다른 사람들의 결혼 소식이다. 1899년 12월 13일, 몽고메리는 외삼촌 존 맥닐의 집에서 치러진 결혼식에서 사진을 찍어줬다. 몇 년 뒤, 몽고메리는 네티 밀러Nettie Millar가 겪은 불행에 관해 말했다. 네티가 신부라는 것을 알리는 기사는 왼쪽 위에 있다. 허먼의 여동생 헬렌의 결혼식 기사(가운데 아래)에서 몽고메리는 어떤 번뇌를 느꼈을까? 1903년 톰슨의 결혼식(청첩장은 봉투 안에 있다)은 레드 스크랩북 11쪽에 실린 톰슨 양의 뉴욕 명함과 연관 있을 것이다.《데일리 에코》에서 만난 사람일까?

14쪽 타버린 성냥과 운명적인 날짜, 그리고 라틴어로 쓴 "바니타스 바니타툼vanitas vanitatum(헛되고 헛되도다)"······ 전부 몽고메리에게 잃어버린 사랑을 떠오르게 하는 것으로 결혼식 페이지의 상석을 차지했다. 프린스오브웨일스 대학 시절의 친구인 메리 캠벨이 1900년에 결혼식을 올린 뒤에는 밤새 춤추면서 다음 날 새벽까지 피로연이 계속됐다. 몽고메리는 사진으로 찍어서 왼쪽 위에 실었다. 핼리팩스 여학교 시절의 친구인 로티 섀퍼드는 몽고메리를《데일리 에코》에 추천했다. 몽고메리는 반나절의 휴가를 얻어 1901년 11월 6일에 열린 로티 여동생의 결혼식에 참석했고(청첩장은 봉투 안에), 청첩장 밑에 붙인 기사도 직접 쓴 듯하다.

When the Transvaal war was at its height, Paul Kruger sent a commissioner to England to find out if there were any more men left there. The commissioner wired from London to say that there were four million men and women "knocking about the town," that there was no excitement, and that men were begging to be sent to fight the Boers. Kruger wired back, "Go north." The commissioner found himself in Newcastle eventually and wired to Kruger: "For God's sake stop that war! England is bringing up men from hell, eight at a time in cages!" He had seen a coal-mine.

NIGHT IS MY FRIEND

BY LUCY LINCOLN MONTGOMERY

Long, long ago
Night was my Foe.
Through each slow and sleepless hour
Ghosts of the Past would creep and lower,
Terrors from the Future loom,
Magnified tenfold by gloom,
The weight of present care and pain
Pressed hopelessly on heart and brain.
Long, long ago
Night was my Foe.

Now to the end
Night is my Friend.
'Tis strange that years must come and go
E'er the blessedness we know—
Such a simple thing and sweet—
'Tis to leave all else complete,
Resting in enfolding Love;
And, though watches wakeful prove,
Learn what strength and comfort lie
In star-set spaces of the sky.
Now to the end
Night is my Friend.

Miss Thompson

Miss Katherine Creighton Thompson.

345 West 94th Street

A Riddle

"I came unto an apple tree,
And apples were upon it.
I took no apples off
And I left no apples on it."

The President's First Trousers

WHEN President Taft was seven years old his mother bought him a pair of short duck trousers. The first time they were washed they shrank badly. The boy was fat, but his mother wedged him into the trousers against his protest. He went out to play, but in a few minutes returned.

"Mamma," he said, "I can't wear these pants; they are too tight. Why, Mamma, they are tighter than my skin."

"Oh, no, they're not, Billy," replied his mother. "Nothing could be tighter than your skin."

"Well, all the same, these pants are. I can sit down in my skin, but I can't in these pants."

BORN
STIRLING.—At the Manse, Cavendish, May 25th, to Rev. and Mrs. John Stirling, a daughter.
MARRIED

Rev. R. H. Stavert, returned today from a trip to Halifax, where he was attending the Post Graduate School at Pine Hill College. Mr. Stavert crosses this afternoon to P. E. Island to spend a few days at his old home in Wilmot Valley. —Moncton Times, May 3.

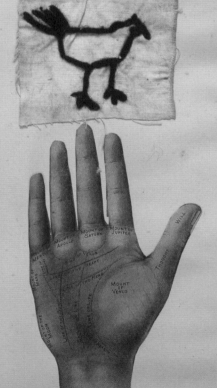

Rev Edwin Simpson of Illinois, and Burton Simpson of Acadia College are visiting in Bay View. The former occupied the pulpit of the Cavendish Baptist Church on Sunday evening.

HIGH COURT
OF FORESTERS
AT TIGNISH

An Interesting Session Closed

AND ADDRESSES DELIVERED

By Dr. Oronhyatekah and Others —A Successful Public Meeting.

PUBLIC MEETING.

The programme was opened by a selection from the 82nd Battalion Band of Charlottetown. This was followed by an address of welcome by Hon Edward Hackett, M P. He briefly reviewed and eulogized the great work that had been accomplished by Dr Oronhyatekah, and concluded his pointed remarks with a reassurance of welcome to the visitors The next number was a well rendered solo by Miss Comstock, who had to respond to an encore. Capt Jos Read, M L A, the oldest Forester on P E Island, on behalf of the High Court thanked the citizens of Tignish for the splendid entertainment they had given. He illustrated the superiority of the I O F over other societies, by a comparison of the modes of travelling now with the stage coach of former days; the latter represented other societies, while the Foresters are emblematic of the Pulman Palace cars drawn by one of the greatest engines that was ever at the head of any train. (Applause)

Miss Lucy Lefurgey read "The Hose Race" in an admirable manner. She responded to a hearty encore with equal acceptance.

Dr Oronhyatekah next addressed the meeting. He was in good form and after telling a few anecdotes, he began the review of the I O F, following its history particularly since the year 1874, showing

the many obstacles which had been met and successfully combated.

He referred to the repeated attacks of the press on the Order and explained how, that instead of being an injury they had been a benefit and the most bitter attacks were always followed by large increase in membership. So much was this so that he had on one occasion written a note to the editor of an attacking paper, who had ceased his criticism, to begin attacking again.

He referred to the publicly expressed opinion of the actuaries of London, who had through their own medium, stated that the O F was organized on a sound financial basis. The Order now extends all over the United Kingdom, United States, France, Belgium, and Australia, carrying with it great possibilities of doing good, such as the sustenance and education of families, enabling them to reach a higher physical, mental and spiritual sphere in life, than they would otherwise. After a well told, well pointed story, he concluded by enumerating some of the benefits to be derived by being Foresters, urging all brethren to stand together in promoting the best interests of the order. The remaining numbers of the splendid programme were a Scotch solo by Dr McDougall, who was encored; a band selection, two readings by Mr Chas Clark, of Ottawa (a returned soldier who figured in the battle of Paardeburg) and a duet by Misses Comstock and Larkin, all of which were exceedingly well rendered and were well received. The meeting closed with the National Anthem.

MR. R. H. MONTGOMERY.

An interesting but quiet affair took place on Wednesday afternoon, May 3rd, at the home of Mr. and Mrs. Peter Millar, Bideford, P. E. I., it being the occasion of the marriage of their eldest daughter, Nettie, to Austin Ramsay of Freeland, Lot 11. Rev. Mr. Murdock tied the nuptial knot. Jas. Millar, brother of the bride, attended the groom, while Miss Alice Ramsay, sister of the groom, assisted the bride. Miss Maud Hayes played the wedding march.

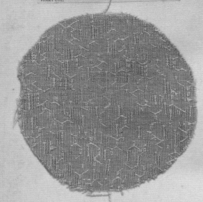

WEDDING BELLS.—On the evening of Wednesday, Dec. 13th, the residence of Mr. John F. McNeil, Cavendish, was the scene of a very pretty wedding, briefly referred to in yesterday's PATRIOT, when his niece, Miss Maggie McLeod, of Kensington, was married to Mr. Alvin Glover, of the same place. At the appointed hour the bridal party entered the parlor to the music of the wedding march played by Miss Fannie Wise, and took their stand under a beautiful arch of evergreens. The bride was simply but beautifully attired, being dressed in white sevis muslin with veil and wreath. She carried an exquisite bouquet of chrysanthemums. She was attended by her cousin, Miss Lucy McNeill, who wore navy blue serge with vest of white satin. The groom was ably supported by his brother, Mr. Robert Glover, teacher, of Carleton. The ceremony was performed by Rev. Chas. McKay, New London, assisted by Rev. Mr. McIntosh, of Cavendish. After a bountiful repast, usual on such occasions, a very enjoyable evening followed. In due time a party of chivariers arrived, and treated the assembled guests to an orderly serenade. Their costumes were particularly good. The many gifts were beautiful and useful; that of the groom to the bride may be specially mentioned—a pair of Persian lamb gloves. On the following morning the happy couple departed, amid showers of rice and old shoes, for their future home in Kensington. Their many friends cordially wish them a happy wedded life.

DECEMBER

Sun	Mon	Tue	Wed	Thu	Fri	Sat
		1	2	3	4	5
6	7	8	9	10	11	12
13	14	15	16	17	18	19
20	21	22	23	24	25	26
27	28	29	30	31		

Mr. Arthur G. Harmon,
Miss Olive DeVore Eby,
Married
Wednesday, July twenty-fifth,
nineteen hundred,
St. Joseph, Michigan.

Miss Montgomery.

December 18th
1899.

WEDDING WEDNESDAY.

The marriage of A. G. Thompson, a well known New York business man and Miss Jean Lyall, daughter of the late Professor Lyall, of Dalhousie College, took place at Miss Tremaine's residence, No. 31 Tower Road. The ceremony was a very quiet one and was performed by Prof. Falconer, assisted by Prof. Forrest. In the afternoon Mr. and Mrs. Thompson left for the United States on their wedding trip. They were recipients of very many wedding presents from friends in Halifax and New York.

Mr. Thompson is a member of the lumber dealing firm of James Thompson and Son whose business is located at Staten Island. Mr. Thompson's home is on Staten Island.

A very pretty wedding took place at the home of Mr. and Mrs. Cornelius Leard, Lower Bedeque, on Tuesday, March 26th, when their daughter, Miss Helen, was united in marriage to Mr Howard McFarlane of Sea Cow Head. The ceremony was performed by the Rev. E P Calven. The bride was becomingly dressed in a suit of pearl gray with white trimmings. After the ceremony a few of the most intimate friends partook of a repast, such as can only be prepared by women like Mrs. Leard. Their many friends join in wishing Mr and Mrs McFarlane a happy journey through life.

At 8 o'clock this evening the residence of Mr. John McLure, North Rustico, will be the scene of a happy gathering to witness the nuptials of Mr. McLure's daughter, Miss Lavinia, to Mr. John A. MacMillan, Brackley Point. Rev. G. C. Robertson will be the officiating clergyman, and about sixty couples will join in the festivities of the occasion. The groom will be supported by Mr. Chester McLure, teacher, Alexandria, and Miss Celia MacMillan, Prince Street, sister of the groom, will act as bride's maid. The costume of the bride will be tastefully trimmed cream silk, and that of the bridesmaid a pretty lavender, both carrying bouquets to match. The wedding gifts are a large and choice variety of the useful and ornamental. After spending the evening in mirthful festivities the bridal party will drive to the groom's home at Brackley Point. Mr. and Mrs. MacMillan have the best wishes of a large circle of friends and in adding congratulations THE GUARDIAN heartily joins.

Friday.
Aug. 26
1898

"Sanitas Sanitatum."

THE subjoined additional particulars of the following marriage have been received. On the evening of Wednesday, the 29th of June, the beautiful residence of Mr. Donald E. Campbell of Darlington was the scene of an exceedingly pretty wedding, when his daughter Mary was united in marriage to Mr. Archibald Beaton of O'Leary Station. At eight o'clock the wedding guests assembled on the lawn, the members of the bridal party took their stand under the arching trees and the Rev. Geo. Millar of Brookfield, assisted by Rev. Malcolm Campbell of Strathalbyn, tied the nuptial knot. The bride was attired in a dress of steel-blue lady's cloth, with trimming of pearl applique and white satin and wore the bridal veil and orange blossoms. She was attended by Miss Euphemia Beaton of O'Leary Station, who wore a pretty gown of flowered muslin, and by Miss Charlotte Campbell, who made a dear little maid of honor in dotted Swiss muslin with a bouquet of white carnations. Mr. Norman Campbell, brother of the bride, supported the groom. After the ceremony the bountiful wedding supper was served, after which the evening passed pleasantly in various amusements while the younger guests danced in the wee sma' hours. Many and beautiful presents testified to the esteem and affection of a large circle of friends. On Thursday morning the unmarried pair departed for an extended wedding tour to the principal cities of Canada and the New England States. Their many friends heartily concur in wishing Mr. and Mrs. Beaton a long, happy, and prosperous wedded life.

SHATFORD-FRASER.

Interesting Event at St. Paul's at Noon To-day.

At noon today St. Paul's Church was the scene of an extremely pretty wedding, when Miss Edna E. Shatford was married to Mr. Edwin Fraser, C. E.

The bride was charmingly gowned in white voile over white taffeta, en traine, with lace trimming and with bridal veil, and carried a shower bouquet of white roses and maidenhair fern. She walked up the aisle alone, to the music of the wedding march from "Lohengrin" and was met at the head of the church by her father, Mr. John E. Shatford, who gave her away.

The service was choral and the ceremony was performed by Rev. W. J. Armitage.

Miss Lottie Shatford was the bridesmaid and wore cream broadcloth trimmed with point d' Ireland lace, with a white picture hat and bouquet of white and yellow chrysanthemums. The groom was supported by Mr. Stonewall Jackson, of New Glasgow. Messrs. Geo. W. and Robert H. Murray and John N. Creed were the ushers.

After the ceremony the bridal party repaired to the residence of the bride's brother, Mr. J. Franklyn Shatford, at 101 Pleasant Street, where a reception was held and luncheon served to about sixty guests.

Many of the groom's old friends from New Glasgow were present, among them being Robert M. McGregor, George Fraser and Frank Macneill.

The rooms were decorated with palms and smilax and streamers of white satin ribbon. Many beautiful gifts were received, including cheques from parents and immediate relatives. The groom's gift to the bride was a pearl pendant and to the bridesmaid a necklace.

Mr. and Mrs. Fraser left on the Maritime Express for their future home in Minneapolis. They will visit several Canadian cities en route. The bride's going-away gown was of otter brown cloth, with hat to match and sable furs. Their

The marriage of Miss Edith England, daughter of Mrs Edward England, of Bideford, to Mr E Bayfield Williams, of the law firm of McKinnon & Williams, Charlottetown, took place at the home of the bride's mother this morning. The ceremony was performed by Rev W E Johnson, B A, of Elgin, N B, in the presence of the immediate relatives and friends. The bride was becomingly attired in white brocaded silk and wore a travelling suit of steel grey broadcloth. The large number of elegant presents testified to the high regard in which the young couple are held. After a wedding breakfast Mr and Mrs Williams boarded the train at Ellerslie for Summerside, and took passage by the Northumberland on a honeymoon trip to Quebec, Montreal, Ottawa and other Canadian cities. They will return about July 1st, and reside in the handsome cottage lately occupied by Mr Benj. Davies, Charlottetown. The PATRIOT joins with hosts of friends in extending congratulations.

The meeting of Cavendish Literary on last Friday evening, Miss Lucy Montgomery read a very interesting on Tennyson. In the course of the many choice selections were quoted the different poems. The paper discussed by Messrs. J. S. Clark, Walter Simpson, Geo. W. Simpson, Geo. R. McGregor, and others.

Professor William Archibald Spooner, of Oxford University, has become famous as a ludicrous word twister. Once, at a special service, seeing some women standing at the back of the church waiting to be seated, he rushed down the aisle and addressed the ushers as follows: "Gentlemen, gentlemen, sew these ladies into their sheets." Being asked at dinner what fruit he would have, he promptly replied: "Pigs, fleas." This is the way in which Dr. Spooner proposed to his wife: Being one afternoon at the home of her father, Bishop Harvey Goodwin, of Carlisle, Mrs. Goodwin said: "Mr. Spooner, will you please go out into the garden and ask Miss Goodwin if she will come in and make tea?" The professor, on finding the lady, said: "Miss Goodwin, your mother wants to ask if you would...

사진 몽고메리의 자작나무 사진 〈하얀 부인White Lady〉은 맥닐가의 사유지에서 촬영한 것으로 아래쪽 자작나무 껍질과 짝을 맞추려고 붙여둔 듯하다. 자작나무 껍질에 적힌 글귀는 이런 것들이다. "좋은 나무였던 것 같다." "숲의 군주." "유령의 숲." 이 세 글귀는 몽고메리가 아홉 살 때 이미 자작나무에 바치는 헌시에서 표현한 것인데, 시의 제목이 〈숲의 군주〉였다.

기사 "캐번디시 소식"과 "백 쇼어 소식"은 몽고메리가 쓴 것으로 보이는데, 캠벨가를 방문하려고 파크 코너에 다녀온 행로를 언급했다. 결혼식 기사는 파크 코너의 프레더리카 캠벨이 신부 들러리를 섰다고 전한다. "마음Psyche(오른쪽 위)"은 레드 스크랩북 3쪽에 실린 데이지 윌리엄스의 "밤의 눈"과 짝을 이루는 기사로, 몽고메리의 필체와 능력을 "실제 모습과 전혀 다르게 보인다"라고 해석했다. 왼쪽 아래에 억지로 밀어 넣은 짤막한 기사는 점점 많이 등장하게 될 이완 맥도널드에 관한 기사 중 첫 번째 것이다.

카드 카드 안쪽(아래 이미지)에는 몽고메리가 비밀 일기에도 썼듯이 노라 리퍼지와 함께 눈 내리는 일요일에 외출했던 일을 기록했다. 저녁 예배를 마친 뒤 제리 클라크가 (자기 말 '올리브'를 몰고서) 노라를 집까지 태워다주겠다고 해서 몽고메리는 프레디 클라크와 함께 가게 됐다. "비열한 속임수"란 제리가 먼젓번 외출에서 노라를 두고 가버린 적이 있어서 그날 밤 잘못을 만회하기 위해 데려다주겠다고 했다는 것을 가리킨다.

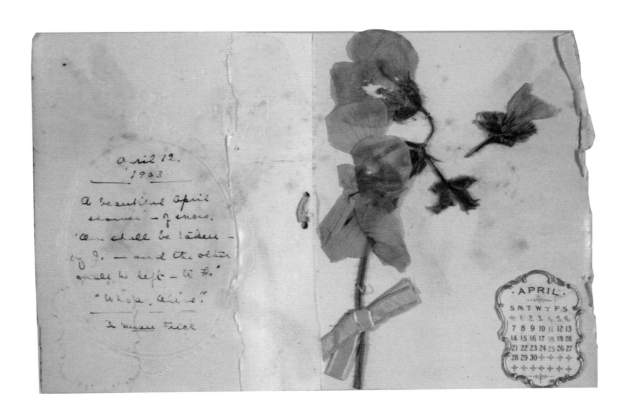

CAVENDISH NOTES.— The season for self-binders to begin their hum, is at hand. Quite a quantity of oats and wheat has succumbed to the sickle, the former crop is very much broken down, but the wheat crop shows quite a lot of rust and weevil, despite all the fine, pure wheat which was sown last spring. —Cavendish is becoming a place of great attractions, particularly in regard to pleasure seekers.—A tea of grand success was held early in July, and picnics galore since then.—The old Presbyterian church, purchased by Geo. Bowness, of Stanley, is now a dilapitated mass of lumber.—The new society at their last meeting succeeded in securing a suitable site for the new church, and hope to see before long a very fine edifice.—Our school is rapidly regaining its former reputation, under the careful, skilful and energetic management of Miss Nellie McNeill.—We are pleased to see Mr. James A. Stewart home again. He has been absent for twelve years in the West and gives our young men great encouragements to go West.—Mrs. C. F. Simpson returned home from Nova Scotia, where she has been visiting her relatives. She was absent two weeks.—Mr. C. W. Jackson accompanied by his mother and sister left last week for their future home in Connecticut. We wish Mr. Jackson every success in his studies. —Miss Lucy Maud Montgomery is visiting friends at Park Corner. She is the guest of Mr. and Mrs. John Campbell.

BACK SHORE NOTES.—The managers of the several factories along the shore are :—Pineo Bros., McLeod & Rattray, LePage & Peters, Thomas Doyle, Moses Gallant, David Marks, James and Albert Graham. Report has it that some of the cleverest of those managers have secured their fishing ground already, by putting out their back lines. —Milk tendering for the drawing to the Stanley Bridge Cheese Factory seems the order of the day, between the farmers. Judging from the number of tenders sent in, the work will be performed at a cheap rate.—Mr. Thomas Doyle, Rustico, has recently disposed of his handsome gelding, Black Sporter, for a handsome sum. We understand Mr. H. S. McLure, teacher at Hope River, was the purchaser. This gelding is sired by the celebrated trotting stallion Bronze Chief, dam Hernando, granddam Morgan. Although young this colt has the breed and actions for being very speedy.—Miss Bertha McKenzie, of Cavendish, who spent the winter at Brackley Point, returned home a few days ago.—The industrious ladies of the C. T. Society still continue to meet at the home of one of the members on Wednesday afternoon of each week the Presbyterian congregations of Rustico, Cavendish and Stanley will miss with regret the aid of their pastor, Rev. G. C. Robertson, who has accepted the call to Bonshaw and adjoining sections. We wish him and his partner in life every success in their new field of labor.—We regret to learn that Miss Katie McPhail has not completely recovered from her sickness of quinsy, but under the careful treatment of Dr. Houston, of New Glasgow, we hope to see her around in a short time.—Cavendish school is greatly progressing under Mr. E Brown's guidance.— COM.

Rev. Mr. McDonald who preached in St. Andrew's congregation on Sunday, made a good impression. He has a fine strong face and his sermons were strong and well reasoned. He preaches again to-morrow.

CAVENDISH NOTES.—Last week's storm of wind and rain did quite a lot of damage to the grain crops, the greater part of that which was standing is now almost totally ruined.—Mr. Chas. E. MacKenzie of South Granville spent Sunday at his home at Cavendish.—Miss L. M. Montgomery is home again after her week's visit to Park Corner.—We feel sorry for your correspondent of 7 h inst and he must certainly be in the ages of man viz dotage when he calls the Presbyterian church a "New Society" perhaps we have a modern Methuselah amongst us when he likens the Presbyterian Church established early in the sixteenth century unto a "new society."—Milk is decreasing at present but the output from Cavendish for this season far exceeds that of any previous year. Cavendish supplies over 6 000 lbs milk daily to Stanley cheese factory more than double the quantity sent three years ago.—Mrs. Seth MacKenzie of Lowell, Mass., who has been visiting her former home here left for home on 8th inst, she was accompanied by Miss Annie McLure who goes for a two months visit to friends in Lowell, Chelsea, Wakefield, etc.— Miss Lucy MacNeill left on 9th for St. John N. B. to attend the exhibition.—It is understood that the mass meeting of the C. G. Club spoken of a few weeks ago has been postponed until after harvest.—The fishermen are slowly gathering their scanty harvest from the sea: very few mackerel have been taken on the North side this year and owing to the scarcity of bait very few cod or hake have been caught and but for the lobster catch which was about the average our fishermen would fare slimly enough. This fact brings vividly to our minds the lines of the poet.

"Companions of the sea and silent air
The lonely fisher thus must ever fare
Without the comfort, hope, with scarce
      a friend
He looks through life and only sees
        its end."

An interesting event took place at the home of Mrs Jeremiah Smith, Orwell, on Wednesday afternoon, Aug 22, when her daughter, Bessie, was united in marriage to Charles H Robertson, of Marshfield. The ceremony was performed by Rev Robt Sinclair assisted by Rev D B MacLeod. The bride, beautifully gowned and carrying a handsome bouquet, entered the room on the arm of her uncle, Mr D McLeod. She was attended by Miss Frederica Campbell Park Corner, and the groom was supported by his cousin N Bannerman Robertson. The ceremony being over, a dainty supper was served, after which the bridal party drove away in the midst of showers of rice to the home of the groom in Marshfield where a reception was held and a very pleasant evening spent. The valuable wedding gifts attested the good will and esteem in which the contracting parties are held by their friends.

"HERBIE, it says here that another octogenarian's dead. What's an octogenarian?"

"Well, I don't quite know what they are, but they must be very sickly creatures. You never hear of them but they're dying."

Psyche—You are of a rather domineering disposition, but knowing how to master yourself just as well as others, are very controlled. You are very fond of elegance and luxury, of aristocratic manners, etc. You know how to suppress and hide your internal thoughts and feelings to such an extent as to appear utterly different from what you really are. You can be extremely amiable, affable and obliging, especially in society. You have a will of your own. You like comfort and ease. You are very economical, very politic and diplomatic, suspicious and distrustful. I could tell you a great many more things from your interesting handwriting.

THOUGHTS OF YOU

시 〈돌이 된 고사리The Petrified Fern〉의 기묘한 아쉬움과 〈꿈꾸는 사람들Dreamers of Dreams〉의 슬픔은 미국 민요 〈케이티 리와 윌리 그레이Katie Lee and Willie Gray〉와 재미 있는 글들로 상쇄된다.

자작나무 이것도 몽고메리가 노라와 외출했을 때를 기념하여 간직한 듯하다. 날짜는 1902년 11월 6일이고, 제목은 "각자 할 일To each man his work"이다. 이날 두 사람은 샘 맥두걸Sam MacDougall의 부흥회에 함께 참석했던 것 같다. 샘 맥두걸은 자기 배경이 탄로 난 뒤에 큰 물의를 일으킨 인물이었다. 몽고메리는 그 사건을 1902년 11월 30일 일기에 상세히 기록했다.

> 11월은 정말 흥미진진한 달이었다. 11월 초에 침례교회는 일련의 부흥회를 시작했다. 교회는 '전도사'를 초빙하여 맥두걸이라고 소개했는데 세례명은 샘이었다.

정말이지 맥두걸은 달콤했다! 그는 잘생겼고, 머릿속에 그의 모습이라도 떠오르면…… 검은 눈동자에 마음이 녹아버릴 것 같았다. 열다섯 살 아이들도 그 눈앞에서는 볼링 핀처럼 쓰러졌다. 그가 탄성을 지르면 가슴이 터질 것 같았다! 찬송 소리도 감미로웠다! 그것을 제외하면 그는 교양이 없고, 선정적이며, 너무 저속해서 내 영혼을 불편하게 했다. 하지만 나는 갔다. 맙소사, 그랬다. 부흥회는 참으로 재미있었다. 부득이 가지 못하는 날이면 너무 아쉬웠다!

그렇게 삼 주가량 흘렀다. 그러다 탄로가 난 것이다. 캐번디시에서 그런 충격적 사건이 일어난 것은 근 십 년 사이에 처음이었다. 샘 목사는 알고 보니 가짜 목사였다. 하지만 그것뿐이라면 참을 만했을 터였다. 그는 장로교인이었다. 어쨌든 자기 입으로는 장로교인이라고 분명히 말했다. 침례교인들은 공포로 피가 얼어붙는 것 같았다. 불쌍한 샘은 교회에서 매몰차게 쫓겨났고, 마을에는 따분한 평화가 다시금 찾아왔다.

KATIE LEE AND WILLIE GRAY.

—A good many years ago a little song popular, which sung the affection of a boy for a small girl. He offers to her basket but she will only let him carry half, and it is the same in later years when he offers to carry life's burdens for her. Their names were Katie Lee and Willie Gray. Ans.—The following verses are probably what you are in search of. We do not know who was the author.

Two brown heads, with tossing curls,
Red lips shutting over pearls,
Bare feet white and red with dew,
Two eyes black and two eyes blue—
Little boy and girl were they,
Katie Lee and Willie Gray.

They were standing where a brook,
Bending like a shepherd's crook,
Flashed its silver, and thick ranks
Of green willows fringed the banks;
Half in thought and half in play
Katie Lee and Willie Gray.

They had cheeks like cherries red;
He was taller—'most a head;
She, with arms like wreaths of snow,
Swings a basket to and fro,
As she loiters, half in play,
Chatting there with Willie Gray.

'Pretty Katie,' Willie said,
And there came a dash of red
Through the brownness of his cheek,
'Boys are strong and girls are weak,
And I'll carry, so I will,
Katie's basket up the hill.'

Katie answered with a laugh:
'You shall only carry half.'
And then, tossing back her curls,
'Boys are weak as well as girls.
Do you think that Katie guessed
Half the wisdom she expressed?

Men are only boys grown tall;
Hearts don't change much, after all;
And when, long years from that day,
Katie Lee and Willie Gray
Stood again beside the brook,
Bending like a shepherd's crook,

Is it strange that Willie said,
While again a dash of red
Crossed the brownness of his cheek:
'I am strong, and you are weak,
Life is but a slippery steep,
Hung with shadows, cold and deep.

'Will you trust me, Katie dear,
Walk beside me without fear?
May I carry—and I will—
All your burdens up the hill?'
And she answered with a laugh,
'No—but you may carry half.'

Close beside the little brook,
Bending like a shepherd's crook,
Washing with its silver hands,
Late and early at the sands,
Is a cottage where, to-day,
Katie lives with Willie Gray.

In the porch she sits, and lo!
Swings a basket to and fro—
Vastly different from the one
That she swung in years agone;
This is long, and deep, and wide,
And—has rockers at the side.

DREAMERS OF DREAMS.

We are all of us dreamers of dreams;
On visions our childhood is fed;
And the heart of the child is unhaunted, it seems,
By the ghosts of dreams that are dead.

From childhood to youth's but a span,
And the years of our youth are soon sped;
Yet the youth is no longer a youth, but a man,
When the first of his dreams is dead.

There's no sadder sight this side the grave
Than the shroud o'er a fond dream spread.
And the heart should be stern and the eyes be brave
To gaze on a dream that is dead.

'Tis as a cup of wormwood and gall
When the doom of a great dream is said,
And the best of a man is under the pall
When the best of his dreams is dead.

He may live on by compact and plan
When the fine bloom of living is shed,
But God pity the little that's left of a man
When the last of his dreams is dead.

Let him show a brave face if he can,
Let him woo fame or fortune instead,
Yet there's not much to do but bury a man
When the last of his dreams is dead.
            —William Herbert Carruth.

The Petrified Fern.

In a valley, centuries ago,
    Grew a little fern leaf, green and slender,
    Veining delicate and fibres tender,
Waving, when the wind crept down so low;
    Rushes tall and moss and grass grew round it,
    Playful sunbeams darted in and found it,
    Drops of dew stole in by night and crowned it,
But no foot of man e'er trod that way—
Earth was young and keeping holiday;

Monster fishes swam the silent main,
    Stately forests waved their giant branches,
    Mountains hurled their snowy avalanches,
Mammoth creatures stalked across the plain;
    Nature reveled in grand mysteries,
    But the little fern was not of these,
    Did not number with the hills and trees;
Only grew and waved, its sweet wild way—
No one came to note it day by day.

Earth one time put on a frolic mood,
    Heaved the rocks and changed the mighty motion
    Of the deep, strong currents of the the ocean;
Moved the plain and shook the haughty wood,
    Crushed the little fern in soft, moist clay,
    Covered it and hid it safe away;
Oh! the long, long centuries since that day!
Oh! the agony! Oh! life's bitter cost,
Since that useless little fern was lost!

Useless? Lost? There came a thoughtful man,
    Searching nature's secrets, far and deep;
From a fissure in a rocky steep
He withdrew a stone, o'er which there ran
    Fairy pencilings, a quaint design,
    Veinings, leafage, fibres clear and fine,
    And the fern's life lay in every line!
So, I think, God hides some souls away,
Sweetly to surprise us the last day.
            —By Mary Lydia Bolles Branch.

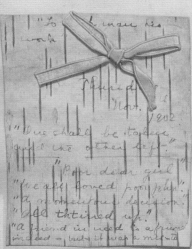

"Who-o?"   "You!"

SHE FELT BAD WHEN WELL.

An old lady in Gloucester was always ailing and "enjoying poor " as she expressed it. Her various ailments were to her the most interesting topic in the world, and she must have thought them most interesting to others, also, for she always talked of them. One day a neighbor found her eating a hearty meal, and asked her how she was. She sighed and answered:

"I feel very well, ma'am, but I always feel bad when I feel well because I know I am going to feel worse

After the rector had announced that the new hymn books were ready, the curate announced the time for the baptism of infants. The rector, being deaf, followed immediately with the surprising statement: "They can be had at the rectory for sixpence each; with stiff backs for one shilling."

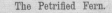

봉투와 기사, 그리고 프로그램 1901년 3월 4일, 몽고메리는 미공개 일기에 다음과 같은 기록을 남겼다.

편지 두 통은 꽤 좋았다. 하나는 앨프리드 메이슨Alfred Mason이라는 사람이 보낸 것이었다. 그는 매사추세츠 피츠필드의 오르간 연주자 같은데, 내 시 〈덧신 한 켤레 A Pair of Slippers〉가 마음에 든다면서 내가 허락해주면 자신이 만든 곡을 붙여 노래로 발표하고 싶다고 말했다. 희한하게도 나머지 한 통 역시 비슷한 편지였다. 보스턴에 사는 채드킨스Chadkins 양이 보낸 편지는 〈낚싯배가 들어올 때When the Fishing Boats Come In〉라는 시에 곡을 붙이고 싶다는 내용이었다. 물론 나는 정말 기쁘고 기분이 좋다.

비슷한 요청은 지금도 몽고메리의 상속자들에게 이어지고 있다.

사진 롭슨 산의 이미지가 다른 뭔가를 대신해 그 자리에 붙어 있고(1930년 즈음, 몽고메리가 서스캐처원으로 가는 길에 캐나다국립철도 사진들을 수집할 때의 기록일 것이다), 이 페이지의 아랫단을 따라 찢어진 흔적으로 보아 교체한 자료가 또 있는 듯하다.

113 South St
Pittsfield
Mass
Feb 16/01

Miss Montgomery

I have taken a great fancy to your poem "A pair of Slippers"

Alfred. T. Mason

A pair of slippers worn, you know,
By grandmamma in the long ago;
Fashioned from satin of ivory hue,
Just the size of a fairy's shoe,
Silver buckles, rosettes and all,
Worn for the first at her birthnight ball.

Somebody thought her sweet and fair,
Somebody praised her golden hair.
Straight into somebody's heart danced she
While the violins tinkled so merrily.
In her dainty slippers and gown of white
Grandpapa found his bride that night.

Long are the years that have passed away,
But hearts of love keep their youth for aye.
Grandmamma's golden hair is white,
But her smile is as sweet as it was the night
She danced, the queen of the maidens all,
With grandpapa at her birthnight ball.

L. M. Montgomery

Mrs L. M. Montgomery

Cavendish

Prince Edwards Island

RECENT MUSICAL EVENTS

IN PITTSFIELD.

MUSICAL CLUB.

The thirty-fourth concert of the Musical Club was given and the last meeting of the season held, at Mrs. J. D. Colt's residence Monday evening. It was well attended and proved a most enjoyable concert. The star of the evening was Mr. Leo Liebermann, of New York City. He was in good voice, and if he had been willing it is probable he would be singing there yet, as his encores were—well, he had to encore everything. Perhaps the response to the song by our own composer was as hearty as any to which he and singer bowed their acknowledgements together. Mr. Liebermann is an artist, one of those big chested tenor robustos that carry you along with them in their crescendos to such an extent you are musically mesmerised, and when he has finished ordinary talking seems gibberish. Mr. Escher did some very clever work with his violin, especially in the softer parts of his numbers. He was ably assisted by Mrs. Stevenson and Miss Bissell. Mr. Mason played all of Mr. Liebermann's accompaniments and evidently is a great favorite with the Musical Club for he is always there. Appended is the program.

Suite for Piano and Organ.
                   Op. 11 Goldmash
  Allegro,
  Andante sostenuto,
  Allegretto Moderato.
  Mrs W. C. Stevenson and Mr. Escher.
Whether we die, or we live,
             Frances Allitsen
     Mr Francis.
Aria.—La Gioconda,   Ponchielli.
     Mr. Liebermann.
a. Herbstlied.   O. Well.
b. Fruhlingslied.
     Violin obl'gato.
  Mr Liebermann and Mr. Escher.
a. I Cannot help loving thee,
           Clayton Johns.
b. A Resolve,   H. de Fontenailles.
     Mr. Francis.
Rondo Capr ccioso,   Saint Saens.
    Piano and Violin.
  Miss M. A. Bissell and Mr Escher
a. I wait for thee,   C. B. Hawley
b. A pair of slippers,   A. T. Mason
c. O come with me, F. Vanden Stucken
     Mr. Liebermann.

It is with regret that the PATRIOT s called upon to chronicle the death of Marie V. Munroe, aged 26, wife of Mr. Fred Compton, St. Eleanors. The sad event took place on Sunday, June 30th. Mrs. Compton had been ill for some time and death was not unexpected. The deceased formerly taught school in Prince County and was a very popular young lady. The funeral which took place yesterday was largely attended.

the pa
s which h been
hose mon s h
I will
nd, Sir
be t
iti

Thirty-Fourth Concert

of the

Musical Club

Entertained by Mrs. James D. Colt,

Monday, March Fourth,

1901

Pittsfield   Massachusetts

Mr. Leo Liebermann
Tenor

Mr. Carl Escher
Violin

Mr. Alfred T. Mason
Accompanist

Mamma—If you eat any more of that pudding, Tommy, you will see the bogie man to-night.
Tommy (after a moment's thought) —Well, give me some more. I might as well settle my mind about the truth of the story once for all.

다음 두 페이지에 담긴 즉 흥성, 재미, 향수가 하나로 생생하게 되살아난 것은 루시 모드 몽고메리가 앤을 상상했을 때였다. 몽고메리의 선생님이었던 해티 고든은 앤이 좋아한 스테이시 선생님으로 재현됐다. 노라와 벌인 모험 같은 장난들도 기억 속에 그대로였고 여전히 대담했다.

여기에는 십 대 시절을 추억할 자료들을 보관한 반면, 레드 스크랩북 19쪽에는 노라와 함께 비밀 일기에 채운 일화들을 기록했다. 1903년 4월 12일, 몽고메리는 전혀 다른 태도로 쓴 자신의 일기에서 비밀 일기에 대해 찬탄했다. "모르는 사람이 그 일기를 읽는다면 덤벙거리는 여자애 둘이서 경솔한 십 대답게 쓴 글이라고 생각할 것이다."

사진 달력 위에 붙인 캐번디시 학교 사진은 몽고메리가 찍은 것이다.

기사 해티 고든이 두 기사에 등장한다. "캐번디시 학교(왼쪽)"는 1889~1890년 사이의 기사인데 당시에 몽고메리는 아직 고든 선생님 밑에서 배우던 학생이었다. "캐번디시 학교 학예회"는 1891년 크리스마스 발표회 이야기를 전한다. 이때 몽고메리는 서부 본토에 나가 아버지, 새어머니와 함께 살다가 일 년 만에 캐번디시로 돌아와서 옛 선생님을 도와 학교를 꾸미고 프로그램에 참여하기로 했다. 기사들을 간직하는 향수에 대해 말하는 것처럼 몽고메리는 감성적인 시 〈이십 년 전에Twenty Years Ago〉를 같이 실었고, 학생 시절에 나누었던 "짧은 이야기"에 관한 재담을 다람쥐 꼬리털 아래에 조심스레 배치했다.

The summer's flower is to the summer sweet, Though to itself it only live and die.

Hourly joys be still upon you!

Tempest

RAPHAEL TUCK & SONS, LONDON, PARIS
COPYRIGHT

Cavendish School.

The regular half-yearly examination of Cavendish school, was held on Friday 27th ult., in the presence of the trustees and parents of the children. Classes were examined in Reading, English Grammar and Analysis, English History, Geography, Arithmetic and Geometry. The examination extended over three hours and was very thorough and minute in the different branches. The pupils showed good progress and creditable proficiency in all the subjects upon which they were examined. The state of the school reflects great credit upon the painstaking and popular teacher, Miss H. L. Gordon. The trustees are to be congratulated upon securing her services for another year.

On the evening of the 30th ult., the scholars of the above school, gave an entertainment in Cavendish Hall, according to the following programme:
Opening Speech—Master John Laird.
Welcome Song—Choir.
Recitation—"Aunt Keziah," Miss Mamie Simpson.
Recitation—"Brave Atta Wayne," Miss Maggie Clark.
Reading—"Burdock's Music Box," Master Nell Simpson.
Instrumental music—"Swedish Wedding March," Miss Maud Montgomery.
Dialogue—"Rival Orators," N J Lockhart and Chesley Clark.
Recitation—"The Arsenal at Springfield," Master John Laird.
Reading Speech—'Buckwood's Wedding,' Miss Maud Montgomery, Master Garfield Stewart.
Music—'Music Everywhere,' Choir.
Recitation—'Little Christel,' Miss Artie McNeill.
Reading—'If I were a Girl,' Master Archie McNeill.
Recitation—'The Last Hymn,' Miss Clara McKenzie.
Instrumental Music—'Medley,' Miss Maud Montgomery.
Recitation—'Neddie's Thanksgiving Visit,' Master Garfield Stewart.
Dialogue, Society for Suppression of Gossip—'Eight Girls.
Recitation—'How to Lighten Troubles,' Miss Lottie Simpson.
Music—'Life is what we Make it,' Choir.
Reading—Miss Witchhazel and Mr. Thistlepod,' Master Chesley Clark.
Speech—Master Frank McNeill.
Recitation—'Katie's Letter,' Charles McKenzie.
Recitation—'A peck of Troubles,' Miss Edith Spurr.
Recitation—'The best Beauty,' Miss Helen Archibald.
Solo—'The Cows are in the Corn,' Miss Maggie Clark.
Recitation—'The Old Farmer's Legacy,' Miss Annie Stewart.
Reading—'The Magic Lantern,' Master Austin Laird.
Recitation—'The Boy's Complaint,' Fred Clark.
Music—'Social Song,' Two Girls and a Boy.
Recitation—'Over the hills to the Poor House,' Miss Maud Montgomery.
Dialogue—'The Census Taker,' Three [ ] Two Boys.
[ ]tion—'Eddie's Treasures,' Miss [ ]ird.
[ ]—'Hiawatha's Departure,' N [ ]
[ ]mental Music—'Battle of Waterloo [ ]s Emma Simpson.
[ ]tion—'The Scholmaster's Guests' [ ]ontgomery.
[ ]tion—'Ship on Fire,' School.
[ ]—'Along the River,' Choir.
[ ]g Speech,—Miss Mamie Simp[ ]

[ ] bye Song—Choir.
[ ]bove lengthy and varied pro[ ] was rendered with great spirit [ ] the scholars. All, from [ ]st to the oldest acquitted [ ] the satisfaction and delight [ ] At the close, compli-

J. C. Spurr, Mr. Walter Simpson and the chairman of the evening, Rev. Wm. P. Archibald. On motion, a vote of thanks to the teacher and scholars, for the excellent entertainment which they had given, was passed unanimously. The unanimous verdict of the audience was that a more enjoyable evening had not been spent for a long time.

Twenty Years Ago.

(Published by request.)

I've wandered to the village, Tom, I've sat beneath the tree,
Upon the schoolhouse playing ground, that sheltered you and me;
But none were left to greet me, Tom, and few were left to know,
Who played with us upon the green, some twenty years ago.

The grass is just as green, Tom; barefooted boys at play
Were sporting just as we did then, with spirits just as gay.
But the "master" sleeps upon the hill, which, coated o'er with snow,
Affording us a sliding-place, some twenty years ago.

The old school house is altered now; the benches are replaced
By new ones, very like the same our penknives once defaced;
But the same old bricks are in the wall, the bell swings to and fro;
It's music just the same, dear Tom, 'twas twenty years ago.

The river's running just as still; the willows on its side
Are larger than they were, Tom; the stream appears less wide;
But the grape-vine swing is ruined now, where once we played the beau,
And swung our sweethearts—pretty girls —just twenty years ago.

The spring that bubbled 'neath the hill, close by the spreading beech,
Is very low—'twas then so high that we could scarcely reach;
And, kneeling down to get a drink, dear Tom, I started so,
To see how sadly I am changed, since twenty years ago.

Near by that spring, upon an elm, you know I cut your name,
Your sweetheart's just beneath it, Tom, and you did mine the same;
Some heartless wretch has peeled the bark, 'twas dying sure; but slow,
Just as she died, whose name you cut, some twenty years ago.

My lids have long been dry, Tom, but tears came to my eyes,
I thought of her I loved so well, those early broken ties;
I visited the old church-yard, and took some flowers to strow
Upon the graves of those we loved, some twenty years ago.

Some are in the church-yard laid, some sleep beneath the sea,
But few are left of our old class, excepting you and me;
And when our time shall come, Tom, and we are called to go,
I hope they'll lay us where we played, just twenty years ago.

—Anonymous

"What is an anecdote, Johnny?" asked the teacher. "A short, funny tale," answered the little fellow. "That's right," said the teacher. "Now, Johnny, you may write a sentence on the blackboard containing the word." Johnny hesitated a moment, and then wrote this: "A rabbit has four legs and one anecdote."—
Exchange.

Entertainment at Cavendish School.

The pupils of the Cavendish School gave an entertainment consisting of music, vocal and instrumental, dialogues and recitations, on the 22d inst., in the Cavendish Hall. The hall was very tastefully decorated for the occasion with evergreen mottoes such as 'We Delight in Our School,' 'Welcome To All,' 'A Merry Christmas.' The pupils, with their teacher, Miss H. L. Gordon, were seated on the platform and all, from the younger to the eldest, had some part to play in the programme. Mrs. L. M. Montgomery, a former scholar, rendered valuable assistance. A large and appreciative audience greeted the children and followed the programme with evident pleasure. The rendering of the programme was carried out with great spirit; all the youthful performers acquitted themselves in a most creditable manner. The teacher deserves much praise for the time and trouble taken by her in preparing the school for this most successful entertainment. Rev W. P. Archibald occupied the chair. At the close a vote of thanks was moved in appropriate terms by the Rev. J. C. Spurr, which being seconded by Mr. Charles Simpson, was carried unanimously. The proceeds of the evening amounted to $15.

PROGRAMME:

Opening Speech..........Master Chesley Clark
Opening Song—Chorus
Rec—A Grievous Complaint.......Freddie Clark
Rec—Little Kitty..........Miss Lottie Simpson
Rec—Daisy's story........Miss Katie McNeill
Music—Inst..........Miss Maud Montgomery
Rec—The Independent Farmer, Austin Laird
Rec—Mrs Mary Jane....Miss Lyla Archibald
Rec—Willie's Breeches......Master Garfield Stewart
Reading Brown's Good Boy......Fresco [ ]
[ ]Mo[ ]

학교 프로그램 기사를 1891년부터 계속 오려내서 보스턴 코미디 프로그램 안에 붙여 넣고, 거기에 노라와 함께하던 시절의 기억들까지 덧붙여 루시 모드 몽고메리는 과거와 현재를 직접 대면시킨다. 노란 띠와 눈 내리는 풍경 속 여인의 청사진, 빅토리아 시대의 동전, 밀짚으로 묶은 나비매듭 모두 몽고메리와 노라가 함께 쓴 비밀 일기 속 추억의 물건들이다.

노란 띠 이 이야기는 한동안 비밀 일기에 계속 이어졌다. 며칠 동안 몽고메리는 노라가 이 띠를 훔쳐 갔다고, 심지어 먹어치웠다고 못 살게 굴었지만, 띠는 결국 두 사람이 함께 쓰는 침실에서 발견됐다. 그 뒤로 비밀 일기는 기념품 슬쩍하기 경쟁과 "영혼이 풍부한" 제임스 스튜어트의 관심을 차지하려는 줄다리기에 집중됐다. 몽고메리는 친구 사이의 장난들을 여기에 익살스러운 차례로 표현하고 문제의 띠와 함께 카드로 보관했다.

청사진 몽고메리는 이 이미지를 비밀 일기에 "뭔가 불가사의한 것"이라고 언급했다. 몽고메리는 응접실에 있던 남자들을 찍었는데, 감광판을 현상하고 나니 노라가 눈을 맞으며 서 있는 사진이 나왔다고 말했다.

동전 이 동전은 몽고메리가 비밀 일기에 "옆방에 몰래 들어가 빅토리아 여왕을 훔쳤다"라고 적은 내용과 관계있는 듯하다. 한 면에는 빅토리아 여왕의 초상이 새겨져 있고 다른 면에는 "뉴브런즈윅"이라고 새겨진 이 1센트짜리 동전은 캐나다 연방정부가 1873년에서 1901년 사이에 발행한 주화일 것이다.

카드 2월 20일, 몽고메리와 노라는 알렉 맥닐의 집에서 열린 무도회에 참석했다. 무도회는 다음 날 새벽 5시까지 이어졌다. 그곳에 있는 동안 몽고메리와 노라는 제임스와 조 스튜어트를 두고 관심 끌기 경쟁에 나섰다.

밀짚 나비매듭 1월 25일 밤, 노라가 아팠고(노란 띠를 삼켜서 그런 듯했다), 노라의 친구인 심프슨 박사와 허니웰 Honeywell 박사가 도왔지만, 몽고메리의 노란 띠를 도로 꺼내줄 수도 없어서 이 밀짚으로 만든 나비 모양의 매듭밖에 대신 줄 게 없었다.

Dialogue—Women's School of Philosophy
...............................Five Girls
Music—Don't Talk (Chorus)
Rec—The Reason .... Master Frank McNeil
Reading—Zephaniah Kreklel .. Chesley Clark
Rec—A Naughty Boy's Lesson .... Miss Edie
    Spurr.
Rec—The Roll Call .... Master Neil Simpson
Solo—My Childhood's Home ...... Miss Mamie
    Simpson.
Rec—When I'm a Man .... Six Boys
Rec—Out of the Old House ...... Miss Maud
    Montgomery.
Speech .... Master Miller Clark
Rec—A Modern Romance. Miss Annie Stuart
Music (Instrumental) .. Miss Emma Simpson
Rec—Entertaining Her Big Sister's Beau....
    Miss Helen Archibald
Dialogue—The Morning Call .... Two Girls
Rec—Rejected .... Miss Ethel Toombs
Rec—A Queer Boy .... Lyle Archibald
Music—Whistling Song .... Chorus
Rec—Mutual Confidences ....
    Miss Nellie McNeill
Rec—A Silly Mouse .... Master W Simpson
Rec—What Women Talk about ....
    Miss Lucy McNeill
Rec Satisfied .... Master Autua Laird
Music Dearest spot of earth to me .. Chorus
Rec When Santa Claus Comes......
    Miss Ellice Laird.
Rec—The Other Side .. Miss Clara McKenzie
Rec—What a Boy Can Do .. Master F Clark
Recitation—Stretch it a Little..........
    Miss Maggie Clark.
Solo—Homeless To-night ...... Miss M Clark
Rec—The Deacon's Confession ....
    Master Chesley Clark.
Rec A Very Bad Case .... Miss Myrtle Laird
Dialogue, Country School........ The School
Music, (Instrumental) .. Miss M Montgomery
Rec Company's Coming, Master F McNeill
Rec, When we were Girls ....
    Miss Emma Simpson.
Rec, Mrs March's Boarders . M Montgomery
Rec, A Fellow's Mother. Master J Simpson
Rec, Hoeing and Praying .... Artle McNeill
Music, Parting Song .... Chorus
Closing Speech.... Miss Mamie Simpson

1903.

Lost, Stolen, or Strayed.

Chap I. A mysterious disappearance.

Chap II. A disconsolate girl.

Chap III. A long-suffering joke

Chap IV. The Lost is found

Friday. Feb. 20
    1903

Last dance before Lent.

A cosy corner on the stairs.

The moon is in its last quarter
at five o'clock in the morning.

OPERA HOUSE

TO-NIGHT

Boston
Comedy Co.

H. PRICE WEBBER, Manager.

The performance will consist of the great
society drama entitled

EAST LYNNE

Or, The Elopement

LADY ISABEL } MADAME VINE }	EDWINA GREY
Archibald Carlyle	George B. Bates
Sir Francis Levison	C. F. Whitman
Lord Mount Severn	B. F. Loring
Richard Hare	H. Andrew McKnight
Mr. Dill	W. H. Bedell
Joyce	Eula Whitman
Barbara Hare	Adelaide Roberts
Miss Cornelia Carlyle	H. Price Webber

Change of Programme Nightly

MURLEY & GARNHUM, Steam Printers, Charlottetown

Jan. 25?
    1903

"A K(night-) of
the Garter.

This is all tis
M. Jbs. could discover

20~21쪽 몽고메리는 핼리팩스에서 경험한 두 가지 일을 하나로 묶었다. 하나는 달하우지 대학생으로 핼리팩스 여학교에서 생활하던 시절(1894-1895)이고, 다른 하나는 신문기자로서 《데일리 에코》에서 일하던 시절(1901-1902)이다.

잡지의 흑백사진들은 핼리팩스 여학교의 외관과 일부 실내의 모습이다. 핼리팩스 호텔의 크리스마스 메뉴에는 빙어 튀김, 크리스마스 쇠고기 등심, "비네그레트소스를 곁들인 송아지 머리 고기" 같은 별미 음식들이 눈에 띄는데, 여기에 보관한 것은 버사 클라크와의 식사를 기념하는 의미일 것이다. 버사 클라크는 몽고메리가 학생일 때 핼리팩스 여학교의 기숙사 사감이었고, 나중에는 핼리팩스 호텔의 객실 책임자가 되었다. 몽고메리는 고향이 그리울 때마다 버사를 찾아가서 맛있는 저녁을 먹으며 즐거운 시간을 보내곤 했다.

시 〈부활절의 가르침An Easter Lesson〉뿐만 아니라 〈새로운 백 년을 맞으며A Century Greeting〉의 작가이기도 한 이디스 M. 러셀은 《데일리 에코》에서 함께 일한 동료였다. J. M. 백스터J. M. Baxter는 몽고메리가 《데일리 에코》에서 사무실을 같이 쓴 그 백스터인 듯하다.

바스러져 나간 듯한 잎사귀에는 검은색 잉크로 "달하우지 대학교 1901년"이라는 글자가 적혀 있다. 몽고메리는 신문사에서 일할 때 달하우지 대학 행사를 취재하러 나왔다.

몽고메리는 신문사에서 "르봉 마르셰Le Bon Marché"와 관련한 기사를 배정받았다고 신나서 일기에 적었다. 몽고메리가 르봉 마르셰에서 판매하는 상품들에 대한 논평을 기사로 써서 《데일리 에코》에 싣게 됐다고 말하자 르봉 마르셰 사장은 몽고메리에게 논평 기사를 잘 써주면 새로 나온 산책용 모자를 선물하겠다고 약속했다. 몽고메리는 그 말을 농담이라고 여겼지만, 사장이 상당히 호의적인 기사에 새 모자로 답하자 아주 기뻐했다. 깃털이 달린 최신 유행 스타일로 앞뒤를 선보이는

사진 속 모자가 최고급 상점에서 보낸 것과 같은 모자였는지도 모른다.

몽고메리의 청사진 속 사람들은 스텔라 캠벨과 오랜 시간 스텔라를 쫓아다닌 라이프 호와트Life Howatt(스텔라와 결혼은 하지 않았다)이다. 커다란 꽃 장식 모자를 쓴 스텔라의 청사진 아래에는 1896년 스탠리 브리지에서 열린 파티에서 가져온 작은 꽃묶음이 있다. 이해에 몽고메리는 달하우지에서 공부를 마친 후 프린스에드워드섬의 벨몬트에서 두 번째 (그리고 행복하지 못했던) 교직 생활을 준비하고 있었다.

23쪽 가까운 베이뷰밀스 농장의 고요한 흑백사진이 캐번디시 해안을 담은 몽고메리의 청사진과 뚜렷한 대조를 이룬다. 몽고메리의 두 친구, 에밀리 몽고메리와 틸리 매켄지Tillie McKenzie가 해안가의 거친 바위에 조용히 앉아서 여유를 즐기는 모습이다. 개봉된 봉투와 "자세한 내용은 안쪽에"라고 적힌 카드는 몽고메리와 노라의 장난과 관련 있다. 봉투 안에는 2월 13일 (존 C. 클라크의 집에서 열린) 밸런타인데이 파티 초대장이 들어 있고, 그 파티에서 두 사람은 기념품 훔치기 경쟁을 벌였다. 냅킨은 그렇게 챙긴 전리품일 것이고, 그 위에 흐릿하게 연필로 쓴 이름들이 보이는데 잭 존스턴Jack Johnston, 에피 심프슨Effie Simpson, 노라 리퍼지, 그리고 이름만 적힌 에버렛Everett(레어드)과 클레미Clemmie(맥닐)이다.

〈용담The Fringed Gentian〉은 몽고메리가 글을 쓰는 데 평생 동안 영감을 주는 시였다.

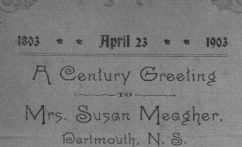

1803 ❧ ❧ April 23 ❧ ❧ 1903

A Century Greeting

TO

Mrs. Susan Meagher,

Dartmouth, N. S.

One hundred years! Oh, joyfully we bring
Our friendly tributes on this crowning day!
What homage is there that we would not pay
To one who of a century can sing!
Glance backward o'er the course of Time's
   swift wing;
What joys and sorrows, happiness and woe
Have marked thy pathway, only thou canst
   know—
Like echoes through Time's corridors they
   ring.

But looking back brings no regretful pain,
For thou hast followed in the narrow way,
Kept by the One above, Who can sustain
His servants by His mercy day to day:
This, then, thy portion; still will He
   maintain
Through life, through death—thy ever-
   lasting Stay.

CHRISTMAS

Halifax Hotel
Halifax, N. S.
H. Hesslein & Sons, Props.

Miss L. M. Montgomery of Sea View,
P. E. I., has accepted a position on the
Halifax Echo. Miss Montgomery as a
writer of short stories and magazine
articles, has gained a high reputation.—
St. John Star.

LE BON MARCHE.

J. M. BAXTER,
Treasurer.

AN EASTER LESSON.

I'm glad that it rained at Easter
To thwart the women that go
To church with no thought of Eastertide,
But only their hats to show;
No Christ and his resurrection
Appeals to them, for they care
For naught but the costly article
That nestles above the hair.

I'm glad that it rained at Easter,
I pity the poor tired men,
Who wish to worship with reverence,
But are oft prevented when
They raise their eyes from their prayer-
books
To seek the clergyman's face,
And all they can see is a surging mass
Of flowers and silks and lace.

I'm glad that it rained at Easter—
It sounds like an unkind thought,
When all should be bright in memory
Of Christ, from the dark grave brought;
But until the meaning of Easter
Comes true to you and me,
The beautiful, holy Eastertide
Is fraught with idolatry.
E.M.R.

March 31, 1902.

Knowing fathers, husbands and brothers will go to the Bon Marche, at the
corner of Sackville and Barrington
streets, to select Christmas gifts this
season for daughters, wives and sisters.
Why? Because to any rightly constituted
woman no gift is more acceptable than a
pretty new hat. And at this establishment all tastes and purses may be suited, for the selections displayed range
from the plain walking hats up to the
most elaborate of imported confections
for smart functions. This year a special
effort has been made to prepare a large
and varied assortment of trimmed hats,
because the large sales of former Christmas seasons has led the proprietor to
believe that hats make most useful and
desirable Christmas presents. They show
two windows filled with charming hats,
both home-trimmed and imported. After
night, especially, these windows are very
attractive, owing to the electric illumina-
tions which show up the millinery to the
best advantage. A fine assortment of
serviceable and natty "ready-to-wear"
hats is a feature of the holiday stock.
Neither are the small folks forgotten, for
there are some exceedingly dainty bon-
nets for them, which need only a chubby
face beneath them to set them off to the
best advantage. One of these should be
mother's present for the baby. A large
assortment of ribbons and silks for fancy
work is also shown, and all the latest
novelties in veilings may be found at
this enterprising and up-to-date millinery
establishment.

RECEPTION ROOM.

"NON-SERVIAM."

O God who reign'st in realms above,
Look down in mercy and in love
Upon Thy children gathered here—
Fill Thou our hearts with holy fear.
The changing skies, the torrent's flow
Proclaim Thy power above, below,
And still resounds, O God Most High,
From ingrate hearts this deathless cry,
"Non Serviam!"

The mountain tops and pine-clad hills,
The mighty seas and sparkling rills,
Thy temple groves and prairie home,
The brilliant studded azure dome,—
All—all with one accord declare
The Greatness that is everywhere,
And yet, a mortal dare defy
Thy sacred laws by ruthless cry,
"Non Serviam!"

"Non Serviam!"—and this to Thee,
Thou God of boundless Majesty!
A marvel great 'twould be to us
But slave address a master thus!
Can we, created by Thy hand,
Dare Thy mandate to withstand?
A "Fiat" still my prayer shall be,
And never more I'll say to Thee
"Non Serviam!"

Halifax. L. C. in Catholic Record.

A Mathmetical Query.

Little six-year-old Harry, while reading a chapter of Genesis, paused and
asked his mother if people in those
days used to do sums on the ground.
He had been reading the passage which
says: "And the sons of men multiplied
upon the face of the earth."

* * *

A Lightning
Change

THE morning after attending a funeral a colored girl told her
mistress she was to be married. "Whom are you going to
marry?" asked the lady. "The corpse's husband," was the
answer. "He allowed I was the life of de funeral, and he said he'd like to
marry me."

Lucy Lincoln Montgomery.

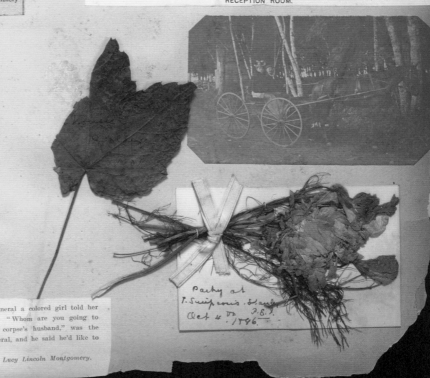

Party at
T. Simpson's House
Oct 4 & 5.
1896.

THE FRINGED GENTIAN.

Lift up thy dewy, fringed eyes,
 O little Alpine flower!
The tear that trembling on them lies
 Has sympathetic power
To move my own; for I, too, dream
 With thee of distant heights,
Whose lofty peaks are all agleam
 With rosy, dazzling lights.

Where aspirations, hopes, desires,
 Combining, fondly dwell—
Where burn the never-dying fires
 Of genius' wondrous spell,
Such towering summits would I reach,
 Who climb and grope in vain:
O little flower! the secret teach—
 The weary way make plain.

Who dreams of wider spheres revealed
 Up higher, near the sky,
Within the valley's narrow field
 Cannot contented lie;
Who longs for mountain breezes rare,
 Is restless down below—
Like me, for stronger, purer air
 Thou pinest, too, I know.

Then whisper, blossom, in thy sleep,
 How may I upward climb
The Alpine path so hard, so steep,
 That leads to heights sublime?
How may I reach the far-off goal
 Of true and honored fame,
To write upon its shining scroll
 A woman's humble name?

BAY VIEW

Best Wishes

몽고메리가 좋아한 시

스크랩북에 많이 담아둔 시는 루시 모드 몽고메리에게 상상력을 불러일으켰고, 그런 시가 전하는 주제들은 몽고메리의 작품들 안에서도 감지된다. 〈용담〉(레드 스크랩북 23쪽)은 몽고메리가 어릴 때부터 영감을 받았던 시다. 엘런 로댐 처치Ellen Rodham Church와 오거스타 데붑나Augusta DeBubna가 쓴 그 시를 처음 접한 것은 외할머니가 보던 잡지《고디의 여성을 위한 책Godey's Lady's Book》1884년 3월 호에서였다. "알프스 산길"과 "반짝이는 소용돌이"가 지닌 은유는 1917년 한 잡지에서 소개했듯 소설가로서 몽고메리가 걸어온 여정의 일부분이 되었고, 그 함의를 바탕으로 세 권 분량의 자전소설인 '에밀리' 시리즈가 탄생했다. "알프스 산길"을 오르려고 고군분투한 덕분에 몽고메리는 1903년 밸런타인데이 즈음에 80편이 넘는 단편소설과 120편이 넘는 시를 발표했다.

스크랩북에 실린 시들은 동시대 작가의 것이든 이미 유명해진 작품이든 신문과 잡지에서 오려낸 것이다. 그런 시들은 슬픈 사랑과 웃긴 사랑과 감상적인 사랑, 영감, 인간적인 약점(허영심과 타인에 대한 험담 등), 자연의 아름다움, 영웅담, 어린 시절과 학창 시절과 부모님과 옛 시절에 대한 그리움, 남녀의 유쾌한 싸움, 귀염 받는 애완동물(특히 고양이)을 얘기했다. 어린 순교자의 비극적인 용기를 노래하는 〈폴란드 소년〉(블루 스크랩북 51쪽)은 앤 셜리에게서 눈물을 자아냈을 것이고, 영웅담인 〈오늘 밤에는 통행금지령을 울리지 마세요〉(블루 스크랩북 57쪽)는 실제로《빨강 머리 앤》에 등장한다. 〈길모퉁이The Bend of the Road〉(레드 스크랩북 26쪽)가 포착한 이미지는 몽고메리가 어린 시절부터 좋아했을 법한 것이어서 삶에서 뜻밖의 순간을 은유하는 "길모퉁이"가 되어 앤 앞에 놓이게 됐다.

몽고메리는 유진 필드의 향수와 찰스 B. 고잉Charles B. Going의 경쾌한 필체에 매료됐다. 기차 승객이 첫눈에 사랑에 빠지는 순간을 익살스럽게 그려낸 고잉의 시 〈도로시, 실망Dorothy: A Disappointment〉(블루 스크랩북 13쪽)에서 몽고메리는 "공중누각"을 짓는다는 시구에 깜짝 놀랐고, 평생에 가장 좋아하는 표현으로 꼽았다. 고잉은 가벼운 자조를 섞어 조롱하는 의미로 그 표현을 사용했지만, 몽고메리는 1904년 작인 〈공중누각〉(이 책에 헌시처럼 위치한 시)에서처럼 줄곧 몽상의 힘과 황홀함을 뜻하는 표현으로 사용했다.

"늑대들과 함께 모험을" 문학적으로 유망주이자 펜팔 친구인 프랭크 먼로 비벌리가 쓴 이 이야기를 몽고메리가 캐번디시 문학회 회지에 실었다(레드 스크랩북 7쪽).

"한눈에 '두 집' 엿보기" 프레더리카 캠벨은 시골 학교 교사로 수년 동안 일하면서 체득한 식견을 바탕으로 훈육에 관해 교훈적인 글을 썼다. 프레더리카와 몽고메리는 서로 든든한 지지자가 되어 교사로서, 그리고 일하는 여성으로서 겪는 시련을 함께 나누었고, 각자 성공을 향해 저마다의 "알프스 산길"을 힘겹게 올라갔다 ("알프스 산길"은 몽고메리가 좋아하는 시 〈용담〉의 한 구절이다).

A Glimpse of "Two Homes."

I am a "school marm," and while sitting at my desk or visiting about the district, have gleaned a certain amount of facts. "Ting, ling, ling," goes the school bell, and in troops the coming generation of Fairville. The teacher glances over the group, and smiles with satisfaction when she notices the "Punctual Four" taking their places, with the promptness for which they are noted. The "Punctual Four" consist of two boys and two girls. If you ever visit Fairville school you will quickly recognize them by their blooming faces, well brushed hair, and immaculate collars, boots, and nails. Their clothes are carefully put on, and neatly mended. The teacher has no need to call on them to "Look alive," every half-second. Oh! no; their mother taught them how to do that long ago, for they are the children of Mrs. Joe. Smart—illustrious for her cookery, thrift, tidiness—and sharp temper. About fifteen minutes after roll-call, two other children saunter in. The teacher frowns, and remarks severely, "Late again." They take their places, and create a clatter, searching for slates, pencils, etc. In appearance, they are the direct opposite of the "Punctual Four." The teacher notes that Jackey is out at the elbows, and that Mintas' boots are minus the required number of buttons. Jackey and Mintas' mother (Mrs. Josh Easy) belongs to the class of good-natured but untidy mothers. School is out. The teacher takes a stroll around the village. Mrs. Joe. Smart has been a trifle more ungracious than usual, therefore Joe Sighs, takes his hat from the peg, and calls on Mrs. Josh. Easy. Joe stays thirty minutes, and arrives at the following conclusions: "Josh is in need of 'mending up;' those children are 'sassy' brats. Josh Easy is going behind, and his temper ain't extry; Mrs. Easy may be good-natured, but she's no wife for a workingman. I guess I'll go home and spend the evening with Martha Sharp." When Joe went home he kissed Martha, and Martha said, "I wouldn't be sich an old fool, Joe Sharp," but somehow her voice did not sound as sharp as usual. 'Reader, which home do you prefer?'

F. E. Campbell,
Sea View,
P.E.I.

FRANK MONROE BEVERLY.

AN ADVENTURE WITH WOLVES.

A great change has taken place in this section of the Old Dominion during the last forty years. Back in the 60's the whole face of the country was almost one uninterrupted forest. Here and there little patches were cleared up, and rude log cabins, the homes of the pioneers, usually marked these "clearings." Game was then plentiful, and the inhabitants depended mostly upon wild meat for their use. Bear, deer and other game roamed the forests in great numbers. The wolf and the panther were frequently met with and were often a source of annoyance to the people.

But the situation has now changed. The forests primeval have given way to the broad fields, the days of log cabins have passed by, and neat cottages (and even more substantial buildings) are to be seen scattered over the country: and the big game has gone. But it is not so much of the present time I wish to write. My narrative has to do with the year of '61, and, having said enough by way of preface, I will now proceed.

On last New Year's night—that is to say, the beginning of the year 1900—I was returning home from a visit to friends over in Cumberland Mountain in company with a man of some 60 years of age, with whom I had fallen in on my way. We were afoot and night had overtaken us. It was not very dark; there was a snow on the ground; and so we had no trouble in finding our way. Along the base of the mountain there flows the Pound River. This stream was frozen over. Just about the time we reached the river the snow commenced falling—a driving snow that met us square in the face. We walked across the stream on the ice and when we

reached the shore my companion said "Here I had quite a serious adventure once. When we get home I will relate it, if you care to hear it." Of course I would hear it; but I did not insist on his relating it then, for I was thinking more of the supper I knew my good dame would have awaiting my arrival and the snug warmth of our fireside than of hearing an adventure related. So I waited till we reached home. After supper I reminded him of his promise and he gave me the following narrative:

"On New Year's night, away back in '61—39 years ago and that's a long time—I was on my way home from the 'Mountain.' I then lived with my parents in a log cabin, a hundred yards perhaps from where this house sets. As I said before, I was coming from the 'Mountain'—the river being frozen over as it is to-night. About the time I reached this side of the river I heard some ugly growls proceeding from the laurel brush above me. I thought of running back across the river; but I hesitated for a few moments, trying to decide what was best to do, when I saw three or four dark looking objects bound out into a little opening near the bank of the stream. The vicious growling was kept up almost incessantly and the objects seemed to be coming towards me. I knew that I must do something: my indecision left me and I sprang to a beech tree up which I climbed, not an instant too soon; for, as I swung myself up by the branches of the tree something caught me by the coat-tail, and, had the cloth not given away, I should doubtless have been pulled down. But as it was I made my way up into the upper branches of the tree minus a coat-tail; but I did not consider it a great loss at that time.

"I was then out of reach of these wolves, as I found them to be; but my fears were that they would stay near the tree and watch for me all night. It was cold; pretty much such a night as this. It was only about half a mile from home; but I had my doubts as to my being able to make Father or the boys hear me,

should I call to them. However, I would try. But, loud as I could halloo, I could get no response. Then my heart sank within me; for I felt sure that I should freeze before daylight should I have to stay up in the tree all night. I grew almost desperate and made another last desperate effort. This time I heard Father's voice in response. He had become uneasy and started out to see if any trouble had befallen me; for he looked for my return home by night. I called to him again upon his nearer approach and told him that I was treed by a pack of wolves. One of my brothers was with him. They both had guns, they said, and our faithful old dog was along. I told them where I was and they ventured up close enough to see the wolves beneath the tree. After assuring themselves that I was in the tree, they discharged their pieces into the pack. Then the old dog ran up, and began a vigorous barking. There was a wild commotion among the wolves, and I could tell from the noise that one of them was badly wounded. I was also sure that some of them were leaving. Then all became quiet beneath the tree. Father and brother then ventured up and found that one wolf lay dead on the ground, while the others had fled. That was the only adventure I ever had with wolves in these here Virginia mountains; but, somehow, I don't yet feel quite [safe] in passing that point after nightfall."

Freeling, Va. F. MONROE BEVERLY.

25–26쪽, 28쪽 여기서는 십 년이 넘는 시간을 펼쳐놓고 그 안에서 로맨스, 시적 이미지, 일상의 사건이라는 몇 가지 주제를 다룬다.

로맨스 25쪽과 28쪽에 나오는 하얀 카드와 26쪽 신년 카드는 모두 노라와 몽고메리가 엉뚱한 장난을 벌이다가 사건으로 발전한 이야기로, 비밀 일기에 숨 가쁘게 설명되어 있다. 몽고메리와 노라가 거짓으로 벌이는 사랑 다툼은 스크랩북을 가득 채우고 빈번히 등장하는 반면, 진짜 비밀과 가슴앓이는 그 페이지들 속에 감추어져 있거나 아예 존재하지 않는다. J. D. 서덜랜드 부부의 명함(레드 스크랩북 26쪽)에는 진심으로 실망감이 담겨 있는지도 모른다. 몽고메리는 잭 서덜랜드의 사진을 벨몬트의 자기 방 침실에 간직했다. 초기 일기에는 그의 이름도 자주 등장했고 늘 좋은 내용이었다. 26쪽(왼쪽 위) 우편엽서 아래쪽에 적힌 "L. D."라는 머리글자는 비더포드에서 몽고메리에게 구애하던 루 디스턴트를 가리킨다. 몽고메리가 캐번디시의 신축 장로교회를 찍은 25쪽 청사진은 아치형 창문과 출입문을 잘 담아냈다. 이 교회는 몽고메리에게 새로 부임한 목사와의 로맨스를 상징하게 되지만, 또한 자신에게 거절당해 끝내 침례교 목사가 된 에드윈 심프슨 때문에 괴롭고 당혹스러운 감정을 떠올려야 했을지도 모르겠다.

시적 이미지 "길모퉁이"는 몽고메리의 삶과 작품에서 가장 눈에 띄면서도 중요한 은유의 형태 가운데 하나이다. 26쪽에 실린 시 〈길모퉁이〉는 알 수 없는 미래가 가지는 거부할 수 없는 매력을 묘사하고, 그 위에 배치한 우편엽서와 잡지에서 오려낸 왼쪽 아래 사진은 길모퉁이를 시각적으로 해석해 보여준다. 앤 셜리는 《빨강 머리 앤》 앞부분에서 매슈와 함께 에이번리로 들어서는 길모퉁이를 돌았을 때 해 질 녘 "기쁨의 하얀 길"의 아름다움에 말문을 잃는다. 끝부분에서는 한층 자란 앤이 길모퉁이를 은유적으로 표현하여 자기 앞에 놓인 삶의 여정을 놀랍고도 멋진 모퉁이들이 있는 길로 이해한

다. 《빨강 머리 앤》의 마지막 장 제목은 "길모퉁이에서"이고, 이 소설의 끝에서 두 번째 문장은 "길에는 언제나 모퉁이가 있었다!"로 앤의 낙관주의가 드러난다. 잡지 사진(레드 스크랩북 26쪽 왼쪽 아래)은 캐번디시 해안이다. 흥미롭게도 몽고메리가 찍은 사진 중에서 많은 사진이 비슷비슷한 굽이를 보여준다. 몽고메리와 앤이 사랑하는 연인의 오솔길도 사진으로 많이 남겼는데 거의 항상 은근히 굽이져 있다.

일상의 사건 28쪽에는 일간지 《몬트리올 목격자 Montreal Witness》가 1889년에 주최한 경연 대회의 수상자들을 평가하는 긴 기사의 첫 부분이 실렸다(오른쪽 아래). 이 대회에 몽고메리는 시 〈르포스 곶〉으로 참가해 주목을 받았다. 1899년에 일부 캐번디시 여성이 재봉봉사회를 결성하여 장로교회를 신축하기 위한 모금 활동에 나섰다. 기금 모금에 관한 기사는 25쪽 중앙에 배치하고 새 교회의 사진을 그 위에 붙여서 그 모금 활동이 성공적이었음을 보여준다.

Men may rise on stepping-stones
Of their dead selves
to higher things.
In Mem.

JULY.

Sun	6	13	20	27
Mon	7	14	21	28
Tue	1	8	15	22	29
Wed	2	9	16	23	30
Thu	3	10	17	24	31
Fri	4	11	18	25
Sat	5	12	19	26

AUGUST.

Sun	3	10	17	24	31
Mon	4	11	18	25
Tue	5	12	19	26
Wed	6	13	20	27
Thu	7	14	21	28
Fri	1	8	15	22	29
Sat	2	9	16	23	30

Entertainment

....IN THE....

Town Hall, Prince Albert,

....ON....

Tuesday, October 3rd, 1899,

UNDER THE AUSPICES OF

Prince Albert Public School.

▲▲▲▲

Miss Marietta La Dell, B.E.,

ASSISTED BY

REV. J. H. LAMBERT

and Leading Local Talent.

SOCIAL AT CAVENDISH.—A very pleasant social and entertainment was held in the Presbyterian Church, Cavendish, on Monday evening, in honor of Rev. George Laird, who is at present on a visit to his native place after an absence in the North West of over twenty years. After a good programme had been rendered tea was served by the ladies. The tables were set in the class rooms and a couple of hours were pleasantly spent in social chat and amusement. Following is the programme:

Chorus, "Send out the Sunlight"—Choir.
Address by Chairman—Rev. M. H. McIntosh.
Solo—Rev. George Laird.
Recitation—Miss Ethel M. Kenzie.
Recitation—Miss Myrtle McNeill.
Solo—Mrs. Roger Simpson.
Recitation—Miss Bertha Hillman.
Speech—Rev. George Laird.
Recitation—Miss Nora Lefurgey.
Solo—Mr. E. J. McKenzie.
Recitation—Miss Elice Laird.
Recitation—Miss L. M. Montgomery.
Solo—Rev. George Laird.
Address—George Simpson, M. L. A.
Recitation—Miss Charlotte Simpson.
Recitation—Miss Hazel McKenzie.
Recitation—Master Ernest Simpson.
Music, "The Beautiful City"—Choir.

Monday, Jan. 12.
1903.

"Where minister meets
money there comes the
tug of war".

"Love in the abstract".

"Sour apples — sweet
apples".

"No wonder they are sour;
you know where she
keeps them".

Three on the platform;
The "disciple" is horrified.
He's going to pray about
it this "Justice".

THE entertainment held in the Cavendish hall on Tuesday evening, the 25th inst., under the management of the members of the Sewing Circle, was a grand success, notwithstanding the unfavorable weather and roads. Rev. M. H. McIntosh occupied the chair, and in a few well chosen remarks, given with his usual eloquence and humor, opened the meeting, and the following program was creditably rendered:

Instrumental Duet—Miss Eveline McLeod and Mr. McClure.
Reading—Selected, Mr. Neil Simpson.
Solo—"Just Break the News to Mother," Miss Ethel Hopgood.
Recitation—"Little Christel," Miss Myrtle McNeill.
Quartette—Dr. and Miss Houston and Mr. and Miss Stevenson.
Recitation—"The Organ Builder," Miss Katie McNeill.
Solo—"I Want My Presents Back," Mr. R. Stevenson.
Reading—"Selected" Mr. John F. McNeill.
Duet—Mr. and Miss McKenzie.
Recitation—"Selected" Mr. McCoubrey.
Solo—"Just to say Good Bye," Miss Janetta McLeod.
Dialogue—"Why we never married," seven maids and seven bachelors.
Solo—Selected" Mr. R. Stevenson.
Recitation—"The Maiden's Sacrifice," Mr. A. E. McKenzie.
Recitation—"The sermon," Miss Eveline McLeod.
Instrumental Duet—Miss Eveline McLeod and Mr. McLure.
Recitation—"Sleepy," Miss Myrtle McNeill.
God Save The Queen.

At the close of the program the ladies of the "Sewing Circle" presented an autograph quilt, to be sold by auction. Mr. John Stewart was then called on and he did justice to the occasion. Mr. James Stewart was the purchaser at the sum of eight dollars. The "Autograph Quilt" contained some two hundred and fifty names from whom a contribution of eighty dollars was received. The proceeds go to the New Presbyterian Church building fund. After the close of the meeting, a supper was given at the home of Mr. and Mrs. John F. McNeill by the Ladies of the Sewing Circle to their friends and visitors who contributed to this entertainment. The party numbered in all about sixty guests.

I. O. F. at New Glasgow.

The claim made by the members of the Independent Order of Foresters that their Society is a social as well as a fraternal organization was fully proved at New Glasgow, on Thursday evening, 11th inst. The At Home given in the Hall by the members of Court Nonpariel was the most enjoyable affair ever held there.

The committee at first decided to sell only fifty tickets, but seventy-five had to be sold, or there would have been charges of partiality. Promptly at 7 30 p. m. the High Chief Ranger of Prince Edward Island, Dr. H. W. Robertson was introduced as the Chairman of the evening, and after delivering a neat and practical address, he stated that the first item on the program would be the public installation of the officers of Court Nonpariel. The important ceremony took place at once. High Secretary L. U. Fowler acting as Marshal. The following are the officers installed:—

Chief Ranger, Artemas Moffatt.
Vice Chief Ranger, Eddie Stevenson.
Rec. Sec'y., J. C. Houston, M. D.
Fin. Sec'y., B. B. Stevenson.
Treas., A. E. Douglas, M. D.,
Orator, James E. Moffatt.
Organist, R. W. Stevenson.
Sr. W., Nelson Orr.
Jr. W., Allan Moffatt.
Sr. Beadle, James Houston.
Jr. Beadle, Frank Andrew.
Past Chief Ranger, Jas. Bullman.
Court Deputy, Geo. Houston.
Physicians, Drs. Houston and Douglas
The balance of the program consisted of vocal and instrumental music, recitations, speeches and readings. Special mention should be made of the solo sung by Miss McLeod of Hunter River; the duett by R. W. Stevenson and his little niece; the recitation by J. Gordon McKay, Miss Montgomery, Miss Stevenson, and Rogers Fowler.

The supper had been arranged in the upper hall by the ladies and if Foresters anywhere are proud of their mothers, wives, sisters and daughters, the members of Court Nonpariel certainly should be, for the High Chief Ranger who is admitted to be a judge of such things, publicly stated that it was the best spread he had ever sat. That there was abundance

A JOB LOT OF JUMBLES.

WHEN one of Nature's lovers poetically wrote in his lady friend's autograph album the lines: "What is rarer than a day in June?" and the ever predatory small brother answered the query in a scrawly hand, "*A Chinaman with Whiskers*," it would seem that the lad had dished up something that is rareness personified.

Little Elmer was playing out on the roof, when suddenly he lost his balance and began to slide. "Oh, God," he prayed, "please don't let me—" but his progress was suddenly stopped. "Never mind, God," he continued, "I've caught on a nail."

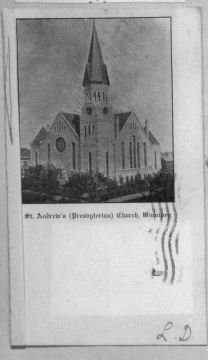

St. Andrew's (Presbyterian) Church, Winnipeg.

L. D.

Mr M J McLeod of Edmonton, Assistant Provincial Treasurer of Alberta, and a son of the late Norman McLeod, St Avard's has arrived in Charlottetown. On Tuesday, next he will be married, at Bideford, to Miss Daisy Williams, a popular young lady of that place. Mr McLeod has been in the West for a number of years and for the past year has been a resident of Edmonton, the seat of government in the province of Alberta. After his marriage on Tuesday next Mr McLeod will return with his bride to the West. Miss Williams, who was formerly on the nursing staff of the Prince Edward Island hospital, is a sister of Mr A E Williams formerly manager of the Bank of New Brunswick and of Mr E Bayfield Williams formerly of this city.

OBITUARY.—The death took place at her home in Cavendish, on Monday, the 19th inst., of Hattie Myrtle, eldest daughter of William Laird, at the early age of twenty-four years. The deceased was a person of quiet and unassuming manner, and by her gentle and lovable disposition endeared herself to all who knew her. During her severe illness which lasted several months she was calm and resigned, and died trusting in the merits of a crucified Redeemer. The funeral service which was conducted by Rev E. Macdonald assisted by Rev A A Smith, of Coldstream, N S, took place on Wednesday, the 21st inst., and was very largely attended. To the bereaved family we extend our sincerest sympathy.

The Bend of the Road

Oh that bend of the road, how it baffles, yet beckons !
What lies there beyond—less or more than heart reckons ?
What ends, what begins, there where sight fails to follow ?
Does the road climb to heaven, or dip to the hollow ?
Oh what glory of greenness, what lights interlacing,
What softness of shadow, what bounty of spacing,
What refreshment of change—aye, what beauty Elysian
The sweep of that curve may deny to the vision !
Oh my soul yearns for sight ! Oh my feet long to follow,
Swift-winged with sweet hope as with wings of a swallow !
Though lonely the way, void of song, void of laughter,
—I must go to the end—I must know what comes after !
GRACE DENIO LICHFIELD, in the *Century*.

TINY SLIPPERS

(ON SEEING A PAIR OF EGYPTIAN SANDALS TWO THOUSAND YEARS OLD)

By Sir Edwin Arnold

TINY slippers of gold and green,
    Tied with a moldering golden cord !
What pretty feet they must have been
    When Cæsar Augustus was Egypt's lord !
Somebody graceful and fair you were !
    Not many girls could dance in these :
Who was the shoemaker made you, dear,
    Such a nice pair of Egyptian "threes ?"

Where were you measured ? In Sais, or On,
    Memphis, or Thebes, or Pelusium ?
Fitting them featly your brown toes upon,
    Lacing them deftly with finger and thumb,
I seem to see you—so long ago !
    Twenty centuries, less or more,
And here are your sandals ; but nobody knows
    What face, or fortune, or name you bore.

Inquire within

My Greeting

Mr & Mrs J D Sutherland.

the coast alternates between bold cliffs and long reaches of sand dunes.

goes without saying seven large baskets were sent the next day to the poor of an adjoining settlement.

The tables in the supper room were not sufficiently large to accomoda'e at once the 150 couples, but while part were enjoying themselves up stairs, some in the lower hall were having a social chat, others explaining Forestry, while others listened to instrumental music given by Messrs. John Marks, Mor't. Harding and P. H. Gallant. It is said that there was a dance and some officers of the high court took part, but for this your correspondent cannot vouch as he left the hall at eleven o'clock. H ping that every "at home" the Foresters have at New Glasgow will have the same success.

THE concert and basket social held in New Glasgow Hall last night was a decided success. Mr. Wm. Laird very ably performed the duties of chairman. The programme was excellent throughout. The recitations given by Miss Montgomery of Cavendish and Miss Ella Bagnall, also the duetts by Miss A. E. Harris and C. McDonald, of Ch'town are worthy of special mention, their renditions proving most pleasing to the audience who evidently appreciate a good thing. Mr. W. D. McCoubrey auctioned the baskets with his wonted ability. The prices obtained averaging 50c each. The proceeds amounted to $32, which sum will go towards the public library. While the entertainment and social were all that could be desired, the pleasure of the audience was considerably marred by four or five uncouth youths from a neighboring locality who evidently consider themselves smart as long as they conduct themselves in the most unmanly manner possible. As those youths are well known and have been repeatedly annoying meetings held by the people of Glasgow, they had better take warning in time, otherwise they will be prosecuted to the full extent of the law. A word to the wise is sufficient.

ANNUAL FORESTER BANQUET

Of Court Nonpareil at New Glasgow Thursday

OFFICERS ARE INSTALLED

Eloquent Speeches Delivered and a Pleasant Evening Spent by all Present,

The annual banquet given by the Foresters of Court Nonpareil at New Glasgow on Thursday night last was an event of more than ordinary note. After the exe cu tion of officers for the

A correspondent writes: "Having oc casion to travel many sections of the Island at different times, I notice some great improvements particularly in the buildings and cemeteries, etc. I see some very fine churches and schoolhouses, but one thing noticeable is the care and pains taken in fixing up some of the cemeteries. Worthy of note is the one at Belfast Church, Vernon River Chapel, and some smaller ones of other denominations—not forgetting to make special mention of Cavendish which is tastefully arranged and a credit to the people. But moving a little further what is found. A large, well finished church with a cemetery in a most disgraceful condition. No doubt there are some very fine monuments but what of that, when it's a very forest; in some places you have to turn up the branches to find the graves. Truly it's a disgrace to find this place made a dumping-ground for stones and sticks of all sorts, where old Scotch settlers who worked early and late to clear and till the soil, are lying in their graves forgotten to a certain extent. Why not appoint a man to clean up and look after this place? If they don't want to pay for it let each one clean of his or her own plot. Where is the clergy man in charge of this parish; can't he make a move in this matter? They want a Doyle or a Sinclair among them, and I hope the next time I have to pass through this section there will be a change for the better."

Foresters and invited guests repa red to he dining hall where under the Forestic decorated room gleamed crystal in magnificent array and intermingled the necessaries to satisfy the most fastidious. At the head of the hall hung a majest c Union Jack and nicely worked were the letters I. O. F. To the left hung the beautiful charter of the Court and to the lower right hung an elaborate picture of Supreme Chief, Dr. Oronhyateka. After ample justice had been done at the table the following toasts were drunk in pure cold water:

The King.—The National Anthem.
Dr. Oronhyateka.—He's a Jolly Good Fellow.
Song.—Bro. R. W. Stevenson.
Forestry.—Responded to by Bro. L. U. Fowler.
Reading—Miss Lefurgey.
Canada—Bro. D. C. Lawlor.
Professions—Bro. W. Simpson, Bro. Dr. Douglas.
Reading—Miss May Macleod.
Island Industries—C. A. Stevenson William Moffatt.
Quartette—R. W. Stevenson, Laura Houston, Miss Raed, Mrs. W. W. Smith.
Sister Societies—Bro. Morley Seller, L. Clark, William Lair'l.
Recitation—Bro. C. E. Mackenzie.
Ladies—R. E. Bagnall and others.
Solo—E. E. Mackay.
Court Nonpariel—Bro. George Houston D. H. C. R.
Every address and number was fittingly neat and appropriate.
We must particularize the reading by Miss Lefurgey whose inimitable style and diction is a drawing card wherever her services are secured.
We could but note the pleasure stamped on all countenances during the evening and as all rose to sing God Save the King. They dispersed feeling repaid amply for their attendance.—COM

CONVENT

—OF THE—

Faithful Companions of Jesus,

PRINCE ALBERT.

Distribution of Prizes

PRESIDED BY

His Honor Joseph Royal, Lieut.-Governor.

WEDNESDAY JUNE 17TH, 1891.

January 15, 1903.

"One shall be taken and the other left."

"He cometh not," she said.

She who will not go when she can, cannot when she would.

A sleigh at the door is worth two across the road.

Blessed are those who expect nothing for they shall not be disappointed.

A Humane Pater.—One reads so frequently of the paternal boot as applied to the undesirable youthful suitor that it is a pleasure to chronicle the more humane method adopted by a wealthy Glasgow merchant for choking off a "follower" of his daughter. The girl was very young, so was the follower, but nevertheless he called formally on the object of his affections. The merchant and his wife entered the room, the latter bearing a glass of milk and a huge slice of bread spread with buttter and jam.

"Now, dear, run away to bed," said the kindly mother to her daughter; "it's time that all good girls should be in bed,"

Then the Glasgow merchant addressed the astonished young man:

"Now, youngster, you drink that glass of milk, and take that slice of bread and jam to eat on the road home—and hurry, for your mother must be anxious about your being out so late by yourself."

The young man did not call again.

DOMINION PRIZE COMPETITION.

REPORT ON THE PRINCE EDWARD ISLAND STORIES.

JUDGE ALLEY'S CRITICISM—A NUMBER OF GOOD STORIES—THE PROVINCE PRIZE GOES TO PRINCE COUNTY.

Prince Edward Island is the banner province in respect to the number of stories sent for the *Witness* Dominion Prize Competition in comparison with the population. The number sent from this Island was seventy-two, which is one for every 621 of population. This is a remarkable showing and one we are very proud of. The report by Judge Alley is a very interesting

JUDGE ALLEY'S REPORT.

CHARLOTTETOWN, P.E.I., 11TH MAY, 1889.

Messrs. John Dougall & Son.

DEAR SIRS,—I beg to return to you the papers—72 in number—written by competitors from this Province for the Dominion Prize Competitions, and to send you the following report regarding them:

QUEEN'S COUNTY.—The number of stories forwarded to me from competitors in this county, according to the endorsement on the wrapper enclosing them was 27, and the number from the city of Charlottetown was five. I found, however, that one of those enclosed in the parcel for Queen's County was from Prince street school, Charlottetown, thereby reducing the number from Queen's County to 26, and increasing that from Charlottetown to six.

The best essay, in my opinion, from Queen's county is from Uigg School, No. 14, and is marked by me Q. A. It is an authentic story, told in a racy and readable way, and though its subject may in one sense be said to be a local incident, it exemplifies a principle which is world wide and universal. Next in the order of merit among the contributions of this county may be ranked three stories, which I have marked Q. B., Q. C. and Q. D. respectively. The first is a well written narrative of an interesting historical incident in the county, and the second is a legend graphically told of a tragedy said to have occurred about the time of the establishment of British rule in the island or spot which has perpetuated the memory of one of the principal actors in the occurrence by h riving from him its name. The third is a sto of a destructive fire which swept over an extensive district in the county some fifty years ago. I would recommend the first two for publication, and the last might also be published, but will require some revision in punctuation and construction of its sentences before it appears in the press. The story I have marked Q. E. is a tragedy told in a tragic as well as in a tragic style, and I am rather disposed to be sceptical as to its authenticity. If true, the experience of the writer was a remarkable one, and the story is worthy of reproduction. The stories marked Q. F. and which relate to...

청사진 레드 스크랩북 26쪽에서 시 〈길모퉁이〉와 이미지를 다시 한 번 돌아본 몽고메리는 자신이 찍은 굽잇길 사진을 29쪽에 실었다(오른쪽 아래). 이 굽잇길을 찍은 곳은 맥닐가의 오솔길로, 집 옆쪽으로 지나가 몽고메리의 "소중한 침실" 창가까지 이어졌다. 이 지면의 상단에는 남향으로 난 창문을 찍은 사진(오른쪽 위)이 있다. 몽고메리는 글을 쓸 때면 이 창문으로 밖을 내다보곤 했다.

잡지 사진 십사 년이라는 시간을 넘나들며 여러 페이지에 걸쳐 공통적으로 이어지는 맥락 속에서 하나의 이야기를 키우고 키워 희망적인 두 이미지를 보여준다. 병아리 사진에 붙은 "갓 태어나다"라는 설명은 잡지에서 오려낸 흑백사진 속 여자를 두고 하는 재미난 논평처럼 보인다. 이완 맥도널드에 대한 기사(왼쪽 위), 몽고메리의 활동에서 교회가 차지하는 중요성, 길모퉁이, 그리고 자신의 박공지붕 밑 창문(그 방을 사랑했지만 맥닐 할머니가 돌아가시면 어쩔 수 없이 떠나야 한다는 것을 알고 있었다)으로 그 여인의 사진을 에워싸면서 몽고메리는 자기 삶에 변화가 생길 수 있다는 걸 말하고자 했을까?

기념품 몽고메리는 렘 매클라우드에게서 받은 감상적 시 〈빛은 충분하다 Light Enough〉를 1893년 3월 4일이라는 날짜가 적힌 종이 바로 위에 붙였다. 이날은 클라라 캠벨과 어맨다 맥닐 Amanda Macneill의 집에서 함께 저녁 시간을 보낸 후 렘 매클라우드와 한바탕 신나게 썰매를 탄 날이었다. 몽고메리는 렘과의 추억을 기념한 지면에 1903년 9월 이완 맥도널드의 성직 서임과 목사 부임을 알리는 캐번디시 소식 기사(왼쪽 위, 몽고메리가 썼을지도 모른다)를 나란히 배치했다. 이와 함께 〈할머니 집에서 At Grandmother's〉라는 시도 붙여뒀는데, 지금은 아무도 없지만 한때는 활기 넘쳤던 집을 향수에 젖어 회상하는 내용이다. 몽고메리는 이 지면을 구상하면서 이미 이완 맥도널드와 자신의 미래를 연관 짓고 있었던 것일까? 할머니가 돌아가시고 자신의 박공지붕 밑 방은 텅 비어버리는, 자신이 대면해야 할 "길모퉁이"를 상상하면서? 1903년 6월 21일 비밀 일기에서 몽고메리는 이완 맥도널드에게 깊은 인상을 받았다고 못을 박아두긴 했다. "오늘 아침에 우리에게 설교해줄 하일랜드 사람을 만났는데 그는 '짱 멋졌다'. 여자아이는 모두 그에게 넋을 잃었다. 나도 가슴이 콩닥콩닥 뛰어서 찬송가를 연주하기 힘들 정도였다."

NOTES FROM CAVENDISH AND VICINITY

The Presbyterian Church, Cavendish, was the scene of a large and interesting gathering on Tuesday the 1st inst., on the occasion of the ordination and induction of Ewen McDonald as the minister of the congregation.

The church was filled to the doors with members of the congregation from different sections of the country. The ladies had the building beautifully decorated with cut flowers and potted plants. After an able and appropriate sermon from Rev. Edwin Smith, the moderator Rev. A. D. McDonald in a solemn service ordained Mr McDonald to the office of the holy ministry and formally induced him into the pastoral charge of the congregation. The new minister was then addressed by Rev Mr McLean on the duties of his office, while Rev. Mr Spencer reminded the congregation of their obligations to their pastor. Mr McDonald was then introduced to the members of the congregation, and received a most hearty welcome. The new pastor is commencing his work under favorable conditions among a people noted for loyalty to their church and pastor and from them he received a most hearty and unanimous call. The PATRIOT wishes Mr. McDonald a pleasant and successful ministry in his first charge. Lieutenant D Stewart is spending a short vacation in Cavendish and Bay View. Mr. and Mrs. James Williams of Fountain Mills were visiting friends in Bay View this week. J J McLeod, of Riverdale was attending the Presbytery meeting in Cavendish on Tuesday representing the Bonshaw and Hampton congregation. This congregation are calling Rev A D McDonald, of Montrose Mr and Mrs George Green, of St John are visiting in Bay View the guests of Mrs (Hon) George Simpson. Considerable harvest is cut in Bay View and Cavendish and promises to be a good crop. At present cutting is delayed by damp weather. Frank Andrew is discharging coal from his schooner at Bay View wharf. Charles Taylor, Esq., Malpeque, paid a flying visit to Bay View and Cavendish on Tuesday and attended the ordination service in the Presbyterian Church.

The rose looks fair,
but fairer we it deem
For that sweet odour
which doth live
in it

It is the mind
that makes the body rich.

Taming of the Shrew.

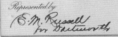

AT GRANDMOTHER'S.

Under the shade of the poplars still,
Lilacs and locusts and clumps between,
Roses over the window sill,
Is the dear old house with its door of green.

Never were seen such spotless floors,
Never such shining rows or tin,
While the rose-leaf odors that came thro' the doors,
Told of the peaceful life within.

Here is the room where the children slept,
Grandmamma's children, tired with play,
And the famous drawer where the cakes were kept,
Shrewsbury cookies and caraway.

The garden walks where the children ran,
Through the flowers and learn their names,
The children thought, since the world began,
Were never such garden walks for games.

There were tulips and asters in regular lines,
Sweet-Williams and marigolds on their stalks,
Bachelor's buttons and sweet pea vines,
And box that bordered the narrow walks.

Pure white lilies stood corner wise
From sunflowers yellow and poppies red
And the summer pinks looked up in surprise
At the kingly hollyhocks overhead.

Morning glories and larkspur stood
Close to the neighborly daffodil;
Cabbage roses and southernwood
Foamed thro' the beds at their own sweet will.

Many a year has passed since then,
Grandmama's house is empty and still
Grandmama's babies have grown to men
And the roses grow wild o'er the window sill.

Never again shall the children meet
Under the poplars gray and tall,
Never again shall the careless feet
Dance thro' the rose-leaf scented hall.

Grandmama's welcome is heard no more
And the children are scattered far and wide,
And the world is a larger place than of yore
But hallowed memories still abide.

And the children are better men to-day
For the cakes and rose-leaves and garden walks,
And grandmother's welcome so far away
And the old sweet Williams on their stalks.
—*Arthur Wentworth Eaton, in the Youth's Companion.*

LIGHT ENOUGH.

What need of light? By far too bright
The fire your dark eyes show.
Mine must reveal the love I feel.
So let the lamp burn low.

Leave me the dark! Too fair a mark
For Cupid's cruel bow
And archer art is my fond heart.
So let the light burn low.

For, if my love should hopeless prove,
Then must I learn to know
Darkness alone till life be flown.
So let the light burn low.

And—if you say the word I pray—
That one sweet word would show
My fate to me so bright to see,
'Twere best the lamp be low.
—J. L. Heaton in "The Quilting Bee.

Mar. 4th 1893

JUST OUT
By W. E. Vilmer

Little Dot: "I know something my teacher doesn't know." Mamma: "Indeed! What is it?" "I know when the world is coming to an end, and she doesn't. I asked her, and she said she didn't know." "O, well, who told you?" "Uncle John. He said the world would come to an end when children stopped asking questions that nobody could answer."—*Exchange.*

루시 모드 몽고메리는 직접 찍은 사진을 사용하여 여기 지면들과 그 이야기의 중심을 잡고서 오래된 자료와 새로운 자료를 나란히 배치하여 때로는 역설적인 유사성을 암시하기도 했다.

32쪽 청사진 두 장이 옛 캐번디시 장로교회의 외관과 내부를 보여준다. 교회는 1899년에 철거됐다. 루시 모드 몽고메리는 1942년에 이 교회 묘지에 안장됐다. 몽고메리가 찍은 "연인의 오솔길" 사진이 1902년 6월 달력에 붙어 있지만 그 달력에 쓰인 날짜는 1902년 9월 16일이다. 이 날짜에 대한 설명을 몽고메리의 일기 어디에서도 찾아볼 수 없다. 몽고메리가 노라 리퍼지와 친구가 된 것은 1902년 여름과 가을이었고, 1902년 8월에는 사촌 프레더리카 캠벨과도 더 깊은 우정을 쌓았다. (왕족에 관한 재담 옆에 익살스럽게 배치된) 풍자만화 "부기A Swell Affair"를 보고, 치아 궤양이 자주 재발하여 고생하던 몽고메리로서는 무척 공감이 갔을 것이다. 기사와 이미지를 창의적으로 배치하다 보면 종종 있는 일이지만, 몽고메리는 여기서도 장례식 소식과 결혼식 소식을 나란히 배치했다.

33쪽 여기에 재미로 수집해둔 다른 자료들처럼 보름달 풍경도 속임수가 숨어 있는 사진이다. 레드 스크랩북 48쪽에도 나오는 대낮 사진에 보름달을 붙인 것이다. 몽고메리가 프린스오브웨일스 대학에 아직 재학 중이던 1894년 《칼리지 레코드》에는 "2학년 교실 쥐의 일기 중에서"라는 재미있는 글이 실렸는데, 1894년 3월 8일 하코트 교수의 수업 시간에 학생들이 2킬로그램 분량의 땅콩을 서로에게 신나게 집어 던지며 한바탕 땅콩 파티를 했던 사건이 담겨 있다(블루 스크랩북 3쪽도 참고). 몽고메리는 이 우스운 추억 옆에다가 샬럿타운 공연에서 본 세이디 캘훈Sadie Calhoun이라는 여배우를 칭찬하는 기사를 배치했다. 잡지에서 오려낸 신부는 뭔가를 떼어낸 자국을 감추려고 붙인 사진이다.

34쪽 캐번디시의 옛 침례교회와 어맨다 맥닐의 집을 찍은 사진은 둘 사이에 어떤 관련성이 있다는 것을 보여준다. 어맨다는 어린 시절부터 몽고메리와 아주 친한 친구였다. 위쪽에 놓인 흰 카드로 기념한 1890년 5월 13일의 소풍길에는 어맨다와 몽고메리, 선생님인 해티 고든을 비롯하여 다른 학생도 여럿 참석했다. 아마도 《에이번리의 앤》에서 "황금빛 소풍"을 떠나도록 영감을 준 소풍이었을 것이다. 십 년도 더 된 학창 시절의 즐거움이 되살아났는지, 몽고메리는 1903년 5월 달력에 노라 리퍼지와 뜻하지 않게 나섰던 침례교회 나들이에 대해 적었다. 가짜 로맨스에 이름을 올린 사람은 루시 모드 몽고메리, 로버트 매켄지, 노라 리퍼지, 헨리 S. 맥루어인데 헨리는 누이의 사망 소식으로 레드 스크랩북 32쪽에도 언급됐다. 캠루프스 다리는 몽고메리가 서부로 여행한 1930년에 수집했을 것으로 보이는데, 일찍이 붙였던 다른 자료를 떼어내고 교체한 사진이지만 로라 프리처드 애그뉴와 함께 즐거웠던 학창 시절을 회상하려는 의도적 표식일 수도 있다. 〈모든 일을 하는 문학소녀The Literary Maid of All Work〉를 같이 수록한 것은 몽고메리가 기자 생활을 마치고 나서 알게 된, 이야기를 엮는 자기 방식을 스스로 비웃는 자신만의 방식일 것이다.

GEMS FOR THE MONTHS.

JANUARY.
By her who in this month was born
No gem save garnets should be worn,
They will insure her constancy,
True friendship and fidelity.

FEBRUARY.
The February-born will find
Sincerity and peace of mind,
Freedom from passion and from care,
If they the amethyst will wear.

MARCH.
Who in this world of ours their eyes
In March first open, shall be wise.
In days of peril firm and brave,
And wear a bloodstone to their grave.

APRIL.
She who from April dates her years
Diamonds shall wear, lest bitter tears
For vain repentance flow; this stone
Emblem of innocence is known.

MAY.
Who first beholds the light of day
In Spring's sweet flower month of May,
And wears an emerald all her life,
Shall be a loved and happy wife.

JUNE.
Who comes with summer to this earth,
And owes to June her day of birth,
With ring of agate on her hand
Can health, wealth, and long life command.

JULY.
The glowing ruby should adorn
Those who in warm July are born.
Then they will be exempt and free
From love's doubts and anxiety.

AUGUST.
Wear a sardonyx, or for thee'
No conjugal felicity.
The August-born without this stone
'Tis said must live unloved and lone.

SEPTEMBER.
A maiden born when autumn leaves
Are rustling in September's breeze,
A sapphire on her brow should bind—
'Twill cure diseases of the mind.

OCTOBER.
October's child is born for woe,
And life's vicissitudes must know.
But lay an opal on her breast,
And hope will lull those woes to rest.

NOVEMBER.
Who first comes to this world below
With drear November's fog and snow,
Should prize the topaz's amber hue—
Emblems of friends and lovers true.

DECEMBER.
If cold December gave you birth,
The month of snow and ice and mirth,
Place on your hand a turquoise blue—
Success will bless you, whate'er you do.

Relic of
Old Presbyterian
Church.
Cavendish. P. E. I.
May 1899.

QUIET HOME WEDDING.

Miss Lottie Shatford and Mr. E. F. T.
Handy United at Hubbard's Cove.

The marriage was solemnized at Hubbard's Cove on Monday morning of Miss
Lottie Shatford, daughter of John E.
Shatford, and Mr. E. F. T. Handy, eldest son of Mr. Edward Handy, of Elmsdale, Ont. The ceremony was performed
by the Rev. Allan P. Shatford, cousin
of the bride and rector at North Sydney,
assisted by the Rev. J. L. S. Foster, of
the parish, in the presence of only the
immediate family. Breakfast followed the
ceremony, the breakfast room being decorated in Christmas decorations of holly
and green. Later Mr. and Mrs. Handy
drove to Halifax to take the Maritime
Express. They will spend Christmas in
Quebec and New Year at the home of
the groom's parents, visiting Toronto
and Montreal before returning to the
Province for the winter. Mr. Handy is
on MacKenzie & Mann's engineering staff
of the Halifax and South Western Railway. Mrs. Handy is a popular and accomplished young lady who has many
friends in Halifax who will join in the
congratulations.

THE death took place at North Rustico
on Sunday Sept 16th of Miss Jennie M
McLure, daughter of Mr and Mrs Hugh
McLure, at the early age of 22 years.
The deceased was a young lady of high
christian character, gentle and loving
disposition, and bore her long suffering
with patience and cheerfulness. She
leaves to mourn a sorrowing
father and mother, two brothers
Aderine of Linkletter and Henry at
home and one sister Mrs Townshend
McNeill of North Rustico, who will
have the deep sympathy of their large
circle of friends in their hour of bereavement. The funeral which was one
of the largest ever held in the vicinity
took place yesterday afternoon to Cavendish Cemetery. The services at the
house were conducted by Revs. Hugh
McDonald, G. N. Stevenson and J.
Belyea and at the cemetery by Rev.
Mr. Belyea.

Tuesday.
Sept 16th
1902

June
Sun Mon Tue Wed Thu Fr. S
1 2 3 4
6 7 8 9 10 11
13 14 15 16 17 18 1
20 21 22 23 24 25 26
27 28 29 30

Prudence and se
spirit bold and
With honour's soul.
united bea thee
Hours of Idleness.

A SWELL AFFAIR

In the jubilee year of Queen Victoria two women were
heard discussing in a tram car the meaning of the word
"jubilee." One did not know the meaning of it; the other did, or thought she did, and gave the following explanation: "Twenty-five 'ears mairit's a silver waddin', an'
fifty 'ears mairit's a golden waddin', an' the jubilee's whan
the maun dees!"

Embarrassing !

A strange minister was preaching in a New
England church recently, and when he opened
the Bible he came upon a notice, which got
mixed up with the regular notices of the day,
and read it out with all due solemnity.

It was a request for the congregation's sympathy and prayers for John Q. Briggs, who had
been deeply afflicted by the loss of his wife.

The regular minister had been using the
notice as a book marker more than a year, and
John Q. Briggs, in a natty grey suit, sat in a
front pew with the new wife he had taken just
the week before.

recognized favorite, Sadie C ▢ appeared before a Charlottetown audience in which, it was easy to perceive, there were many of her admirers. The house was crowded and Miss Calhoun and her company of players should feel flattered by the attention and applause bestowed upon them—even if the same was richly marited as happened to be the case. In the dramatization of Mary J. Holmes' well-known novel "Lena Rivers" Miss Calhoun in the title role did some very effective work. She really is worthy of more than the usual application of complimentary terms handed out on occasions of this sort, for her talent is manifest to the senses, and her charm is more than ordinary. Her delineation of the part excited the liveliest sympathy and admiration and her success was testified by generous applause. Miss Calhoun received a handsome boquet as a tribute to her skill. The other members in the cast acted well their parts presenting the play in a manner that was well balanced—no one part detracting from the high quality marking the whole performance. It will be good news to theatre-goers to know that "Lena Rivers" is to be repeated on Friday night, the closing night of Miss Calhoun's engagement here. To-night the play will be "Miss Calvert of Louisiana." The Knickerbocker Quartette between the first and second acts sang some selections in good taste and their music was harmonious and pleasing.

Monday's Child is fair of face.
Tuesday's Child is full of grace.
Wednesday's Child has far to go.
Thursday's Child is full of woe.
Friday's Child is loving and giving.
Saturday's Child must work for her living.
But the Child who is born on the Sabbath Day
Is witty and wise and gentle and gay.

Mixed Up.—At a trial in a German ▢urt a man appeared as a witness.
"Your name?" asked the judge.
"Vell, I calls myself Fritz, but may be I don't know if it is Henrich. You see, Judge, dat mine moder she haf two poys; one of them was me and one mine proder, and toder was myself; ▢n't know which, and my moder, she ▢t know, too; and one of us was named ▢z, and toder Henrich, or one Henrich ▢ toder Fritz. I don't know which it ▢ and one of us got died, and my ▢r she could never tell which it was, ▢ mine broder, who got died. So you ▢r. Judge, I don't know whether I ▢itz or Henrich, and my ▢

EVOLUTION OF THE ENGAGEMENT RING:

MARRIED
HOUSTON-FRASER— ▢ the Manse,
Cavendish, April 1 ▢ the
Rev. John Stirling, ▢
Houston and Ann ▢
both of Mayfield.

Mayflower Picnic.
May 1890.

AN ANGLER'S PARADISE—McNEILL'S POND

Old Baptist Church.

The old Baptist
church Lower dial
P. E. Island.

THE LITERARY MAID OF ALL WORK.

In spring I chant the glowing hue
    Of autumn's gay apparel ;
With mercury at ninety two,
    I write a Christmas carol ;
When all the land, in snowy dress,
    Lies sunk in winter slumber,
We're hustling 'round to get to press
    The Great Midsummer Number.

When life is glad with singing birds
    And bright with sunny magic,
The order comes, "Two thousand words ;
    You'd better make it tragic."
When all my being seems to merge
    In fierce and somber passions,
Or I would chant a funeral dirge,
    I'm set to writing fashions.

I'm Grandma's Specs for Little Fry,
    Receipts of Auntie Plenty's.
A Word to Men and Maidens—I,
    A spinster in the twenties !
I tell what springs from drink and dice,
    How carpets should be shaken ;
I give young mothers sage advice—
    God grant it isn't taken !

I set at naught the season's laws ;
    I violate my nature
By posing as a set of bores
    In foolish nomenclature.
And yet there's humor in the fray ;
    'Tis only this that pinches—
" We want a poem, right away,
    " And make it just four inches !"

```
              MAY.
     S M T W T F S
               1  2  3  4
      5  6  7  8  9 10 11
     12 13 14 15 16 17 18
     19 20 21 22 23 24 25
     26 27 28 29 30 31
```

May 10th 1903.

A fair exchange is no
    robbery.
"no nights in heaven".
A matrimonial arrange-
    ment.
L. N. M. R. A. M. N. L. H. S. M.

THE concert and pie social held in
Granville Hall on Thursday night, under
the auspices of Pearly Stream Division
of the Sons of Temperance, was a decided success. Although the night was
cold and somewhat stormy, yet a goodly
number were present to enjoy a few
hours listening to the best local talent
that could be secured for the occasion.
The programme was carried out in a
very able manner, and reflected credit on
those who took part in what might be
called the very best entertainment
that has taken place in Granville
for a number of years. The following
is the programme: Opening chorus, by
the choir; recitation, Miss Ella B Brown;
solo, Mr. Wm. Morrison; speech, Mr.
Geo. Simpson; instrumental duett Miss
Florence Haslam and Mr. Neil McNeill;
solo, Miss Lilla Morris; recitation, Miss
Maud Montgomery; solo, R. M. Lamont
(encored); stump speech, A. J. Corbett;
solo and chorus, W. Haslam and choir;
recitation, Mr. Chas. E. McKenzie; solo,
Miss Gertie McLeod; stump speech,
Mr. W. Morrison; solo, R. M. Lamont
(encored); closing chorus, choir. After
this excellent programme was rendered
the auctioneer, Mr. R M. Lamont, sold
the pies, all of which brought good
prices. Over $20 was realized, which
goes towards buying an organ for the
Division. Special mention must be
made of the solo of Miss Lilla Morris, a
little girl of six, who made her first
appearance in public and delighted the
audience with her clear sweet voice.
Mr. Chas. McKenzie performed the
duties of chairman, while Miss Florence
Haslam presided at the organ.

CONVENIENT.

"What are marsupials?" asked the teacher, and
Johnny was ready with his answer.

"Animals that have pouches in their stomachs,"
he said, glibly.

"And for what are these pouches used?" asked
the teacher, ignoring the slight inaccuracy of the
answer. "I'm sure that you know that, too."

"Yes'm," said Johnny, with encouraging promptness. "The pouches are for them to crawl into
and conceal themselves when pursued."

레드 스크랩북 34쪽

고양이에게 헌정하는 이 지면은 주로 헨리에트 론네르 크닙(블루 스크랩북 22쪽 참고)이 잡지에 그린 삽화들을 오려 붙인 것이다. 카드 안쪽에는 몽고메리의 사촌인 토티 (애니) 맥닐Tottie (Annie) Macneill이 소중히 여기는 고양이 밥스를 안고 찍은 청사진이 있다. 몽고메리가 찍은 맥닐가의 농장 마당 사진은 외할머니의 부엌문에서 찍었다. 가운데 아래에 있는 고양이는 밥스일까? 밥스는 원래 코코Coco라고 불렸는데, 보어전쟁의 영웅이자 영국군 지도자였던 육군원수 칸다하르의 로버츠 경을 부르는 애칭이 "밥스"였다. (흰 카드에 적혀 있는) "감성 충만soulful"은 몽고메리와 노라가 비밀 일기에서 제임스 알렉산더 스튜어트를 부르는 별명이었다. 노라는 제임스가 밥스와 비슷한 이유를 수수께끼로 낸 적이 있는데, 이 카드로(이 페이지 전체를 말하는 듯도 하다) 몽고메리는 분한 척 대답한 셈이다.

고양이

루시 모드 몽고메리는 고양이를 무척 좋아했다. 1887년부터 가지고 있던 톱시의 털과 아버지의 결혼 청첩장은 블루 스크랩북과 레드 스크랩북에서 가장 오래된 소장품이다. 다른 고양이들의 이름과 털도 스크랩북 곳곳에 보관되어 있다. 카리시마, 파이어플라이, 맥스, 톰스, 밥스, 래디, 대피 1세와 대피 2세를 가장 좋아하는 고양이로 꼽았다. 고양이 그림을 구하여 캐번디시의 침실 벽에 걸었고, 나중에 온타리오에 살 때는 잉크로 검은 고양이를 그려서 서명에 포함하기도 했다(이 책의 헌시 참고). 이완 맥도널드도 몽고메리만큼 고양이를 좋아했고, 몽고메리의 두 아들도 자라면서 고양이를 좋아하게 됐다. 두 아이가 친구들과 찍은 사진에 고양이가 같이 찍힌 사진이 수십 장은 된다. 고양이만 사진에 담기도 했다. 몽고메리에게 마지막 두 번째 작품이 된 소설 《랜턴힐의 제인Jane of Lantern Hill》(1937)은 "십사 년 동안 매력적이고 다정한 동지"였다면서 사랑하는 회색 줄무늬 고양이 럭키와의 추억에 헌정했을 정도이다. 몽고메리는 자기 가정을 꾸린 뒤로는 늘 고양이를 한 마리 이상 길렀고, 1911년에 결혼하여 온타리오에 정착했을 때는 대피(일기를 봐도 대피 3세를 말하는 것인지 정확하지 않다)를 나무 궤짝에 넣어 데려올 준비를 했을 정도이다. 프레더리카 캠벨도 고양이를 사랑했고, 스코틀랜드 펜팔 친구인 조지 보이드 맥밀런도 그랬다. 어린 앤의 삶에 고양이가 거의 등장하지 않는다는 것은 수수께끼다. 물론 고양이를 허락하지 않았으리라고 짐작되는 마릴라의 생각은 고양이는 집 안이 아니라 헛간에서 살아야 한다고 믿었던 외할머니의 생각을 그대로 반영하고 있을 것이다. 외할머니도 나이가 들고는 회색 얼룩 고양이 대피를 점점 좋아하여 대피에게서 위안을 얻기도 했다. 고양이는 앤이 성인이 된 이후의 삶에 두드러지게 나타난다. 외할머니가 더 이상 세상에 없어서 그 이야기를 읽지도 못할 터이기 때문이다. 몽고메리는 에밀리 버드 스타에게는 고양이를 대단히 아끼고 사랑하는 마음을 선물한다.

All
Good
Wishes

Cats

Whose faith in
humanity is great
— but —
who is not like
the Soulful.

Cruel, but composed and bland,
Dumb, inscrutable and grand;
So Tiberius might have sat,
Had Tiberius been a cat.

여기에서는 루시 모드 몽고메리가 자신과 다른 사람들의 사진들까지 모아서 자기가 좋아하는 것들을 얘기한다.

36쪽 로라 프리처드 애그뉴가 아들을 낳았다는 소식을 아기 사진 여러 장과 함께 붙여뒀다. 많은 학교 친구가 결혼하고 아이도 낳았다. 몽고메리 개인의 삶에서 이완 맥도널드 목사가 점점 더 중요한 위치를 차지하게 됐다는 점을 감안하면, 우리에게 친숙한 교직에 대한 재담과 더불어 종교적인 농담이 늘어간다는 사실에도 특별한 의미가 담겨 있을까? 〈젖소가 집에 올 때When the Cows Come Home〉는 몽고메리와 노라가 같이 읽은 작품인지도 모른다.

37쪽 로라 프리처드 애그뉴의 여동생 에벌린은 1903년에 결혼했다(청첩장은 봉투 안에 있다). 그로부터 칠 년도 더 지난 1911년 7월 5일, 에벌린의 결혼식에서 연주됐던 찬송가 〈에덴 동산 위에서 속삭이는 목소리The Voice That Breathed O'er Eden〉가 똑같이 연주되는 소리를 들으면서 몽고메리는 파크 코너의 캠벨가 응접실에서 자기 결혼식을 맞게 된다. 사진 속 호랑가시나무는 인조 호랑가시나무와 짝을 이루는데 로라가 여동생의 결혼식 기념으로 몽고메리에게 보내준 것인 듯하다. 찢어진 트럼프 카드는 몽고메리와 노라가 1903년 비밀 일기에서 언급한 오래된 카드 한 벌에 들어 있던 것인 듯하다. "내 교향곡My Symphony"에 제시되어 있는 하모니는 그 중간에 끼어든 카드들과 상관없이 에벌린의 결혼을 축복하는 듯하다.

38쪽 몽고메리는 자신이 좋아하는 "연인의 오솔길"의 청사진을 낡은 달력 위에 붙여놓았다. "어느 여자의 마지막 말A Woman's Last Word"은 서로 멀어진 연인의 자존심에 관한 우스개 이야기다. 앤 셜리가 길버트를 무시하는 정도와 거의 비슷하다. 연극 광고에서 한 가지 항목이 눈에 들어온다. "특별 출연Specialty Stars" 아래에 있는 "적갈색 털을 가진 개와 함께 있는 소녀The Girl with the Dog with the Auburn Hair" 말이다. 몽고메리는 학창 시절에 빨간 머리인 오스틴 레어드Austin Laird를 골려먹느라 〈적갈색 머리카락을 가진 소년The Boy with the Auburn Hair〉이라는 시를 썼던 기억을 떠올렸을까? 몽고메리와 오스틴은 그 뒤로 한동안 서로 말을 하지 않았다. 양 떼 목장 사진은 또 다른 기억을 떠올리게 했을 것이다. 일기에 따르면 1893년 9월 4일에 몽고메리는 오스트레일리아에 사는 여자아이에게서 "'귀여운 적갈색 양 한 마리만' 보내달라는 편지를 받는 꿈을 꾸었다. 오스틴이 내 머리맡을 맴돌고 있는 게 틀림없다고 생각한다". 몽고메리는 그 상황을 거꾸로 바꾸어 《빨강 머리 앤》에서 앤 셜리가 빨간 머리를 "당근!"이라며 놀리는 길버트 블라이드의 머리에 석판이 부서질 정도로 내리치게 만들었다.

Born.

AGNEW—On July 9th, 1902, the wife of A. Agnew, of a son.

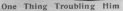

One Thing Troubling Him

AN old Scotch fisherman was visited during his last illness by a clergyman, who wore a close-fitting clerical waistcoat, which buttoned behind. The clergyman asked the old man if his mind was perfectly at ease. "Oo, ay, I'm a' richt; but there's just ae thing that troubles me, and I dinna like to speak o't." "I am anxious to comfort you,' replied the clergyman. "Tell me what perplexes you." "Weel, sir, it's just like this," said the old man, eagerly. "I canna for the life o' me mak' oot hoo ye manage tae get intae that westkit."—N. Y. Observer.

WHEN THE COWS COME HOME.

(Edith Hunter, St. Etienne De Beauharnois, very kindly sends the words of "When the cows come home' by Mrs. Agnes E. Mitchell, which was asked for by 'Prairie' in a recent issue of the 'Witness.')

With klingle, klangle, klingle,
Way down the dusty dingle,
The cows are coming home.
Now sweet and clear, and faint and low,
The airy tinklings come and go.
Like chimings from the far off tower,
Or patterings of an April shower
That makes the daisies grow;
Koling, koling, kolinglelingle,
Far down the darkening dingle,
The cows come slowly home.
And old-time friends, and twilight plays,
And starry nights, and sunny days,
Come trooping up the misty ways,
When the cows come home.

With jingle, jangle, jingle,
Soft tones that sweetly mingle,
The cows are coming home;
Malvine and Pearl, and Florimel,
DeKamp, Red Rose and Gretchen Schell,
Queen Bess and Sylph and Spangled Sue,
Across the fields I hear her 'loo-oo'
And clang her silver bell;
Goling, goling, golinglelingle,
With faint far sounds that mingle,
The cows come slowly home.
And mother songs of long-gone years,
And baby joys and childish fears,
And youthful hopes and youthful tears,
When the cows come home.

With ringle, rangle, ringle,
By twos and threes and single,
The cows are coming home,
Through violet air we see the town,
And the summer sun a-slipping down,
And the maple in the hazel glade
Throws down the path a longer shade
And the hills are growing brown
To-ring, to-rang toringleringle,
By threes and fours and single,
The cows come slowly home.
The same sweet sound of wordless psalm,
The same sweet June day rest and calm.
The same sweet scent of buds and balm,
When the cows come home.

With tinkle, tankle, tinkle,
Through ferns and periwinkle
The cows are coming home,
A-loitering in the checkered stream
Where the sun rays glance and gleam;
Clarine, Peachbloom and Phoebe, Phyllis,
Stand knee-deep in the creamy lilies,
In a drowsy dream;
To-link, to-lank, to-linklelinkle,
O'er banks with buttercups a-twinkle,
The cows come slowly home.
And up through memory's deep ravine
Come the brook's old song and its old-time sheen,
And the crescent of the silver queen,
When the cows come home.

With klingle, klangle, klingle,
With loo-oo, moo-oo, and jingle,
The cows are coming home,
And over there on Merlin Hill,
Sounds the plaintive cry of the whippoor-will
And the dew-drops lie on the tangled vines,
And over the poplars Venus shines,
And over the silent mill.
Ko-ling, ko-lang, kolinglelingle,
With a ting-a-ling and jingle,
When the cows come come slowly home.
Let down the bars; let in the train
Of long gone songs and flowers and rain,
For dear old times come back again,
When the cows come home.

Mrs. F. Bennett. Mrs. Garvock H.C.

Schoolmaster (turning round sharply): "Which of you is it that is daring to make faces at me?" Six Youngsters (in chorus): "Freddy Brown, sir." Schoolmaster: "Ah! Then you six boys stand up and be caned. If you saw Freddy Brown making faces, it shows that you were not attending to your lessons."

레드 스크랩북 36쪽

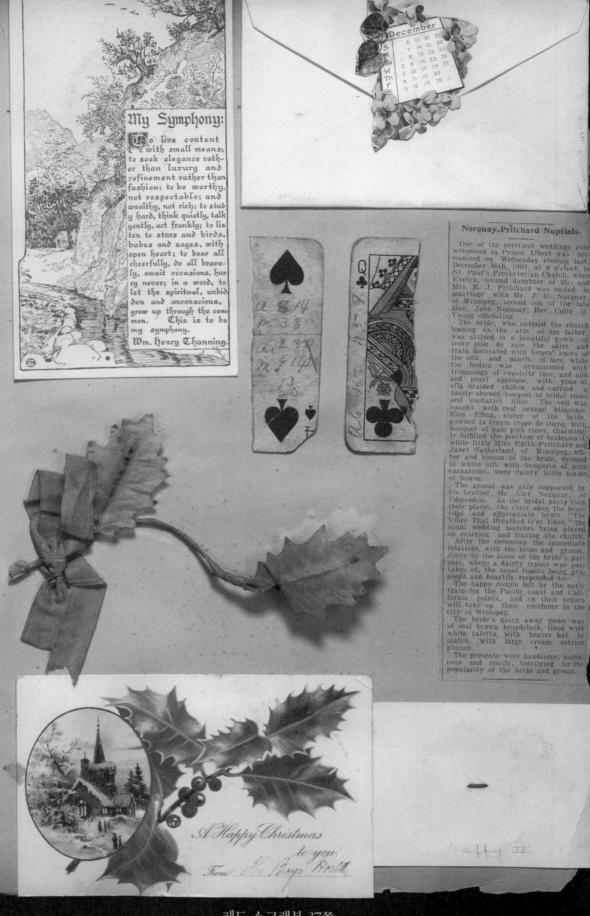

My Symphony:

To live content with small means; to seek elegance rather than luxury and refinement rather than fashion; to be worthy, not respectable; and wealthy, not rich; to study hard, think quietly, talk gently, act frankly; to listen to stars and birds, babes and sages, with open heart; to bear all cheerfully, do all bravely, await occasions, hurry never; in a word, to let the spiritual, unbidden and unconscious, grow up through the common. This is to be my symphony.

Wm. Henry Channing.

December

	S	M	Tu	W	Th	F	S
	6	13	20	27			
	7	14	21	28			
	1	8	15	22	29		
	2	9	16	23	30		
	3	10	17	24	31		
	4	11	18	25			
	5	12	19	26			

Norquay–Pritchard Nuptials.

One of the prettiest weddings ever witnessed in Prince Albert was solemnized on Wednesday evening last, December 30th, 1903, at 8 o'clock, in St. Paul's Presbyterian Church, when Evelyn, second daughter of Mr. and Mrs. R. J. Pritchard was united in marriage with Mr. J. G. Norquay, of Winnipeg, second son of the late Hon. John Norquay, Rev. Colin G. Young officiating.

The bride, who entered the church leaning on the arm of her father, was attired in a beautiful gown of ivory poie de soie, the skirt and train decorated with lovers' knots of the silk, and panels of lace, while the bodice was ornamented with trimmings of exquisite lace, and silk and pearl applique, with yoke of silk braided chiffon, and carried a lovely shower bouquet of bridal roses and eucharist lilies. The veil was caught with real orange blossoms. Miss Elma, sister of the bride, gowned in cream crepe de chene, with bouquet of pale pink roses, charmingly fulfilled the position of bridesmaid, while little Miss Edith Pritchard and Janet Sutherland, of Winnipeg, sister and cousin of the bride, dressed in white silk with bouquets of pink carnations, were dainty little maids of honor.

The groom was ably supported by his brother, Mr. Alex. Norquay, of Edmonton. As the bridal party took their places, the choir sang the beautiful and appropriate hymn, "The Voice That Breathed O'er Eden," the usual wedding marches being played on entering and leaving the church.

After the ceremony the immediate relatives, with the bride and groom, drove to the home of the bride's parents, where a dainty repast was partaken of, the usual toasts being proposed and heartily responded to.

The happy couple left by the early train for the Pacific coast and California points, and on their return will take up their residence in the city of Winnipeg.

The bride's going away gown was of seal brown broadcloth, lined with white taffeta, with beaver hat to match, with large cream ostrich plumes.

The presents were handsome, numerous and costly, testifying to the popularity of the bride and groom.

A Happy Christmas to you.

From The Boys World

OPERA HOUSE

Four nights commencing Monday, September 24th

The Nineteenth Edition of CHARLES H. YALE'S
Forever and Ever

DEVIL'S AUCTION

Re-written, re-arranged and staged under the personal direction of

CHAS. H. YALE

and produced with new scenery by John W. Wilkins and T. A. Manning

Costumes and Armour by Van Horn & Son, and Armour from designs of McIlvaine. Wig by A. M. Buch & Co. Shoes by Bertrand & Co. Tights by Nolan & Co. Mechanical Effects, A. J. Overpeck and Stephen MacNeill. Properties, William Ullrich. Light Effects, William P. Currans.

CAST

MORTALS

Carlos, a poor shepherd..................Miss Beatrice Clements
Toby, a donkey, afterwards transformed into a man.........R. T. Brown
Pere Andoche, an old Flemish Farmer................W. H. Lorella
Count Fortuno, created by Mephisto's art to resemble a mortal
......................................Miss Madge Torrence
Going Gone, an auctioneer...................James A. Franks
Tresbem, a bailiff............................George Cole
Madeline, Andoche's daughter..........Miss Florence Clements
Janet, a milkmaid.......................Miss Annie Lloyd
Peasants, Villagers, etc.

MONGOLIANS

Kow Wow Chang, Grand Mandarin.............W. H. Lorella
See Shing, his astrologer...................Henri Earle
Hoang Kan, his doctor...................Thomas Saelyr
Moon Show, Soothsayer....................Wm. Speurl
Koket.................................Miss Julia Lake
Oriental attendants of the Mandarin

IMMORTALS

Crystalline, the fairy protectress...........Miss Alice Stoddard

INFERNALS

Mephisto, the evil one................Henry P. Thomas
Chaos, an imp of darkness.................Ben Leando
Witches, Gnomes, Goblins, Skeletons and Demons

PRINCIPAL DANCERS

Amelia Maveroffer....................Premier Absolute
Hilda Maccari.....................Premier Characteristic

SPECIALTY STARS

Richard T. Brown................Comedian and Mimic
Annie Lloyd......................The Vital Spark
The Three Brothers Leando..........Comedy Acrobats
Irene and Zaza......The Girl with the Dog with the Auburn Hair
Sisters Clements...................Descriptive Duetists

AND

THE SIDONIA TROUPE......... of Eight English Singers and Dancers.
Direction Alfred and Madame Phasey

Overture—Forever and Ever Devil's Auction.............Perle
Leon M. Polachek and Orchestra

SYNOPSIS OF SCENERY, INCIDENTS, BALLETS AND FEATURES

ACT I.—Scene 1.—The Caverns of Gloom (new). Revolving Transformation to Andoche Valley (new).
THE SISTERS CLEMENTS, in their Singing and Dancing Specialties
First time of the new Comic Divertisement, arranged by Madame Phasey, entitled
LES DANSE GROTESQUE, introducing Entire Corps de Ballet and Principal Dancers, AMELIA MAVEROFFER and HILDA MACCARI, Grand Finale and Comic Tableau
ACT II.—Scene 1.—Flemish Landscape. MISS ANNIE LLOYD, THE VITAL SPARK, in Unique Specialties. Scene 2—The New and Comical Trick Scene CASTLE INSOMNIA. Mechanical change to Scene 3. THE GARDENS OF THE MANIKINS. Brilliant Mongolian Ballet arranged by Madame Phasey.
THE FEAST OF THE DRAGON, introducing the Corps de Ballet and European Premieres, AMELIA MAVEROFFER and HILDA MACCARI

THE THREE BROTHERS LEANDO, Comedy Acrobats
RICHARD T. BROWN, Comedian and Mimic
The Laughable Manikin Scene—Imposing Tableau

ACT III.—Scene 1.—The New Electric Sensation. THE DANCE OF THE ELEMENTS, interpreted by Amelia Maveroffer and Hilda Maccari
THE MUSICAL DOLLS, Misses Wasserman, Lake, Young, Stoddard, Munn Sisters, Maccari and Troy. Scene 2.—The Palace of Flora. THE FAMOUS SIDONIA TROUPE, the English Singing and Dancing Octette Direction of Alfred and Madame Phasey
IRENE and ZAZA, the Girl with the Dog with the Auburn Hair
Scene 3.—The Realms of Despair. Scene 4.—A new magnificent transformation scene, entitled "The Flight of Time," concluding with the magnificent missen scene, "The Palace of Hours."

Sweet is it to have done
the
thing one
ought.

The Princess

SEPTEMBER.

Sun	7	14	21	28
Mon	1	8	15	22	29
Tue	2	9	16	23	30
Wed	3	10	17	24
Thu	4	11	18	25
Fri	5	12	19	26
Sat	6	13	20	27

OCTOBER.

Sun	5	12	19	26
Mon	6	13	20	27
Tue	7	14	21	28
Wed	1	8	15	22	29
Thu	2	9	16	23	30
Fri	3	10	17	24	31
Sat	4	11	18	25

RAPHAEL TUCK & SONS 67 LONDON.

SHEEP RANCH IN CALIFORNIA
By Nellie E. Stiffler

A WOMAN'S LAST WORD.

IF the two young people of whom *Answers* tells this story were not reconciled by their own absurdity, they at least furnished amusement for others.

They had been engaged, but had quarreled, and were too proud to make up. Both were anxious to have people believe that they had entirely forgotten each other.

He called at her home one day to see her father—on business, of course. She answered the door-bell.

Said he: "Ah, Miss Jepkin, I believe. Is your father in?"

"No, sir," she replied, "father is not in at present. Do you wish to see him personally?"

"I do," he answered, feeling that she was yielding, "on very particular personal business," and he turned proudly to go away.

"I beg your pardon," she cried after him, as he reached the lowest step, "but who shall I say called?"

❖ ❖ ❖

소설 집필을 시작하기 전이면 그동안 기록해 둔 쪽지와 자투리 대화들을 자세히 살펴봤듯이, 루시 모드 몽고메리는 수집품과 오려낸 기사를 모아둔 상자들을 샅샅이 찾아보고, 최소한 1889년부터 최대한 1906년까지의 자료들을 골라 이 지면들을 꾸몄다. 종이로 덮인 풀 자국, 부분적으로 가려진 너덜너덜한 가장자리를 보면 몽고메리가 이야기를 고치거나, 스크랩북 자료를 떼어서 일기에 삽화로 썼다는 것을 짐작할 수 있다.

39쪽《프린스에드워드섬 매거진Prince Edward Island Magazine》에서 오려낸 심프슨가의 제분소(몽고메리 시대의 명소였다), 같은 잡지에서 오려낸, 몽고메리가 존경하는 프린스오브웨일스 대학교수 존 케이븐John Caven의 시, 몽고메리가 찍은 르포스 곶의 청사진(훨씬 오래전에 같은 곳을 촬영한 사진을 레드 스크랩북 3쪽과 48쪽에 실었다)은 모두 고향에 대한 사랑을 보여주며, '앤' 시리즈에서도 책장을 넘길 때마다 그 사랑을 느낄 수 있다. 부총독Lieutenant Governor의 명함은 1910년 가을에 캐나다 총독인 그레이 백작에게 초대받았던 날의 기념물일 것이다. 그레이 백작도《빨강 머리 앤》을 무척 좋아했다.

40쪽 레드 스크랩북 26쪽에 실린 〈길모퉁이〉라는 시의 제목같이《빨강 머리 앤》의 팬이라면 시 제목에 들어간 "연인의 오솔길"이라는 구절(왼쪽 위)에 관심이 쏠릴 것이다. 낙엽, 〈연인의 오솔길에 내린 겨울Winter in Lovers' Lane〉, 〈데이지의 노래The Daisies' Lane〉 속 봄과 여름(펜팔 친구 이프리엄 웨버의 글에서 은유적으로 표현한 상록수는 사계절 전체에 속한다)처럼 사계절로 모아지는 표현들이 '연인의 오솔길'이라는 장소를 이 지면의 주제로 제시하는 듯하다. 하지만 그 자료들을 하나로 묶는 것은 연인 자체인지도 모른다. 허먼 리어드의 형제가 결혼한다는 소식을 클린턴 스콜라드Clinton Scollard의 시와 나란

히 배치하면서 몽고메리는 분명히 세상을 떠난 허먼을 생각했을 것이다. 잘생긴 유부남인 에드윈 스미스Edwin Smith는 1901년에 캐번디시에서 보이기 시작해 1903년 친구인 이완 맥도널드의 부임 예배에서 설교를 했는데, 맥도널드 부부가 온타리오에 정착하여 생활할 때도 그들 앞에 자주 나타났다. 잡지에서 오려낸 패션 모델은 이 지면에 남은 자국으로 보아 몽고메리가 누군가의 사진을 떼어내고 그 사진으로 대신했다는 것을 알 수 있다.

42쪽 1904년 여름, 몽고메리는 1894년에 썼던 옛 일기를 읽으며 자신이 얼마나 변했는지 가늠하고 있었다. 1894년 프린스오브웨일스 대학 교지《칼리지 레코드》에 짧은 희극인 〈정해진 법칙The Usual Way〉을 기고했는데, 스스로 열심히 공부한다고 굳게 믿는 밀리센트와 로즈가 초콜릿을 먹으면서 지나가는 행인들을 구경하고 잡담을 나눈다는 내용이다. 몽고메리는 자신의 졸업 10주년 기념으로 열린 발표회(뮤지컬 작품과 2막극) 프로그램을 간직했다. 포인트 플레전트 공원은 몽고메리가 핼리팩스에 살 때 거닐기 좋아했던 곳으로,《레드먼드의 앤》(1915)에서 앤이 "킹스포트"의 "레드먼드 대학"에 다닐 때 자주 산책하는 장소로 나온다. 우스꽝스러운 노새 지표는 십 년 후 몽고메리의 전진을 역설적으로 보여준다.

AT THE DUNK.

By John Caven.

AUSE here,—and look upon a sight as fair
  As ever painter limned of poet's dreams :
g the forest-tops the sun's last beams
  ger caressingly, while here and there
purple patch drops through the heated air
n Dunk's clear waters, as, with graceful sweep,
hey lave the forest roots or noiseless creep
  eneath the flowers the meadow's margins bear.
A thoughtful stillness reigns : on earth or sky.
o sound to jar, no cloud the blue to dim :
ith chirp and croak, the night-hawk hurries by,
d high-perched robin chants his compline hymn ;
  up, the rapids seem to heave a sigh,—
nk, mourning meets the tide—a grave to him.

"Children," said the teacher, while instructing the class
in composition, "you should not attempt any flights of
fancy, but simply be yourselves, and write what is in you.
Do not imitate any other person's writings or draw in-
spiration from outside sources." As a result of this advice, Johnny Wise turned in the following composition :
"We should not attempt any flites of fancy, but rite what
is in us. In me there is my stummick, lungs, hart, liver,
two apples, one piece of pie, one stick of lemon candy, and
my dinner."—*Selected.*

Let Them Do It

A FARMER'S wife who had no very romantic
  ideas about the opposite sex, and who,
hurrying from churn to sink, from sink to shed,
and back to the kitchen stove, was asked if she
wanted to vote.
  "No, I certainly don't!" she said. "I say if
there's one little thing that the men folks can do
alone, for goodness' sake let 'em do it!"

The Board of Education insists that scholars in the first and second year's course in
higher elementary schools shall spend at
least four hours per week in the study of
science, half of which time must be devoted
to practical work. The ages of these
scholars will vary between ten and twelve.
Half of them are girls. Touching this a
Halifax correspondent, who signs himself
' W. D.,' sends us the following :—

Seated one day at my lessons,
  I was wearily trying to cram
A problem in hydrostatics—
  Something about a gramme.
I know not if I was dreaming,
  I fancy I wanted my tea ;
But I heard a melodious murmur
  Like the sound of A, B, C.

It flooded the dreary class-room
  Like an echo from long ago,
It filled my soul with yearnings
  And my eyes with H_2O.
I couldn't think where I had heard it,
  My memory seemed to halt ;
It brought back the days when children
  Called sodium chloride 'salt.'
It made me forget for a moment
  The smells and formulae,
And it trembled away into silence
  With a sound I thought was D.

I have sought, but I seek it vainly,
  That A, B, C, divine ;
I heard it in my childhood,
  But now I am nearly nine.
I learn about nitric acid,
  I learn about NH_3 ;
Perhaps when I go to the Technical School
  I shall learn my A, B, C.

AN UNFORTUNATE PITCH

A MUSICAL ANECDOTE

Copyright 1899, by Ivers & Pond Piano Co.

Now it happened one morning, not a very ♪ ago, that a
farmer by the name of 𝄞♩♩♩♩ set out for Boston to sell
a load of ♩♩♩♩ and to buy a new ♪. His horse had not
been young very recently, and his ♩ movement was about *largo*
tranquillo; but when he had gone a little more than 𝄞♩♩
of the distance, he unexpectedly took fright at a stranger who
carried a large ♩ in one hand and a ♩ of ducks in the
other, and rushing down a 𝄞♩♩♩♩♩ where
the road made a ♯, he upset the load, throwing the farmer
to the ground ♭ on his 𝄞♩♩. At first he seemed a
little dazed and somewhat off his ♩. He got a ♩ into his
head that an earthquake had made his load 𝄞♩♩ so that he
lost his ♩, and that a great ground ──── made the road
pitch and roll like a ship in a 𝄞♩♩. However, in a 𝄰
time he recovered his consciousness in a great *poco a*
poco. The stranger came up to help on a *Presto* 𝄞♪♪♪♪♪♪
and said they would have things fixed in 𝄰 It took them
but a 𝄰 to get some ──── from the fence, right up the
wagon, put every 𝄞♩♩ in place and ♩♩ them on
with a 𝄞♩♩ making everything *Allegro.* The horse had
ceased to ♩ with fear, and they started again. Having reached
Boston, the farmer sold his grain to a dealer in ♩♩♩,
then bought a new ♪ ♩ at the rooms of Ivers and Pond, who do
business on a large 𝄞♩♩ He paid 𝄞♩♩
of the price in cash and gave a ♩ over his own ♩ for the
──── On the way back he did not ♩♩♩ his morning experience,
but safely reached his journey's 𝄰   Ben Marcato.

LITTLE BROWN HANDS.
(By Mary H. Krout.)

They drive home the cows from the pas-
   ture,
Up through the long, shady lane,
Where the quail whistles loud in the wheat
   field,
  That is yellow with ripening grain,
They find, in the thick waving grasses,
  Where the scarlet-lipped strawberry
    grows,
They gather the earliest snowdrops,
  And the first crimson buds of the rose.

They toss the hay in the meadow,
  They gather the elder-bloom white,
They find when the dusky grapes purple
  In the soft-tinted October light.
They know where the apples hang ripest,
  And are sweeter than Italy's wines,
They know where the fruit hangs the
   thickest,
  On the long, thorny blackberry vines.

They gather the delicate seaweeds,
  And build tiny castles of sand ;
They pick up the beautiful sea-shells,
  Fairy barks that have drifted to land.
They wave from the tall, rocking tree-tops,
  Where the oriole's hammock nest
   swings,
And at night-time are folded in slumber
  By a song that a fond mother sings.

Those who toil bravely are strongest ;
  The humble and poor become great ;
And from those brown-handed children
  Shall grow mighty rulers of State.
The pen of the author and statesman,
  The noble and wise of the land,
The sword and chisel and pallette,
  Shall be held in the little brown hand.

Ecclesiastical Humor.

Some stories about children collected by
the late Bishop How of England are amusing.
  A little cousin of his being asked who was
the first man, promptly answered Adam.
Asked next who was the first woman, he
thought a little and then hesitatingly replied Madam.
  A boy being asked the meaning of Archangel replied, "An angel who came out of
the ark." Another derived Pontifex from
Pons a bridge, adding, "It means the Chief
Priest, just as we say Archbishop."
  "John Wesley," wrote a boy in an examination paper, "invented Methodist cha-
pels, and afterward became Duke of Wellington."
  Unusually bright is this:—"A parable is a
heavenly story with no earthly meaning."
  The mother of a pupil in a school for physiology conducted by a country rector wrote
to the latter, saying:—"Reverend sir,—
Please not to teach our Susan any more
about her inside; it makes her so proud."
  Ignorance was quite as common among
the oldsters as the youngsters. The Bishop
tells of a parish school where the teacher
giving an oral lesson on the English language pointed out that there are many
words pronounced the same, but spelled
quite different.
  "Now," he said, "there's the word 'har.'
There's the har you breathe and the har of
your head and the har that runs in the 'fields
and the har to an estate, all spelled quite
different, but all pronounced the same."

The Lieutenant Governor

Prince Edward Island

WINTER IN LOVERS' LANE

BY CLINTON SCOLLARD

IN LOVERS' LANE 'TIS WINTER NOW
(WILL SPRINGTIDE NEVER COME AGAIN?),
AND NOT A BIRD FROM ANY BOUGH
VOICES THE OLD DIVINE REFRAIN.

THE PATH THAT GLEAMED WITH GREEN AND GOLD
SHOWS STAR ON EVANESCENT STAR—
PALE FRAGILE BLOSSOMS OF THE COLD
WHITER THAN JUNE'S WHITE LILIES ARE.

AND NOT A FOOTFALL WAKES THE HUSH
WHEN THE FAINT SILVER OF THE MOON
GLINTS O'ER THE COVERT WHENCE THE THRUSH
SPILLED, SUMMER-LONG, ITS JOCUND TUNE.

THOSE TREMULOUS TRYSTINGS, ARE THEY DONE,—
THE MEETING JOY, THE PARTING PAIN?
WILL HEARTS NO MORE BE WOOED AND WON
IN MEMORY-HAUNTED LOVERS' LANE?

AH, WAIT TILL APRIL'S BUGLE-CALL
RINGS, RICH WITH RAPTURE, UP THE GLEN,
TILL MAY ONCE MORE HER FLOWERY THRALL
WEAVES AMOROUSLY—AND THEN—AND THEN!

THE home of John and Mrs Bowness, Bedeque will be the scene of a happy event this evening at seven o'clock when their daughter Carrie T. will be united in matrimony to W. Calvin Leard, son of Cornelius Leard of Lower Bedeque. The ceremony will be performed by Rev Neil McLauchlin in the presence of immediate relations and friends. The bride is to be attended by her sister Miss Lizzie Bowness and she will wear white organdie trimmed with lace and insertion, and white roses. The dress of the bridesmaid will be of white organdie, trimmed with lace, and pink roses. The groom will be supported by A. H Affleck of Searletown. The presents are very beautiful and testify of the popularity of the happy couple. After spending the evening at the bride's parents where music will be furnished by Miss Carrie Pridham and Mis May Leard, Mr and Mrs Leard leave for their future home in Lower Bedeque. The Guardian joins with other friends in extending sincere best wishes.

Cultivating Evergreens

By Ephraim Weber

LET us keep fresh. The mildew of egotism has a hundred subtle fungi, which are withering many nice people around the tips and edges. That central self-reference eats the chlorophyl out of a character, and leaves us pale mullein stalks by the wall, when we ought to be evergreens by the veranda. A man and his wife, having settled in a bleak country, drove twenty miles on a difficult trail for a few little spruces and jack-pines to plant by the door. Have we taken half that trouble to freshen our beings with a new taking to heart the lives of our fellows? Have we even gone as far as visiting a mission or a soap factory to sensitize our sympathy? Something of this kind might not be a bad way to begin the evergreen work.

REV. EDWIN SMITH, M. A.

THE DAISIES' SONG.

(For the Transcript.)

We had a peaceful sleep
All through the winter night,
But when winds of March were blowing,
And soft April rains were flowing,
We crept slowly toward the light.

"Come," said May, "my dear ones,
And put your green gowns on."
Then, cried June, "My darling daisies,
All around your yellow faces
Your white-frilled caps now don."

Then began the frolic,
The wild and merry fun,
The wind piped up a lively tune,
Our pulses throbbed with joy of June;
We laughed, we danced, we sang and pranced,
We swayed, we whirled, we sprang and twirled,
We bobbed to the ground in our glee;
No flowers so jolly as we
Under the smiling sun.

A dandelion near
In solemn tones cried out—
"Daisies, daisies, do be quiet,
You are making such a riot
You disturb my meditations
With your comical gyrations;
You 're crazy without doubt."

"O moon-faced dandy, dear!
Half asleep 'mong the grasses,
Would n't you dance with legs like these,
And broad-frilled caps to catch each breeze,
That o'er the meadow passes?"

So again to the wind's gay tune,
We started in joyous motion,
Now with drooping heads and lazy,
And now in a circle mazy,
Each little white-capped daisy
Bobbed about as if crazy,
In mad and wild commotion.

LUCY LINCOLN MONTGOMERY.

Old Gentleman: "Do you mean to say that your teachers never thrash you?" Little Gentleman: "Never. We have moral suasion at our school." Old Gentleman: "What's that?" Little Boy: "O, we get kep' in, and stood up in corners, and locked out, and locked in, and made to write one word a thousand times, and scowled at, and jawed at, and that's all."

WHERE JONES WENT

A series of revival services was being held in a Western and placards giving notice of the services were posted in cons ous places. One day the following notice was posted: " Its Location and Absolute Certainty. Thomas Jones, ba soloist, will sing 'Tell Mother I'll Be There.'" L. Mc Lib

Miss L. M. Montgomery

The College Record

"Non Collegio sed vitæ discimus."

VOL. I.　　　P. W. COLLEGE, CHARLOTTETOWN, MARCH, 1894.　　　NO. 2.

The College Record.

THE RECORD will be published monthly during the remainder of the term.

Subscription price 25 cents, in advance. Single copies 10 cents.

EDITORS—E. N. M. Hunter, H. McKinnon.

BUSINESS MANAGER—T. R. MacMillan.

☞ Address all communications to
BUSINESS MANAGER,
P. W. College,
Charlottetown.

P, W. COLLEGE, MARCH, 1894.

The College Record.

This is the second number of The Record, and we have to thank the students and others for the generous manner in which they received the first, and for the mild criticism which was passed upon it. We are well aware of its many defects, but how to remedy them is much more difficult to perceive. Any suggestions that would tend to the improvement of the paper would be thankfully received.

We would like to see more of the students contribute some articles,—not poetry(!) alone, but some good prose compositions or letters on any subject of general interest. Some of the poetical effusions which we have lately received are marked by the " prodigal exuberance of early genius," and give unmistakable evidence of the approach of Spring.

As time goes by, and the students increase in numbers, it becomes more apparent that the present College building is wholly inadequate to meet the demands made on it for accommodation. This year there are nearly 170 students, and as it is almost impossible to seat so many, the need of a new and larger building is felt to be urgent.

The system of ventilation—the windows —is bad, and, in cold weather, is injurious to the health. When we go home this summer, let us impress on our parents the necessity of a new building, that, when the time comes for footing the bills, they may know that the money is wisely expended

It is with pleasure that we see Prof. Earle engaged as Musical Director. The students take quite an interest in the music, and will, no doubt, profit much from the instruction. Let us all do our best, that we may have some good singing at commencement.

We are in receipt of a new publication, —" Prince Street School Times,"— which we welcome to our table. It is a bright and interesting journal, and we must congratulate the young ladies on their new departure, and wish it a successful future.

GRAND DRAMATIC AND MUSICAL

ENTERTAINMENT

BY THE
PUPILS OF NOTRE DAME

AT THE

OPERA HOUSE, CHARLOTTETOWN

JUNE 8, 1904

EXAMINER ❧ JOB PRINT.

June 9. 1904.

Charlottetown
P. E. I.

"who can put up the biggest bluff?"

MULE BAROMETER
(HANG OUTSIDE)

DIRECTIONS.
If tail is dry
FAIR
If tail is wet
RAIN
If tail is swinging
WINDY
If tail is wet and swinging
STORMY
If tail is frozen
COLD

"Page Fences wear best" under any weather conditions.

Get the Page
WHITE BRAND

DON'T BE LIKE THE MULE'S TAIL - - BEHIND - -

The Page Wire Fence Co., Ltd
WALKERVILLE, TORONTO, MONTREAL, ST. JOHN

A PRETTY BIT OF SCENERY IN POINT PLEASANT PARK, HALIFAX.

레드 스크랩북 42쪽

결혼 소식과 마을에 관한 기사와 재미있는 이야기 사이에는 쥐구멍에 숨고 싶어지게 하는 두 가지 이야기가 있다. 루시 모드 몽고메리가 파혼으로 겪은 수치심은 에드윈 심프슨이 마을을 방문하거나 편지를 보내와 주변을 맴돌 때마다 끊임없이 되살아난다. 몽고메리는 올리버 맥닐(미국에서 찾아온 먼 친척이다)에게 육체적으로 끌렸을 때도 비슷한 고통을 받았다. 그러나 올리버와는 사랑에 빠지지 않았다(사실 당시에는 이완 맥도널드와 비밀리에 약혼을 한 때였다). 이런 상황이 허먼 리어드를 향한 비슷한 감정 안에 오래도록 감춰진 상처를 건드리지 않았을까 싶다.

44쪽 여기에 몽고메리는 3월 달력을 붙이고 다른 해의 8월 달력을 그 위에 덧붙인 뒤 달력의 아래쪽에는 "불의 시련"이라 적고 에드윈 심프슨에게서 마음 아픈 편지를 받은 날짜도 써놓았다. 에드윈이 프린스에드워드섬을 방문해 머무르는 동안, 몽고메리는 다행히 캐번디시를 찾은 그를 피할 수 있었다. 그에게서 달갑지 않은 편지를 받은 날, 몽고메리는 자기 행운이 결국 다했다는 것을 직감했다. 1903년 8월 12일, 미공개 일기에서 몽고메리는 이렇게 괴로운 심정을 토로했다. "잠시 숨을 돌리고 나면 결국 고통만 더 커지고 만다는 것을 뼈저리게 느꼈다. 펼친 손바닥을 자로 때리기 전에 내려치는 시늉만 몇 번씩 하던 선생님이 기억난다. 삶을 살다 보면 같은 경험이 반복되는 것 같다." 펜팔 친구인 루시 링컨 몽고메리의 시 〈불멸의 희망Immortal Hope〉은 에드윈 심프슨을 기억하는 자료 옆에 배치되어 해석이 쉽지 않아졌다. 몽고메리는 그가 이제 그만 자신을 내버려두기를 바랐을까? 아니면 그가 다시 한 번 희망을 불태우기를 바랐을까?

46쪽 흑백 단체 사진에 스코틀랜드 펜팔 친구인 조지 보이드 맥밀런이 보인다. 맨 뒷줄 오른쪽 끝에 서 있다. 한가운데에는 몽고메리가 캐번디시 장로교회 연단을 찍은 사진이 있고, 그 아래에는 "이완 맥도널드 목사"

가 집전한 결혼식 기사가 있다. 이 기사 옆으로 배치된 1909년 기사 두 편은 사우스다코타주의 올리버 맥닐과 관련된 소식을 전한다. 올리버 맥닐은 몽고메리를 보자마자 뜨거운 사랑에 빠졌다. 1909년 9월 21일, 그가 단 몇 주만 머물다 간 뒤에 몽고메리는 "절대로 더 이상은 올리버 맥닐과 연인의 오솔길을 걷지 말아야겠어"라고 깨달았다. 올리버 맥닐이 청혼했을 때 몽고메리는 거절했지만, 그에게 강하게 끌렸고 일기장에 이렇게 고백했다. "하지만 오늘 밤 내가 또다시 불장난을 하고 있다는 것을 깨달았다." "또다시"라는 표현은 허먼 리어드를 향한 감정과 비슷하다는 뜻이다. 로어 비데크에서 생활했던 1897년에서 1898년까지 몽고메리는 심프슨과 약혼했고, 이제 1909년에는 이완 맥도널드와 약혼한 사이가 되어 있었다.

47쪽 많은 꽃과 순수한 새끼 고양이들의 깜짝 놀란 표정이 축하 분위기를 자아낸다. 눈길을 끄는 꽃다발은 이완 맥도널드와 함께했던 시간을 기념한 것이거나, 노라 리퍼지와의 즐거운 외출길에 꺾어 온 것일 수도 있다. 노라가 캐번디시를 방문한 것은 1904년 7월 보름께였다.

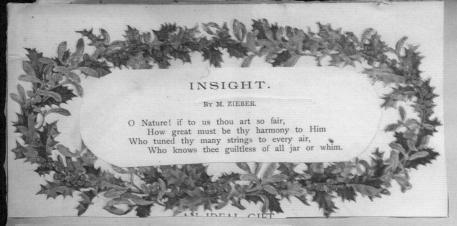

INSIGHT.

By M. ZIEBER.

O Nature! if to us thou art so fair,
   How great must be thy harmony to Him
Who tuned thy many strings to every air,
   Who knows thee guiltless of all jar or whim.

AN IDEAL GIFT

Announcement

A missionary concert will be held here on thursday next at 7 Oclock Miss Martha M Clark returned missionary will be present A silver collection will be taken up for the mission band

August 12. 1903.

Trial by Fire.

IMMORTAL HOPE.

Out to the starry night
I took my hope deferred,
My hope, that sought in vain for years,
Through troubled days and nights of tears,
One heart-inspiring word.

I chose a shining star
From hosts above my head,
And said, "I'll watch that through the
   night;
When its last gleam shall fade from sight
Then will my hope be dead."

So through the evening dim,
And midnight's chilling air,
My dying hope held to my heart,
I strove, in anguish, e'er we'd part,
To breathe a willing prayer.

O'er the horizon far,
And out of sight they swept;
Pleiades faded like a mist,
Orion, too, the boundary kissed,
And my star onward crept.

Till, trembling on the verge
Of dawn, it passed away.
I kissed my dead hope on the eyes,
So still it lay in that pale guise,
Then turned to face the day.

In amber air there shone
The glorious star of morn,
My hope sprang up and oped its eyes,
I caught a glimpse of Paradise
In that first glow of dawn.

        LUCY LINCOLN MONTGOMERY.
In the Waverley Magazine for October.

Thursday. July 9 1903

Hours splendid as the past may still be thine.

November

Sun	Mon	Tue	Wed	Tho	Fri	Sat
+	1	2	3	4	5	6
7	8	9	10	11	12	13
14	15	16	17	18	19	20
21	22	23	24	25	26	27
28	29	30	+	+	+	+

December

Sun	Mon	Tue	Wed	Tho	Fri	Sat
+	+	+	1	2	3	4
5	6	7	8	9	10	11
12	13	14	15	16	17	18
19	20	21	22	23	24	25
26	27	28	29	30	31	+

And bless thy future as thy former day.

Elegy on Newstead Abbey

garden looks very
— by moonlight.

Abbey.

Do You See the Point?

"Any idiot knows," said Rex the Riddler, "that the real reason the Boers sleep with their boots on is that they want to keep De Wet from defeat. But can you tell me this. Why cannot a deaf and dumb man tickle nine women? You'll never guess it. Give it up? Well, a deaf and dumb man can't tickle nine women because he can only gesticulate. See?"

* * *

A pretty home wedding will be solemnized in this city, at seven o'clock this morning at the home of T. C. and Mrs James, when their daughter, Miss Mary, will become the wife of Rev. W. A. McKay of Wick, Ontario. The bride, who will be unattended, will wear an imported tailored suit of blue cloth, with black and white picture hat. Rev T. F. Fullerton performs the ceremony in the presence of the immediate friends of the family, after which the young couple will leave by the Northumberland for Nova Scotia, the groom's former home, and then proceed to New York. The happy couple will have the best wishes of a large circle of friends, the bride being a general favorite who will be greatly missed.

PROF. HOWARD MURRAY, LL.D.

The home of W. A. and Mrs. Macneill, Cavendish, was the scene of a pleasant social event on the evening of Monday, September 6th, when several of their friends gathered in to meet Mrs Emma Wright of Oakland, Cal, and Oliver Macneill of Dakota. A delightful evening was spent in games, music and recreations, among which latter must be mentioned those of his own composition given by the genial host. At a late hour the guests seperated, unanimous in their expression of thanks for the kindness of host and hostess.

A VERY pleasing event took place on Tuesday evening, 25th inst, at 7 o'clock, at the residence of John T. and Mrs Hillman, Bay View, when their daughter, Miss Margaret M, was united in marriage to H L McReavy, senior member of the firm of H L McReavy & Co. of Boston, in the presence of sixty of their immediate friends and relatives. The ceremony was performed by the Rev J G Belyea, assisted by the Rev. Ewen McDonald. The bride looked charming in a dress of white crepe du chene over white satin. She wore a birdal veil and carried a bouquet of white American Beauty roses. She was attended by her sister, Miss Bertha M., who was gowned in pale blue silk and carried a bouquet of carnations. The groomsman was D. O. Harvey, of Cape Traverse, cousin of the bride. Immediately after the ceremony the company repaired to the dining room where they enjoyed the bounteous repast prepared for the occasion. Mr and Mrs McReavy left for a tour of the principal places of interest on the island. They will leave for their future home in Boston on Saturday 29th inst. The groom's present to the bride was a gold bracelet and to the bridesmaid a gold signet ring. The numerus and costly presents from friends at home and abroad attest to the popularity of both bride and groom. The PATRIOT joins with many friends in extending hearty congratulations.

On Wednesday, September first, Mr and Mrs Laird of Cavendish gave a very enjoyable afternoon tea in honor of their sister, Mrs Emma Wright of Oakland, Cal., and their nephew Oliver McNeill, who are at present visiting them. After tea a very pleasant evening was spent, with an impromptu program of music, readings and speeches by the guests. Among the latter were the four sisters and her mother, Mrs W. who has attained to the ninety years. Com

195-
H.S.C.

May CHRISTMAS be a time of rest and peace.

8411
They're rather tiny, and rather afraid,
The world's such a wonderful place;
When told to look pretty, they all three obeyed
With the utmost politeness and grace!

ROTARY PHOTO. EC

ON the evening of Wednesday June 22, the residence of Archie Best of Mount Royal was the scene of a very pretty wedding when his sister, Euphemia, was united in marriage to R. Bruce Hayes, of Ellerslie. At 7 o'clock the bridal party amid the company of about thirty guests assembled in the parlor and Rev. D. McLean of Springfield tied the nuptial knot. Miss Bertie Hayes of Ellerslie, cousin of the groom played the wedding march. The bride who was given away by her brother was attired in a suit of white silk, trimmed with over lace and white ribbon and wore the bridal veil and orange blossoms. She was attended by Miss Annie Campbell of Darlington who wore a pretty gown of white dimity, trimmed with valenciennes lace and white ribbon. The groom was ably supported by Dr. G. P. McDougall of O'Leary. After the ceremony the usual bountiful wedding supper was served after which the evening passed very pleasantly in various amusements. Many beautiful presents testified to the esteem and affection of a large circle of friends. The happy couple will start in a few days for Winnipeg where they intend to reside.

THE annual examination of Hope River school took place on Friday. There was a good attendance from the district and several visitors from Cavendish, including Rev Ewen McDonald, Miss L M Montgomery and Miss Brown teacher of Cavendish school. The various classes were examined by the teacher, Miss Brown, Rev Mr McDonald and Miss Montgomery and acquited themselves in such a way as to win the warmest encomiums from the various examiners. After the examinations were over Master Ernest Simpson on behalf of the pupils presented the teacher Miss McKay with an address and dressing case. Rev Mr McDonald, Messrs George Simpson, Walter Simpson and Misses Brown and Montgomery congratulated the pupils and teacher on the efficiency of the school. Miss McKay who is leaving the school for a rest has endeared herself to the scholars in a marked degree during the three years she has been in the school, and her efficiency as a teacher won the confidence of the parents. —CORR.

Friday. July 10th
1904

The dawn of
Murphy.

여기에서 루시 모드 몽고메리는 일찍이 머릿속을 사로잡았던 결혼 생활의 꿈과 작가로서의 삶을 함께 엮어냈다.

48쪽 소피아 몽고메리Sophia Montgomerie(1863-1942)는 14대 에글링턴 백작의 딸이었다. 몽고메리의 아버지는 에글링턴 백작과 같은 가문이라고 주장하면서 서스캐처원의 집을 에글링턴 빌라라 불렀다. 메리언 키스Marian Keith는 캐나다 소설가인 메리 에스터 밀러Mary Esther Miller(1874-1961)가 쓰던 필명으로, 1909년에 덩컨 맥그레거Duncan MacGregor와 결혼했다. 여기에 메리언 키스의 사진이 있다는 것은 몽고메리가 캐나다 문학계에서 자신과 비교될 만한 다른 작가들을 의식했다는 뜻이다. 몽고메리가 처음 메리언을 만난 것은 1911년 12월 토론토에서였다. 캐나다여성기자클럽Canadian Women's Press Club에서 두 작가를 위해 열어준 연회 자리였다. 몽고메리는 메리언이 자기 작품에 열광적인 반응을 보이는 바람에 당혹스러울 수밖에 없었다. 메리언의 작품 중에서 그녀가 읽은 것은 《예의 바른 던컨Duncan Polite》(1905)밖에 없었고, 별로 마음에 들지도 않았기 때문이다. 코믹 정치시인 〈실패한 행동A Defeated Motion〉은 《데일리 에코》 시절의 동료인 이디스 러셀의 작품이다. 오래된 잡지 사진은 레드 스크랩북 3쪽에도 실렸던 것인데 어린 시절 르포스 곶의 모습이다(이곳을 주제로 시를 써서 첫 성공을 맛봤다). 아치 모양의 문처럼 뚫린 바위 사진은 몽고메리가 직접 찍었고, 달빛이 비치는 풍경으로 둔갑시켜 33쪽에 붙여놓았다. 머리카락 뭉치는 모드 비턴Maud Beaton의 것이다. 모드라는 이름은 몽고메리의 이름을 딴 것으로, 프린스오브웨일스 대학 시절부터 절친한 친구였던 메리 캠벨 비턴의 딸이다.

50쪽 구두끈으로 묶은 나비매듭은 깔끔하게 하나로 엮어낸 이야기를 암시한다. 신문 기사는 1906년 8월에 작별 인사를 겸하여 캐번디시에서 열린 소풍을 다루었는데, 그 주인공은 스코틀랜드로 유학을 떠나게 된 이완 맥도널드였다. 몽고메리가 직접 쓴 듯싶은 이 기사는 이완 맥도널드 목사를 한껏 칭송한다. 10월 12일, 몽고메리는 이완 맥도널드가 떠났으며 자신이 그와 약혼했다는 게 새삼스레 놀랍다고 일기에 썼다. 희한하게도 소풍을 언급한 일기에서, 몽고메리는 (이완 맥도널드가 아니라) 에드윈 심프슨과 만난 사실에 더 집중하면서 다행히도 칠 년이나 지난 끝에 마침내 창피하거나 당혹스러운 감정 없이 그와 이야기를 나눌 수 있게 됐다고 적었다. 봉투에 든 내용물은 1905년 버사 클라크(핼리팩스 여학교 시절의 친구)의 결혼식 청첩장이다. 버사의 신랑은 블랙Black 씨였다. "캐나다의 선 라이프Sun Life of Canada"를 대표하는 남자들의 사진 사이에 자리한 여성은 이디스 러셀이다.

52쪽 프린스에드워드섬에서 만든 스크랩북에서 《빨강 머리 앤》과 관련된 이야기를 직접 언급하는 곳은 이 페이지가 유일하다. 소설을 출간하고 이 년이 지난 1910년, 《빨강 머리 앤》은 이미 캐번디시와 떼어놓고 생각할 수 없는 작품이 되어 있었다. 웹 농장에서 열린 정원 파티에 대해 다루는 기사에서는 손님들이 웹 과수원에서 "반짝이는 호수"를 볼 수 있고, "아름다운 길을 따라 걸을 수 있는데, '연인의 오솔길'이라 알려진 이 길은 이제 《빨강 머리 앤》의 작가 덕분에 널리 알려졌다"라고 자랑스럽게 말한다. 이 기사가 다른 자료들 틈에서 특별히 더 눈에 띄도록 배치되지 않았다는 점이 재미있다.

Lady Sophia Montgomerie

(Photo. by Lafayette)

By Marian Keith

His Last Request.

Pat was in the habit of going home drunk every night and beating his wife Biddy—not because he disliked her, but because he thought it was the thing to do. Finally Biddy lost patience and appealed to the priest. The priest called that evening, and Pat came home drunk as usual.

"Pat," said the priest, "you're drunk, and I'm going to make you stop this right here. If you ever get drunk again I'll turn you into a rat—do you mind that? If I don't see you I'll know about it just the same, and into a rat you go. Now you mind that."

Pat was very docile that night, but the next evening he came home even worse drunk than ever, kicked in the door, and Biddy dodged behind the table to defend herself.

"Don't be afraid, darlint," says Pat, as he steadied himself before dropping into a chair, "I'm not going to bate ye. I won't lay the weight of me finger on ye. I want ye to be kind to me to-night, darlint, and to remember the days when we was swatehearts and when ye loved me. You know his riverince said last night if I got dhrunk again he'd turn me into a rat. He didn't see me, but he knows I'm dhrunk and this night into a rat I go. But I want ye to be kind to me, darlint, and watch me, and when ye see me gettin'

little, and the hair growin' out on me, and me whiskers gettin' long, if ye ever loved me, darlint, for God's sake, keep yer eye on the cat."—Selected from the Ladies' Home Journal by Miss L. M. Keller, Buffalo, N. Y.

A DEFEATED MOTION.

The motion is that we resolve
  This parliament to now dissolve,
'Tis wrong our country's state affairs
  Be run by men of sixty years.
The seniors all are in the lead;
  'Tis plain this garden we must weed.

There's Member B—— from County Clare,
  Although he pompadours his hair
And sets his glasses on just so,
  And has what all the world calls "go,"
He's in his sixties, there's no doubt,
  So he is one to hustle out.

The honorable Mr. Jay——,
  Like Mr. B——, has had his day;
Though eloquent in a debate,
  We all lament he's out of date,
And so resign his stately form
  To perish 'neath the chloroform.

But what the need to thus compare?
  It drives us to a dull despair;
For each seems useful in his place,
  Performs his part with easy grace,
Takes active interest in each bill,
  Except this one, which strives to kill
The men of sixty years, because
  Doc. Osler adds it to our laws.

Now, gentlemen, shall we retire
  At this eccentric man's desire?
Or shall we stay alive and show
  That, though the years may come and go,
We're never older than we feel,
  And vastly wiser by a deal.

A sage at sixty and a fool
  At thirty is the common rule.
The question, then, for you and me,
  Is this: "To be, or not to be?"
I, for my part, am sixty-seven,
  But want more years this side of heaven,

And you, no doubt, all feel the same,
  For suicide's a crying shame.
Just then the ballots round were passed;
  Then scrutineers worked hard and fast.
The verdict was one mighty "Nay!"—
  The old men's parliament would stay.

EDITH M. RUSSELL.

Dartmouth, N. S.

Maud M. Beaton.

Rev. R. H. Stavert, Grand Worthy Patriarch of the Sons of Temperance paid a visit to Carsonville yesterday and last evening gave an illustrious lecture on the subject of temperance. John Leiper occupied the chair and introduced the speaker. The hall was well filled and all went away feeling that they had had a pleasant and profitable evening. Mr. Stavert left this morning on return to Harcourt.—Exc. (Rev. Mr. Stavert is a native of this province.)

A kindergarten teacher was explaining to the little ones what wool was. "Feel my dress," she said. "It is made of wool. Many of our winter clothes are woollen."

A little later, to refresh his memory, she asked, "John, of what are your trousers made?"

"Of papa's old ones," shouted Johnny.

Lucy Lincoln Montgomery.

A FEW OF NOVA SCOTIA'S REPRESENTATIVES.—SUN LIFE OF CANADA.

A. R. McQUEEN, New Glasgow,   M. N. DAVISON, Windsor,   A. H. MACKAY, Salt Springs, Pictou Co.

B. W. MOSHER, Spring Hill.   MISS E. M. RUSSELL, Women's Dept.

G. A. GADBOIS, pt. Thrift Dept.   E. W. W. SIM, Cashier.   W. J. MARQUAND, Manager for Nova Scotia, Halifax.   DR. A. F. BUCKLEY, Med. Examiner, Halifax.   R. D. BELL, Inspector for N.S., Halifax.

A. McARTHUR, Pictou.   J. G. WORTH, North Sydney

W. WOODHEAD, Halifax.   J. W. BETCHER, Sydney.   J. PERCY MILLER, Halifax.

A FAREWELL picnic and social gathering was held on the manse grounds at Cavendish on Friday, in honor of Rev Ewen McDonald who is resigning as pastor of that congregation. There was a large gathering from Stanley and Rustico and the Baptist and Presbyterian congregations of Cavendish. After a most enjoyable afternoon the people assembled in the church which was crowded many being unable to gain admittance. After suitable music from the choirs of Cavendish and Stanley churches the Hon Mr Simpson on behalf of the Presbyterian congregation of Cavendish, Stanley and Rustico presented Rev Mr MacDonald with a very complimentary address and a substantial sum of money. Mr McDonald replied in fitting terms. After addresses from the Rev Mr Belyea of the Baptist Church, Rev Edwin Simpson of Monmouth Ill, and others, and a closing piece of music from the choir, the large gathering dispersed. The Rev Mr McDonald during his three years pastorate has endeared himself to the people of his congregation in no ordinary way. A man of broad mind and generous heart, an indefatigable worker and genial companion his place in the congregation and community will be hard to fill.

(Guardian please copy.)

Hon. T. R. Black, a leading Nova Scotia agriculturist, who is a strong supporter of the Maritime Winter Fair.

Permanent address Box 1254
Boston U S A

Mrs. David Crownfield

59 W. Vernon St.
Boston—U. S. A.

In Memory of

Mr. W. D. MacIntyre

Inspector of Schools

FOR PRINCE COUNTY

1899—1905

THE LATE HON. GEO. SIMPSON

THE funeral of the late Hon. George Simpson will take place tomorrow at 2 p.m., to Cavendish Cemetery, about two miles from his home in Bay View. He was a member of Court New London, I. O. F. and that Order, including the Royal Foresters from Summerside will have charge of the funeral arrangements. Members of the Provincial Government, and other friends from this city will be present.

AN ENJOYABLE GARDEN PARTY HELD

A garden party was given on the 18th inst by Ernest and Mrs Webb of Cavendish in honor of George and Mrs Abbott of Lawrence, Mass, who have been spending a vacation at Bay View the guests of Walter and Mrs Simpson. A number of invited friends were present and among them was Miss Maggie G. McNeill who has lately returned to her native isle after sixteen years absence, eleven of which were spent in Klondike. The tables were spread under the shade of the apple trees in "Old Orchard" in full view of the Lake of shining water, and a bounteous repast was served by the hostess assisted by the ladies of the party. After ample justice had been done at the tables, some engaged in games while others enjoyed a walk through the beautiful path known as "Lovers' Lane" now made famous by the author of "Anne of Green Gables." After an afternoon of thorough enjoyment the party separated to their homes after expressing their hearty thanks to the host and hostess. Mrs (Rev) L. G. McNeill of St John was one of the guests and enjoyed the

"**슬**픈 자살," 악마 같은 기질, 검은 고양이가 여기에 구성된 시각적 드라마를 짐작하게 한다.

기사 윌리엄 C. 맥닐William C. Macneill은 몽고메리가 어린 시절에 절친했던 친구이자 먼 친척인 어맨다의 아버지였다. 맥닐이 스스로 목숨을 끊었던 1907년 5월 3일, 몽고메리와 어맨다는 이미 성장하여 멀리 떨어져 살고 있었다. 사실 몽고메리가 그 사건을 일기에 쓴 것은 그로부터 십 년이 지난 뒤, 불행한 결혼 생활을 하고 있는 어맨다에게서 남편에 대해 끝없이 불평을 늘어놓는 편지를 받고서 실망한 뒤였다. 1917년 9월 27일, 몽고메리는 이렇게 적었다.

어맨다가 자신의 악마 같은 기질을 자제하기만 한다면 남편도 친절하게 굴 것이다. 그 기질을 다스리지 못하면 어맨다는 그 옛날 자신의 불쌍한 아버지가 그랬듯이 광기에 빠져 자살로 생을 마감하고 말 것이다. 그날 밤 아버지가 죽은 후에 어맨다가 보여준 행동을 잊을 수 있을까! 악마에게 홀렸다는 전설 같은 이야기를 믿을 수밖에 없을 정도였다.

메피스토펠레스 사진 몽고메리가 핼리팩스에서 〈파우스트〉에 출연한 루이스 모리슨Lewis Morrison을 본 것은 달하우지 학생 시절인 1895년이었고, 연극 광고 전단도 블루 스크랩북(68쪽)에 붙여놓았다. 모리슨의 광고 사진은 당시 수집품 사이에 보관했던 것일 수도 있고, 좀 더 최근의 것을 자살 사건이 있었던 시점에 꺼내 든 것일 수도 있다. 어떤 경우든 악마와 나란히 자살 기사를 배치하는 것으로 자신이 십 년 뒤 일기에 적은 상황에 대해 말없이 강한 논평을 남긴 셈이 되었다. 몽고메리는 어맨다가 보낸 괴로운 편지를 읽고 나서 이 지면을 들춰봤을 것이고, 자기 기억 속에서 악마 같은 이미지를 새로이 떠올렸을 것이다. 십 대 시절, 서스캐처원에서 지낼 때 몽고메리는 검은 고양이를 잠시 키운 적

이 있었다. 고양이 이름은 메피스토펠레스였는데 어느 날 사라졌다. 몽고메리의 새어머니가 더 이상 고양이의 변덕을 참아줄 수 없었기 때문이다(몽고메리의 말에 따르면 새어머니도 곧잘 욱하고 성질을 내는 사람이었다). 메피스토펠레스가 흘리고 간 털 뭉치는 블루 스크랩북 37쪽에 남아 있다(왼쪽 아래, 찾아보기도 힘들 만큼 얼마 안 되는 양이다).

강 사진 이 지면은 서스캐처원에 다녀온 뒤 1930년에 다시 들춰보고 재구성했을 것이다. 1930년 10월 10일 일기에서 몽고메리는 프린스앨버트의 리버 스트리트 풍경이 강을 가로지르는 다리를 제외하고는 1890년 당시와 거의 달라진 게 없다고 적었다. 몽고메리는 흰 잉크로 다리를 지워버려 프린스앨버트를 젊은 시절에 알던 풍경과 더 비슷한 모습으로 만들었다.

결혼 소식 결혼식과 장례식을 곧잘 짝지었던 전례대로, 몽고메리는 1909년 사촌인 로라 매킨타이어Laura McIntyre의 결혼 소식을 자살 기사 바로 아래에 배치했다(청첩장은 레드 스크랩북 59쪽에 실었다).

A SAD SUICIDE

Victim Was William C. McNeill of Cavendish.

BODY WAS FOUND LAST NIGHT

Lying Face Downward in Clark's Pond, in a Foot and a Half of Water.

A sad suicide occurred yesterday in Cavendish, the victim being William C. McNeill, aged 77, a prominent, highly respected resident, with many relatives in that section of the country.

He left home in the afternoon and his friends becoming uneasy organized a searching party.

At seven o'clock they found Mr McNeill's body lying face downward in Clark's Pond in a foot and a half of water.

The unfortunate man although in good circumstances, and the owner of a farm of two hundred acres, had been in poor health recently and his mind had given away under the strain.

He leaves to mourn three sons and two daughters, some of whom had been residing with him at Cavendish. There is one son in Kensington.

AYLESWORTH—McINTYRE.

A pretty wedding took place at two o'clock yesterday afternoon at the home of E. M. Carpenter, Fourth street, when Mrs Carpenter's brother, R. B. Aylesworth, of Calgary, was united in marriage to Miss Laura McIntyre, of this city. The ceremony was performed by Rev C. A. Myers, pastor of Westminster Presbyterian Church, in the presence of a few immediate friends, including Mrs. (Dr.) Alesworth, Collingwood, Ontario, mother of the groom, and Miss Beatrice McIntyre, Charlottetown, P. E. I., sister of the bride. After the ceremony Mr and Mrs Aylesworth left on the afternoon train on a trip to the coast. They will make their residence in Calgary, where Mr Aylesworth conducts a drug business. — Edmonton Bulletin, Aug. 17.

Photograph by Marceau, Los Angeles, Cal.

LEWIS MORRISON, ONE OF THE OLDEST OF ROAD STARS, IN HIS FAMILIAR CHARACTER OF *MEPHISTOPHELES* IN "FAUST."

두 번째 스크랩북이 끝나가자 루시 모드 몽고메리는 캐번디시 고향 집을 떠날 준비라도 하듯이 오래된 자료들과 새로운 자료들을 하나로 엮었다.

55쪽 봉투 안에는 프린스오브웨일스 대학 동창이자 소중한 캐번디시 친구인 패니 와이즈의 1904년 결혼식 청첩장이 들어 있다. 비더포드 시절이 떠오른 이유는 베이필드 윌리엄스의 누이가 사망했다는 부고 기사 때문인 듯하다. 결혼 소식을 전하는 기사에는 캐번디시 학교 교사였던 웰링턴 맥커브리Wellington McCoubrey가 신혼여행지를 프린스에드워드섬으로 정하여 돌아온다는 이야기가 자세히 실려 있다. 직물 견본들은 패니 와이즈의 결혼과 관계있는 것으로 보이는데, 몽고메리가 패션과 옷감에 평생 관심을 두었다는 징표이다. 펜팔 친구인 프랭크 먼로 비벌리의 시(왼쪽 가운데) 옆에는 앞발을 둘 다 들고 서 있는 고양이 두 마리 그림이 놓였다. 짐작건대 헨리에트 론네르 크닙의 작품일 것이다. 몽고메리는 교회와 관련된 재담과 그 옆에 찻잔 사진을 나란히 오려 붙였는데 그 사진에는 "수배, 셜록 홈즈"라고 호기심을 자극하는 문구가 적혀 있다. 찻잔은 레드 스크랩북 47쪽(왼쪽 위)에 붙인 카드의 앞부분이다. 47쪽 카드는 꽃으로 장식되어 있고 해티 고든의 머리글자와 1895년이라는 날짜가 적혀 있다. 셜록 홈즈 같은 명탐정이라도 있어야만 호기심에 빠진 캐번디시에서 몽고메리와 이완 맥도널드의 관계를 알아낼 수 있었을까?

57쪽 아일랜드계 미국인 작가인 제럴드 칼턴은 몽고메리의 펜팔 친구였을 것으로 보이는데 주고받은 편지는 모두 사라지고 없다. 당시 문학계에 발을 들여놓기 위해 고군분투하던 몽고메리는 칼턴의 성공이 감탄스러웠을 것이다. 〈상처 입은 제비갈매기에게To a Wounded Tern〉를 쓴 제레마이아 S. 클라크는 노라와 몽고메리의 비밀 일기에서 심심찮게 등장하던 "제이들" 중 한 사람인 제리 클라크이다. 제리의 시는 《프린스에드워드섬 매거진》1900년 3월 호에 실렸다. 몽고메리가 스크랩북에 붙인 잡지 사진과 기사의 일부는 그 잡지의 초기 발행본들에서 오려낸 것이다.

58쪽 몽고메리는 프린스앨버트에서 지냈던 1890년과 1891년에 루시 마거릿 베이커Lucy Margaret Baker와 잘 아는 사이였다. 베이커가 "우리 집에서 두 집 건너"에 살았다고 말하는 몽고메리는 저녁 식사도 같이할 때가 많았다고 한다. 1930년 10월 11일 일기에 따르면 베이커는 큼직한 초콜릿 케이크도 만들었다. "수족의 전사champion of the Sioux"에 관한 기사를 읽고 몽고메리는 제리 클라크의 시를 앞쪽에 배치해야겠다고 생각했다(거꾸로일 수도 있다). 제리 자신이 캐나다 원주민들의 열정적인 선생님이었기 때문이다. 침례교 프로그램은 몽고메리에게 머지않아 언젠가 목사의 아내로 살아야 한다는 사실을 떠올리게 한 듯하다. 침례교 프로그램과 사랑하는 집과의 작별을 묘사한 시 〈출발Departure〉 사이에 백조와 아기 백조의 사진이 놓였다. 몽고메리는 결혼 뒤에 아이를 바라는 마음을 에둘러 표현한 것일까?

—The sudden death of Mrs. Rev. E. S. Weeks, Bideford has cast a gloom of sadness over many hearts. She was in her usual health up to a few days before her death, when she became suddenly ill of penitonitis and passed away on Wednesday last, at the early age of 28 years. Mrs. Weeks was a daughter of the late Albert Williams and leaves to mourn her husband, an infant five months old, her mother, who is now in Edmonton, Alberta, one sister, Mrs. Murdock McLeod, Edmonton, and five brothers, A. E. of Moncton, N. B., Clifford of Boston, E. Bayfield, Edmonton, Teacher and Claud, Bideford, besides many friends. The funeral will take place today at two p. m.

A TICKET FOR BONNYWICKET

By Frank Monroe Beverly

SHE looked somewhat dejected,
The girl at Coalbrook did;
The agent at the window
The surging crowd kept hid—
She wanted a ticket
For Bonnywicket.

Though hard she tried to see him,
The throng had kept her back;
The more she tried to enter,
The denser grew the pack—
She'd get no ticket
For Bonnywicket.

Then helpless and appealing,
Her eyes on me she cast;
She looked like one who passes
Through trouble sharp and vast—
"I want a ticket
For Bonnywicket."

"And thus comes your dejection,
My gentle lass," I said.
"Well, I will make an effort—
This throng seems quite ill-bred—
To get a ticket
For Bonnywicket."

I pressed on to the window,
By crowding through the pack,
And saw the busy agent,
Then forced my slow way back—
I had a ticket
For Bonnywicket.

But those sweet eyes, appealing,
I thought without design,
Had fled, and left me minus
Two dollars-forty-nine!
To sell: A ticket
For Bonnywicket.

Father and Son

The Sydney Post of Tuesday says: "At 6.15 this morning the wedding was solemnized at the residence, George St., of Miss B. Blanche Taylor, eldest daughter o. the late George W. Taylor, formerly of De Bert, Colchester County, to H. A. Wellington McCoubrey, of New Glasgow, P. E. I., senior member of the firm of McCoubrey & Bulman, of this city. Rev. O. N. Chipman, pastor of Pitt St. Baptist Church, tied the nuptial knot. The bride wore a charming going away gown of brown panama cloth, with hat to match, a costume that looked exceedingly becoming. Both the principals were unattended. The happy couple were the recipients of a large number of handsome souvenirs from their host of friends, suited to the occasion. Mr. McCoubrey's fellow guests of Alfonse Hotel tendered their departing bachelor friends a timely gift in the shape of a finely-finished chocolate set. After the wedding breakfast, Mr. and Mrs. McCoubrey left by the early train on a month's visit to Prince Edward Island, and arrived in this City on Tuesday evening.

X The late Bishop Selwyn delighted to tell the following racy incident in his varied experience: While Bishop of Litchfield he was walking one day in the Black Country, and observing a group of colliers seated by the roadside in a semicircle, with a brass kettle in front of them, inquired what was going on. "Why, yer honor," replied a grave-looking member, "it's a sort of wager. Yon kettle is a prize for the fellow who can tell the biggest lie, and I am the umpire." Amazed and shocked, the good bishop said reprovingly, "Why, my friends, I have never told a lie that I know of since I was born." There was a dead silence, only broken by the voice of the umpire, who said in a deliberate tone, "Gie the bishop the kettle."

Brimful of good wishes.

GERALD CARLTON

Of the many stars of Park Row, none is of greater magnitude than Gerald Carlton. Though this is the third generation in which he has lived and labored, he is as young and active as when he first won his spurs in the fields of literature and journalism.

The secret of his success as well as of his popularity is intense activity. No man has ever led a more strenuous life or has achieved more than has he. Within the compass of forty years, he has made his mark as a soldier, traveler and consul, as poet, playwright and novelist, as editor, staff writer and man of affairs.

No one among modern American writers better represents the genius of Ireland. Carlton was born in the Emerald Isle, educated and brought up under the best traditions of Irish social life. This chapter of his experience gives a delicious flavor to his speech, and is forever being betrayed by the keen wit and droll humor that mark the Milesian temperament.

It was long ago noticed by Voltaire that the highest wit went hand in hand with the deepest thought, and Carlton's case is no exception to this rule. In his advocacy of novel reforms and of lofty ideals, his best work has been marked by a brilliancy and hearty fun which made his scholarship all the more attractive and irresistible. Yet is must not be supposed that his genius is of a polemic or didactic character. He has always sought to please and make happy rather than to argue or to teach. But in his work he has so used all the powers of the human mind as to give his lightest utterances a more than ephemeral value.

He is probably best known through his poems, short stories and novels. The first are delightful bits of versification, such as might be expected from a compatriot of Moore and Yeats. In fiction, he has been indefatigable and has produced over two hundred novels and novelettes. Not one has sold less than 5,000 copies, and some have passed the 100,000 mark.

In his methods of work he belongs to past rather than present schools. He avoids the problem novel and all the sex questions about which so many volumes, bright and dull, have been written. His characters have always been taken from actual life, and in the last analysis are the very people whom the reader meets in New York, London, San Francisco and Hong-Kong. In the selection of characters he has always been guided by a fine sense of fitness. He eschews morbidity and monstrosity, preferring to sin, if possible, on the side of naturalness rather than that of eccentricity. For that reason

his stories are clean and wholesome and are filled with fresh air, sunlight and good health.

As a member of the consular service. Carlton proved himself tactful, energetic and efficient. He was one of the big army of Government representatives who uphold the honor of the American flag abroad and who make the American gentleman loved and respected in other lands.

WILLIAM E. S. FALES.

Edward F. Feist has assumed charge of the Cassville (Mo.) *Daily Herald.*

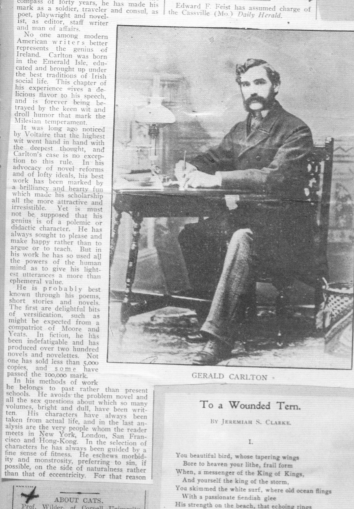

GERALD CARLTON

The marriage of Miss Janet Irene MacNeill, only daughter of Dr. R. and Mrs. MacNeill, of Charlottetown, to Mr. John K. Macdonald, merchant of Wycocomagh, Cape Breton, will take place at half past six this evening, at the home of the bride, 135 Pownal Street. The ceremony will be performed by Rev. T. F. Fullerton, pastor of St. James Church, city, in the presence of near relatives and intimate friends of the bride and groom. The bride will be attended by Miss Mame Hughes, daughter of Hon. George Hughes, and the groom by Mr. Charles D. Herman, of Dartmouth, N. S. The bridal costume is of ivory silk eolienne. It is trimmed with ball fringe and handmade Irish crochet, the gift of the bride's cousin, Mrs. A. E. Morrison of this city. The veil and orange blossoms and a bouquet of bride's roses and carnations complete the beautiful costume. The bridesmaid will wear pale green eolienne with lace trimming, and carry a bouquet of pink carnations. There are many beautiful wedding presents from friends in this province and in Cape Breton. The groom's gift to the bride will be an amethyst and pearl pendant, and to the bridesmaid a pearl pin. After the ceremony supper will be served, and Mr. and Mrs. MacDonald will leave by the evening express on a wedding trip to Albany, New York, Quebec, Toronto, Montreal, Niagara Falls, Buffalo, Halifax and other cities. The bride's travelling costume is a blue tailor made suit with hat to match. She will wear a fur lined coat with mink trimmings, a gift from her parents. The enjoyable event is creating great interest in this city, where the bride, who is one of our most estimable and accomplished young ladies, has many warm friends. The groom who is well known in commercial circles in Cape Breton as a successful and enterprising business man is also widely popular. The Patriot joins with their acquaintances in THE Island and the other island, in wishing Mr. and Mrs. MacDonald an overflowing measure of happiness and prosperity.

ABOUT CATS.

Prof. Wilder, of Cornell University, wrote a description of the cat some years ago, from which we take the following:

'Its anatomical structure considered, the cat is more decidedly specialized and more finely differentiated than man, and is in some respects a finer creature. It is as nearly perfect as an animal can be in anatomical structure. The muscles are more delicate, they are prettier, and in some cases they are more complex. The eye is protected in a way ours is not, there being a third lid. The shape of the cat is beautiful. It uses all its force to advantage, and never wastes any. When it makes a leap, it will light in just the right place. It can turn in the air in a very slight space, and it always alights on its feet.

'The cat has extreme keeness of apprehension. It recognizes its friends, and its foes. A single spank will alienate the dearest pet of a cat for at least a month.

'If cleanliness is next to godliness, the cat is the most religious of animals. Cleanliness is not only a habit, but a fad with it.

'The affection of cats for human beings and for each other is remarkable. Their homing faculty is extraordinary.

'In Germany thirty-seven cats were carried in sacks twenty-four miles in various directions, and all of them were home within twenty-four hours.

'How a cat purrs nobody knows, and nobody is likely to find out, because the cat purrs only when it is happy, and it is not likely to be happy when an investigation is going on to discover how it purrs.'

To a Wounded Tern.

BY JEREMIAH S. CLARKE.

I.

You beautiful bird, whose tapering wings
    Bore to heaven your lithe, frail form
When, a messenger of the King of Kings,
    And yourself the king of the storm,
You skimmed the white surf, where old ocean flings
    With a passionate fiendish glee
His strength on the beach, that echoing rings
    With a wonderful harmony;
While your mate's shrill screech to my warm heart brings
    A melody pleasing to me;

II.

Your joy is no more, for a cruel ball
    By a mischievous sportsman aimed
Has pierced your bosom, so shapely and small,
    And left you—Oh fairest one—maimed.
Alone—on a stone—too feeble to call,
    You are waiting for death's cold hand.
O, have I a heart in my bosom at all
    If I pass you, or pitiless stand,—
Nor help you to bear, nor throw on the pall?
    Ah! sad ending of life so grand!

III.

I clasp in my hand your fluttering breast,
    Though I sigh as you struggle there.
I close—a moment—and you are at rest;
    Then I almost breathe a prayer
For your mate and brood in the lonely nest
    On the sand-dune over the bay,
As the wind blows cool, and the glowing west
    Announces the close of the day.
[Must your feathers rest on a lady's crest
    While your body moulders away?]

PROGRAMME

—OF—

N. W. Queen's Sunday School Convention

Cavendish Baptist Church

July 15, 1909

MORNING SESSION

10.00—Devotions led by Mr. Arthur Simpson
10.30—Review of Year's Work, by the President
    Appointment of Committees
11.00—Reports of District Superintendents of Departments
    Discussion
12.00—Closing

AFTERNOON SESSION

2.30—Devotions, led by Rev. John Gillis
    Minutes
3.00—Report of the District Secretary-Treasurer
    Discussion
3.30—"How Did Jesus Teach?" By Rev. W. I. Green
    "Teaching of the Sunday School Lesson." By Mr. A. Moffatt
    "The Home Department." By Rev. J. Stirling
    Conference, led by the Field Secretary
    Music. Offering
5.00—Closing

EVENING SESSION

7.45—Song Service, led by Mr. Theodore Pickering
8.15—Minutes
    Reports of Committees
8.30—Address—"The Sunday School as an Educational Opportunity
    of the Church." By Rev. H. R. Bell
    Music
9.15—Address, by the Field Secretary
    Music. Offering
9.45—Closing

---

the outlaws to make doors and windows and sashes for the houses are all stories in themselves.

To-day Miss Baker is worshipped by those Indians, who would have murdered her, and by their children's children. When a salary at last came from the church and the reserve was finally granted the outcasts by the Government, the old chief came to her. 'Miss Baker,' he said with puzzled look, drawing a circle on the new ground with his cane, 'if we build on the new reserve here,' pointing to the rim of the circle, 'will you build here in the centre? Will you stay in the centre if we go into houses?'

DEPARTURE

BY

CAMILLA L. KENYON

O LITTLE house, so plain and bare,
My slow feet linger on your stair
For the last time. I shall no more
Come hither. When I close the door
Upon you now, I shall be through
With all the dear, sad past, and you.

Dear house! And yet, I did not guess
Before there was this tenderness
Hid in a heart that often swelled
With angry yearning, and rebelled
At your low walls, the humble guise
You wore to careless stranger eyes.
I chafed so at the meager ways,
The narrow cares, the fretted days,
The life you were the shell of; yet
Now, for your sake, my cheeks are wet.

Oh, wild dark sea of change and chance!
Oh, varying winds of circumstance!
How kind, how sure, this haven seems,
How dear the past — its hopes, its dreams,
The old, old love, the toil, the care,
Forth to the future now I fare,
Yet still with backward gaze that clings
To the old, worn, familiar things;

With backward gaze that seems to see,
Bidding their still farewell to me,
Dim shapes, whose wistful eyes entreat
Remembrance. Ah, unechoing feet,
Ah, unheard voices, sad and kind,
These too, these too, I leave behind!
Here, with the old dead years, alone
I have you safe — you are mine own.

Farewell; my hand has left the door
That opens to me now no more.

A MODERN HEROINE

The Funeral of Miss Baker Took Place at Dundee To-day.

STORY OF HER MISSION WORK AMONG THE SIOUX WAS A THRILLING ONE.

The remains of the late Miss Lucy Margaret Baker, the pioneer lady missionary among the Sioux Indians, who died at the Royal Victoria Hospital on Sunday evening, were conveyed this morning on the 7.25 train from Bona-

THE LATE MISS LUCY BAKER.

venture station to her old home at Dundee, Quebec, where the funeral will take place this afternoon. The body was accompanied on its last journey by Mr. W. A. Baker and Mr. J. R. Baker, brothers of the deceased.

The nature of Miss Baker's life work was recently described in 'Collier's,' in an article on 'The Borderland Woman,' by Miss Agnes C. Laut. Miss Laut said in part:

'One day we went to call at a cottage in Prince Albert, where lived a little lady of the old school—the kind who wear lace and black silk...

to the West in the seventies to inaugurate some sort of academy for the frontier. Clergymen came out at the same time on the same errand; but they did not stay. The post was perilous and lonely, six weeks from the nearest town by fastest travel; and one after another—there was a twenty-year procession of them—the white-shirted gentlemen chucked their commissions (got a 'call' elsewhere) and withdrew; but Miss Baker, with blue blood in her veins and high living behind, stayed on. Then, when settlement came, the academy gave place to modern institutions; and the little lady seemed stranded high and dry, like other good things of the old school left behind by the tide of progress; but wait a bit. The borderland woman doesn't strand easily.

Across the river from the new town was a band of 'outcast dogs,' outlaw Sioux, driven from the United States after the massacres with prices of $1,000 reward on their heads and girdles round their waists, made of scalp locks from the murdered down in Minnesota. Canadian tribes would have nothing to do with the outlaws. They were a hunted, hounded, haunted band, living no one knew how, keeping to themselves, suspicious of all comers.

'The Canadian Government would, of course, do nothing for these American Indians; but to the little Christian lady of the old school this didn't seem a very Christian-like policy, and without any prospect of the salary which came from the church afterward, she told Commander Perry, of the Mounted Police, that if he would put up a tent for her over on the Sioux camping ground, she would see what could be done for the outcasts.'

The Sioux resented any white coming among them. They thought she might be a spy, after that $1,000 reward; and they would not answer when she accosted them for passage across the river. Watching her chance, she followed a young hunter, who had been selling his game in the town, down to his dugout on the river, and when he jumped in to push himself off, she jumped in after him; that was the way she got her first passage across. Later an old dugout was procured, and in this she punted herself back and forth, through all kinds of weather and ice runs.

'How the little lady won the arab outcast youngsters to school, mastered the Sioux xtongue, pouring over the Riggs Missouri Dictionary till four in the morning, forgetting to eat; how she and Miss Cameron, a kindred spirit, who had joined her, with their own hands, taught

---

레드 스크랩북 58쪽

이 뒤쪽 스크랩북 페이지에서 가장 흥미로운 자료는 타자기로 쳐서 접어놓은 별점 종이다. 여기에는 아래 축소된 크기로 실어놓았다. "게자리의 둘째 주"에 대한 경고가 눈에 띈다. 루시모드 몽고메리의 결혼식 날짜는 7월 5일이었다. 자신을 작가이자 물병자리 여자라고 밝힌 사람은 몽고메리의 사촌인 버티 매킨타이어였을 것이다. 그녀의 여동생인 로라가 결혼한다는 소식을 에드먼턴 우체국 소인이 찍힌 봉투로 알려온 그 버티다. 버티의 생일은 1월 24일인데, 한편으로 별점상 장차 작가가 될 가능성이 있는 또 한 명의 인물은 프레더리카 캠벨이다. 프레더리카는 물고기자리로 2월 22일에 태어났다. 조지 보이드 맥밀런은 꽃과 우편엽서를 사랑했으니 튤립 엽서는 그가 보낸 것인지도 모른다. 이디스 러셀의 〈두 그림Two Pictures〉은 암울한 이미지를 묘사하며 알록달록한 우편엽서와 확연한 대조를 이룬다. 어머니들을 찬양하는 시 〈용맹한 사람들The Valiant〉은 케이프 트래버스 학교가 프레더리카 캠벨에게 보내는 헌사를 다룬 기사(왼쪽, 기사에는 H. E. 캠벨이라고 잘못 표기되어 있다), 그리고 프레더리카와 몽고메리의 스탠리 브리지 친구인 마거릿 로스Margaret Ross의 결혼 소식을 다룬 기사(오른쪽) 사이에 배치했다. 몽고메리가 금전적으로 지원한 덕분에 프레더리카는 1910년 몬트리올의 맥도널드 대학이 새로 개설한 2년제 가정학 프로그램에 들어갈 수 있었다. 그해에는 영혼의 단짝인 몽고메리와 프레더리카에게 커다란 삶의 변화가 찾아왔다. 몽고메리는 그 변화를 온타리오 스크랩북 첫 페이지에 기록했다.

SAGITTARIUS Nov. 22d to Dec. 21st.

Sagittarius people are the industrious ones of the earth. They work unceasingly and with the greatest zest. They are far seeing and possess quick thought, enterprise, and great perseverance. Sagittarius people are honorable, truthful, and safe guardians of a secret, but are apt to be too blunt of speech and too impetuous. Their ideals are high, and an appeal to their heart is always sure of a response. These people give freely without thought of the morrow. Many great musicians and writers are born under this sign. The women are affectionate, and will deny themselves everything for the benefit of those they love. These people are bright and witty, and misfortunes are powerless to crush them. Sagittarius gives magnetism, talent, and ability. Those under its influence possess great occult power if developed and exercised. Rheumatism is the disease most likely to trouble these subjects. Sagittarius is a fortunate sign. All Sagittarius people are most likely to succeed while under the influence of their own sign. These subjects are warned that the 2d week in Cancer may prove unfortunate to them.(This will account for any rejected M.S.S. that you may have sent away or received from June 28th to July 5th.)

MARRIAGE-- A union will prove happiest with Aries, Aquarius, or Pisces people. (That would be Mar. 21st to Apl. 19th; Jan. 20th to Feb. 19th; Feb. 19th to Mar. 21st. I'm an Aquarius, so that with the above knowledge there would be danger of my proposing to you were I a man.)

GOVERNING PLANET-- Jupiter. (That may account for your admiring him so much. Did you recognize him as your boss when you were regaling me with an account of his beauty?)

ASTRAL COLORS-- Gold and green.(I have observed that people are usually fond of their astral colors. You certainly are. Trees, grass, daffodils, buttercups and goldenrod will bear me out in my assertion.)

BIRTH STONES-- Diamonds and Turquoise.

FLOWER-- Clover.
' I have shaken the dew in the meadows
From the clover's pale-hued gowns.'

'And fleet winds steal from clover slopes
The fragrance of the new-mown hay.

'And all the golden air is sweet
With incense rose-red clover yields.'

I am glad to find you so loyal to the flower that destiny has decreed for you.

I wrote this in the twilight, hence many blunders.

TWO PICTURES.

(A Fresh Air Sermon by Edith M. Russell.)

Sturdy little bare legs wading in the surf—
"Gee! but ain't this bully! bestest fun on eurf!
Makes me awful hungry. Seems jes like a dream—
Buttermilk an' curd balls, strawberries an' cream!
Say! but won't to-morrer be the biggest day—
Me an' t'other fellers goin' ter help make hay!
Guess I won't git homesick; wusn't that way yet.
Like ter stay here allus—dandy place, you bet!"

Little tear-stained features pressed against the pane—
"Nothin' much a-doin' here is this ole lane.
Wished I wus a kiddie like them ones they say
Has a week o' picnic down there at Cow Bay.
Mother goes out washin', father's worse'n dead;
Much es we kin manage git a loaf er bread.
Wish that nice kind ECHO'd ketch a sight o' me—
Never seen no ocean; never climbed no tree."

Hear the children pleading—list their plaintive cry—
Give them aid refreshing lest they droop and die;
Give them one small pleasure far from city strife.
They are but existing—teach the joy of life.
Will you heed their pleading?—ye who hoard your tin.
Scripture says that rich men scarce' can enter in.
Would you seek the city that is paved with gold?
Practice then the motto: "Nothing! withhold."

Groeten uit het Bollenland

EDMONTON, ALTA
AUG 18
12 — M
1907

Miss L. Maud Mon.

Cavendish

P. E. Island

—The following address and presentation was made to Miss H. E. Campbell who is principal in Cape Traverse school. Miss Campbell's ability and popularity is very much in evidence. Miss Stella, her sister, who is in charge of the primary department was also remembered by the scholars in her room. The teachers in turn returned the compliment and the children arrived home to the bosom of their parents beaming with smiles. Cape Traverse has been favored with exceptionally good teachers of late years, and continue to feel that their happiness is complete in regard to school matters. The address was signed on behalf of the school by Annie C. Irving and Oliga J. Crosby: "It is with feelings of deep appreciation and gratitude in recognition of your kindness to us since you have become our teacher that we humbly ask you to accept this small token at our hands. We are quite conscious of your untiring devotion to the arduous task you are engaged in and we have fully appreciated your lofty motives in trying to cultivate in each of us the attributes of a higher and grander life. But this small gift at our hands is not a measure of compensation. This debt we shall always owe you. It is only a mere symbol of how we admire your high aims, your moral and genial character, and your amiable and pleasant face. In after years in whatever part of the great field of life we may be called to labor, we shall look back with pleasure to our school days and cherish the remembrance of the happy hours which we spend at school while under your care.

THE VALIANT

Not for the star-crowned heroes, the men that
conquer and slay,
But a song for those that bore them, the mothers
braver than they!
With never a blare of trumpets, with never a surge
of cheers,
They march to the unseen hazard—pale, patient
volunteers;
No hate in their hearts to steel them,—with love
for a circling shield,
To the mercy of merciless nature their fragile selves
they yield.
Now God look down in pity, and temper thy sternest
law;
From the field of dread and peril bid Pain his
troops withdraw!
Then unto her peace triumphant let each spent
victor win,
Tho' life be bruised and trembling,—yet, lit from a
flame within
Is the wan sweet smile of conquest, gained without
war's alarms,
The woman's smile of victory for the new life safe
in her arms.
So not for the star-crowned heroes, the men that
conquer and slay,
But a song for those that bore them, the mothers
braver than they!

M. A. De WOLFE HOWE.

A very happy event, in which the communities of Stanley Bridge and Cavendish were much interested, was celebrated in the Presbyterian church at the former place yesterday, when Rev. John Sterling and Miss Margaret Ross were united in the Holy bonds of matrimony. The ceremony was a very joyous one and was performed by Rev. Mr. Strathie assisted by Rev. Mr. Sterling, brother of the groom. The bride was attended by her sister Miss Winnifred Ross and was given away by her brother J. Stanley Ross. The groom was supported by Rev. Mr. Miller of Hopewell, N. S. After the ceremony the bride and groom were driven to the station where they took passage for Summerside from whence they will proceed to Montreal, Toronto and other Canadian cities, being absent on their wedding tour for about a month. Mr. and Mrs. Sterling were departed on their journey by the best wishes of the large number of friends gathered to speed them off. One of those present said : "We gave them rice—not by the handful but by the bagful." Mr. Sterling will be much missed by his congregation during his absence, but all join in wishing him a very happy wedded life.

루시 모드 몽고메리는 극적인 느낌을 주려는 듯이 두 번째 스크랩북을 핼리혜성 사진으로 끝냈다. 핼리혜성은 몽고메리가 같은 지면에서 다른 주제들을 강조하려고 사용한 이미지였다. 혜성의 머리 쪽은 시간이 흘러도 변하지 않는 로맨스를 의미하고, 꼬리 쪽은 인간의 나약함을 뜻한다. 좀 더 큰 맥락에서 보면 혜성은 성숙한 예술가의 목표와 힘에 대한 선언이라 할 것이다.

몽고메리는 핼리혜성 사진을 클린턴 스콜라드의 시 〈혜성The Comet〉과 짝지어 "신의 손안에 있는 횃불"로 묘사했다. 이토록 아름답고 낭만적인 이미지들은 이 페이지의 맨 위에 있는 〈이집트의 비문An Epitaph of Egypt〉으로 한층 강해진다. 이 시는 파라오 시대의 어느 "마음씨 고운" 소녀가 영생을 얻게 된다는 이야기를 담고 있다. "사랑은 별과 함께 그대를 떠나갔어도 / 여전히 그대는 비길 데 없음을 죽어서도 입증하는구나."

아래쪽은 몽고메리의 풍자적인 유머 감각을 보여준다. 핼리혜성 자체는 몽고메리에게 실망이었다. 아마추어 천문학자라도 되고 싶었던 몽고메리는 핼리혜성을 볼 수 있기를 고대했다. 1910년 5월 23일, 안타깝게도 혜성은 너무 희미했다! 오려 붙인 기사와 청첩장(봉투 안)은 1910년 7월 20일에 올리버 맥닐이 결혼한다고 알려준다. 일 년 전에 그토록 열렬히 자신에게 구애했던 남자였다. 몽고메리에게 허먼 리어드에 대한 기억을 되살리며 수치스러운 격정에 불을 지펴 고통스레 가슴이 타들도록 만든 남자였다. 아마도 몽고메리는 혜성을 빌려서 올리버 맥닐의 덧없는 열정을 비웃고 자기 마음도 반추하려 했을 것이다. 이런 단신들 가까이에 자리한 것은 여자아이가 결혼 생활을 어떻게 묘사해야 할지 몰라서 결국 종이를 비워뒀다는 우스개 이야기다. 몽고메리는 결혼을 앞두고 있었다. 결혼할 남자를 열렬히 사랑하지는 않는다고 말했던 몽고메리도 이 지면을 채우기가 두려웠을까?

혜성은 목표가 확고함을 뜻하기도 한다. 질주하는 빛은 자기 길을 따라간다. 몽고메리는 윌리엄 헨리 William Henley의 유명한 시 〈인빅투스Invictus〉를 제목은 생략한 채 이 지면과 마주 보는 지면(이 책에는 포함되지 않았다)에 청첩장과 짧은 기사들 사이에 풀로 붙여놓았다. 헨리가 공격적으로 그려낸 이미지는 몽고메리가 무척 좋아하는 시로 문학적 여정에 영감을 얻은 〈용담〉(레드 스크랩북 23쪽)의 잔잔한 느낌과 비교하면 뚜렷하게 대조된다. 헨리의 시적 이미지는 몽고메리가 혜성을 자기 긍정으로 읽을 수 있도록 용기를 주었다. 헨리의 시에서 마지막 시구는 그러기에 적합해 보인다.

> 지나야 할 문이 아무리 좁아도
> 나를 기다리는 형벌이 아무리 많아도
> 그건 중요하지 않아.
> 나는 내 운명의 주인,
> 나는 내 영혼의 선장.

수년 동안 자료를 모으고 배열하면서 스크랩북 두 권을 만드는 동안, 몽고메리는 성숙한 여인이 되고, 다재다능한 작가가 되었다. 유머 감각과 풍자 정신과 순수한 용기로 무장한 몽고메리는 굳은 결심으로 자신만의 "알프스 산길"을 올라서 불후의 명성에 도달했다.

An Epitaph of Egypt

BY ETHEL M. HEWITT

"Within the tomb of a young girl, probably a daughter of Mena, the founder of Memphis, was found the simple inscription that she was 'Sweet of heart.'"

HERE, in this weltering, western world,
  The veil of sixty centuries lifts,
And strews a crowded London floor
  With trove of Egypt's sandy drifts.
Here, among goblets kings have quaffed,
  Love laughs to scorn the goldsmith's art,
Where one small stone in brief attests
  Mena's young daughter "Sweet of heart."

Oh, surely, crowned with praise like this,
  She found the gods' dread judgment kind;
The Secret Faces at the Gate
  Smiled like the ones she left behind.
So long it has been well with thee,
  Since joy and sorrow sealed thy sleep,
That even Egypt fails to stir
  Thy memory in its shrouded sleep.

So long upon thy happy brows
  The Overcomers' Crown has pressed,
It cannot hurt that strangers' eyes
  Break in upon thy quiet rest.
No space within the Fields of Peace,
  Nor any earth-strayed winds recall
How the last lotus on life's brink
  Flung the first whiteness on thy pall.

Yet well through all the changeful years
  Thy tomb has kept its ancient trust!
The love that left thee with the stars
  Still proves thee peerless in the dust;
More splendid than these gems which light
  Death's way for kings with quenchless flame,
A chisel steeped in tears has traced
  The legend of thy fragrant fame.

THE COMET.

(Clinton Scollard in The New York Sun.)

Fashioned of fire and flame,
Out of the dawn you came;
Now you have taken flight
Into the nether night.
Courier of the dark,
  What is the word you bring,
Flashing across the sky's wide arc
  In your ceaseless wandering?

Guest of the constant stars,
Aldebaran and Mars,
Worlds of the upper seas,
Orion, the Pleiades,
Have you for them a sign?
  Symbol are you of the soul,
Of that inscrutable power divine
  That moulded the cosmic whole!

Yesterday—to-day—
And never a sage can say,
Probing with mortal skill
To fathom immortal will!
And still as the ages steal
  O'er us, who are kin to the sod,
Through the outer vast you will burn and
    wheel,
  A torch in the hand of God!

Rev. H. R. Stavert, Harcourt, N. B., a native of this province, has returned after a visit to Portland, Boston and other American cities.

AS A SLIGHT diversion the teacher suggested that each child in the class draw a picture from which she could guess what the child wanted to be when grown. All sorts of articles were illustrated: books for bookkeepers, hats for milliners, etc. One little girl, however, had a blank sheet.
  "Why, Doris, don't you want to be anything when you are grown?"
  "Yessum," said Doris; "I want to be married, but I don't know how to draw it."

Married

Wednesday at the home of Mrs. Frank Campbell occurred the marriage of Mr Oliver McNeill, of Tulare and Miss Mabel Lee, of Summerside, Prince Edward Island, Canada. Reverend Harkness officiated.

Miss Lee is the only daughter of R. C. Lee of Summerside. Miss Lee was born in Minneapolis but she has spent the greater part of her life in Summerside where her parents have resided for a number of years.

Mr. McNeill is well and favorably known in Tulare and Spink county. He is a native of Canada but has spent the past twenty-eight years of his life in Spink county. At the present time he is engaged in farming near Tulare where he has large land interests.

The many friends of Mr. McNeill join in wishing him the greatest of happiness in his new life.

Mr. and Mrs. McNeill will be at home to their friends on their farm near Tulare after the first of August

Northville Chapter O. E. S.

에필로그

    루시 모드 몽고메리는 프린스에드워드섬을 깊고도 뜨겁게 사랑하는 마음으로 그곳을 《빨강 머리 앤》의 가장 매혹적인 특징 가운데 하나로 재탄생시켰다. 프린스에드워드섬의 풍성한 색채와 윤곽은 몽고메리가 풍경을 묘사하는 곳마다 그 모습을 드러내면서 아름다운 것을 사랑하고 고향을 그리워하는 등장인물들의 마음을 전했다. 다채로운 기념품으로 가득한 블루 스크랩북과 레드 스크랩북은 그 자체로 몽고메리에게 사물을 바라보고 상상하는 힘을 키워준 프린스에드워드섬 생활에 대한 찬사이다.

    몽고메리의 개인적인 생활에 급격한 변화가 생긴 것은 1911년 7월 5일에 이완 맥도널드 목사와 결혼하면서부터였다. 이완 맥도널드는 프린스에드워드섬에서 온타리오의 리스크데일과 제피르로 부임지를 옮겨 다녔다. 결혼한 뒤로 몽고메리는 다시는 프린스에드워드섬에 정착해 생활하지 못했다. 대신 결혼 생활을 하면서 아이들을 돌보고 글을 쓰는 틈틈이 시간 나는 대로 섬을 방문했다. 또한 꿈속에서도, 일기와 스크랩북에서도, 그리고 그곳을 새롭게 탄생시킨 소설을 통해서도 섬을 찾아갔다.

    몽고메리는 1939년 영국 왕 조지 6세와 왕비 엘리자베스의 방문을 기념해 준비한 소책자인 《캐나다의 정신The Spirit of Canada》에서 프린스에드워드섬을 생각하는 자신의 감정을 그대로 담아냈다. 몽고메리는 이렇게 적었다.

    평화! 이슬이 내리고, 늙디늙은 별들이 내려다보며, 바다는 밤마다 사랑하는 작은 뭍으로 다가와 밀회를 이어가는 여름날 황혼 녘에 아벡웨이트의 구불구불 붉은 길을, 또는 그 들판이나 바닷가를 거닐어보면 평화가 무엇인지 비로소 알 수 있으리라. 그제야 우리에게 영혼이 있음을 발견하고, 젊음은 환영처럼 사라지는 것이 아니라 가슴속에 영원히 살아 숨 쉬는 그 무엇임을 알게 된다. 어둠에 물들어 으스스한 언덕과 길게 뻗은 백사장과 파도가 철썩거리는 바다를 둘러보고, 농가의 불빛들과 이미 죽었지만 이 땅을 사랑했던 이들이 경작했던 오래된 밭들을 돌아보면 (…) 아벡웨이트에서 태어나지 않았더라도 누구든 말할 것이다. (…) "아…… 집에 왔구나."

    프린스에드워드섬은 언제나 몽고메리에게 고향이자 영감을 주는 곳이었다.

프랜시스 W. P. 볼저Francis W. P. Bolger, CM

참고 문헌

Bolger, Francis W.P. The Years before "Anne." Charlottetown: Prince Edward Island Heritage Foundation, 1974.

Cavendish Literary Society Minute Book. Prince Edward Island Public Archives, Cavendish Literary Society Fonds (1896–1924), acc. 2412.

Epperly, Elizabeth R. "Approaching the Montgomery Manuscripts." In Harvesting Thistles: The Textual Garden of L.M. Montgomery, edited by Mary Henley Rubio, 74–83. Guelph, ON: Canadian Children's Press, 1994.

—. The Fragrance of Sweet-Grass: L.M. Montgomery's Heroines and the Pursuit of Romance. Toronto: University of Toronto Press, 1992.

—. Through Lover's Lane: L.M. Montgomery's Photography and Visual Imagination. Toronto: University of Toronto Press, 2007.

—. "Visual Drama: Capturing Life in Montgomery's Scrapbooks." In Gammel, The Intimate Life of L.M. Montgomery, 189–209.

—. "The Visual Imagination of L.M. Montgomery." In Making Avonlea: L.M. Montgomery and Popular Culture, edited by Irene Gammel, 84–98. Toronto: University of Toronto Press, 2002.

Gammel, Irene, ed. The Intimate Life of L.M. Montgomery. Toronto: University of Toronto Press, 2005.

—. Making Avonlea: L.M. Montgomery and Popular Culture. Toronto: University of Toronto Press, 2002.

—. "'… where has my yellow garter gone?' The Diary of L.M. Montgomery and Nora Lefurgey." In Gammel, The Intimate Life of L.M. Montgomery, 19–87.

Kouwenhoven, John A. Half a Truth Is Better Than None: Some Unsystematic Conjectures about Art, Disorder, and American Experience. Chicago: University of Chicago Press, 1982.

Kunard, Andrea. "Photography for Ladies: Women and Photography at the Turn of the Twentieth Century." Picturing a Canadian Life: L.M. Montgomery's Personal Scrapbooks and Book Covers. lmm.confederationcentre.com/english/collecting/collecting-3-1d.html.

L.M. Montgomery Institute. The Bend in the Road: An Invitation to the World and Work of L.M. Montgomery. CD-ROM. Charlottetown: L.M. Montgomery Institute, 2000.

McCabe, Kevin, comp., and Alexandra Heilbron, ed. The Lucy Maud Montgomery Album. Toronto: Fitzhenry and Whiteside, 1999.

Montgomery, Lucy Maud. Anne of Green Gables. 1908. Toronto: Penguin, 2006.

—. Jane of Lantern Hill. 1937. Toronto: McClelland and Stewart, 1989.

—. My Dear Mr. M: Letters to G.B. MacMillan from L.M. Montgomery. 1980. Edited by Francis W.P. Bolger and Elizabeth R. Epperly. Toronto: Oxford University Press, 1992.

—. "Prince Edward Island." In The Spirit of Canada, 16–19. Foreword by Sir Edward Beatty. n.p.: Canadian Pacific Railway, 1939.

—. The Selected Journals of L.M. Montgomery. 5 vols. Edited by Mary Rubio and Elizabeth Waterston. Toronto: Oxford University Press, 1985–2004.

—. The Story Girl. 1911. Toronto: McGraw-Hill Ryerson, 1944.

—. Unpublished diary entries, 1891–1929. L.M. Montgomery Papers, University of Guelph Archives.

Picturing a Canadian Life: L.M. Montgomery's Personal Scrapbooks and Book Covers. Virtual Museum of Canada. lmm.confederationcentre.com.

Rubio, Mary Henley, ed. Harvesting Thistles: The Textual Garden of L.M. Montgomery. Guelph, ON: Canadian Children's Press, 1994.

West, Nancy Martha. Kodak and the Lens of Nostalgia. Charlottesville: University of Virginia Press, 2000.

감사의 글

이 사랑스러운《루시 몽고메리의 빨강 머리 앤 스크랩북》을 새로운 판본으로 출판해준 님버스 출판사Nimbus Publishing에 막대한 감사를 표하면서, 특히 터릴리 벌저Terrilee Bulger와 매의 눈을 가진 휘트니 모런Whitney Moran, 그리고 성실하고 부지런한 디자이너들과 출판사 직원들에게 고마운 마음을 전한다. 이 책과 함께하는 모든 동반자(연방미술전시관부터 루시모드몽고메리생가재단, 루시모드몽고메리연구소LMMI, 엘리자베스 에펄리까지 루시 모드 몽고메리의 유산을 이어받은 사람들)는 독자들이 이 책을 손에 쥘 수 있게 해준 출판사의 결단에 고마워하고 있다. 독자들은 몽고메리가 보여주는 다양한 형태의 창의성을 감상하며 환영할 것이다.

2008년을 지나면서 우리는 스크랩북들을 출판하는 데 열렬한 지지를 보냈던 몽고메리의 친척과 학자 네 명을 잃었다. 루스 맥도널드Ruth Macdonald(몽고메리의 셋째 아들인 스튜어트의 혼자 남은 아내), 데이비드 맥도널드David Macdonald(몽고메리의 장남인 체스터의 아들), 존 맥닐John Macneill(몽고메리의 사촌으로, 아내 제니 맥닐Jennie Macneill과 함께 몽고메리의 소중한 캐번디시 집을 소유하고 개발한 장본인), 프랜시스 W. P 볼저 박사(저명한 프린스에드워드섬 역사학자이자 몽고메리 전문가로서 수십 년 동안 몽고메리생가재단의 이사장이었다)가 그들이다. 몽고메리가 통찰하고 창조해낸 글과 세계를 보물처럼 귀하게 여기는 사람들은 이 영웅들의 노력과 비전에 큰 은혜를 입었다.

이번 판본은 2008년도와 같은 내용과 이미지로 다시 인쇄하되 그 일부를 수정해 바로잡았다. 기쁘게도 이 책의 본문에서 "미공개 일기"로 인용하는, 겔프 대학교 문서보관소에 소장되어 있는 몽고메리의 캐번디시 일기가 현재 두 권의 책(옥스퍼드대학교출판부)으로 출판되어 있다. 메리 루비오 박사와 엘리자베스 워터스턴 박사가 2012년과 2013년에 출간한《루시 모드 몽고메리 일기 완전판Complete Journals of L. M. Montgomery》이다. 우리가 루비오와 워터스턴에게 진 빚은 점점 불어나고 있다. 몽고메리를 주제로 한 훌륭한 책과 연구는 2008년 이후에 무수히 등장했다(www.lmmontgomery.ca 및 새로운 정기간행물과 관련해서는 www.journaloflmmontgomerystudies.ca 참고).

우리는 도나 제인 캠벨Donna Jane Campbell 박사가 루시모드몽고메리연구소에 선물한 라이리 캠벨 컬렉션Ryrie-Campbell Collection에 대해 감사 인사를 전한다. 이 소장품은 현재 프린스에드워드아일랜드 대학교의 로버트슨 도서관에서 보관하고 관리하는데, 여기에는 몽고메리가 작품을 발표한 잡지 수백 권이 저장된 온라인 자료(www.kindredspaces.ca)를 비롯하여 몽고메리가 즐겨 수집했던 기사와 이미지 상당수가 포함되어 있다. 고故 크리스티 워스터Christy Woster(및 가족)와 캐럴린 스트롬 콜린스Carolyn Strom

Collins는 감사하게도 2018년에 그들이 소장하던 잡지와 카탈로그 이미지 수백 장을 LMMI에 기증해줬다. 그들은 이 자료들이 몽고메리가 블루 스크랩북과 레드 스크랩북에 오려 붙인 원본이라고 밝혔다. 그들이 수집한 자료를 보면 당시에 몽고메리가 잡지를 통해 얼마나 방대한 글을 읽었는지 알 수 있다.

스크랩북을 편집하고 그에 대해 설명한 장본인으로서 나는 파트너들과 함께 일하고, 여러 마음 넉넉한 개인과도 함께 작업할 수 있는 특권을 누렸다. 고마워요, 린다 아미찬드Linda Amichand, 케이트 맥도널드 버틀러Kate Macdonald Butler, 조지 캠벨George Campbell과 모린 캠벨Maureen Campbell, 메리 베스 캐버트Mary Beth Cavert, 샐리 키프 코헨Sally Keefe Cohen, 엘리자베스 드블루아Elizabeth DeBlois, 멜라니 피시베인Melanie Fishbane, 아이린 가멜Irene Gammel, 리처드 구달Richard Goodall, 캐스린 하비Kathryn Harvey, 벤저민 르페브르Benjamin Lefebvre, 바버라 레이턴Barbara Leighton, 제니 릿스터Jenny Litster, 사이먼 로이드Simon Lloyd, 제니 맥닐Jennie Macneill, 진 미첼Jean Mitchell, 도널드 모지스Donald Moses, 맬브 피터스만Malve Petersmann, 주디 필립스Judy Phillips, 케빈 라이스Kevin Rice, 로라 로빈슨Laura Robinson, 젠 루비오Jen Rubio, 케이트 스카스Kate Scarth, 필립 스미스Philip Smith, 버지 윌슨Budge Wilson, 에밀리 워스터Emily Woster. 조너선 웹Jonathan Webb(이 기획이 옳다고 믿었다)과 헬렌 리브스Helen Reeves(가장 처음에 이 일을 밀어붙였다)에게도 고맙다고 말하고 싶다. 개인적으로 깊은 고마움을 표하고 싶은 사람은 가장 먼저 나의 파트너인 앤 루이스 브룩스Anne-Louise Brookes이다. 그의 비판적인 사고 덕분에 우리의 대화는 엄청난 모험으로 변하고, 나는 질문하고 웃게 된다. 그리고 우리의 아이들과 손주들인 도널드Donald와 마크Marc(마크의 아이들인 칼린Karlyn과 레이드Reid), 제시카Jessica(마이크Mike)와 그 아이들인 오거스트Auguste와 엘리너Eleanor에게, 나의 화가 자매인 캐럴린 에펄리Carolyn Epperly와 몽고메리를 사랑하는 그 딸들(킬리Keely, 시애라Ciara, 케이트린Caitrin), 손녀딸 리애나Liana에게, 로레타 영Loretta Young을 알아본 형제인 존 데이비드 에펄리John David Epperly Jr.(와 똑같이 사건을 캐는 데 열정적인 올케 로리 덩컨Laurie Duncan, 두 사람의 아들 알렉스Alex와 대니얼Daniel)에게, 몽고메리를 존경하여 내 여동생에게 "앤"이라는 이름을 지어준 새어머니 주디Judy에게, 모두모두 축복이 깃들기를.

옮긴이 **박혜원**

덕성여자대학교에서 심리학을 전공하고 현재 전문 번역가로 활동하고 있다. 옮긴 책으로는《곰돌이 푸 1 - 위니 더 푸》,《곰돌이 푸 2 - 푸 모퉁이에 있는 집》,《빨강 머리 앤》,《에이번리의 앤》,《비밀의 화원》,《소공녀 세라》,《자기만의 방》,《퀸 - 불멸의 록 밴드 퀸의 40주년 공식 컬렉션》등이 있다.

루시 몽고메리의
빨강 머리 앤 스크랩북

1판 1쇄 발행 2020년 9월 25일

지은이 엘리자베스 롤린스 에펄리
옮긴이 박혜원
펴낸이 장영재
펴낸곳 더모던
전화 02-3141-4421
팩스 02-3141-4428
등록 2012년 3월 16일(제313-2012-81호)
주소 서울시 마포구 성미산로32길 12, 2층 (우 03983)
전자우편 sanhonjinju@naver.com
카페 cafe.naver.com/mirbookcompany

ISBN 979-11-6445-317-7 03840

＊파본은 책을 구입하신 서점에서 교환해 드립니다.
＊책값은 뒤표지에 있습니다.